Pra

"A sexy page-tu

...ng New York Times
bestselling author

"Julie Leto's *Phantom Pleasures* is a delicious story with equal parts passion and adventure. The plot moves quickly, with the relationship building as intensely as the danger. With a Gypsy touch of magic and a flaming redhead, one can't go wrong."
—Fresh Fiction

"Dark magic and the endless quest for power kick off an exciting new paranormal series by the versatile Leto. A fast and fun start to a most promising series!"
—*Romantic Times*

"Leto has done a great job setting up an engaging paranormal universe." —Romance Readers at Heart

"This is one magical tale, with mystery and twists and turns you don't expect." —Romance Reviews Today

"A *big* twist I never saw coming—which I absolutely *loved* about this book."
—The Romance Reader's Connection

Praise for other novels by Julie Leto

"Nobody writes a bad girl like Julie Leto!"
—Carly Philips, *New York Times* bestselling author

"Sizzling chemistry and loads of sexual tension make this Leto tale a scorcher." —*Romantic Times*

"Smart, sophisticated, and sizzling from start to finish." —Fresh Fiction

"Wow, what a stunner . . . breathtaking action and sexy fun. Heart-stopping scenes, scorching sensuality, and snappy dialogue . . . a Perfect 10."
—Romance Reviews Today

DERBY ACRES BOOKS
LOCAL SEPARATE
TAFT AND 00 93200

ALSO BY JULIE LETO

Phantom Pleasures

PHANTOM'S TOUCH

JULIE LETO

A SIGNET ECLIPSE BOOK

SIGNET ECLIPSE
Published by New American Library, a division of
Penguin Group (USA) Inc., 375 Hudson Street,
New York, New York 10014, USA
Penguin Group (Canada), 90 Eglinton Avenue East, Suite 700, Toronto,
Ontario M4P 2Y3, Canada (a division of Pearson Penguin Canada Inc.)
Penguin Books Ltd., 80 Strand, London WC2R 0RL, England
Penguin Ireland, 25 St. Stephen's Green, Dublin 2,
Ireland (a division of Penguin Books Ltd.)
Penguin Group (Australia), 250 Camberwell Road, Camberwell, Victoria 3124,
Australia (a division of Pearson Australia Group Pty. Ltd.)
Penguin Books India Pvt. Ltd., 11 Community Centre, Panchsheel Park,
New Delhi - 110 017, India
Penguin Group (NZ), 67 Apollo Drive, Rosedale, North Shore 0632,
New Zealand (a division of Pearson New Zealand Ltd.)
Penguin Books (South Africa) (Pty.) Ltd., 24 Sturdee Avenue,
Rosebank, Johannesburg 2196, South Africa

Penguin Books Ltd., Registered Offices:
80 Strand, London WC2R 0RL, England

First published by Signet Eclipse, an imprint of New American Library,
a division of Penguin Group (USA) Inc.

First Printing, December 2008
10 9 8 7 6 5 4 3 2 1

Copyright © Bookgoddess LLC, 2008
All rights reserved

SIGNET ECLIPSE and logo are trademarks of Penguin Group (USA) Inc.

Printed in the United States of America

Without limiting the rights under copyright reserved above, no part of this
publication may be reproduced, stored in or introduced into a retrieval system, or transmitted, in any form, or by any means (electronic, mechanical,
photocopying, recording, or otherwise), without the prior written permission
of both the copyright owner and the above publisher of this book.

PUBLISHER'S NOTE
This is a work of fiction. Names, characters, places, and incidents either are
the product of the author's imagination or are used fictitiously, and any resemblance to actual persons, living or dead, business establishments, events, or
locales is entirely coincidental.
    The publisher does not have any control over and does not assume any
responsibility for author or third-party Web sites or their content.

If you purchased this book without a cover you should be aware that this
book is stolen property. It was reported as "unsold and destroyed" to the
publisher and neither the author nor the publisher has received any payment
for this "stripped book."

The scanning, uploading, and distribution of this book via the Internet or via
any other means without the permission of the publisher is illegal and punish-
able by law. Please purchase only authorized electronic editions, and do not
participate in or encourage electronic piracy of copyrighted materials. Your
support of the author's rights is appreciated.

I dedicated *Phantom Pleasures* to new beginnings.
For *Phantom's Touch*, I say, "Here's
to second chances."

ACKNOWLEDGMENTS

Every book provides new opportunities to interact with people who know so much more than I do about a great many things. Special thanks to authors Deborah Hale and Laura Resnick for sharing so many fascinating resources on Georgian England with me. You both expanded my knowledge and my ever-growing library! I also send a special shout-out to my agent extraordinaire, Helen Breitwieser, who influenced this book in many ways—some obvious and some not. But in addition to lending some of her personality traits to the character of Helen Talbot (her loyalty and smarts being top of the list!) her knowledge of not only the Hollywood machine but of the landscape of Los Angeles was invaluable. Our tour of downtown LA on a breezy Saturday opened my eyes to the beauty of a city not often recognized for its architecture and design—I'll have to write another book set in LA sometime soon so I can use more of what I learned. I also could not have completed this book without the eagle eyes of my longtime critique partner, Susan Kearney; my sister-in-law and reader, Joy Leto; and Amy P., whose expertise in many areas of writing and publishing influenced this book greatly. I'm very appreciative! And of course, as always, to the amazing publishing team at Signet Eclipse/NAL, especially Laura Cifelli and Lindsay Nouis. I bow yet again to you both. And without doubt, to the art department, who has gone above and beyond to give me amazing covers. Thanks so much!

Finally, there comes a time in a woman's life when

she realizes that although writing is the most solitary of professions, there are certain aspects of success that could not be attained without her closest and dearest friends. In my case, I have Leslie Kelly, who somehow has come to possess the other half of my brain—the half that I need when I'm plotting a book. Luckily she always lets me borrow it when I need it most. I also am fortunate enough to have Carly Phillips and Janelle Denison, who are the caretakers of my heart and soul, respectively. Together, we're "the Plotmonkeys," a wacky name for women who are seriously my best friends in the universe and who keep me together—mind, body, and soul. I love you guys!

Prologue

"I don't think this is a good idea."

Catalina Reyes circled the table, her eyes darting between noted Gypsy researcher Paschal Rousseau and his mouthwateringly sexy son, Ben. They sat across from each other, arms folded tightly as they competed in a frowning contest that, in Cat's opinion, could have neither winner nor prize. Between them, still cradled in plain brown paper and nestled in a cardboard box, was a quarter-size piece of brass. A casual observer might see only an old button inside the package, but to the Rousseau men, the fastener was a major bone of contention.

"Cat's right, Dad," Ben insisted. His eyes, lighter than his father's yet still stormy gray, darted to her. "After last time, you were too weak to protect yourself. You were kidnapped the very next day."

Paschal's eyes shone with the cockiness that Cat had come to associate with both Rousseau men, as well as their Forsyth ancestors. She supposed it was a blessing to women everywhere that they didn't make men like them anymore.

"Won't happen again," Paschal blustered. "You and Cat will protect me."

"From kidnapping, sure," Cat argued, "but not from the toll that physically connecting with that button will take on your body. You may look younger than ninety, Paschal, but you're actually how old?"

As Ben leaned forward, his dark hair, which he hadn't cut since he and Cat had met nine months ago, hung rakishly over one eye. "Well, let's do the math, shall we? You were born in 1717, correct?"

Paschal frowned and refused to answer.

Cat rubbed her arms. Despite her experiences as a paranormal researcher, she still shivered when she thought about how Paschal Rousseau was actually Paxton Forsyth, the fourth son of an English earl. Through magical means that defied modern explanation, Paschal had been trapped inside a cursed Gypsy object—a mirror—and released sometime during World War II by Ben's mother. Over the last sixty-plus years, he'd aged—exceptionally well—and had used his latent psychic abilities to try to locate the sister and five brothers who had been ripped away from him so many centuries ago.

So far, he'd found one family member. Now, with the aid of the button, he might find another.

Cat slid into the empty chair beside Paschal. "Ben's right. Let me try."

Though her own psychic abilities had been dormant for most of her life, connecting with Rousseau and his son had sparked skills that Cat now could use with a fairly decent success rate. Perhaps if she touched the button, which was stamped with the Forsyth crest, she'd be able to focus in on the energy of Aiden Forsyth, the brother who'd reportedly worn the notion on his army uniform sometime before, during or after the Battle of Culloden. They desperately needed a clue as to what had happened to him all those years ago. Damon, the eldest, recently released brother, had found the button while scouring Europe for evidence about the fate of his family. The least they could do here in the States was coax some information from the tarnished bit of brass.

There was, at least, precedent. Through a seascape

painted by Damon over two centuries ago, Paschal had discovered that despite the passage of time, his brother lived. And with help from Cat's best friend, the hotel heiress Alexa Chandler, Damon was now entirely free of the curse. The new couple, currently in Dresden searching for other items that might have been used by the Gypsies to imprison his siblings or, as in this case, articles that might have belonged to them, relied on the Rousseaus and Cat to take the search to the next level.

"You can't do it," Paschal said, his voice hearty, even though she'd noticed a few more wrinkles on his face lately, more visible thanks to an increasing paleness both she and Ben tried to ignore. He spent nearly all his time in his house or at his university office, searching, hoping. Trying to find his brothers and sister in whatever time he had left.

"I can try," she assured.

"Go ahead," he replied with a confident swing of his hand, gesturing at the box. "Try if you like, but you'll never connect to the past when you haven't lived it—you're not that good a psychic yet. No offense."

Cat slid the box closer to her and smirked. "None taken."

She peered inside, then, with a determined inhalation, took the button into her palm. Paschal crossed his arms and leaned back in his chair, the certainty of her failure etched on his face.

Ben, however, shifted forward and slid his warm, supportive palm over her knee. She allowed herself a split second to enjoy the feel of his flesh against hers and the memory of how much higher those fingers had sneaked up her thigh only a few hours ago.

When he cleared his throat guiltily, she guessed the same memory had occurred to him as well.

"Go ahead," Ben urged. "Show the old man that he's not the only one who can do this."

Great. No pressure.

She inhaled again, but this time she allowed the breath to fill her lungs to maximum capacity. She concentrated on the oxygen expanding in her system, and when she felt entirely full, she blew out the air through her mouth, tightened her fingers around the button, closed her eyes and concentrated. The voodoo chants taught to her by her grandfather looped in her brain. She called upon the Santería spirits invoked by her grandmother to guide her way.

The button's age instantly struck her. A blast of odors. Stuffy rooms. Stale sweat. Piquant perfumes. Images popped across her inner eyelids like tiny, fragile bubbles. Boxes. Cartons. Envelopes. Even a beaded sachet. Hand after hand after hand. Some warm and gentle. Some cold and hard. Cruel.

She dropped the button.

"Too many people have touched this," she said, wincing from the icy ache in the center of her palm.

Paschal's grin was maddening. "You don't say?" His expression darkened. "Without knowledge of the precise person we're looking for in all that psychic detritus, he's impossible to find."

She supposed he was entitled to his omniscient tone, but she still shoved the button back into the box angrily, then glanced at Ben.

"He's right," she conceded.

With a harrumph, Paschal snatched the box from Cat.

Ben opened his mouth to argue, but Paschal had already grabbed the button and tossed the box aside. He clutched the brass tightly in his gnarled hand, closed his eyes and fell utterly silent. If not for the way his empty hand gripped the edge of the table, they might have thought he was asleep.

But Cat recognized the trance for what it was. With any luck, he was even now psychically jetting back into the past and then, hopefully, into the present, where they'd find his brother Aiden. Only when they found out what had happened to the entire Forsyth brood, including the sister who betrayed them all, would Paschal finally find peace.

When Paschal gasped, both Ben and Cat shot forward. His closed eyelids rippled from the rapid movements underneath. His jaw slackened, and a barely audible moan mixed with the sounds of his suddenly shallow breathing.

"Paschal?" Ben asked, his voice so deep and desperate, Cat knew the ever unflappable man was teetering on the edge. "Dad?"

Paschal groaned.

She swallowed deeply, said a silent prayer, then whispered, "He'll be okay."

"You don't know that," Ben snapped.

"Do you want me to know?"

Ben's gaze locked with hers. "How can you?"

With another wordless plea for help to the God who had bestowed her with her gift, Cat held on tight to Ben with one hand. With the other, she slid her fingers into the thick white hair at Paschal's temple and attempted a connection.

After all, what did they have to lose?

Valoren, outside Germany
October 1747

With his hand clutching the hilt of his sword, Aiden Forsyth reined in his skittish steed and watched his youngest brother, Rafe, ride across the craggy wasteland that separated their family estate and Umgeben, the village of the banished Gypsies.

When he reached his brothers, Rafe slid off his horse's back, stomped into the center of the circle of brothers, and reported to Damon, the eldest.

"The mercenary army advances at dawn."

Damon nodded. "Then we have time to find Sarina."

"Not if Rogan has spirited her away." Aiden drew his weapon, admiring the pull of its weight against his hand. This was what he knew—dueling, honor, war. No matter how tired of bloodshed he was, he'd rather face the oncoming horde of mercenaries than the infinite mysteries of magic. "He's brought this danger on our sister. On us. He must pay for his betrayal!"

Aiden's heart thudded against his chest in heavy, painful beats. His battle would not be for king or country this time, but for something more precious—family. After the madness at Culloden, Aiden had never wanted to kill again. But then he'd arrived home in Valoren, the colony for exiled Gypsies, governed by his father, to find his sister missing, an oncoming death squad headed toward his family, and his beloved brothers preparing to ride to the rescue of all. He'd instantly slipped back into his role of consummate soldier, with no time for regret over how much this action would cost his soul.

Damon grabbed the hilt of Aiden's weapon, which flashed silver as lightning streaked across the sky. "Remember, we must find Sarina *before* we kill Rogan. He cannot die until we know where she is."

Aiden bit back his protest and, in the eyes of his brothers, saw that they did the same. Damon's order was cool and logical, but still Aiden chafed under any edict that would allow Rogan more time among the living. Still, honor dictated that Rogan would die at the hand of a Forsyth son. Which one made no difference, as long as the murder happened soon. Very soon.

Men Aiden had once served with in the king's army were gathering close by, preparing to slaughter the Umgeben villagers Aiden had known since childhood. Lord Rogan, who must have bewitched Sarina with his reputed sorcerer's magic, had invoked the king's wrath by usurping his governor's power and demanding autonomy for the Romani wanderers. Even their father, who'd devoted his life to serving the king and protecting the Gypsy tribe, was in danger. If the Forsyth sons did not act quickly and decisively, the bloodshed at dawn would rival that of the massacre of Bonnie Prince Charlie's last supporters.

"We must ride!" Damon declared.

And so they did. When they emerged through the valley, lightning illuminated more than just the black sky and the forbidding mountains on either side. The village within was wholly untouched—and yet deathly still.

There was no sign of the people who lived here . . . but no sign of evacuation, either. All remained peaceful and calm. Eerily so.

Aiden grabbed Rafe by the arm as he trotted past him. "Did you not send warnings?"

Rafe nodded, then shook him off and rode onward.

Colin, the third born, stopped at Aiden's side. "We sent a groom as soon as your message arrived. Father had called us together to decide how to lead the Gypsies to safety when we found Sarina's letter, declaring she'd run off with Rogan. Then you arrived."

Aiden nodded. He was thankful his father was, at least for the moment, safely hidden with his wife and servants at their estate on the other side of the mountain. "Father is fortunate the Gypsies rebelled against him of late and barred him from the village. He can remain loyal to the king, at least in show."

"If only the Gypsies had rebelled similarly against Rogan," Colin said darkly, "we wouldn't be facing this massacre at all."

Their gazes locked on the looming structure at the far end of the village, abutting the mountainside. Rogan's castle. He'd come to Valoren as Damon's guest, then settled here like a king among the Gypsies. Shockingly, the normally suspicious Romani had accepted him like a prodigal son. Aiden had met Rogan

only once, years ago in London, but had been struck
by the iciness beneath the man's considerable charm.
Aiden vowed to never turn his back on such a blackguard, but Damon had declared the nobleman merely
eccentric and intriguing and had invited him to the
family home in Valoren. At the time, Aiden had been
too concerned with his own interests and upcoming
campaign against the Scottish rebels to challenge his
brother's judgment. But now certainly wasn't the time
for regrets.

"God help us," Colin continued. "In a few hours
this will be the site of a bloodbath."

"Not if we can stop it," Aiden assured him.

They rode to each dwelling, knocking on the
hollow-sounding doors and tearing curtains aside with
drawn blades. Curious signs met them at every turn.
Prized possessions sat out in the open, untended. Fires
burned with food on the spit, as if the owners had
only wandered a few steps away. And yet, locked pens
were empty of livestock. And the handcrafted talismans that normally hung around the village were
gone.

"What sort of magic spirits away an entire town?"
asked Logan, the older of the twins.

Paxton, the younger twin, shook his head. "They
had but an hour's warning. They could not have abandoned their homes without our meeting them on the
valley road."

Rafe did not respond. The youngest Forsyth son
had been born to their father's Gypsy second wife, as
had Sarina. Rafe had spent more time among the villagers than he had with his own family. If the disap-
pearance had caught him unaware, how would they
find Sarina before it was too late?

Not by standing still and wallowing in their surprise.

Aiden shot off orders. Colin he sent to the chapel.
Rafe to search out the *Chovihano*, anticipating that
the Gypsy elder might have stayed behind, too lame

to travel. He directed the twins to the tinker's hut, hoping the only Umgeben Gypsy allowed to travel outside the boundaries of Valoren had heard about the mercenaries and had warned the Romani before Aiden had stumbled across some of his former cavalry mates on his journey home.

Without question, his brothers obeyed. Aiden froze when Damon placed a calming hand on his shoulder.

"We'll find her," he said.

"I'll seek out Rogan," Aiden insisted.

Damon's eyes hardened. "I brought that viper into our midst. It is my right to slay him. But only after Sarina is back in our care."

Straightening tall in his saddle, Damon looked more like a general than Aiden would ever have dreamed. His eldest brother had once wanted nothing more than to inherit his title, serve in the House of Lords and continue to bring honor to the Forsyth name. He'd had no interest in dueling, for sport or insult, preferring more solitary pursuits and reasoned resolution of conflict. Aiden, on the other hand, had once relished a good fight. Settling scores with the aid of his sword or the occasional pistol was as natural to him as breathing. Yet each and every one of his brothers, even pious Colin and studious Paxton, had the capability to draw blood on behalf of their sister. But Damon blamed himself for this turn of events. He deserved the first chance to call Rogan out.

"Check the armory," Damon said. "See if the Gypsies armed themselves before they disappeared."

Aiden started to tell his brother to take care, but changed his mind. The time for care had passed. Aiden rode west, concentrating solely on his aims: Find his sister. Find the Gypsies. Organize an escape from King George's mercenaries. Spit on Rogan's corpse. After that, Aiden had no plans except living without the constant barrage of violence from rebellion and war.

Though he'd lived in Valoren the least of all his brothers, he knew his way around the village as expertly as the rest. Barren at first glance, the land possessed a powerful magic, strong enough to keep the itinerant wanderers rooted to one place. Though they refused to build more than rickety homes, preferring their wheeled *vardos*, the Romani had otherwise created a thriving village, funded by the sale of crafts and natural remedies to nearby hamlets. They existed in peace, healthy and safe, begrudgingly content with their lot.

And then Rogan had come to Valoren.

With a quick tug on his horse's reins, Aiden headed toward the dark cavern where Rogan had trained the Gypsies to forge weapons even the king's master blacksmiths would have coveted. He'd hoped to find the gated cave empty of the armaments, but he was quickly disappointed. Torchlight flickered over a full containment of swords, battle-axes and bayonets, all glowing red-silver in the light from the untended yet smoldering forge.

"Hello?"

His voice echoed through the warm, dry space. The dirt showed a single set of footprints, and the indentations did not indicate that the person they belonged to had been in any hurry. In fact, as he approached the weapons, Aiden noticed a thin layer of dust on the table, likely blown in by the storm.

Disheartened, he turned to leave. *Damn Rogan.* Not only had the sorcerer enticed Sarina into a romance despite the disparity in their ages, but he'd challenged the king's authority over Valoren. George II had no choice but to act swiftly. Images of torn and bloodied bodies flashed in Aiden's brain. He'd seen incredible carnage in Scotland. He had no desire to see such human wreckage again.

With a bitter taste in his mouth, he took one last look at the weaponry, then turned to leave.

A light flashed, and inside his head he heard a desperate scream. Feminine. Needful. Afraid.

"Sarina?"

He dashed back into the cave, but found no inner chamber, no path that led anywhere but into shadow. In a curve in the darkness, however, he spied a strange, bluish light. He drew his weapon and advanced into the alcove, shocked to find a single sword fastened to the stone wall.

The blade gleamed, reflecting a light that could not exist. A chill slithered through him as the unnatural glow swelled on the hilt, flashing red in the strange gems fastened there.

Rogan's sword?

He'd heard about the weapon. The beauty and elegance of the deadly double edge had been legend among all who'd been invited into Rogan's inner sanctum. How ironic would it be if he killed Rogan with a thrust from his own infamous blade?

The honed steel was exquisite—perfectly smooth and, Aiden guessed, utterly balanced. The wraparound handle, reminiscent of coveted Spanish foils, was a stunning web of fine gold. And the jewels? Aiden had never seen gemstones of that color—the color of fury. The color of rage.

Aiden grabbed the handle. Instantly the red stones flamed against his palm. He yanked his hand back, but the metal fused with his skin, burning hot. His legs buckled against the pain, but though he expected to suffer the crack of his kneecaps against the stone floor, he felt nothing.

Absolutely nothing.

1

"You're all mine."

Lauren Cole chuckled greedily, holding the package close to her chest as she flipped the light switch and locked the door behind her. No one would think to look for her here. With her new movie scheduled to start filming in less than a week, the studio soundstage was normally a beehive of activity—except in the middle of the night. She had less than six hours to enjoy her stolen treasure.

And enjoy it she would.

She kicked off her soft-soled shoes and, with a squeal of delight, fell to her knees on the nearest mat in the studio exercise room, clutching the objet d'art she'd liberated from her ex-husband's house. Even wrapped in a cashmere throw, the metal underneath bit deliciously into her skin.

The sword was hers. The last and final gift she'd ever accept—or, in this case, *take*—from Ross Marchand. Her body thrummed with excitement, and she had to remind herself to breathe. Adrenaline overload caused some of her dizziness, but mostly she was simply jazzed to have returned, even for just one night, to the girl she used to be. The conniver. The street kid. The thief.

Ross Marchand, her ex, had made it his business, literally, to drum her felonious tendencies out of her. He'd taught her to speak properly, dress with style and channel her expert lying skills into genuine acting talent. In the end, she'd worked his red carpets and movie premieres so adeptly, every paparazzo within a two-mile radius of Hollywood Boulevard had wanted to know everything about her—especially the name of her next film, which, of course, the internationally known Marchand would produce. Thanks to Ross, she'd glided onto the Hollywood A-list before her made-up name had ever rolled across a silver screen.

But as she caressed the cashmere wrap, she knew that sometimes being bad felt oh, so good.

Then a knock on the door stopped her cold.

The pounding in her ears kept her from identifying the intruder until he said, "Who's in there?"

She exhaled. Marco. Studio security. Diligent, but sweet. She shoved the sword out of the line of sight, then scrambled across the workout mats and unlocked the door.

"Hey, Marco," she said, using all of her considerable acting skill to appear relaxed, if not slightly guilty for breaking a rule she and the security guard had confronted on more than one occasion.

The older man arched a bushy, salt-and-pepper eyebrow. "Ms. Cole, you know you're not supposed to be on the set alone."

She grinned at him prettily, having learned the power of her smile years ago. "Technically, I'm not *on* the set. I'm in my favorite rehearsal room."

"The one with all the weapons," he pointed out, attempting to look over her shoulder, but at five-foot-nine, Lauren had a few inches on the guy. Tightening her grip on the door, she blocked his view.

"We're shooting the first fight scene the day after tomorrow," she explained in a whisper that echoed in the cavernous silence of the soundstage just behind him. Though filled with lighting, sets and equipment, the bulding was off-limits to everyone but security until morning. Lauren had come here on autopilot, figuring Ross wouldn't think to look for her on the set when filming hadn't yet started. "I just wanted to get in some more workout time."

"Without your trainer?"

Lauren suppressed a smirk. "I've done how many of these Athena movies now, Marco? I could train the trainer."

Marco snorted. "You could kick my ass, and I'm the one carrying the gun."

She squeezed her arm through the opening and then laid her hand on Marco's shoulder. "That's about the nicest thing any man has ever said to me."

She batted her eyelashes, which made Marco laugh and forgive her trespassing, despite the item he may or may not realize she'd lifted from the film producer's private study. Well, it used to be her study, too. She'd shared his home, his bed and—at least on paper—his last name until a year ago, when she'd caught him fucking her ingenue costar in the cabana by the pool.

The divorce had been relatively quick and pain free, the final decree having been delivered just that morning, severing their marital bond. Thanks to Ross, she'd learned how to manage her own money, so she wouldn't be returning to the streets anytime soon. California law and an ironclad prenup had taken care of the rest. She got the town house in Beverly Hills. He kept the Malibu beach house. She got Apollo, the dog whose favorite pastime was chewing on Ross's Bruno Maglis, and he'd taken the art. All the art. Including, unfortunately, the magnificent sword he'd purchased for her from a shady Dresden antiques dealer in a dicey part of the bustling German town.

From the moment she'd caught sight of the intricate inlaid gold handle glittering above a polished steel blade, she'd wanted it. Needed it. The tug in her chest had instantly reminded her of her days on the streets, when she'd been so hungry that her entire body ached. And Ross, so magnanimous and generous (she'd thought at the time), had paid the exorbitant price in cash to appease her ravenous need for the weapon. But then he'd snatched the prize away before she'd even touched it, insisting that the sword had to be authenticated before anyone handled it.

Once the ancient weapon had arrived in Los Angeles with papers declaring it an amazingly de-signed double-edged sword likely forged in the eigh-teenth century, he'd immediately had it sealed in a glass case.

The familiar pull of the sword forced her to cut her conversation with Marco short.

"Thanks for not snitching on me," she said hope-fully. "I think I owe you another case of that Austra-lian wine your wife likes so much."

He frowned deeply at first, glanced at his watch, and then patted his nightstick.

"You don't have to do that, Ms. Cole," he an-swered.

"Don't you have your daughter's wedding coming up? I bet that wine would be perfect for the re-hearsal dinner."

His grin returned, and after assuring her that no one would interrupt her private workout session, he left. She released the breath caught in her chest, then relocked the door. It was barely midnight. She had at least until five a.m. to figure out what the heck she was going to do next.

Because stealing the sword was one thing. Keeping it was something else entirely.

She slid across the mat and dropped to her knees again. At Ross's house, she'd barely had time to re-move it from the case, wrap it in the blanket, and hightail it out of there. The last thing she needed was to be caught by someone on Ross's staff. She had the legal right to the sword. Her attorneys had assured her that she was entitled to anything Ross had purchased for her as a gift during their marriage. But legal mumbo jumbo aside, taking the sword could mean the end of her career.

Ross had been indulgent during their marriage, but only when it suited his needs. Right now he needed her to star in the final Athena film, the fifth in an action-adventure series that had made her an international sensation. She'd agreed, since pocketing her generous salary, as well as a healthy portion of all residuals, had been her plan all along. One more movie with her ex and then she'd be free of him forever.

But he'd balked at letting her use the sword for the film. He'd laughed at her request in front of everyone from the director to the key grip during a preproduction meeting.

In private, he'd reminded her with pointed ruthlessness of what he could do to her career if she challenged him so boldly again. There were things he alone knew about her past that could destroy her. One tip from him to the tabloids and she'd be finished.

That threat had been the final straw.

The old Lauren, the Lauren who'd once made her own way in the world and didn't depend on anyone else—ever—would not have asked permission to use the sword. She wouldn't have worried about consequences or folded under some jerk's bullying.

And even if Ross gave up her secrets, he'd pay a hefty price himself—not only for keeping her secret, but for harboring a few of his own.

So tonight, to celebrate the final divorce decree, she'd broken into her former home and stolen the sword. Now, gingerly grasping the edges of the camel-colored blanket, she peeled aside the buttery soft wool until the lights above her flashed off the sword's polished blade. She gasped, then moved to touch the steel, stopping when she realized that her fingerprints would mar its beauty. No, the only part of this sword she needed to touch was the handle.

She shifted so that her fingers slipped into the masterfully crafted grip, which seemed to enclose her hand. Immediately warmth spread through her flesh, causing her fingers to buzz as if she were gripping . . . her vibrator? She snickered at the thought, but erotic images quickly filled her brain. The impressions deepened. Darkened. Expanded.

Like the gold on the handle, naked bodies intertwined in her mind. Not anyone she knew—or did she? His hard sex pressed against her skin like the pommel and hilt of this magnificent sword.

Her nipples tightened painfully, and she released the weapon. A gentle throbbing intensified between her legs.

What the hell? She knew swords were the ultimate phallic symbols, but she'd been around the damned things since her first turn as Athena six years ago. She enjoyed swordplay, but she certainly never got all hot and bothered over it.

Laying the blade gently on the blanket, she tore off the cropped jacket she'd worn over layered tank tops. The room had suddenly become stifling, so she scrambled to the door, lowered the thermostat and doused all but the few dim blue lights her trainers used to simulate fighting in the dark. When she turned and caught sight of the sword, she gasped. The handle sparkled and glowed.

Intrigued, she crept forward. The mat shifted beneath her, moving the sword as she walked. Jewels in the handle, fiery red amid the polished gold, captured the scant light and reflected back a brilliance that was nothing short of ethereal.

Damn, she'd known the sword was beautiful, but she'd never truly seen it, had she? The antiques shop had been dingy and dusty and gray. The case that Ross had enclosed the sword in had diminished its real beauty. Now she could see it. Now she could touch it.

She wanted to fight with it—cut the air with the blade and make the weapon sing as she parried and thrust. This was the weapon Athena would carry during this film, Ross be damned. Her final hurrah as the warrior goddess summoned to an alternate universe to smite the sadistic and pummel the unpure demanded a sword of unparalleled beauty and scarlet power. Invigorated, Lauren hurried to the video camera. Once Ross saw how she used the sword, once he witnessed the magnificence of it, he'd never deny her.

Not, at least, in front of the production crew, who would be wholly bowled over by the way the sword captured the light and reflected back pure power. They'd save a bundle on special effects, she was sure. At least, that was the argument she intended to use.

Once she had the video rolling, she dashed back to the sword and lifted it again, this time holding the weapon with a straightened arm to get a full feel for the weight. She'd never held anything so perfectly balanced. Warmth washed over her again, and in response her heartbeat accelerated.

She sliced the sword through the air once, then twice, instantly finding a controlled rhythm marked by the quiet swish of the blade. She spun and chopped downward, skillfully pulling up before the blade touched the ground. She turned and, with a precision that shocked even her, stopped dead before she connected with the hanging workout bag she imagined was an attacking foe.

"Wow," she said, breathing hard, not from the exertion of lifting or wielding the sword, but from the overpowering surge of electricity shooting through the handle and into her arms. The steel reflected a luminous ruby gleam. It was as if the blade were . . . alive.

I am alive.

The voice was deep, masculine, but so quick, so soft, she knew she'd imagined the words.

"Marco?" she called out.

No response.

She bent her arms at the elbows, bringing the sword parallel with her body, the blade shining a fiery red, the same color as the jewels prickling with heat on the handle. Leaning close and then gazing upward, she realized the steel couldn't reflect the light from this angle.

And besides, it was the wrong color.

The light was coming from . . . within?

Touch me. Don't be afraid.

The voice, louder and more insistent this time, echoed in her brain. She hadn't heard the command; instead the message had vibrated up her arms. She tried to drop the sword, but the handle seemed to curve tighter around her hands, tangling her fingers, encircling her wrists, holding her captive.

She knocked into the hard canvas workout bag, then, flying on the momentum, threw herself hard against the wall. Nothing dislodged the sword from her hand. Her vision swam. The blue lights above her merged with the luster of the blade, nearly blinding her in a purple haze. She turned the sword again, more slowly this time, trying to find a way out of the twist of metal, when she saw them.

Eyes.

As silver as the blade.

Powerful. Hypnotic.

Do not forsake me, Lauren Cole. Only you can set me free.

Desperate and afraid, Lauren ran toward the light switches. Was this some sort of trick? Special effects? Was Ross paying her back for stealing the sword, or was her conscience twisting her triumph? But Ross couldn't know she was here. And even if Marco had alerted him, he wouldn't have had time to do anything more than burst in and demand her weapon back.

Forget him. You want me.

"Who are you?" she asked desperately.

Embrace me and find out.

Lauren struggled all the way to the door. She tried to reach for the lock, but her hands remained imprisoned by the handle's coil. Stunned, she slid to the ground and lifted the blade.

Images flashed again. The naked bodies. The hard sex. The muscled man with hair the color of night and eyes as silver as storm clouds. She knew him. She'd wanted him.

Did she want him now?

"Tell me who you are," she demanded.

Touch me and know.

She swallowed thickly. Her heart slammed hard against her ribs. She squeezed her eyes shut, then forced them open, trying to see clearly, trying to figure out what the hell was going on. The ghostly red light had not diminished. If anything, as her fear increased, the glow intensified.

And so did her desire.

She dropped the blade. The flat side of the metal touched her calf and stretched over her thigh. Intense sensations nailed her to the floor. Not pain. Not blood. She hadn't been cut. She'd been . . . captured?

"I . . . can't . . . breathe."

2

Every muscle in Aiden's body tightened as if he'd been pressed between two hot iron walls. Pain erupted in his skull, and for the first time in centuries Aiden Forsyth remembered what it felt like to face death. He lifted his chin, determined to face his demise straight-on, but a slice of fiery steel burned across his middle and he doubled over. He waited, panting, expecting to feel the ooze of bloody heat from his disemboweled innards, but the sensation never came. Instead he dropped onto a soft, leathery surface.

He opened his eyes, but he could see nothing but shadows and a dim blue light. The odors that assailed his nostrils were instantly familiar, yet completely foreign. He smelled no blood, but the distinctive salty sweetness of sweat and the cold sharpness of forged steel. And woman. Oh, yes, the unmistakable scent of warm, clean skin and musky desire raked through his senses and brought him to full consciousness.

The floor he lay on was soft and scuffed. Above him he spied the source of the odd blue gleam, but he wondered how stars could be contained within four walls. Though the corners of the room were muted by shadows, he knew he was closed in. Captured. Contained. And yet freer than he'd felt in hundreds of years.

Cautiously he moved his arms and saw that he

hadn't been cut open. He bore no injuries that he could see. The more he moved, the more his blood pumped through his body. With a great breath he inhaled every bit of air he could take into his lungs. The sensation was marvelous. Was he free? Finally? After all these years?

He spotted the woman just a few steps away. Her cascade of flaxen hair draped across her face, then fell in a soft veil over her generous breasts, which rose and fell with weak but steady breaths. She'd collapsed against the wall, the sword that had been his prison lying across her leg, the pommel nestled between her thighs.

At once aroused and shocked, Aiden crawled to her, his hand hovering above the hilt, above her skin. He'd been trapped inside the weapon for centuries. If he touched it, would he end up back inside?

But touching her? She was worth the risk. Familiar and powerful lust spiked through him, and he couldn't resist brushing aside her hair and curving the golden strands behind her ear. Her cheeks were flushed. Despite the blue light above her, her skin was pink with exertion. And he remembered. . . .

She'd wielded a sword like no woman he'd ever watched, though he'd sensed more than seen her prowess with the weapon. Now more than ever he craved her. Winning her could be the greatest victory of his sorry, sordid existence.

"Lauren." Her name croaked from his lips, his tongue and teeth unused for so long.

She stirred, but didn't wake. The sword slid off her body, and almost instantly her eyelashes fluttered.

He smiled, remembering the blueness of her eyes. Since the first time he'd become aware of her in the dusty Dresden shop, he'd longed to possess her. Years had passed since she'd coaxed her lover into purchasing the sword, and when Aiden had finally become aware of her presence again, she could not hold him.

He was encased in glass out of her reach, even as he'd
known somehow that only her touch would release
him. How many times had she pressed her fingertips
against the barrier between them, clearly wanting him
with as much passion as he wanted her? Each instance
had caused a surge in his awareness, a spike in the
torture that was his prison.

Aiden glanced down at his hands. Scars cut furrows
in the flesh around his knuckles. A few from early
duels. Some from training. Some from battle. All from
the time, centuries ago, when he'd been nothing more
than a soldier and a son. Was he now truly free of
Lord Rogan's Gypsy curse?

With effort he stood, shifting his weight from side
to side to regain his balance. His breeches and shirt
retained the dampness from his night ride all those
years ago. He tore off his waistcoat, desperate to re-
move the restraint of the snug material across his
chest. If not for the presence of the woman who'd
kept him clinging to consciousness for the past few
years, he would have stripped his body bare and run
out immediately into the daylight. Only moments before it seemed, he'd been trapped in the house above
the ocean, but clearly she'd moved him somewhere
else.

A doorknob was just above her head. He glanced
around, but between the clutter of crates and machin-
ery in the room and the deceptively mirrored walls on
one side, he saw no other exit.

Frowning, he dropped to his knees beside her. Even
unconscious, with her lips slightly parted, her skin
gleamed with life. The ebb and flow of her breathing,
marked by the gentle swell of her breasts, made his
mouth water, not only because of the obvious fullness
of her flesh, but because of what she was. Who she
was. A living, breathing woman. A woman who could
touch him. A woman who *had* touched him. A woman

who would touch him more intimately, if he had his way.

And it had been so very long since Aiden had had his way.

He drew his finger over her cheek, causing a moan to escape her lips. The sound resonated through him, tugging hard from his heart to his groin.

"Lauren, love. Time to awaken."

Her mewl told him she was resisting, or else was having trouble finding consciousness again. He had no idea why she'd collapsed, but no doubt Rogan's black magic was to blame.

Shifting onto his knees, he cupped her cheek and spoke to her in an insistent tone. "Lauren, open your eyes."

Her lashes fluttered and she groaned. The sound tore through Aiden. Was she in pain?

"Lauren?" he barked.

She instantly reacted. She sat up, flattened her back against the wall and wrapped her hand around the sword's handle. He backed away, but not before she had the tip of the blade leveled against his chest.

"Who are you?"

He raised his hands in capitulation. He could disarm her, but he did not want their first interaction to be violent. "I am Aiden Forsyth, my lady."

She squinted her eyes. "Who? Are you an actor?"

"Absolutely not," he said, shocked by her assumption. Men of his station did not take to the stage, though he'd seen a fair amount of lively productions in his day. "I loved an actress once, though, if that makes any difference. Breathtaking creature. Threw me over for the son of a duke."

Her gaze bored into him, but she did not speak. Then she made a quick scan of the room, all the time holding the blade steady. When she looked at him directly again, her eyes lingered, but not in any way he'd describe as flirtatious or coy. She was measuring him as a man would measure any opponent who'd thrown down the proverbial gauntlet.

"You're on the set," she said calmly. "But you're not one of the crew."

She pressed the tip of the sword against his shirt, and the bite on his skin raised his ire. He fought to remain still. Cheeky wench, this one.

"I am neither sailor nor actor, madam. I'm a soldier, albeit one from a different time."

With practiced skill, she slid her legs beneath her and, using the wall behind her as leverage, stretched to her feet. The blade, buoyed against the ties of his shirt, remained steady. Potentially deadly. Clearly Lauren Cole was not unskilled with weaponry, and that knowledge added another layer of excitement to their interaction. He'd wanted her, longed for her for years, and now she was driving him entirely mad with lust even as she threatened to run him through.

"You're a soldier? What . . . Are you a consultant on the film?"

"I know not what you mean. I am not from this time, my lady. I was, until moments ago, trapped within the sword you are now holding against me."

"Trapped?"

Confusion flitted across her keen blue eyes and gave him the advantage he needed. He snatched her wrist, twisted, pulled and shifted his weight until she was not only disarmed, but the sword was tossed into a shadowed corner. His manuever ended with her beneath him, her arms pinned on either side of her head and her body flush against his.

The sensation of woman—the feel, the scent, the sound—nearly undid him. His cock tightened and blood rushed downward, leaving his brain deliciously befuddled with need. How long had he fantasized about this very woman, in this very position? Well, not exactly *this* position.

"Let go of me!"

He groaned. "If only 'twere that easy."

She narrowed her gaze until twin slits of sapphire burned into him. "It's not hard," she said, flicking a glance downward, as if she were talking about his private parts. "You just shift to the side before I make you sorry you ever touched me."

"Actually, my lady, 'twas you who touched me. Had you not, I would not be here, but captured still inside that infernal sword."

She struggled, but Aiden outweighed her and easily kept her in check. He rather enjoyed the way her hips and groin writhed beneath him. His behavior was wholly ungentlemanlike, but he was too aroused, too alive to care.

He'd free her momentarily. Once he was certain she'd listen. For as much as he'd always craved his freedom, he'd known for many years that this world was entirely unlike the one from which he'd come. The way she spoke testified to drastic change in time and place. Aiden had no idea where he was, how he'd gotten here, or whether any of his brothers had suffered the same fate as he, but he intended to find out at the first opportunity. And chances were, he'd need her help to proceed.

Unfortunately, she didn't seem the least bit cooperative. She raised her head and, in a whirl of movement, slammed her forehead hard against his. Dazed, he had no defense when she shoved hard against one shoulder and rolled him off her body.

When he'd regained clear vision, he found her standing, legs balanced on bouncing feet, arms curved, hands open, eyes wide and focused. She was ready for battle.

He rolled over onto his back and tried to contain his laughter.

"Stand down, my lady. I am not here to hurt you."

"As if you could if you wanted to, you thug," she

said, kicking out with her foot. Her heel connected with his knee and he yelped.

She moved to repeat the painful strike, but he reacted quickly, grabbing her foot and yanking upward so that her momentum sent her flying onto her curvaceous backside. She landed with a thud, but before he could offer an apology for his unthinking reaction, she arched her back, kicked up both legs and landed upright, back in the fighting stance.

Air rushed into his gaping mouth.

She quirked a grin. "Thought all my moves were special effects and stunt doubles, did you?"

Aiden drew himself to his full height. A good row was an excellent way to work through pent-up need. But having the woman who'd fueled his carnal desires as his opponent? He thought he might explode for the lascivious beauty of it.

"I have no idea what you are talking about, my lady, but it would be ghastly of me to take advantage of you in physical combat."

She laughed. "Think you can?" With a curl of her fingers, she invited him to strike. "Bring it, brother. Let's see what you've got."

Aiden grinned. The fear he'd caught in her eyes earlier had totally disappeared. The woman oozed confidence, and while Aiden knew he should have been scandalized by her attitude, instead he was enamored. He'd seen such feminine bravery only once before—in Scotland. On the opposing side. One of the rebellious clans had allowed a few chosen women to fight, though under great subterfuge. Nonetheless, once their ruse had been discovered, Aiden had been thoroughly disgusted that men would allow their womenfolk to face death . . . completely unlike the way he felt now.

He feinted left, then charged right, but she'd been ready for his false move. Grabbing him by the forearm, she spun, using his own momentum to twirl him around, then kicked his midsection with her powerful leg so that he went flying across the soft floor. Tucking his shoulder, he rolled and popped back to standing, just in time to catch her foot before he suffered another hard kick to his stomach.

He held her steady.

"You fight like a man," he assessed.

"No need to insult me," she countered, leveling a punch to the side of his jaw.

He staggered and released her foot. She spun behind him, then flattened him with a kick to his back.

Expecting her to pounce, he rolled over. Instead of diving atop him, as he so desired, she soared overhead in an arc worthy of an acrobat. When she emerged on the other side, she'd reclaimed the sword he'd so carelessly tossed aside. Once again the blade was leveled at him, but this time she didn't seem so intent on cutting him to ribbons.

The edges of her mouth tilted upward in a tentative grin while her breasts bounced lusciously.

"Tell me . . . honestly," she demanded, breathless. "Who . . . are you?"

With a sniff, Aiden stood, took two steps back and bowed as he would have to any of the gentle ladies he might have met at the court of King George II, his sovereign monarch. "I cannot tell you more than I already have, my lady. My name is Aiden Forsyth. I'm the second son of Lord John Forsyth, Earl of Hereford. I was a soldier in the army of George the Second, victorious under Cumberland at the Battle of Culloden, and was journeying to my family at the colony in Valoren when I was cursed by a black-hearted, vile sorcerer named Rogan and trapped in the sword you are now pointing at my heart."

She blinked. "You're either a very good actor or you're a crazed fan."

"I'm no actor," he assured her. "And frankly, I have no idea what a 'crazed fan' is. So I can neither confirm nor deny if I am one."

Her cynicism shone in her eyes. He could not blame her. He'd hardly believe the story himself had he not lived it. He considered leaving, but as a soldier he knew better than to charge into any situation without proper exploration and planning. Lives were lost when fools rushed in. Or out, as the case might be.

The world outside these mirrored walls was hers, not his. He guessed as much from his time on the mantel in the house above the ocean. The curse had trapped him, but from the moment Lauren had discovered the sword in the antiques shop, his awareness of his surroundings had increased. And yet he knew he'd need her help to navigate this time. To help him return to England. Perhaps to what was left of his family.

Unfortunately, in order to ensure her assistance he knew of only one way to prove that he was who he claimed to be.

"You bought the sword in a disgustingly dusty shop in Dresden."

The sword wavered as she shook her head. "Ross could have told you that. He loved showing off his prize."

He nodded. True enough. Aiden had been aware of the powerful man who'd bought the sword for Lauren, parading various people by the case and boasting of the minimal price he'd paid for such a worthy specimen—and how he'd had offers ten times the amount to sell to other collectors.

"But he purchased the sword for you, did he not? As a gift. A gift he kept from you, no matter how angry you became. You spent hours admiring the sword in his study, oftentimes after you'd had a swim in the pool just visible from the study where the sword was kept."

She pulled the sword up tight. Had he made a tactical error?

"What are you? A stalker?"

"Another word I do not understand, my lady."

She stepped back. "Ross has incredible security in his house. His staff has been with him for years." Suddenly she charged forward and grabbed him by the collar with her free hand.

"I don't recognize you. You couldn't have been anywhere near Ross's house without my noticing."

"Unless I was in the sword," he countered.

"That's impossible," she insisted.

She had a point. To anyone unfamiliar with the power of magic, what he claimed was insane. But he'd had centuries to come to terms with the magic. He was living proof.

He glanced at the sword. The curse had been imbued into the metal; of that he was sure.

"Then I will simply have to prove that what I've said is true," he said, then disappeared into the darkness.

3

Lauren screamed. After sprinting to the door, she flipped on the lights, gasping, her heart racing as she scanned the room for any sign of the man she'd just sparred with. He'd seemed so . . . familiar. So . . . solid.

Where had he gone?

Her gaze darted to the sword on the mat. With complete fascination, she realized that beside the weapon were two thick indentations in the cushioned floor—two indentations the size of a rather large man's feet. Two indentations that suddenly started toward her.

She doused the lights again, hoping she could slip away in the darkness, but he grabbed her by the arm and reeled her in to him. She connected with his chest with a thud. He was hard and hot and very, very real.

And also very, very invisible.

"How are you doing this?"

When he spoke, his breath teased the side of her cheek. "Magic."

Even though she couldn't see him, she could feel his gaze rake down her body. Her nipples tightened, and the quiver of fear in her belly dipped lower and changed into something deeper, darker and hungrier. She'd seen him for only a few flashes in the deceptive blue light, but his attractiveness had been hard to miss. Dark hair worn past his shoulders. Light eyes. Pale blue, perhaps gray. And a body lean, muscled and honed for battle. She'd gotten in her licks, but she knew he'd held back, toying with her—not out of arrogance, but out of a clear intention not to hurt her. Lauren had seen enough street fights in her youth to know when a guy was holding back from kicking ass.

She reached out and found his shoulders precisely where she imagined they'd be.

"Holy—"

He cut off her curse. "Now do you believe me?"

"I don't know what to believe," she answered honestly, and was thankful he was holding her, because she suddenly felt on the verge of collapse. "In my line of work, there are geniuses who could make the Statue of Liberty disappear."

A chuckle lilted his voice. "I assume this statue is very large?"

She closed her eyes tightly. This couldn't be happening. Magic didn't really exist. Magic was what the technicians and engineers and special-effects wizards created on the screen. Even in the studio, during a shoot that hadn't yet been turned over to the CGI guys, she'd been amazed at the effects that could be achieved the old-fashioned way: with mirrors, wires and other cinematic sleights of hand.

But an invisible man holding her so tightly against him, her entire body was reacting in traitorous, yet delicious ways?

"Are you a ghost?" she asked.

"Do I feel ghostly?"

She swallowed thickly. Ghostly? No. Amazingly hard and warm and powerful? Oh, yeah.

"Why are you here?"

"You freed me from the curse. Released me from the sword."

"How?"

"I am afraid, my lady, that I do not know."

Every word he spoke aroused her as the adrenaline

from their fight morphed into something even more elemental. His voice was incredibly confident and smooth, in keeping with his fighting style—restrained, yet brimming with power.

"I need to sit down," she said, her voice shaky.

He did not release her. "You will not run?"

She took a deep breath. "Make yourself solid again."

"I assure you, my lady, though you cannot see me, I am still quite solid."

Yeah, she could feel that. There was a telltale bulge near her hip that she was trying—wholly unsuccessfully—to ignore.

She licked her lips, attempting to alleviate the sudden dryness there. "I stand corrected. Please make yourself visible. I don't like talking to the air. Even in the dark."

Seconds later he not only materialized into view, but the dim blue lights she'd doused bloomed again with their suddenly strange sapphire glow. If she hadn't been standing so close, holding him with her own hands, she would not have believed the magic that was so clearly real.

"Okay, now I really need to sit down."

After another slight bow that was totally congruous with his costume, which consisted of snug breeches and a stiff white shirt that smelled vaguely of rain, he led her across the room to a stack of trunks. Lauren hopped on top, spread her legs and lowered her head between her knees. Gulping in huge breaths, she tried to come up with a rational explanation for . . .

"What is your name again?" she asked.

"Aiden Forsyth."

. . . for Aiden's unbelievable appearance in her life.

"And you were trapped in the sword?"

"By a Gypsy curse, yes."

The rush in her ears somehow made his story easier to believe.

"And what year did this happen?"

"Seventeen hundred and forty-seven."

She wasn't up to doing the math, but needless to say it was a hell of a long time ago. Centuries, even.

"You said Gypsies. Did this happen in France?"

The whole of her knowledge about Gypsies came from Disney's *The Hunchback of Notre Dame* and the various warnings she'd received prior to traveling to Europe.

"Valoren, actually," he replied.

She sat up. Imaginary stars flew around her as her optical nerves adjusted to the retreat of blood from her brain. "Whoa," she said, her balance skewed.

He grabbed her hand. God, he was warm. And strong. His fingers were slim sinews of muscle. His palm was rough and scarred.

"Are you—"

"I'm fine," she said, swallowing thickly. "Look, I know crap about geography except what I've learned jetting around for location shoots. Where is Valoren?"

With a glance at the trunks, Aiden silently asked for permission to sit beside her. She scooted over to give him room.

"You are quite talented with a sword," he said.

She rolled her eyes. "Yeah, yeah. Honey. Vinegar. It's all the same to me. Tell me more about Valoren."

He pursed his lips, hopefully attempting to condense a large chunk of information into a quick sound bite. This was too crazy. Insane, even. She couldn't help but wonder if she'd finally cracked and her divorce, the stress of trying to make the move from action-adventure heroine to more serious dramatic roles, the constant hounding from the paparazzi and her tragic lack of sex over the last year were driving her, like so many other actresses before her, beyond the edge of reason.

"Have you heard of King George?"

"I saw *The Madness of King George*," she replied. "My ex is a movie producer. We watched a lot of movies."

"What is a movie?"

"Never mind. You fill me in on your history first; then I'll do my best to catch you up to this century."

"Agreed. You do know that King George ruled England?"

"That much I know," she responded, somewhat proud of herself for retaining that tidbit. George, if she remembered correctly, was the crazy king who taxed the tea and caused the colonists to revolt. She'd caught that much knowledge during her sixth-grade play, when she'd been awarded the role of Betsy Ross.

"He was German; did you know that?"

"A German king of England? How did that happen?"

Aiden took a deep breath, exhaling loudly. "Very complicated succession. Let's bypass that discussion."

She smiled. "I'm starting to like you."

"Likewise, my lady," he replied, a glitter in his eyes. Which were, by the way, the most stunning platinum color she'd ever seen.

"London was quite overrun by Gypsies, who, with their very different ways, tended to live on the fringes of even the lowest society."

"They were thieves and con artists?"

His mouth pinched a bit. Had she hit a nerve? Was he Gypsy?

"They were considered so, yes. And in many cases this was true. Those in the upper echelons of society wanted the king to imprison them all or, at the very least, expel them from the country. As you may know, Gypsies have no homeland."

She shook her head. "No, I didn't know that. I figured they all came from Romania or something."

"They are wanderers," he explained, and she guessed his advanced knowledge of the Gypsies came from a better source than her cartoons and travel guides. "The Romani believe in borrowing the earth, not owning it, which is why they do not stay in one place, if they can help it, for very long. However, the Gypsies of London were quite entrenched, having built a community that thrived. When I was but a boy, George the First was convinced by a rather kindhearted nobleman to move the Gypsy population to a colony of sorts, a track of land under the Hanoverian king's control in Germany. The colony was called Valoren, and the village of the Gypsies, Umgeben."

"I've never heard of it."

"The place wasn't discussed much in polite society. There the Gypsies, having no choice, established a small community. They lived peacefully under the watchful eyes of this earl, who had been appointed governor."

"Are you the earl?"

Aiden chuckled. "He was my father."

"So you were next in line?"

"No, that delight would have fallen to my eldest brother, Damon."

"You have more than one brother?"

"Five. And a sister. Half sister, truth be told. My youngest brother and sister were born to my father's second wife. She was a Gypsy."

"And she cursed you?"

"On more than one occasion, I'm sure," he said with a rueful snort, "but not into the sword. She was a good woman. Made my father very happy. I wonder . . ." His voice trailed off, but he quickly snapped his spine straighter and continued his story. "The curse was placed, I believe, by an evil sorcerer by the name of Lord Rogan."

Lauren listened intently while Aiden recounted the night he'd ridden with his brothers from the family's estate into the village of Umgeben, not but a mile or so away, though tucked between two mountains in a treacherous valley that both protected the Gypsies from invaders and trapped them there for slaughter. She marveled at his matter-of-fact tone when she could see a swirl of emotions playing over his face. His jaw had tightened so that she thought it might snap the next time he spoke Lord Rogan's name.

Instinctively, she cupped his chin with her hand. He stopped speaking, and his eyes, full of surprise, locked with hers.

"What?"

"This hurts you. To tell me, I mean," she said.

He closed his eyes briefly, and when the lids lifted again the regret and anger she'd seen only seconds before were gone.

"Does it pain you to listen?"

She nodded. "Of course. A whole village vanished? An evil sorcerer who'd entranced them all into making him their leader?"

She shivered, thinking about Powers Boothe's creepy portrayal of Jim Jones in that flick that had won an Emmy. And for a split second she wondered at her own blind obedience to Ross. She'd once followed that man around like a puppy: done what he told her, when he told her. She'd created a whole persona, from her hair to her clothes to her film roles, all on his "advice." Advice, her ass. He'd been her Svengali, and she'd done nothing to fight him until she'd found him screwing his next creation.

"I know my tale sounds unbelievable," Aiden muttered.

"Not really," she said wryly. "Okay, overall, yeah, your story sounds like an expert pitch for a supernatural flick, but pared down, this Rogan guy sounds totally believable. There are men who can be very convincing, even to the most suspicious people."

Aiden shook his head. "None were more suspicious of outsiders than the Romani," he said. "But Rogan had a way with them. Perhaps it was the magic."

"Real magic?" she asked, breathless. This was all so overwhelming. Gypsies? Magic? Cursed noblemen?

"I am here, am I not?" Humor lit his eyes for a

brief moment, but was gone as quickly as a flash of lightning. He held his emotions close to the vest, Lauren thought. Reminded her of . . . her.

"I can't argue with what I see. Or can't see, as the case may be," she joked.

The wordplay clearly escaped his attention. Instead his gaze locked on the mirror on the other side of the room. When she looked, she saw only the two of them and while they were a striking pair—her blond hair bright against his darkness, their body types both buff and formidable—she didn't know why he was so intrigued with how they looked.

"I'd been away for many years," he said, his voice tinged with bitterness as he turned back to her. "I did not witness how Rogan ingratiated himself into the lives of the Romani or into my sister's heart, but the outcome proved the magic incontrovertible. I touched the sword and was sucked into it. Over all this time, I've been only vaguely aware of my surroundings, becoming fully conscious only on the day you wandered into the shop in Dresden and somehow awakened me."

"That was three years ago," she said.

"And I've wanted you ever since."

Longing. Pure and simple and clear. The sound wrapped around her like a velvet rope and pulled her to her feet. She was used to men making her the object of their desires, but not like this. In Hollywood, few guys kept their lusty appetites private. Men she'd never met before thought nothing of coming up to her at a movie premiere or a club, or hell, even at the gym after a workout, and telling her precisely where they'd like to stick their tongues or other body parts in relation to her body. Some guys had more finesse, dressing up their base desires with fancy words and glittering gifts, but it was all the same: They wanted to nail the famous actress who portrayed the sensual goddess Athena on the silver screen. They couldn't wait to add a notch to their bedposts or sell their sordid stories to the celebrity rags.

Or, at the very least, they itched to mold her into a woman they could own, body and soul, until the next blank canvas came along.

But something in Aiden Forsyth's cadence told her he wasn't a man who propositioned a woman without consequence. He wasn't Ross. He wasn't like any man she'd ever met.

"You only wanted me so I could free you," she said.

He stood, stepped intimately into her personal space and cupped her elbows gently. "Yes. Because once I was free I would make love to you."

Rooted, Lauren blinked rapidly, wondering if he would disappear again. Maybe this was all a dream. Maybe she'd bonked herself on the head during her workout with the sword. Maybe she'd never even stolen the sword at all, but had tripped and fallen on that loose tile in Ross's entryway, knocked herself unconscious and was even now waiting for Ross's snooty butler to call 911. Maybe her overactive imagination cooked up Aiden as a delicious distraction from the fact that she was dying. What better way to go than in the arms of a glorious, sexy soldier from another time and place?

Suddenly his smile turned reticent. He stepped back, breaking the spell that had held her in thrall. "I speak too boldly."

"No," she found herself protesting, her hand instinctively pressing to his chest. His heart beat rapidly beneath the rock-hard muscles, lulling her into a calm she hadn't felt in months. "You're a guy who's been trapped in a sword for two hundred and fifty years, give or take. Can't blame you for wanting to have a little fun once you're free."

Her laughter sounded hollow, even to her own ears. As if she were on the brink of a complete breakdown. Very *One Flew Over the Cuckoo's Nest*. Very, very.

He hooked a finger beneath her chin, lifting her eyes to his, all humor gone from his slate gray gaze. She hadn't realized until that moment that she'd been staring at the floor. What the hell had come over her? Lauren Cole wasn't a shy, shrinking violet. She'd lost her virginity at thirteen, and after her marriage to Ross she'd discovered the advantages of being a tigress in the bedroom. But in this sweaty, dusty room, with nothing but torn mats, bad lighting and a wall of mirrors, she felt different. Uncertain, maybe. Vulnerable, definitely. Frightened? Without question.

Aiden traced the angles of her chin and cheeks with his fingers, as if he were a blind man trying to learn an important face. "You speak of *fun* as if mutual enjoyment is a bad thing."

"Not bad." She shook her head softly, hoping not to break from his soft touch.

"You are a woman of great sensuality. I've watched you. For so long."

As he spoke, his face drifted closer and closer. When his lips swiped softly across hers she heard a hiss, as if his holding back caused him physical pain. She'd fisted her hands at her sides, hardly trusting herself not to tear off his clothes and give him what he wanted.

"You've watched me?"

Her mind raced. How often had she sneaked into the study fresh from a swim or a shower to take a peek at the weapon she coveted? How often had she found herself drawn into that room in the middle of the night after her sleep had been disrupted by erotic images and sensations? Those were the times, deep in the night, when she'd found herself most enamored of the sword. Just like tonight, when her haunted dreams had pushed her over the edge, spurred her to break into Ross's house and take what was rightfully hers. Even as she'd slipped on her dark clothes and then driven with her headlights off up Ross's curved driveway, she'd fantasized about the men of courage and valor who had wielded a sword of such deadly beauty in times past—never imagining one of those men's souls had been trapped inside the steel.

"Then watch me now, Aiden," she said, a thrill shooting through her as she switched places with him. "Because there's something I've wanted to show a man like you for a very long time."

4

Burying her hands in his shirt, Lauren pressed between his thighs to stare at him eye to eye. Their noses brushed, and, with their lips less than a breath apart, Aiden had to engage all his self-control to keep from capturing her mouth and plundering it with utter disregard for anything but his own pleasure. In his old life he'd not been a patient man, but over the last two and a half centuries he'd learned the value of the virtue. A few minutes of restraint tonight could earn him what he'd sought since the first minute he'd sensed Lauren's presence in the Dresden shop all those years ago.

Without a word she turned and padded to the door. When her hand skimmed the knob, his breath jammed in his throat, but he relaxed after realizing she was only checking the lock to make sure it was secure. When she cast him a brief but potent smile over her shoulder, lust flooded through him. He could hear his blood rushing through his veins and feel the exquisite tightening of his groin. This woman, this modern woman who had once reminded him so much of a trapped bird, now reveled in a freedom that he—more than any man alive—understood.

At a strange metallic box near the door, she flipped switches until the lights in the room glowed a warm, exotic red. This world was a mystery to him, but long ago he'd learned not to care, not to compare the ways of his past with this strange environment in which he'd awakened. He'd figure out the specifics when necessary. For now he wanted nothing more than to be fully alive. Raw. Unchained.

When she'd achieved the atmosphere that pleased her, she started toward him, her arms softly curved at her sides, her chin dipped, her eyes alight with a desire as strong as his own. He imagined her as he'd seen her once, many nights ago, hair mussed from sleep, wearing a delectable confection of silk in a fine sapphire blue that matched her eyes.

Her sharp intake of breath brought him back to the present.

She stood frozen in front of him, no longer dressed in pants, but in the sapphire gown.

"How did you . . . ?" she managed.

Aiden wondered, then grinned. "I only wished to see you in this gown, and there you are."

The corner of her mouth tilted in an amazed smile that intensified his desire.

"You really are magic," she said.

He glanced at the sword and wondered how he'd come to command Rogan's powers. But when she stepped into his arms, he forgot about the weapon and the curse and the sorcerer who'd trapped him there. He thought only about the sensation of smoothing his hands around her waist and clutching her tightly from behind, pressing her flush against his body, groaning as need, white-hot as forged steel, shot through him.

"I see your sword isn't the only thing hard and lethal around here," she quipped.

He arched a brow. "You are as bold as you are beautiful."

"I guess in your time period, such talk would make me a shameless hussy."

"I care not for the past," he said honestly. "I am here now."

Their kiss recalled a clash of predators. Tongues collided. Teeth grazed. Lips pressed hard and harder until Aiden feared he might not ever take another breath. The ache in his chest only invigorated him, made him hungrier, thirstier, harder. Her flesh, so soft beneath his ravaging touch, responded instantly. He yanked off his shirt and thrilled to the feel of her hardened nipples grazing his chest.

He slipped his hands beneath the straps of her gown, and seconds later the material fell away. The moment he cupped her breasts she groaned, threw back her head, arched her back and offered him full access, which he took greedily.

Sensations overwhelmed him from everywhere. The stiff responsiveness of her nipples, the hot buoyancy of her flesh, the sweet, scented flavors of her skin, the aria of pleasured moans she sang without hesitancy, without any attempts at modesty. And unlike the women who followed near the soldiers of his regiment to service the men as needed, Lauren's focus for the moment was on her own pleasure. Not his. And he was perfectly willing to give her whatever she desired.

Pushing himself off the trunks, he dropped to his knees and plied his lips across her belly. When she lifted a leg over his shoulder, giving him access to her sweet mound, he nearly fell backward in ecstasy. Instead, he steadied his hands on her buttocks, tilted her slightly and inhaled.

The scent was intoxicating. Hot. Wet. Crisp, yet musky. Unable to resist, he tasted her, and the flavors on his tongue, coupled with her cry of delight, shot straight to his cock, which pulsed with need. He lapped at her insistently, loving how she gripped his hair tightly, tugging as he found the hard nub within and flicked it until she cooed in pleasured delight.

But he did not want her to come. Not yet. Not until he was buried deep inside her, the sound of her climaxing cries loud in his ear. He shifted her body until he could kiss a path up to her neck, suckling for a moment at the spot where her veins pulsed thickly. She'd skewered her fingers into his hair as she whispered his name over and over in his ear.

"Tell me what more you want, my lady," he whispered, drawing his tongue around the shell of her ear.

"I want you," she said simply.

In seconds he was free of the fastenings on his breeches. And yet he could not bear the idea of making love to her without the comforts he hadn't enjoyed in centuries.

Looking over her shoulder a second later, he smiled as a simple bed materialized. White linen sheets. An array of pillows. All he needed. In a swift move that earned him a yelp of surprise from her, he lifted her into his arms, then moved to the bed, where he laid her amid the sheets, tinged scarlet from the lights above.

He stood above her, suddenly frozen in place.

"What's wrong?" she asked, leaning up on her elbow.

"What on earth could be wrong?"

She eased back onto the pillow, throwing her arm casually above her head, comfortable with her nudity in ways Aiden had rarely appreciated until now.

"Then what are you doing way up there?" she asked. "If this is all a dream, then I have no idea what we're waiting for."

He climbed onto the bed beside her. "Is that what you think this is? A dream?"

"There's no other explanation."

"There's magic," he offered.

"I can't believe in magic."

"Yes, you can," he said, kissing the tip of her nose. "You already do. If you did not, you would have run screaming from this chamber by now."

Her smile rippled with confidence. "I don't run screaming from anywhere, buddy."

"A fine policy."

Suddenly dark, her eyes reflected the frown bowing her delicious lips. "This can't be real," she breathed.

He leaned over her, his mouth inches from hers. "You may tell yourself this is a dream if that is what you wish, but I will show you how very real I am."

"You could," she said, her eyes suddenly twinkling with a wicked gleam. "But why don't you let me be the reality tester?"

She slid her hands around him sensually but, in one quick move, flipped him onto his back and pinned him to the mattress. When he shifted to counter her attack, she grabbed his hands and held them above his head.

"You do realize I could unseat you, yes?" he said.

She licked her lips, her gaze raking down his skin with raw appreciation. "Of course you could. You're bigger and stronger. But honestly, why would you want to?"

Why indeed? When her stare continued to drift hungrily over his body, he immediately gave quarter. She kissed him soundly, shifting until her sweet center pressed hard against him. She didn't make him wait, but moved until the tip of his head met her slick opening.

He slid neatly inside her, her flesh tight around his, pulsing and hot and needful. He cursed at her restraint, which caused her to laugh, and the vibrations heightened the pleasure building inside him.

"Maybe," he said, his chest tight, "this *is* a dream."

She arched her back, tempting him to near madness. "Trust me," she admitted, "it is."

Releasing his hands, she stretched, her skin glistening under the red lights. Aiden clasped her hips, and together they established a rhythm that was slow and languorous, yet greedy and voracious. He closed his eyes tightly and concentrated on the feel of their bodies, conscious of every thrill, every sensation, every escalation of need. She braced her hands on him, her right palm just inches from where his heart beat in a wild, building crescendo. When she tugged on the hair peppering his chest, he thought he'd go insane.

"Yes," she cried, undulating atop him, increasing the maddening tempo of their lovemaking until Aiden lost all track of time and space. It was as if they were floating in midair, nothing to anchor them except each other, nothing to stop them from toppling into bliss-ful oblivion.

When his sex surged and spilled, he cried out in hot abandon, then watched her climax as well. Then, in a move as quick and unexpected as her initial attack, he spun her beneath him and kissed her long and hard and desperately. Only when she pushed on his chest did he stop his assault, panting.

"Slow down, tiger," she said with a laugh in her voice. "I'm not going anywhere."

"Perhaps," he said, "but what of me?"

"You planning to leave?" she asked.

He shook his head, his lips aching for hers. "I am not a fool, my lady. But I am cursed. This pleasure cannot last."

Lauren knew it was morning only because her stomach growled loudly enough to wake her. Unlike the pampered little starlets who could subsist on a few leaves of lettuce and a snort of blow, Lauren needed real food first thing in the morning. And a comfortable bed, she thought with an ache stabbing between her shoulder blades. What the hell was wrong with her mattress?

She sat up and forced her eyes open. A red light beamed into her eyes, and she rolled over, catching a rather rancid sniff of leathery sweat.

Where was she?

The workout room?

Memories flooded her: powerful images of a magic man and the sword and—*Oh God*. She realized then that she was naked. But where was the bed? The sexy gown? Hell, where was Aiden?

"Aiden?"

Her voice echoed, hollow in the empty space.

She sat up.

"Aiden!"

He didn't answer, but just outside she heard the dull thump of hammers and the tinny whine of table saws. Holy crap, she'd spent the night in the workout room next to the soundstage. Had she locked the door? Because if she hadn't, she was going to provide one hell of a show if someone decided to pop inside.

She found her clothes and threw herself into them as quickly as possible. She hit the lights, and, though momentarily blinded, she rubbed and squinted until her eyes watered and the room came fully into view. No Aiden. No simple bed. No sign that the aches in her body—the delicious, languorous aches—were anything but a powerful dream.

Until a whisper teased across her neck. "Good morning, my lady."

Only Aiden wasn't anywhere to be seen.

She glanced at the sword, cradled once again in the cashmere blanket.

"Don't do that," she insisted. "Make yourself visible."

"Alas, I cannot."

"Are you back in the sword?" she asked.

"If I were, could I do this?"

She gasped as an invisible hand copped a gentle feel of her left breast, followed by the press of moist lips at the center of her breastbone. She reached out and the atmosphere stiffened, but provided no real resistance. He was there, but not there, doing decadent things to her body that no one could see. Not even her.

But she could feel. *Oh, boy.* Could she ever.

She gulped. "Then . . . you . . . are . . . real."

Her voice shot upward as his lips rounded on her nipple and suckled through the fabric of her tank top.

"Did I not prove that last night?" he murmured against her flesh.

The hammering outside grew louder, and she could hear the rough voices of the crew shouting over the power tools. She attempted to push him back, flailing when she could not feel him.

"It's daytime, sweetheart. Time to end this fantasy."

He chuckled, the sound oddly echoed. "We're nowhere near the end of our fantasy, my lady."

Lauren couldn't suppress the smile that teased the edges of her mouth, particularly when his warm fingertip traced her jawline, leaving behind an imprint of intoxicating heat.

"Why are you invisible?"

"I am apparently corporeal only in the night. The curse remains."

"Why didn't I free you all the way?"

"I know not."

Her chest tightened. "Maybe you are a ghost."

"I am not or I would have been only a spirit last night. Ghosts do not become corporeal—they have left their earthly bodies behind."

A curl of heat tickled Lauren intimately. He had an earthly body, all right, and he wasn't afraid to use it.

"You're a phantom, then," she surmised.

"Pardon me?"

"A phantom. I read a script about a being that could flit in and out between reality and fantasy— ghostly sometimes and other times solid. Very solid," she said, a flush of heat pinkening her skin as the muscles in her inner thighs instinctively tightened. He wasn't even touching her there, yet her body ached to compress around him.

"I shall be whatever you wish me to be," he promised, "but I fear you must keep the sword near you."

"Forever?" Not that she minded a lover who was

invisible during the day and amazingly solid at night, but as an actress whose first order of business once she finished this film was to shed her Athena image, she couldn't imagine carrying a sword around with her everywhere she went.

"I am bound to the sword," he explained. "I cannot make my way in your world until you free me completely."

"How am I going to do that?"

"I'm not entirely certain you can," he said, intoxicating her yet again with breathy words against her skin. "But imagine the delight we'll both enjoy while we find out."

5

Ross Marchand shoved his hands into his pockets, his teeth grinding and his jaw aching. He stopped himself by remembering the cost of his veneers. He wasn't going to lose control. Not for her. At least, not yet.

He had other things to worry about. Bigger things than his ex-wife and that stupid sword. Like a film about to go into production without a leading man. And that little problem with his finances.

"Do you want me to call the police, sir?"

Nigel lingered a few steps behind him, in the space between the Louis XIV settee and the wing backed chair once reputed to have been owned by Winston Churchill. His butler had left himself enough space to make a quick getaway from Ross's home office. Smart man.

"No," Ross croaked, glancing down at the tool, so carelessly discarded, that had cut through the case. He'd seen the high-tech gadget before. Hell, he'd paid for it. He wondered if the crew on his latest spy thriller, which had wrapped two weeks ago, realized it was missing. "I know who took it."

"Well, of course you do," Nigel muttered, his British accent, which Ross had long suspected was an affectation, slipping a bit. "Shall I put in a call to the former Mrs. Marchand and ask her to return your property?"

Ross snorted. As if Lauren would do anything Nigel asked her to. Even the entire U.N. wouldn't attempt anything as hopeless as trying to barter peace between his second wife and his butler. Nigel had nearly been a casualty of the endless warfare during his seven-year marriage.

"Don't bother."

"You think she'll deny taking the sword?"

Nigel's voice rose an octave. He seemed to be taking the whole situation as a personal affront, especially since Lauren had been clever enough to charm her way past security on the butler's night off.

"Of course she won't deny it," Ross said. He took one last look at the empty case atop his mantel. He needed a drink. Something rare. Something expensive.

After a second Ross realized the butler had mentioned, prior to the news about the missing sword, that he had a second matter that required his attention. He slid into the custom-fitted Aeron chair behind his desk, took two cleansing breaths and then spoke.

"You had something else to tell me?"

The butler's lips tightened into a pucker. "There's someone waiting for you on the lanai, sir."

"Someone?"

The butler straightened to his full, if not quite average height, and adjusted his shoulders until his gray suit molded to his fit frame. "The gentleman was averse to giving his name, sir, but achieved entrance to the house by showing the guard this."

A business card? That was all it took to make it past security?

Ross snatched the small rectangle and knew immediately by touch how the stranger had bypassed his front gate. Custom designed and embossed on hand-tanned leather, the cards came from Ross's very private collection. He handed them out to only the biggest movers and shakers in the entertainment industry—and a select few power brokers from outside the film world. There had been quite an uproar in the gossip rags two years ago when one of Ross's cards had been entered into evidence in the murder trial of a notorious mobster. It was an uproar he couldn't quite shake—and he had no one to blame but himself. His expensive tastes meant that the company he kept often left a lot to be desired.

"What's the guy look like?"

A twitch of a smile itched the corner of Nigel's mouth. "Rather cosmopolitan, sir. Impeccably dressed and groomed."

"Not an actor?"

Nigel's nostrils flared, as if he'd suddenly caught a whiff of rotten eggs. "Certainly not, sir. I'd guess a businessman of extreme influence. And if he's local, then I'll eat my hat."

Ross chuckled, picturing Nigel taking a bite out of the bowler he liked to wear, particularly when he ran errands in Ross's classic Aston Martin, like stopping by the tailor or the dry cleaner or the gourmet market. "Yeah? Well, let's see just what sort this joker is. Grab a bottle of Macallan and two glasses and meet me on the lanai."

Nigel nodded and instantly disappeared. Good man, Nigel, even if the British butler was straight out of central casting. Ross had hired him fifteen years ago, when he was more interested in creating a persona for himself than he was in collecting genuine articles. But whether Nigel was from Birmingham, England, or Birmingham, Alabama, had made no difference to Ross. The man knew Ross's secrets, and without exception Nigel had kept them all.

After checking his hair in the mirror, Ross ambled onto the patio to find a well-dressed man standing near the ledge overlooking Malibu. When he turned and nodded in greeting, the sun glinted off dark eyeglasses, further obscuring his face. He didn't look familiar. But he had to be, if he had one of Ross's cards.

Ross strode forward and accepted the man's proffered hand.

"Mr. Marchand. The view is truly stunning," the stranger said, gesturing to the blue-green Pacific sparkling just below the house. "I'm surprised you bother to make films when you can sit here and watch the waves. Amazing. Terrible and beautiful."

Ross forced a grin, but had other things on his mind beyond the ocean, which admittedly was awe-inspiring, though he certainly hadn't bought this house for the view.

"You have me at a disadvantage. You know my name. I can't say the same."

The stranger whipped off his glasses, revealing sharp, dark blue eyes. "I apologize. We spoke on the phone about six months ago in regard to an item you purchased from a Dresden collector. An item I was—still am, actually—interested in taking off your hands."

The blood Ross had managed to cool down to a simmer before Nigel had announced his mysterious guest flared again.

"You mean that damned sword?" he barked, yanking his hand back.

The stranger nodded coolly.

Ross took a deep breath and tempered his anger. Slowly he pushed his ire at his ex-wife aside and brought his negotiating skills to the forefront. Clearly this man had gone to a lot of trouble to bid for the weapon in person.

"I've had many inquiries about the sword," Ross admitted. "But I certainly don't recall sending any collectors my business card or inviting them to my home."

The man grinned, then moved toward the shaded granite table near the edge of the infinity swimming pool. He slid into a cushioned chair with ease, extracting a handkerchief from his pocket to mop his barely perspiring brow. "I thought you'd appreciate my tenacity," he said in a tone that implied Ross actually did. Which, he supposed, was true. "A friend acquired your card on my behalf. Talking over the telephone can be so cold and impersonal. A possible exchange of cash for a commodity of this magnitude requires a personal interaction."

Nigel opened the sliding glass door, a tray with two Riedel glasses and Ross's prized bottle of single-malt balanced expertly in his hands. With a barely perceptible shake, Ross stopped Nigel from striding forward. He wasn't pouring out his best stuff for some asshole who'd managed to breach his security, no matter how clever he'd been in arranging a face-to-face.

"What's your name?"

"Farrow Pryce."

"And your business?"

"Varied and diversified. You can have your man check me out, if you wish. I'll wait."

Ross narrowed his gaze. Over the years he'd learned to read people. Observe. Make judgments. His instincts came from his gut, and so far he'd been wrong only once. Twice, if he counted Lauren. But their nasty breakup and divorce notwithstanding, she wasn't a bad person. Stubborn and headstrong, sure. Tricky and conniving, absolutely. But without those qualities, she might have buckled under the stress of Hollywood. Happened all the time.

He motioned to Nigel, who proceeded forward and delivered the scotch to the table.

"What was your name again?" Ross asked.

The stranger turned and answered directly to Nigel. "Pryce. With a y. First name Farrow. Family name. Cumbersome, really, but unique. Makes me particularly easy to investigate."

Brief eye contact with Nigel assured Ross he'd have background information on this man in a flash. In the meantime, Ross could at least find out how a collector interested in that damned sword could manage to show up on the very morning it had been discovered missing.

"What brings you here today, of all days?" Ross asked, sliding the scotch to his visitor.

Pryce took a sip, hummed in appreciation of the smooth scotch, then set down his glass. "Is this a bad time?"

"No worse than usual," Ross replied.

Farrow chuckled. "Then I'd like to make your day considerably better."

Slipping his hand into the pocket of his tailored suit jacket, he pulled out a slip of paper. He flattened it on the table, then slid it silently across the table to Ross. A cashier's check. Ross glanced down, raising an eyebrow as he eyed the amount.

"That's about fifteen times what I paid for the sword," Ross commented.

"Twenty. When I want something, I do my research."

"Have you been collecting swords long?"

"Not at all," Farrow replied, swirling his finger around the tulip edge of his glass. "I honestly couldn't care less about any but the Dresden sword."

"Think that's wise," Ross asked, sliding the check back toward Pryce, "telling me how desperate you are?"

"Under other circumstances, no, it wouldn't be wise at all. Giving you that much power in the negotiations would be quite detrimental. But you see, money is not all I have to offer you, Mr. Marchand. Though honestly, I can't imagine what commodity you need more. Particularly now."

Ross stiffened, but forced another sip of scotch. "I'm a movie producer. I always need money. And in much larger amounts than what you're offering."

"If I were offering to finance a film, of course you'd

need more." Finally Pryce lifted the scotch glass and took an appreciative sniff. "But what exactly is the price of saving your life?"

Ross slammed his glass down. "Is that some sort of threat?"

Men a hell of a lot scarier-looking than this one had asked Ross the very same question recently, but there was a cold malevolence in this man's eyes that made Ross wish he hadn't sent Nigel away so quickly. How in the hell did this guy know about his troubles? So far he'd defied the Hollywood rumor mill. The bastards riding his ass tended to keep very low profiles.

Farrow Pryce looked entirely unruffled, as if discussing the longevity of Ross's life bored him to tears. "Calm down, Mr. Marchand. I did not come here offering you an obscene amount of money for an antique sword to insult you. And I see no need for us to work against each other when working together can be so much more beneficial. You have something I want—the sword—and I have something you need: money."

Ross didn't have time for this shit. He wasn't going to play into the hands of some outsider who'd somehow stumbled onto the truth about Ross's financial situation. Besides, the damned sword was just one more reminder of his fucked-up marriage to Lauren. He should be glad she'd taken it. Now, once the movie was over, they'd be entirely through.

"I hate to disappoint you, but I don't have the sword anymore, Mr. Pryce. You're too late."

If Ross had thought the man's eyes were icy before, he was mistaken. They were suddenly glacial. "You sold it?"

Ross snorted. "If only. It was stolen."

"When?"

"Last night. You're about twelve hours too late."

Pryce immediately whipped out his cell phone and hit a speed-dial button. Before Ross could stop him, he was shouting to someone on the other end about finding out whether some man named Rousseau had gotten the sword. The name didn't sound familiar, but Ross had so many offers for the sword since he'd shown it off to his associates that he hardly kept track of names anymore.

Glancing over his shoulder at the windows to his study, he wondered why he'd held on to the damned thing so long anyway. At first he'd simply wanted to show Lauren that she couldn't have everything she wanted. Then, when things between them had deteriorated, he'd used the antique to hold on to her. Long before he'd turned his eye toward her buxom costar, he'd sensed her moving away from him, exerting her independence in little ways that ate away at the bonds of their marriage. He'd given up so much to make her a star. And this was how she repaid him? By robbing him in the dead of night?

"Find out if and how he got it and where it is now," Farrow snarled. "You have an hour. Don't disappoint me."

Ross had to admit the man had the intimidation factor down pat.

"You're wasting your time," Ross informed him, snatching his scotch and downing the last of the smooth liquor in one fiery gulp. "I know who stole the sword."

"You've called the police?"

"No point. Proving the sword doesn't actually belong to her is more trouble than my lawyers say its worth."

"Her?" Farrow asked, his eyes narrowed. "Who?"

"My ex-wife."

It took the man a second, but his scowl relaxed into a confident grin. "The stage producer or the actress?"

"Lauren Cole."

He tucked the check securely into his pocket. "Clearly, then, I am dealing with the wrong Marchand."

He stood to leave, but Ross leaned across and

pressed his hand to the man's shoulder, forcing him back into his chair. "You're dealing with the only Marchand who might have listened to you. That woman has wanted that sword for years. She risked her career last night lifting it from me. I could fire her ass for pulling that stunt. She's not going to sell it to you."

"I'll make her an irresistible offer."

"Money? She's got more than she needs, believe me."

Farrow's grin curved his sharp cheek. "There are other ways to persuade someone to part with a valuable."

At this, Ross's chest clenched. He knew a threat when he heard it, even when couched in a deviously benign tone. He might be totally pissed off at Lauren, but she was the principal player in his latest soon-to-be blockbuster film. If something happened to her, the movie wouldn't get made, and without his anticipated income from the box-office receipts, he might never get himself out of the financial hole he'd fallen into.

"Now, wait just a minute, Pryce. My ex-wife might be a total pain in my ass, but I won't stand by while you—"

The man held up his hand. "Calm down, Marchand. I know she's your meal ticket."

He dropped his overly sophisticated demeanor, chugged back the scotch and slid the glass toward the decanter for a refill. Ross sensed that now was the time to negotiate. Clearly, the man knew things. If word got out that Ross Marchand was hip deep in debt to people who'd shoot you dead and steal your cannoli without a backward glance, many of his more respectable investors would cross his name off their guest lists quicker than he could say Roman Polanski. His smarter move would be to work with this guy— or at the very least, to make him think he was willing to strike a deal.

"Why do you want this sword so badly anyway?"

Farrow Pryce assessed him quickly, then, apparently deciding he was worth the trouble, leaned forward and spoke in an even tone. "Have you ever heard of an organization called the K'vr?"

Ross searched his memory and came up empty. "Should I have?"

"No," Pryce replied. "And no amount of research by your butler will yield much information, either. He certainly won't be able to connect me or my millions to the organization, though I assure you I wouldn't have a penny without the legacy of the K'vr. It's an organization devoted to . . . well, let's just say we're devoted to the acquisition of great power."

"What kind of power?"

"The kind of power you conjure in your movies, although you have to use computer-generated effects."

In the span of the next ten minutes, Farrow Pryce wove a tale straight from a high-budget B movie. A wicked sorcerer named Rogan. A Gypsy curse. A missing source of unimaginable power that had been sought for centuries by people like him who believed Rogan's legacy would bestow the means to world domination. When he was through explaining how the sword could very well be the hidden magical source of unimaginable power, Ross applauded.

"I have to say, Pryce, this goes down in history as the most innovative pitch I've ever heard. You had me going there for awhile," he said, pouring himself another measure of scotch. He couldn't believe he hadn't seen this coming. "But as fascinating as your story is, and as resourceful as you've been in setting up this meeting, the idea's not right for me. I already have the Athena franchise for fantasy films. But if you want to type up a treatment, I'll keep it on file."

Farrow glared at him. "I'm not an aspiring screen-writer, you idiot!" He shot to his feet. "I know all about your sour deals and the fact that if this next

Athena film loses a single penny, you'll likely see that ocean at a much closer range after being fitted with cement loafers. I need that sword. I've waited my entire life to inherit the power of my forefathers, and I'm not waiting any longer. You're going to get that sword for me, do you understand?"

The sound of a throat clearing alerted Ross to Nigel's appearance. The butler didn't say a word, but the way he stared at Pryce spoke volumes.

The man was for real—and he was dangerous.

"You're serious?" Ross asked.

Farrow calmly returned to his chair. "Deadly serious. Now"—he gestured to Nigel, calling him closer with the wave of his hand—"we have some planning to do, you and I. Nigel, is it? Do ensure that Mr. Marchand and I are not interrupted. And perhaps you can call around and discover the location of his former wife? I believe she and I have business to execute, and Mr. Marchand will be our intermediary."

Ross cursed under his breath. He hadn't meant to drag Lauren into his mess. He'd gone to great lengths to protect her so far, if for no other reason than because he'd invested so much in the Athena franchise—money he couldn't afford to lose.

But she'd made a serious mistake in stealing that sword. Now it looked like there was nothing Ross could do to keep her out of trouble—in fact, it looked like he would be a pawn in dragging her down unless he could figure out how to double-cross this K'vr wacko without getting himself killed in the process.

6

Helen Talbot strode onto the soundstage, clutching the file that contained what might be her last chance to salvage this film. Plucking off her Roberto Cavalli sunglasses and sliding them like a headband into her seriously-in-need-of-new-highlights hair, she opened the folder and scanned the head shots one more time.

Production on *Wrath of Athena* was set to start in a few days, and as of last night the film was without a leading man. Again. The role was clearly cursed, though she wasn't ready to let anyone in on that secret yet. She was working her way into becoming one of the most sought-after casting agents in the industry, and one cursed role could ruin her career.

Helen had already presented dozens of perfectly sculpted paragons of male perfection to the director and the production team. Though the character amounted to little more than eye candy for the film's leading lady, no one had been good enough. And even though Helen was excellent at her job, she wasn't the cause of the hiring glitch.

Lauren Cole, the star, was being a big pain in the ass.

Which Helen considered both telling and ironic, since the woman had been nothing but easygoing and cooperative in the past.

"Hey, Marco," she called out to the security guard

who stood, arms folded across his chest, watching a gaggle of grips adjusting the lighting equipment overhead.

The pudgy man turned and eyed her suspiciously.

"Helen Talbot, remember?"

His expression didn't change.

"The casting director on our sweet little project here?"

Finally recognition dawned in his eyes. She wouldn't have bothered except that Lauren insisted everyone in management on her films play nice with the crew. And today she needed Lauren in a good mood. A very good mood.

"Sorry, Ms. Talbot," the security guard said with an apologetic smile. "It's been a long night. I'm just about to clock out, but I wanted to, er, wait around and see if everything was all right."

Helen eyed the man narrowly. "Why? Did something happen?"

She'd been on the lot for less than fifteen minutes. Definitely not long enough to pick up on any gossip. If ever the stars were aligned against a film production, it was this one. Not only was Mercury in retrograde again, meaning there were bound to be technical issues up the wazoo, but the fact that the divorce between the primary talent and the executive producer had become final only a few days before shooting did not bode well.

Not that Helen wanted Lauren to stay married to the freakishly controlling Ross Marchand, but she was counting on this film's making it to the big screen on time and under budget. The Athena movies were by far the biggest films Helen had ever worked on. With this, the last production, and the studio watching her with eagle eyes, she had to make all the right choices or she'd find herself back to casting small-budget indies, or worse . . . having to return to acting.

Marco glanced sideways. Twice. Helen followed the direction of his stare to the workout room where Lauren spent inordinate amounts of time playing with her weapons and ensuring that her trainers, who hopefully had stock in prescription painkillers, earned every dime they were paid.

"Marco," she said, straightening to her full five-foot-seven-inch height. "Tell me what's wrong this instant or I'll have you tossed off this lot."

He slung his hands into his pockets and shifted nervously. "It's Ms. Cole. She came in late last night."

"Came here? Why? What time?"

"Just before midnight. Not sure why. I guess she wanted to work off some frustration, you know?"

Helen nodded. Yes, she knew, and so did every other person who stood in the supermarket line and had the literacy level of a turnip. The divorce had been splashed on every tabloid headline for weeks.

"Okay, so she came to the studio to work out late. What's the problem?"

Marco's mouth twisted and his shoulders hunched upward, as if he were afraid to say.

Helen patted his arm lightly and turned on her best smile. "It's okay, Marco. You know Lauren and I are friends. If she needs something, I'm the woman to get it for her." She gave the folder she now held against her chest a possessive squeeze. First and foremost, Lauren needed a new leading man. In more ways than one, in Helen's opinion.

Marco leaned forward. "She stayed all night."

"Really?"

That was unusual behavior, even for Lauren. She had a top-notch workout space in her house. Why would she come here when filming hadn't even started? It wasn't like she had an early morning call.

Marco's eyes darted left and right. "She hasn't come out. Her car is still in the parking lot."

Helen stepped close and gripped Marco's arm a little tighter, her voice a whisper as her stomach cramped with worry. "Are you sure she's okay?"

Before he could respond, Helen moved past the man and headed straight to the workout room and banged on the door.

"Lauren! Open up this instant. Lauren!"

Without a full crew in the soundstage, Helen's voice echoed and amplified up into the rafters. The sounds of hammers and table saws stopped dead. She winced. This was all she needed—more personal crap from the cast causing a disruption to the production.

If Lauren was in trouble, Helen was bound and determined not only to fix the problem, but to do so with the minimum of intrusion from the press. She should have become a publicist, but thanks to her dubious first career as a "teen" star, she hated publicists.

She turned to the crew. "Sorry, guys. Just yelling because all that hard work of yours is noisy. Nothing to gape at. Proceed."

After a moment of hesitation and muttering, someone in charge started barking orders and the noise returned. Helen, determined to gain entrance to the locked room, knocked louder. When she pressed her ear to the door, she heard what she thought was an annoyed, "Hold your horses."

Suddenly the door swung open. Lauren stood just inside the threshold, looking like she hadn't brushed her hair in days, her expression clearly aggravated.

"What? Oh," Lauren said, glancing behind her quickly, then opening the door wider. "It's you."

Helen slipped inside and immediately shut the door before someone on the crew snapped a picture with a cell phone camera of Lauren Cole looking like hell and sold it to the tabloids for a small fortune.

"Yeah, it's me. Question is, who are you, and what have you done with the drop-dead-gorgeous star of this film?"

Lauren locked the door, schlepped over to a pile of workout mats in a corner and threw her obviously exhausted body on top.

"She doesn't report to the set until day after tomorrow," Lauren muttered.

"You didn't get the call, then?"

Lauren removed the arm she'd slung across her eyes. "What call?"

"The one that informed you we needed you on the set today to read lines with the prospective actors vying for the role of your booty boy?"

"Booty boy? Where's Joey?"

Ah, Joey Villarosa. What a major-league hottie. Helen allowed herself a few wistful memories of the hunk's first "audition" with her. And the second. And, ooh, the third. Yeah, the third one had been the charm. He hadn't even wanted a part in the movie. He'd been brought in as a potential consultant and trainer for the action sequences.

Well, he'd done a damned fine job consulting her on the sexual advantages of a good workout. Maybe he could do the same for Lauren. And fast.

"Helen?"

"Hmm?"

"Where's Joey?" Lauren repeated.

Lauren spoke slowly, with exaggerated enunciation and suspicious eyes, as if Helen had been sampling her signature pomegranate martinis again with breakfast. She was about to shoot off a sassy comeback when she remembered that Lauren hadn't heard.

"Sweetheart, I'd tell you to sit down, but if you were reclining any further, I'd be picking out your casket."

"Rough night," Lauren said. "Don't tell me Joey got pummeled in another Ultimate Fighting competition. I keep telling him he's too pretty to slap down with those punks."

"He's in the hospital."

"What?"

Lauren shot up, then caught herself on an unsteady hand.

"Must have been some workout," Helen quipped, before picking her way gingerly across the leather mats, crinkling her nose at the smell of stale sweat. But suddenly, as if on an unseen breeze, another scent teased her nostrils. Sweaty, but sweet. Warm. Raw.

Like sex.

"What exactly did you do here all night?" she asked, suspicious. "I don't see tequila bottles or lime rinds, so clearly the party started somewhere else."

"I wasn't drinking," Lauren said, giving herself a shake. Leaning on her elbows, she skewered Helen with a look that stopped her cold. "What happened to Joey? And why didn't anyone call me?"

"I did call you," Helen snapped. "Funny little thing about cell phones. You have to turn them on before you can hear the ring."

"Is he all right?"

Helen frowned. "He'll live, and the scars will give him character, I'm sure."

"Scars?" Lauren swung off the pile of mats. "Helen, tell me what happened right now or those mats you're trying to balance your Prada shoes on aren't going to be enough cushion when I knock you on your bony ass."

Helen inhaled, delight overriding her adverse reaction to Lauren's colorful but completely bogus attempt at intimidation. She swung around halfway, her hands framing her Pilates-shaped backside. "Do you really think my ass is bony? God, I love you."

"Helen . . ."

This time the threat was real.

"Some sort of accident. He's going to be fine, but he's off the film. His agent called me around midnight."

Joey had trained Lauren in the first four films. Their

rapport, while not inherently sexual, was undeniable. Michael, the director, had agreed to take on an inexperienced actor because it meant Lauren was happy and Helen was off his back.

Since Lauren's breakup with Ross Marchand, she had closed herself off from men in a way that, frankly, Helen couldn't imagine. Helen had quite a list of divorces to her name, and not one of them had stopped her from taking lovers. Of course, lovers had usually been the reason for her divorces. Either way, she couldn't understand Lauren's inability to put her hurt behind her and have some bedroom therapy with a costar. But no matter how many gorgeous, six-packed, hot-bodied actors Helen had brought in to read with Lauren for the part in the final Athena film, not one inspired any chemistry.

Until Joey had been recruited, the writers had actually considered making Athena a lesbian. Or at the very least, pissed off at men, which, fortunately for them, was in keeping with the myth. Unfortunately, part of the success of the series so far had been the steamy love scenes between Lauren and her costar du jour. And since this was the last film, no one wanted to mess with the formula.

So with Joey out of the boy-toy business, it was time to select another choice piece of meat for the powerful Athena to love—and, alas, lose.

Lauren, lost in thought, had wandered to where a sword lay on one of the filthy, sweaty mats. When she picked up the weapon, a strange light flickered off the blade. Helen looked around, but couldn't see where the spot was coming from.

"What's that light?"

Lauren had dropped to her knees and was running her fingers along the rather wicked-looking blade. Stepping closer, Helen realized the weapon didn't look at all like a prop, and remembered her friend bemoaning the fact that her ex-husband had withheld some sword from her in the divorce settlement—a fact that hadn't been sitting well with Lauren for quite some time.

"Lauren, is that . . . ?"

But Lauren didn't respond.

"Lauren!"

Lauren's hands jerked back from the blade. "What?"

"Is that Ross's sword?"

"No," Lauren snapped. "This was never Ross's sword."

Holy shit. Lauren had done it now. If the lack of a costar hadn't blown up production, the lead actress's stealing from the producer certainly would do the trick. Helen rushed forward to remove the sword before someone saw it, but the moment her hand shot out, she was caught in a crushing grip.

"No! Don't touch him."

Helen jerked her hand free. "What do you mean, *him*?"

"I mean *it*. Don't touch *it*. It's very sharp. You could cut yourself."

"Maybe then I'll bleed out and won't have to deal with the fact that my entire career is over if you don't get that sword out of here."

Lauren looked confused.

Helen grunted. Clearly Lauren hadn't gotten much sleep. She was usually quicker on the uptake.

"I've got a movie scheduled to start filming in forty-eight hours, and the costar we had lined up for you is out of commission. Now, imagine if you, the star of the film, were thrown in jail for grand theft or whatever it's called. . . ."

"Ross would never have me arrested. The sword is technically mine, and he knows it. Besides, he'd lose a bundle if this film shut down."

"Would he?" Helen asked. The rumors had been insidious this time. Not like the typical gossip-culture whisperings that surrounded each and every production in town. Ross Marchand, people claimed, had some kind of money problems. Since disparaging remarks about moneymen like Ross were floated around this town more often than balloons at a kid's birthday party, she hadn't paid too much attention at first. But then the innuendos and scandalous blather hadn't died away. That usually meant truth was anchoring the rumors inside the mill.

Helen hadn't wanted to say anything to Lauren, who'd fortunately divorced herself from the Hollywood glitterati the minute she chucked Marchand. She needed to have her head in the movie, not on worrying whether her paycheck was going to bounce—or worse, if creditors were coming after her for debts incurred before the end of the marriage.

"If the movie doesn't get filmed, he'll lose millions. You know that," Lauren insisted, turning, her mind momentarily off the sword still gleaming so oddly on the ground. "Wait a minute. What aren't you telling me?"

Sounds from outside the rehearsal room reminded Helen that this wasn't the time or the place to discuss Ross's dicey financial situation. Grabbing Lauren's wrist, she glanced at the door, making the reason for her reticence perfectly clear.

"Get rid of the sword, Lauren. Go to your trailer, clean up, and meet me back here in a half hour. I have five actors coming in to do a read-through at ten, but there's time for us to grab a cup of coffee beforehand. Off the lot, if you know what I mean."

Lauren's brow furrowed. She clearly wanted to know more, but a loud bang just on the other side of the door spurred her to action. She grabbed a blanket, wrapped up the sword, gave Helen a hug and then promised to return in twenty.

Once the door was closed, the tension in Helen's shoulders relaxed somewhat, but not enough for her to cancel the masseuse who was coming at two. She tossed the folder she'd been carrying onto a trunk, then looked around, wondering, first, what the hell her friend had been doing in the rehearsal room alone all night long, and second, how she was going to weasel a confession out of her before their lattes got cold. She and Lauren were close, but since Ross had strong-armed Lauren into making this last film, she'd been edgy and sullen. The last thing Helen wanted to do was set her off right before production started in earnest.

Turning, she caught sight of a flickering red light. A flickering red light atop a video camera aimed in her direction. *Interesting.* What could Lauren have been doing last night that she felt the need to record?

Well, only one way to find out.

7

Lauren shot into her trailer and collapsed against the door, the sword clutched tightly against her chest, her breathing labored. Her mind swam, and she wasn't sure what to focus on first. Joey's accident? Helen's quest for her new costar? Ross and the stolen sword? The parade of as yet unnamed actors coming in to read with her? Or the insane belief that she'd just spent the night with Aiden Forsyth, a man who claimed to have been cursed by Gypsies in 1747, but who had made mad, passionate love to her all night long before disappearing with the dawn?

Lovingly, she placed the sword across the coffee table, but kept the blanket closed.

"Aiden? Are you here?" she asked the air.

She heard nothing. Felt nothing. Fear jabbed at her chest. Had it all been a dream? She'd suspected it before, but the pleasure of making love with Aiden had been too intense, too complete, to come from her subconscious. Maybe she'd lost her mind? She'd always wondered if and when her lie of a life would catch up to her and start chipping away at her sanity. Clearly the divorce had pushed her over the edge. Funny. She would have put her money on the marriage doing the trick.

"Aiden?" she asked again, desperation lilting her voice.

After another tense minute, the atmosphere shifted. Warmed. Filled. Aiden's scent, a mixture of leather and rain, reached her nostrils and eased the rapid pounding of her heart.

She sighed. "You're here."

"Yes," he replied, his voice as rich as dark chocolate.

"Where?"

"Where do you want me to be?"

She closed her eyes. His hands smoothed over her hips and around her backside, which he clutched possessively. How easy it would be to surrender and indulge again in a few hours of mindless lovemaking. And with an invisible lover? Damn, how many of her private fantasies was he going to deliver?

"Let me see you," she requested.

"I cannot," he replied.

"We're in my trailer. No one will find us here."

"I do not fear discovery, my lady. I have not the ability to make myself corporeal. I suspect the dawning of a new day has changed my circumstances."

"Convenient," she snapped.

After checking to make sure she'd locked the door, Lauren unwrapped the sword from the cashmere blanket. She touched the handle, then remembered that she'd experienced the sword's magical effect fully only after her skin had made contact with the blade. How many other people had handled the sword over the years? Why had none of them freed Aiden from his prison?

Why *her*?

The question would have to wait. She sat on the couch and scooted the table closer, then stretched her hands above the polished steel. The reddish silver gleam had diminished, but the sword still sparkled with potent power, causing the hair on her arms to stand on end.

"Ready?" she asked.

"Proceed," he replied.

She took a deep breath and placed her palms flat on the sword. She glanced around, but noticed nothing different.

"Anything?" she asked. "Aiden?"

"Nothing."

Damn.

"Maybe you can only come out in the dark?"

She dashed to the light switch, plunged the trailer into relative darkness and then waited for her eyes to adjust to the shadows. She caught the glimmer of the sword and groped her way back to the table.

Again she touched the sword.

And again nothing happened.

"Sorry," she apologized. "Maybe I'm doing something wrong."

"No," Aiden said. "The exhaustion trapping me in this insubstantial state is hard to fight. Perhaps the magic must rejuvenate during the day."

"Magic with a time limit? Who writes these rules?"

"Rogan," Aiden spat. "His motives for creating such a trap in the first place are incomprehensible. And right now I am too fatigued to untangle his intentions. For now I prefer to focus only on you."

The lights popped back on. Then off. Then on.

"Amazing," he said on a wonder-filled breath.

"Are you doing that?" she asked.

"Yes," he replied. "I seem to possess some of Rogan's magic."

She couldn't help but smile, even though Aiden didn't seem happy about this turn of events. The man was trapped in a curse and fighting intense exhaustion, and yet the light switch amused him; the ability to manipulate it did not.

Still, she understood his conflicting emotions. She hadn't had a chance to think too hard about last night, but she'd been lonely enough over the last year—hell, possibly the last five—to know how much she'd missed by cutting herself off from the male species. Lauren had never denied her sexuality for so long. Being touched and aroused had always been a welcome escape. The thrill of seduction. The madness of orgasm. Yet before she'd released her phantom lover from the sword, the only satisfying action she'd gotten recently had been in her dreams—dreams of a dark-haired, gray-eyed stranger whose soul had felt as old as time.

Aiden?

Of course.

She glanced at the sword.

All this time he'd been haunting her, reaching out to her. She could kick herself for not defying Ross sooner. The shame she'd fought since she'd finally grown the balls to walk out on the cheating bastard flooded over her again. She'd been so young. Starstruck. Stupid. Ross had played on her vulnerabilities like a virtuoso. Was Aiden doing the same, catering to her sexual needs as Ross had appealed to her fantasies about stardom and financial independence?

Aiden's invisible hands curved around her, softly pressing against the small of her back with a touch that was both light and erotic. With concerted effort she pushed her desires aside. She needed time to think.

"Will you return inside the sword?" she asked.

"You do not wish that," he countered.

Despite the ephemeral quality of his voice, she heard his surprise loud and clear.

"No, I don't wish it," she admitted. "I'm just wondering where you'll go."

"Not far," he replied.

With a chilled whoosh, Aiden moved away from her, the sensual quality of the air instantly lost in the cold, sterile environment of her trailer. She hadn't yet had time to personalize her dressing area with more than a few of the leftovers from the last film. Her first Athena costume, encased in glass and hanging on the

wall until the charitable donation she intended to
make at the premiere of *Wrath of Athena*. The hand-
embroidered gold cushions left over from the harem
scene in *Athena's Revenge*. The empty picture frames
that used to hold photos of her and Ross. Knickknacks
and memories, few of which reflected who she really
was anymore.

"Who was that woman?" Aiden asked.

"What?" Did his magic give him the ability to read
her thoughts? "Who?"

"The woman you spoke with? The one who in-
truded on our privacy."

"Oh, Helen?" Lauren volunteered, happy to address a topic other than her damaged psyche. "She's
my best friend and, conveniently, the casting director
on my latest film."

Lauren marched into her bathroom to turn on the
shower. She untied the drawstring on her pants, shaking off the unfamiliar shyness that came from knowing
Aiden was watching her undress.

"A film?"

She stopped moving. *Wow.* How did you explain
video and film to a man who'd likely never even seen
a photograph?

"You said you'd seduced an actress once, yes?"

She could almost feel a wink in his voice when he
replied, "I believe I'm up to two now."

"I meant in the past."

"Ah, yes. She was portraying Léonide in *Le Triom-
phe de l'Amour* in Paris when we first met. I was in
a regiment assigned to escort an ambassador to the
court of Louis the Fifteenth. I was instantly entranced.
I found her again in London, where she played Titania
in *A Midsummer Night's Dream*."

Geez, could he have personally known Shake-
speare? No, that wasn't the right time period. Not that
she knew shit about history, but she'd seen *Shake-
speare in Love*, and Joseph Fiennes had clearly worn

pantaloons. Aiden, while briefly in his clothes, had looked more like Jason Isaacs in *The Patriot*.

She shivered. In a good way. A very good way.

"A film is like a play," she explained, "only it is recorded so that other people can see it later."

"Ah," he said, as if he understood.

But how could he? If he was from the past, as he claimed, then he'd have no way of knowing what a movie was. She'd just have to show him. Maybe use the video she'd taken last night.

The video. She hadn't turned off the machine, not even after Aiden had materialized. Which meant they'd made love within full view of the camera. *Shit*. She hadn't removed the tape, meaning that Helen or anyone else who stumbled into the room might soon see exactly what Lauren had been doing . . . with Aiden. All night long.

8

Lauren shot out of the dressing room and nearly knocked over two interns in her dash to the workout room. When she flung open the door, her heart, pounding hard against her chest, dropped like a stone to the pit of her stomach.

"Helen!"

Her friend was standing at the tiny six-inch monitor, her eyes fixed on the screen and a wicked smile lighting her face.

Lauren jumped inside, locked the door behind her and dashed over to where her friend stood, her arms crossed and one manicured fingernail tapping her chin.

"You weren't supposed to see this," Lauren said, attempting to turn off the machine.

Helen slapped her hand away. Pleasured moans—clearly her own—issued from the tinny speaker.

"Or hear it," she said, managing to at least snap off the volume. When she tried to shut down the power, Helen's hand shot out and encircled her wrist.

"Don't you dare," her friend warned.

Lauren tried to laugh it off. "Into voyeurism much?"

Helen's grin elongated. "Tell me watching other people doing it doesn't get you hot?"

"It doesn't," Lauren lied.

Helen arched a doubtful brow. "Well, it gets me

hot. Especially when . . ." Her eyes widened. "Oh, did he just—"

Lauren twisted out of Helen's grasp and turned off the machine.

"Spoilsport," Helen groused.

With a jab, Lauren pushed the eject button and re- trieved the tape, which she shoved in her pocket.

"I'm going to forget you ever saw that," Lauren said.

"I'm not. In fact, as a reward for letting me watch you get what you've so desperately needed over the last year, I'm going to cancel the auditions for your next leading man."

Lauren eyed her friend suspiciously. "How? We start production in two days."

"I know."

The cat-in-the-cream expression on Helen's face was not reassuring.

"Helen Wilhelm Talbot, what are you thinking?"

Helen reached around and patted Lauren's back pocket, which was now hard and square with the evi- dence of her tryst. "I'm thinking I just found your leading man, and I'm willing to hire him sight unseen. Well, audition unseen. Otherwise, I've seen more than my fair share, and he's delicious."

Lauren jumped back as Helen headed toward the door. Her friend had clearly lost her mind. Aiden wasn't real. Aiden was a ghost. Er, a phantom. Alive, but not completely part of this world. At least, not yet. And it would be damned hard to put him on film, since he was mostly invisible.

"You're nuts," Lauren announced.

"Maybe, but the chemistry you two showed on that tape nearly melted the acrylic off my nail polish."

"That's not chemistry," Lauren argued. "That was sex."

"You can't have one without the other. The man is gorgeous. And that fight scene! He was holding back;

I could see it. Toying with you. It's been a damned long time since any of your costars looked like they could best you in a fight and make that tough-girl attitude of yours crumble with a touch. Michael is going to kiss my feet," Helen said, her eyes gleaming now in the particular way they did when she'd made up her mind about something.

Only a few months ago Michael Sharpe, the director, had said something to Lauren about making sure the last film paired her with a hero worthy of Athena's strength and power. He'd instructed the scriptwriters to pen a romantic story line that would satisfy the hordes of female moviegoers who had become her loyal fan base. Guys flocked to the movies, too, but it was the women who bought the tickets and the merchandise, who dressed their daughters in Athena Halloween costumes and made Oprah's ratings shoot even higher whenever Lauren appeared on the talk show to promote a film.

Helen rubbed her hands together like the proverbial silent-film villain—only this time she was entirely on Lauren's side. If the film did well, they'd be hot properties in Hollywood and beyond.

Lauren had to admit Aiden was perfect. Strong, clever, sexy. A combination of rogue and warrior. She could easily imagine him pulling a sword over some dishonor or slight, just as easily as she could see him seducing a theater full of women with one heady glance, magnified in breathtaking glory on a silver screen. Oh, and IMAX? The possibility stole her breath.

But she couldn't forget that he wasn't real. Even the latest advances in film technology couldn't get around that little detail. However, the video proved he would show up on camera. If he was filmed at night, at least.

Still strategizing, Helen went on: "With this hunk as your leading man, Michael will get exactly what he wants, and you'll get a little—well, maybe not so little—action on the side. And affairs between costars can be good for a film if the publicity is handled right. Can you imagine how insane with jealousy Ross will be? Oh! This is so fucking perfect! Now tell me who he is and how I can find him. Who's his agent?"

"He's not an actor," Lauren insisted.

"Oh, well . . . who fucking cares? He's got enough charisma and intensity to pull this off. The rest we'll fake."

"Fake?" Lauren wasn't sure when she had started to get offended by comments like that. It wasn't as though she'd won an Oscar. But since she'd started playing Athena, she'd worked hard at her craft. Just *anybody* couldn't pull it off, especially not someone from the eighteenth century.

"The only actor who has to act in this film is you. Everyone else is window dressing."

"That's not true," Lauren insisted. She wanted to feel flattered, but she'd been doing this too long not to understand how having talented costars pushed her to shine. Ross Marchand had spared no expense to bring in A-list actors to play opposite her or to take high-profile cameos. She couldn't deny that he'd done all the right things to make her who she was—but it was now up to her to keep her reputation golden.

And while that wasn't the reason she couldn't pursue Aiden as her costar, the excuse would work great for Helen.

"I think I rate better than amateurs, don't you?" she asked haughtily.

Helen rolled her eyes. "You can play diva with someone else, Lauren Cole. You just don't want to share your boy toy with the rest of the world."

"Does he look like a boy?"

"He looks like heaven, but if you don't tell me his name and how I can find him, we're both sunk, and you know it. You could, of course, read with each and

every model-turned-actor scheduled to show up in"—
she glanced at her watch—"thirty minutes."

Lauren opened her mouth to argue, but groaned
instead. She knew Helen would punish her further by
choosing a sensual love scene to read with all the auditioning actors, which would mean hours of awkward
chitchat as a prelude to inept fake kissing, moaning and
orgasms. She could either waste time with Helen, who
would undoubtedly find no one who floated Lauren's
boat, or she could take a chance that she could . . . what?
Work something out with the phantom so he'd be her
costar? Demand that they shoot his scenes only at night?
She supposed she'd heard of wackier demands in Hollywood. Most people probably wouldn't raise an eyebrow.

Of course, most people didn't have Ross Marchand
as their producer.

"I'll talk to him," she promised, hoping to stall.

Helen's smile was entirely too confident for someone who'd gotten just a *maybe*. Then again, *maybe*
didn't exist in Helen's professional vocabulary. She
was the ultimate do-or-die film executive, which was
why she had so much on the line with this movie.

So did Lauren. So what did she have to lose by
asking?

She'd left the door to the trailer open. Despite the
increasing fatigue that made it hard for Aiden to remain entirely aware of his surroundings, he could not
pass up the opportunity to explore. He'd been trapped
in one place so long, he longed to move, survey the
landscape and assess his situation from a broader
angle. His instinct, born of many duels and battles,
could not be waylaid. Rogan's cursed magic would
simply have to wait its turn to torment his soul.

A surge of power shot through him. He gave a cursory glance at the sword, then concentrated and
pushed his diaphanous form into this new and fascinating world.

Sadly, the world he anticipated did not exist outside of Lauren's domicile. The trailer, as she'd called it, stood within a building the size of the cathedrals of Paris or the palaces of London. The ceiling stretched six or seven stories high, and the walls, a dull charcoal gray, were obscured by stage sets the like of which he'd never seen.

To his left he spied the interior of a mountain cavern, replete with dark stone walls and a river of glistening black ooze piping through the middle. To his right a wide expanse of sheer material fluttered in an unnatural wind across walls that shimmered with angelic luster. The furnishings within were all gold-leafed and worthy of a sultan's harem.

Everywhere he looked, men and women milled about, tools in their hands as they strung thick cords from one end of the space to the other or tested lighting that turned day into night and then back again. Some of the workers were high in the air, adjusting strange mechanisms from a web of metal frames that crisscrossed the ceiling. All of them shouted and joked with one another as they worked, or else barked orders, reminding Aiden of his regiment shortly before battle. A sizzle of excitement rang through their voices. They enjoyed their work. They anticipated the opening of their production, of which, he realized, Lauren must be the featured performer.

The star-shaped plaque on her door with her name in the middle clearly gave her away.

Two men strode past him, both wearing pants of a rough blue fabric that looked at once sloppy and incredibly comfortable. "Did you hear about Joe?"

"Yeah, freaky, huh? Hasn't hit the news yet. Marchand must be keeping it hushed. Anyone know what caused the explosion?"

The first man shrugged his bulky shoulders. "Gas leak, probably. What else? This isn't exactly a war zone."

"Maybe he pissed off some bruiser whose wife he was screwing."

They laughed heartily and disappeared around a corner. The language of this time was different in so many ways from his own, but the actions and suppositions of the people clearly were not. Gossip and interest in lurid details still existed. Men still battled against other men for the affection of women. Centuries had passed, but the basics of love and war remained the same.

Luckily, Aiden had hung with the sword in Ross Marchand's office long enough to understand the vernacular of the conversations going on around him—about investments and the massive scope of the entertainment undertakings of one Ross Marchand.

While he was under the control of Rogan's magic, his awareness had been limited. But now that Lauren had explained what a film was, Aiden realized that he had observed Marchand screening scenes from his films on a box that sat on his desk. While entrapped by the magic, Aiden hadn't cared enough to be shocked or surprised by the advancements in technology, but now he couldn't help but wonder how he could ever find a place of significance in a society that had so expanded without him.

A few feet away a man sat on a tall stool pressing buttons on a device like one he'd seen Ross use to retrieve information. Aiden concentrated on joining the worker, and soon was there.

"Hey, Gibbs," the man shouted to a well-dressed bloke holding a thick book overflowing with photographs. "What's the name of that doohickey that Athena found in the third flick? This database is useless without the right name. You know . . . the thing she wore that made her irresistible to men?"

"As if she needed any help." The man named Gibbs chuckled as he flipped through the pages of the book.

Aiden agreed. With Lauren playing the role of the

goddess Athena, any man within a mile radius was likely helpless to resist her.

Gibbs slammed his hand on the appropriate page. "You mean Aphrodite's girdle?"

The man at the keyboard punched the buttons of the corresponding letters and spelled out the word inside a thin white block. He then clicked a button and a photograph of a thick gold belt appeared.

"Yeah, that's it," he confirmed. "Is she using it in this film? I didn't see it with the costume drawings."

"Don't think so," Gibbs replied.

"We should add it to the background of her room, though, don't you think? I think it's in storage. Hey, you . . ."

The man snagged the collar of a young woman who'd been hurrying by with a tray of steaming coffee and shouted orders for her to retrieve the girdle from "wardrobe." She mumbled her agreement, then darted away. The longer Aiden observed, the more this organized chaos resembled the preparations before a battle. Generals and lieutenants poring over plans, shouting orders to infantry peons, who nodded their quick assent. The energy surging through the room was soothingly familiar, even if the situation was as foreign to him as the eighteenth century would be to Lauren.

He returned his attention to the machine. He had a vague understanding that the device was a repository for varied sources of information. Could it, perhaps, lead him to his family?

Stepping directly beside the man whose fingers flew over the keys, he called upon the magic that held him and whispered the name Forsyth into the man's ear.

"What?" he asked.

Gibbs replied. "I didn't say anything."

"You didn't ask about Forsyth?"

"What's a Forsyth?"

"No idea," the man muttered to himself, then continued about his business.

But Aiden would not be deterred. He concentrated harder, focusing his attention onto the man's hands. Seconds later he watched as the name appeared in the little white box.

The words "No results found in Athena database," flashed on the screen.

Damn.

And yet he'd discovered that he was not only trapped by Rogan's cursed magic, but that he had some measure of control over the power as well. This could prove quite interesting, and he wondered what else he could do once he returned to solid form.

With a glance back in the direction of Lauren's trailer, which remained empty, he continued his exploration. A young woman passed so close to him he felt her penetrate his space. The jolt was immediate and unnerving—for both of them. She yelped. But when no one noticed she hurried away.

Finally he spotted a door in a far corner that flashed with daylight whenever opened. He immediately moved toward it, wondering whether the sun was as hot as it had been in his time, whether the air outside smelled putrid like London or invigorating like the valleys of Valoren. But the closer he came to the door, the heavier he felt. And then weaker. With only twenty feet between him and freedom, a painful pull yanked him back to Lauren's trailer, inches from where she'd left the sword.

He'd been tethered again. Bound in ways that clamped the very essence of his soul. Despite the iciness coursing through his bloodstream, he shouted in rage. Several frames dropped off Lauren's wall with a crash.

"Aiden?"

It was the last thing he heard before he fell into a dark and bottomless void.

9

Lauren had no idea where Aiden had gone. She'd been in the trailer for over an hour, calling his name intermittently into the air, stroking the sword, wavering between feeling his arousing presence somewhere near her and then convincing herself that she was entirely alone. At least she knew now that Aiden's appearance had not been a dream or a side effect of some sort of head injury. Helen had seen him, too, in the video, though she'd clearly either missed the part where he'd materialized out of nowhere, or else she'd written off his unexplainable appearance as a technical glitch. How he got there wasn't nearly as interesting as what had happened shortly thereafter. The practically pornographic digital recording she now toyed with in her hands.

She'd always said she'd never make a skin flick, but apparently all her common sense had flown out the window last night. Now she was considering actually watching the thing, curious whether the chemistry Helen had insisted translated onto film truly existed.

Did she dare?

She knew they were hot together in person. She had the sweetly sore muscles to prove it. But it took a special connection to translate that incendiary quality onto the screen.

Just thinking about the possibility raised her internal temperature. She splashed over ice cubes a bottle of room-temperature club soda she found in the bar, blanched at the bitter taste, but drank anyway.

While chewing on an ice cube, she slipped the tiny tape into an adapter, then attached it to the VCR and flipped on the television. She hit rewind and waited until the tape queued to the right spot. Adjusting the volume to a bare minimum, she then grabbed a nearby footstool and dragged it close to the TV so she could sit close. She watched her workout impassively, but gasped when she witnessed the moment when the sword touched her leg. She passed out, and Aiden appeared as if stepping through an invisible barrier.

Leaning nearer to the screen, she saw him kneel over her, his hand hovering just beside her cheek, as if he wanted to touch her, but didn't dare. An odd glow illuminating from the sword added just enough light to make the scene crisp and sharp. He smoothed a single lock behind her ear, so softly, so carefully, she couldn't resist mimicking the gesture. The action progressed, and she watched with utter fascination as she reacted to him, fought him and then brazenly made love to him as if she'd known him forever.

When she threw her leg over his shoulder so he could lick her through and through, she muttered, "Damn. I didn't realize I was so easy."

"I've met many easy women in my days," a cocky male voice replied, so close to her ear she could feel his breath, "and you, my lady, are anything but."

She remained still, a smirk curving her lips. "How long have you been . . . back?"

"Mere moments. Your pleasured moans enticed me from my sleep."

She glanced around and, as expected, saw no sign of him, though his presence now completely filled the trailer. "You were napping?"

"In a manner of speaking," he replied.

She clicked off the television, grinning when he made a disappointed noise. She shoved the recording into the safe she'd had installed in an armoire, then returned to the couch and sat directly across from the sword. She should erase it. Get rid of it forever. She certainly didn't want to end up like Pam Anderson or Paris Hilton. And yet she couldn't quite imagine destroying such an intimate record of what had been one of the best nights of her life.

"There was so much more to see," he said.

"Yes, well, now you've seen a film firsthand."

"And I also understand why men cannot tear their eyes away from you when you are on the screen."

"You're picking up the lingo," she noted.

"I'm a quick learner."

"That's good," she said, knowing that now was as good a time as any to broach the topic of his joining her in the movie. Because—*hell and hot damn*—Helen was right: They sizzled together on the screen. Even before they'd had sex, their banter and byplay had overflowed with the kind of sexual tension that might put her in the same league as Julia Roberts when she'd starred opposite Richard Gere, or, even better, Ellen Barkin playing a coy attorney opposite the corrupt and carnal Dennis Quaid. "Because I have a proposition for you."

His chuckle made her realize that the word had the same naughty connotations in his century as it did in hers.

"Proposition away, my lady."

"You need me to free you again from the sword, right?"

"Again, yes. I am free, but not untethered by the curse that captured me," he said, and she noted hints of anger and resentment in his voice.

"If you could have freed yourself on your own, or

with anyone else who'd handled the sword, it would have happened long before I came around, right?"

"This seems a logical deduction, my lady. The sword had not always resided in that antiques shop. Several owners possessed it over the years, though I was not truly aware of their presence until you came into that shop."

Her mind worked overtime. She'd had a bit of time while she was waiting for him to reappear to work out the situation and come up with a strategy for broaching the subject. He needed her and she needed him. Sure, she could look for a new costar among the many talented actors she was sure Helen had lined up for auditions, but what was the fun in that? She couldn't resist the appeal of flaunting her new lover right under Ross's nose while enjoying the company of a man who intrigued her in ways she'd never thought possible. While she fully intended to help Aiden no matter his decision to join the cast, he didn't have to know that right away.

"Well, then. You need me and I need you."

His hands, still invisible, were on her immediately, splayed on her waist, his fingers magically long enough to reach not only the bottom swell of her breasts, but the lowest curve of her backside.

She tried to slap him away, but could not.

"That's not what I meant," she said loudly.

The brazen contact did not stop. "How do you need me, then, if not to pleasure you?"

"I need you to become an actor."

Instantly his touch disappeared.

"Woman, have you been brained?"

Aiden stalked about the room, honestly concerned for the sanity of the woman who'd freed him and become his lover in the span of one day. He'd had women make unreasonable demands after he'd sexually satisfied them before, but Lauren Cole brought the negotiation to a higher standard. "Have you no idea who I am?"

"You're Aiden Forsyth," she replied, her tone clipped.

Aiden wasn't one to throw his family's name about—he'd taken great pains to ensure that the soldiers in his regiment saw him as an able commander rather than the son of an earl who'd bought his commission—but this wild idea had stunned him beyond measure.

"Do you have any idea what that name means?"

"It's English for 'closed-minded'?"

He growled, fighting the fatigue that still lingered in his consciousness. He needed Lauren in order to gain his freedom from the sword; of this he was certain. But could he subject himself to the indignities of the stage simply to please her?

Unthinkable.

"You could at least hear me out," she argued.

Aiden stifled a grin with a sniff, inhaling the unmistakable scent of weakness. She needed him. He'd survived bloody battles by exploiting such vulnerability to his advantage. He'd been victorious in violent skirmishes with the Scots because of his knowledge of weapons and strategies. His long military career had taught him that the negotiation between men and women bore a hefty resemblance to the battlefield between kings.

"I am not visible. I expect this part of the curse causes a problem even your"—he tried to recall the wording she'd used—"'modern filmmaking techniques' cannot overcome."

"We'd have to film at night," she said calmly, as if she were a paragon of logic rather than a lovely woman who happened to need him desperately. Nearly, he guessed, as desperately as he needed her.

"I'm a soldier, my lady," he said reasonably. "The

son of an earl. For me to take to the stage would be scandalous."

She turned her head ever so slightly, as if straining to hear whether his voice betrayed his true feelings on the matter. He was suddenly very thankful that she could not see him. Although he'd been a fine liar in his lifetime, he suspected that Lauren Cole was better than most at ferreting out untruths and manipulations. She had, after all, survived a marriage to a master manipulator like Ross Marchand.

"In your time period, maybe. But now you'll be this mysterious, intriguing, powerful man who will sweep Athena off her feet, and then . . ."

"Then what?"

Lauren's eyes narrowed, though her glare was focused about two paces to his left. He'd known her for a very short time, but he already understood that she was a woman of great resourcefulness and cunning. He had to admire her pluck, even if he also had to guard against it.

"Then you'll have the whole new world at your disposal. Look," she said, then sighed in frustration. "Where are you?"

"Can't you sense me?"

"I know you're here."

"You can hear me, of course. But can you sense me?"

Aiden watched as she closed her eyes and concentrated.

Determining the scope of their connection could help him outwit the curse, and it also gave him a moment to think. He had to explore the full breadth of his control over the magic, and perhaps his influence over her. Could he use Rogan's magic to bend Lauren to his will? Did he want to?

Open your eyes, he thought, swooping closer and watching her lids vibrate, the lashes fluttering against her cheeks.

She lifted her hand, but her eyes remained shut. "You're right here."

He didn't reply, but tried again to force her to open her eyes.

They squeezed tighter.

He moved away. Only then did he realize how the tightening in his chest meant he'd been holding his breath. Unexpected relief flooded through him. He was pleased that he could not will her to do his bidding. He wanted her, despite his better judgment, to help him of her own free will.

"You moved," she said, her eyes flashing open.

"Try again," he replied.

She smiled, closed her eyes and concentrated.

He couldn't help admiring the sculpted beauty of her fair cheeks and proud chin as she searched for him. He'd made love to his fair share of women, but Lauren Cole had been his equal, offering intimacy as he'd never experienced. The way she spoke to him with a glint of humor in her eyes, the way she cajoled and influenced with no pretense about her true intentions, was wholly intriguing. Women of his time had no trouble asking for what they wanted, but none he'd met had ever appealed to him with such an irresistible combination of need and confidence. Lauren knew she would get precisely what she wanted—without bribery or coercion or blatant seduction.

She took a step closer. After a moment she closed her eyes again, took a deep breath; then, with a smile curving her generous lips, she walked straight through him. Into him. His essence surrounded her, penetrated her, and the vibrations of her need struck him at his core. He knew then that he could deny her nothing— even this outrageous request.

"You're here," she said confidently.

"My lady, you are irresistible."

She opened her eyes, which sparkled bright blue.

"Does that mean you'll tarnish your good name and lower yourself to my vocation?"

"I'll lower myself," he said, dropping onto invisible, insubstantial knees so that he could blow a heated breath across the exposed flesh of her stomach. "As to my new vocation, we shall have to wait and see."

10

Lauren allowed the sweet sensation to tickle across her tummy, and for an instant forgot what she'd asked Aiden to do. She had a whole new request for him that had absolutely nothing to do with movies or Athena or swords, except for the fleshy kind he'd wielded on her last night. The needs of her body instantly overrode the requirements of her mind. When his hot breath swooshed intimately between her legs, she nearly lost her balance.

"Stop that," she said in a voice she found entirely unconvincing.

Luckily, so did he.

He blew again, harder this time, so that a concentrated curl of heat spiraled into her.

"Honestly," she insisted, "I can't make love to you again. Not like this."

"Why on earth not?"

He was behind her now, and she nearly jumped out of her skin when she felt the luxurious pressure of his touch on her breasts.

"I need . . ." she started, her thoughts derailed the moment pinpricks of pressure lengthened and pleasured her nipples.

"Oh, yes, my lady," Aiden purred into her ear. "You do need."

Slowly the sensation of her blouse bunching at her

waist lured her deeper into sensual hypnosis. In seconds she'd lifted her arms. He tugged the blouse until she was bare breasted and open to whatever magical seduction he had to offer. Only she shouldn't be doing this, should she? Not before she'd ensured his agreement. Women were supposed to use sex to get what *they* wanted, right? Not just for pleasure. But, ooooh, the pleasure.

"Stop!"

This time her voice reverberated in the emptiness of the room. Instantly her heated flesh chilled. Had he left?

"Aiden?"

A knock shook the trailer. Lauren crossed her arms quickly to cover her nudity, but then remembered she'd locked the door.

"Who is it?"

"Oh, Lauren! You're inside? You're not supposed to be on the set yet!"

Lauren struggled through her muddled mind to recognize the voice.

"Cinda?"

Her assistant. Great kid. Bad timing.

"I was just coming to stock your fridge and tidy up," she explained.

Lauren coughed and shook her head, trying to restore her equilibrium.

"Can you come back later? I was just about to jump in the shower."

Lauren knew the excuse sounded totally bogus. Actresses, by their trade, were not shy or prudish. Cinda had seen Lauren in her altogether more times than Lauren could count. Then again, so had most of the cast and crew of her films, since she'd never shied from nudity on-screen if it enhanced Athena's sensual nature, which it often did. But the last thing Lauren needed right now was people around. She had her hands full with her phantom. If he hadn't left.

But then, he couldn't leave, could he? Not without her? Without the sword?

"Oh, sure," Cinda answered. "You need anything?"

"Just about an hour of privacy," Lauren replied, wincing at the way that sounded. Cinda might have been the gofer assigned to her by the studio two films ago, but they'd become friends. Now she was blowing the girl off.

Lauren walked over to the door, but denied her urge to open it. "Could you do me one favor before you leave?"

"Sure!" Perky, as always.

"Could you head over to my place and feed Apollo? Take him for a walk?"

That she had gone this long without thinking of her dog was criminal. Sure, the housekeeper would let him out into the dog run first thing, but the poor guy had to be miserable without real company. He'd been the only loyal male in her life since . . . well, since *ever*.

"Why don't you pick up your Princess, too, and take them on a play date at the dog park? It's supposed to be a gorgeous day today."

Cinda's squeal of delight told Lauren that she'd not only fixed any hard feelings with her assistant, but she'd just gotten rid of her for the better part of the day.

"Really?"

"Honestly," Lauren reassured her. "I'm going to be here all day working on the casting of my costar."

"You'll call me if you need anything?" Cinda asked.

"Before I call anyone else, I promise."

After a shouted, "Thank you," Lauren heard Cinda fly down the metal steps outside the trailer.

Her assistant was gone. She was alone.

Or was she?

"Aiden?"

He did not reply. She closed her eyes and concentrated as she'd done before, conjuring his scent in her mind as she attempted to find the leathery essence lingering around her. She smelled nothing but the cold crispness of newly recycled air.

Though Cinda had already dumped Ross's pictures out of the now-empty frames, Lauren realized she'd been married the last time she'd used this space. The other pictures were candid shots of her with costars, crew and fans who'd won trips to the set. Still, the gaping holes made a statement. About loneliness. About betrayal. About lies.

Aiden's sudden appearance, however, had torn away the veil she'd kept over her emotions for so long. She *was* lonely. She *was* starved for intimacy and sex. Lauren needed those things in her life—and preferably on a regular basis . . . preferably with a man like Aiden: Strong. Honorable. Not entirely real.

Which made her wonder . . . was she going from an earthbound, human Svengali to an ethereal one? Over the course of her life, she'd gone from depending on no one to relying on Ross's money, Ross's contacts, Ross's advice and approval. Now she was finally on her own again. Did she really need another man in her bed, even one who was solid and visible only during the night?

Actually, she couldn't think of a better way to ease into her life as a single woman again. Aiden needed her more than she needed him. He wanted his total freedom, and she could, once they figured out how, give that to him. Maybe he could give her the same.

On that hopeful note, she pushed into the bathroom at the back of the trailer and tore off the rest of her clothes. She really did need a shower. And a nap.

If she hadn't watched part of the video, she might have believed that her rendezvous with Aiden had been nothing more than a very hot dream. Or maybe—what was the word her therapist would use—

a "manifestation" of some deep-seated, unfulfilled desires. Well, if that was the case, Aiden put the "man" in "manifestation."

But despite everything she knew about reality and dreams, Lauren believed Aiden was real, a phantom of his living self, trapped by an ancient curse in the blade of a magical sword. The evidence on the recording was incontrovertible. He'd seduced her last night, just as she'd seduced him. The heat they'd generated could have started a California wildfire during the rainy season. She knew all this, and yet she wasn't afraid. Why should she be? In her life before she became the famous Lauren Cole, she'd certainly dealt with greater dangers. So far the only risk Aiden had brought into her life was the risk of orgasmic overdose.

The shower door was stuck, so with a grunt she tugged it open, reached in and turned the lever, allowing the water to run through the long-unused pipes. Steam instantly blossomed, so she opened the door to the living area and turned on the vent. For an instant she glanced longingly at the sword nestled on the table and wondered whether Aiden would come out to play again anytime soon. Just the thought sent a gentle throbbing between her legs. God, how long had it been since a flash of erotic memory had wound her up so tightly? How long since she had had anything remotely erotic to remember?

Lauren tested the temperature, found the scalding water irresistible and stepped beneath the stream. She was so caught up in the delicious way the heat eased into her stiff and constricted muscles, she didn't bother to close the door completely. She wasn't entirely surprised when the chill of its falling open blasted her bare backside.

Then the feel of Aiden's hands against her skin nearly sent her flying.

She spun.

"Aiden?"

A sensation began at a precise spot between her inner thighs and knees, much like the tips of fingers tracing over her skin. Primal heat immediately suffused her body from every direction: Inside, from the needfulness. Outside, from the water. She leaned forward against the tile and concentrated on the sweet pressure rising higher and higher up her leg and then disappearing into the tawny curls at the juncture of her thighs. Somewhere between a breath and a probing touch, the invisible finger parted her feminine lips and slipped inside, slim at first, teasing the tip of her clit, then broadening, stretching, touching every sensitized part of her. She gasped, choking down water as her heart sent needful pulses through her veins. Her hands itched for someone to touch, someone to cling to, even as she tripped on to the edge of a climax. With no male flesh to hang on to, she grabbed the showerhead for balance.

Her breasts made exquisite contact with the chilled tile, adding to the explosion of sensations detonating across her body.

She was panting, moaning uncontrollably as pleasure built to the pressure point. Then the contact disappeared.

"Aiden?"

"I'm here," he said, his whisper barely audible over the shower, his form entirely unseen, even amid the steam.

Though her body throbbed for him to finish what he'd started, Lauren forced herself to breathe. Not to sound anxious. Or worse—desperate. "I hoped it was you and not some other phantom haunting my trailer."

"I am not dead," he replied, his voice deep and throaty and decadent. "I cannot haunt you."

"You're sure?" she asked.

Once again the sensation of having a man inside her—and yet . . . not—threw her body into extrasensory overload. She gasped, then cried out when an added force tightened around her nipples. She squeezed her eyes tight as an orgasm rocked through her, prolonged and exquisite and maddening.

"Why are you," she asked, spinning around, "doing this to me?"

"Do you not enjoy my attention?" Aiden teased.

She swiped water out of her eyes. "You know I do."

A slither of a touch snaked across her neck and shoulders. "You found me, my lady. Fate drew you to me."

"I don't believe in fate," she argued.

"I'd venture to guess that less than a day ago, you did not believe in phantoms, either."

She couldn't resist laughing. At him. At herself. She pushed the water out of her eyes again and decided she'd better get lathered soon or risk running out of hot water. She loved her luxury trailer, but it was a trailer, not a suite at the Crown Chandler Beverly Hills.

"You've got me there," she agreed.

Suddenly he was surrounding her again. In front. In back. Over. Beneath. Inside. She gasped for breath, sputtering when water flooded her mouth and nose.

"I want you everywhere," he admitted.

She forced herself to move to the other side of the shower stall. "Slow down, phantom boy. You're going to drown me. Unless," she said, suddenly suspicious, "that's your intention. Take me into the afterlife with you?"

His presence rushed at her in a wave, but the change in atmosphere remained inches away.

"I told you," he said, "I am not dead."

"How can you be so sure?"

Suddenly all she could feel was the cold draft from the opened shower door and the hot sizzle of the water against her skin.

Was he gone?

Had she insulted him?

She had no idea what constituted a faux pas in the world of phantoms and ghosts, but she did know she had to get out of the shower. She made short work of lathering her body with a squeeze from a fresh bottle of her favorite aromatherapy wash, courtesy of Cinda, no doubt, and then took the time to wash and condition her hair. After doing a quick check to make sure all necessary parts were sufficiently buffed and clean, she shut off the shower and reached for a towel.

Stepping into the cold bathroom, she wondered how far Aiden had wandered. Still dripping, she closed the shower door behind her and began to call his name.

But the instant the metal trim touched the stall, the lights above her flashed. A hot spire of electricity shot through her body, seizing her muscles until she dropped, unconscious, to the ground.

Aiden waited for Lauren to emerge from the tiny room where he'd left her bathing beneath a shower of water with soap suds on her skin and in her hair. The scent of vanilla and lavender drifted on the steam, reminding him of his childhood, when flowers had bloomed heartily in his mother's cherished garden. He'd been so young when she died. Unlike his brother Colin, Aiden was not a religious man. He wasn't sure he believed in an afterlife of any kind. But this place where he'd emerged, this California, shared qualities with both heaven and hell.

Despite Lauren's misgivings, Aiden was sure he was still alive. Ghosts or cursed spirits did not experience the rapture he'd felt last night, nor the torture of being unable to join with her now beneath the cleansing water.

No longer willing to torment himself with the sounds and smells and tastes of her sensual delight while he could not fully feel his own, he had watched her bathe for as long as he could stand the agony.

Aiden had never seen anything like the contraption that rained water down on her hot and hard, but he longed to experience the sensations while in his solid state. There would be time enough, he mused, willing himself into the other room. He had no idea how yet to break the barrier between his phantom state and true life, but he knew the wall between worlds existed, just as certainly as he knew he was not dead.

Contact with the sword all those years ago had brought him quick pain, yes, but he'd been aware of his entrapment just as immediately. Somewhere in the recesses of his memory, he recalled raging against Rogan, knowing he'd been bound by a curse the dark sorcerer could have conjured. Over the course of two-hundred and fifty years, any moment of awareness had been dominated by the desire to run the bastard through with his own cursed sword. Now, part of Aiden wanted to thank the black-hearted liar for setting in motion his meeting with Lauren.

Suddenly the lights around him flickered. He heard what sounded like a feminine squeak from behind him and then a thud that was unmistakably the sound of a body dropping to the ground.

"Lauren!"

He whirled back into the room and froze. Lauren. Naked. Wet. Unconscious.

And there was nothing he could do to help her.

11

David Drake, as he was calling himself these days, scanned the increasingly busy set for signs of the casting director he'd been told was somewhere inside the soundstage. He glanced at the portfolio he clutched in his hand and refamiliarized himself with the stats printed on the back of the professionally produced eight-by-ten glossy. He supposed his agent's insisting that his height was six feet when he was only five-eleven and three-quarters wasn't so much of a lie, but the rest seemed to have come out of the ether.

Hometown: Boise, Idaho. Sure, he'd been born in the potato state, but he hadn't lived there for more than the week it had taken his mother to break out of the hospital and hitchhike to L.A.

Eyes: blue. Thanks to contacts.

Hair: black. Gotta love that L'Oréal Men.

He supposed his weight was accurate. He worked out three hours a day to make sure he never tipped over one eighty. Lean and hot as he was, he was primed for the role as the goddess Athena's lover du jour. He'd watched the first four movies long before he'd been in a position to audition for a role. He'd memorized most of the dialogue, even though he wasn't wonked-out enough to actually recite them in tandem with the actors, like some über-fans he'd met. But since the series had had the same team of writers for all four films, he'd learned the cadence and rhythm of their words. He was going to nail this audition. And then he'd get exactly what he'd come for.

"Can I help you?"

He turned to face a striking woman in a bold blue blouse. Matching eyes flashed against porcelain skin. Thick, dark blond hair. Thin waist. And the mouth . . . Good thing she chose such a light shade of lipstick or the luscious lips would overpower. Her confident smile threw his thoughts in a lusty direction that took him by surprise.

"I'm here to see Helen Talbot."

The woman crossed her arms tightly over her chest, and he couldn't help but watch how her breasts rounded from the tension.

She cleared her throat, but when he met her eyes again she didn't seem offended by his blatant stare. "I'm Helen Talbot."

He flashed his best bad-boy grin and offered his hand. "David Drake."

She raised an eyebrow.

"I'm here for a read with Lauren Cole? My agent told me to be here at two o'clock."

After taking a quick glance at her watch, she slipped her hand into his. But instead of giving it the hearty, "I'm a woman but I can do business rougher than any man" shake he'd become so accustomed to in Hollywood, she just held his hand, as if she were determining the size and texture of it. After a moment, a satisfied grin turned those plump lips into the stuff of erotic fantasies.

"The audition has been canceled, Mr. Drake. Last-minute decision. The role has been cast. Your agent probably missed you."

He took his cell phone out of his pocket, and though he'd turned the device to vibrate, there was nothing indicating a missed call. "Sorry, my agent must not have gotten the message."

She took a step to the side so she could get a better view of his backside. There was no slyness. No pretense. After a few high-profile guest roles on the New York soap scene, he'd been auditioning in Hollywood for over a year. And yet he couldn't remember ever being so audaciously assessed. At least, not by a woman. Despite the urban legends about casting couches, David's experience so far ran along the lines of movie executives so harried and single-minded, they barely had time to look up from stacks of résumés and scripts, much less seduce the stampede of wannabe actors and actresses called to each audition. He was lucky to get one glance before he heard a yea or nay.

Clearly this woman liked to take her time.

Clucking her tongue, she glanced over to the trailer behind her. The one with the gold star on the door. *Lauren's.*

"Crying shame," she lamented. "You would have looked very nice next to Ms. Cole."

He shifted his stance to better accentuate his . . . assets. He'd done worse to get jobs before, though not usually as an actor. But now that he knew how close he was to Lauren, it was time to put his theatrical skills to good use. This woman wanted to be seduced, though her motives seemed entirely more personal than professional. Not that he cared. He smoothed a fingertip along the curve of her elbow. Intimate and yet . . . not. "Then maybe you should rethink your casting decision," he suggested.

She nibbled on her bottom lip, and David couldn't help but feel a twitch of arousal as he imagined her teeth grazing his own mouth. He pressed his lips tightly together and glanced aside. It wasn't like him to get the hots for a woman after only a few seconds of conversation. In California he'd learned that barracudas operated mostly on land. Since he had his own prey to hunt, he had to remain out of this one's

clutches. He could tease and toy, but nothing more—
no matter how much the deprivation might hurt.

"Hmm," she hummed wistfully. "Wish I could."

"Any smaller roles not yet cast?" he asked.

Her gaze drifted up from his chest and met his.
"Bold as brass, aren't you?"

"This is Hollywood. Can't survive otherwise."

Without warning the lights above them blinked, then
went off. The power tools sputtered to a halt. Cursing
echoed all around them while dim emergency lights
clicked on near the exits. Then, just as quickly, the
power came back on. "Wait here. Let me consult with
my leading lady. It might be a good idea to have backup."

As Helen Talbot curved around him, brushing his
arm even though there were yards of empty space on
either side of him, he turned and watched her walk
away. Either she was swinging her ass especially for
his perusal, or the woman had a walk that could stop
traffic. On the L.A. freeway. At rush hour.

Even with the carpenters and scenery technicians
working their table saws and forklifts with screeching
accuracy, he heard Helen's knock on Lauren's trailer
intensify to an insistent pounding. He walked closer.
She was calling out the star's name with a definite
tinge of concern in her voice.

"Something wrong?" he asked.

Helen waved her hand dismissively. "She's probably
in the shower. But where the hell is that assistant of
hers?"

She dug into her pocket and extracted her phone,
tapped a few times until Lauren's picture flooded the
screen, and then held the device to her ear. Seconds
later they heard Lauren's phone ringing inside.

"Maybe she's not there," he offered, though the
tight worry on Helen Talbot's face kicked his instincts
into overdrive. Helen was more than a little concerned. Why?

"She's in there. She hasn't left her trailer."

"You think something's wrong?" he asked, trying not to sound too anxious to get involved.

Helen skewered him with a look that made him feel like a complete idiot. *Wow*. The woman had clearly honed that expression to a fine point.

"Move," he directed, giving her a gentle push to get her out of the way and digging in his pocket for the tool he kept there. Always.

He had the sharp end inserted into the door lock before Helen could say, "Let me call security."

The click was hard to hear amid Helen's warnings that she had to go in first and that he should stay outside and that if anything he might or might not see inside the trailer made it into the tabloids, she'd make sure he never worked in this town again. Obediently he swung the door open for her and stepped aside. She called out Lauren's name, and despite the threat to his career, he couldn't help but glance into the small but clearly plush trailer.

Helen burst through an open door at the other end. She screamed, swung around with a pointed finger and ordered him to call 911, then disappeared through the door.

He did as she asked, waving over two of the crew who'd stopped dead at the sound of Helen's shout. He handed the phone to one of the guys, told him to order an ambulance and dashed inside. He found Helen in the back room, dragging a towel over Lauren's naked body, the star's flesh wet and the distinctive smell of smoke and singed flesh lingering in the air.

"What happened?" he asked.

Helen, her face stoically passive, shook her head violently as she smoothed the hair away from Lauren's face. Her hands wavered over Lauren, as if she wanted to do something to help, but had no idea what.

"Does she have a pulse?" David prompted, dropping to his knees beside her.

Helen's hands shook so much that her charm bracelet rattled. David leaned across and checked the vein at Lauren's neck. He tried to feel some movement, but if it was there, it was slight.

"The ambulance is on its way," the crewman shouted, rushing in with the phone.

"Is that nine-one-one?" Helen asked.

He handed her the phone. Helen ordered him to alert the gate to let the ambulance in, commanded his cohort to stay by the door and ensure that no one else came in, then rattled off the circumstances to the emergency operator on the other end of the phone, conveniently leaving out the name of the woman lying on the floor.

"Do you know CPR?" Helen asked David, clearly repeating the question posed by the operator on the other end of the phone.

David was by no means an expert, but with his past, he knew a few emergency medical tricks. With a quick nod he checked Lauren's breathing, and after he found nothing, he did what he'd wanted to do for a very, very long time.

He covered her sweet mouth with his.

Aiden instinctively sought the sword, but just as quickly resisted the pull of the handle and the call of the blade. Overwhelming instinct told him that the wastrel lowering his lips over Lauren's was doing more than accosting her as she lay unconscious on the floor. Otherwise he would have struck the man down on the spot. Despite the terror ripping through him, he heard enough of the conversation to know that these people were trying to help.

He, on the other hand, was helpless. Or was he? He moved closer to the sword and felt a surge of something dark, dangerous, but powerful. Could Rogan's magic help Lauren? He placed one invisible hand on the hilt of the sword and held the other toward her, concentrating completely on restoring her life.

Seconds later she gasped, but did not regain consciousness. As Aiden strained to see her more clearly, the number of people in the room doubled. All sorts of foreign apparatus were dragged inside, and the voices grew to a near-hysterical cacophony that kept him from understanding what was going on. After men in dark uniforms strapped her to a cot with wheels and took her away, he tried to follow. But just as he caught sight of the sunlight, he was yanked back into the tiny trailer.

He cried out in frustration, a howl that burned as it ripped from his soul. Was she dead? Had Rogan's dark magic killed her or saved her?

The door to the trailer was flung open. The dark blond woman named Helen burst back inside. Aiden was careful to move out of her way. Clearly she could not see him, but had she heard him?

"Ms. Talbot," the man who'd put his lips on Lauren called from just outside the door. "The paramedics are leaving."

"Did you hear that?" she asked the man.

"Hear what?"

"That scream."

The man stuck his head inside and eyed her as if she'd lost her mind.

"Don't you want to ride along with her?" the man asked.

She shook her head. "Michael knows the chief of staff at the hospital. He wants to go with her." Her eyes betrayed that she'd been ordered to stay behind. "I'll be right behind them. I just want to . . ." Her voice drifted off as her eyes narrowed on the sword. She then spun on the man and pointed out the door. "Can you wait for me at the gate? I have something I need to do."

The man's jaw tightened, but with a silent nod he disappeared and shut the door behind him.

Helen Talbot dashed into the bathroom and did a quick search of the cabinets, drawers and floor. She shot back into the main room and checked the closets and under the cushions on the couch. She sniffed the glass Lauren had left on a table, then took a tentative sip.

"Water," she said aloud, then pressed her lips into a thin, flat line as she surveyed the room with eyes that would miss nothing.

Eyes that landed again on the sword.

Aiden stiffened. Did she mean to steal the weapon? Could he stop her?

Seconds later she'd wrapped the sword inside the blanket and shoved it into a canvas bag she found in a closet. He expected to be wrenched back into the weapon, but though he felt a tug on his stomach, as if the tether between him and the metal had tightened, he remained where he stood. Or floated. Or . . . existed.

He had much to learn about this new reality—until, at least, he figured out a way to free himself entirely. To find his family. To defeat the curse.

Something he could not do without Lauren Cole, who at this moment might very well be dead.

12

"She's dangerous," Ben warned.

"I've dealt with dangerous women before," Paschal assured him, though his voice was weak and his face pale. Sitting at his father's bedside, Ben had watched a veil of advanced age unfurl over his father's usually robust body. The aftereffects of Paschal's psychic episode, brought on by his contact with the antique button, had knocked the ninety-five-year-old man into a terrifying state. Paschal had slept nonstop since that morning, but had gotten very little rest. His muttering testified to disturbing dreams and secrets Ben had not wanted to know about. Though his father had finally woken half an hour ago, a haunted glaze still shadowed his silver-gray eyes.

"Speaking of dangerous women," Paschal said, a shadow of a smile playing over his dry, cracked lips, "where is Cat?"

"Doing some research on how to find your friend Gemma Von Roan before she finds us."

A sneer curled Paschal's mouth. "Gemma Von Roan is not a friend. She's a means to an end. As Farrow Pryce's lover, she'll be an invaluable ally. If nothing else, she'll be able to tell us what that rat bastard lover of hers has found out about my brothers."

"She could lie," Ben countered.

"She could," Paschal admitted. "But if she does, I'll know."

Ben's frown was starting to make his jaw ache. He rubbed his unshaven face and wondered how the hell his life had turned from roller coaster to kiddie ride back to roller coaster in such a short period of time. He'd had a profitable career trading in valuable antiquities. Then his mother had died, leaving him responsible for his father's care. Until a few months ago that task entailed becoming his father's teaching assistant and grading derivative, undergrad essays on Gypsy lore and tradition. Now he was in a race to find a cursed sword and a missing uncle, all while dodging a ruthless cult that had already attacked Paschal once. If not for Gemma Von Roan, Paschal might have been killed. But Ben still didn't trust her. And clearly neither did Paschal.

"You like her, though," Ben said, catching a sudden twinkle in Paschal's eyes.

"She's interesting."

"Like a close personal friend would be?"

His voice had dipped low with innuendo on the words "close" and "personal."

"Means to an end," Paschal repeated.

Ben chuckled. "Make all the denials you want, old man, but I haven't left your bedside all day. You talk in your sleep. This Gemma Von Roan was more to you than just a means to an end."

Paschal's scowl evoked childhood memories Ben would have rather repressed. Normally a peaceful man, Paschal could be formidable when the situation warranted.

"I'm over ninety years old," Paschal grumbled. "On a good day, any woman who is more than a means to an end could send me to an early grave."

With a cough, Ben covered his laughter. His father's face had gone from pasty to an enraged red. No doubt thinking of Gemma, the woman whose name he'd muttered quite a few times since his interaction with the button, had added fuel to the old man's fire.

"Technically, you're nearly three hundred years old. You missed your chance at an early grave years ago," he quipped.

"Impertinent," his father snapped.

"Just calling it like I see it."

"Maybe you should spend more time worrying about your own love life and leaving mine the hell alone."

Ben shoved away from the bed, needing distance from his father's crotchety attitude. Or perhaps from his on-the-mark comment.

His father had shut his eyes and drawn his mouth into a tight line. Ben turned to the shaded window. Cracks of sunlight filtered from around the curtains, reminding him of a sunny afternoon three weeks ago when he and Cat had made love against the picture window facing the ocean until the clouds had rolled in. In the maelstrom of thunder, lightning and the whistling strains of wind, they had explored each other's bodies in ways that made him long for the days when seducing a woman had been his one and only concern.

With a groan he pushed the memories aside. Now that Paschal was awake, Ben had to concentrate on finding out what his father had seen after touching the button—what new aspects of this mystery he'd keyed in to. Ben could no longer fool himself into believing that his father would live forever—the curse had not made Paschal immortal. While he'd been trapped by the Gypsy magic, the aging process had stopped, but immediately on his release it had restarted. Ben suspected that Paschal's unusual robustness and age-defying energy had been a residual effect of the magic, but his father could rely on that power no longer. Searching for his brothers had sapped it out of him.

The old man had had enough verve nine months

ago to seduce a woman who might be the key to their next move. Either Paschal Rousseau was more of a dog than Ben had ever suspected, or this Gemma Von Roan had her own nefarious reasons for succumbing to his father's charm.

Ben fingered the curtains in front of the window. "If Gemma Von Roan is still Farrow Pryce's lover, you can't deny that she's our best bet for finding out whether he's gotten his hands on the sword."

Paschal shook his head. "He doesn't have it. If he did, Aiden would be dead."

"Maybe he is," Ben said, wondering when he'd become the voice of doom. "The fact that you got Damon back after all these centuries is inconceivable. There's a very good chance he's the only brother you'll ever reunite with. You need to prepare yourself."

Paschal smirked, then coughed before he snapped, "Did you have Defeatist Flakes for breakfast?"

"I'm trying to be realistic," Ben insisted.

"Since when? I miss the old Ben."

The old Ben. He hardly remembered the guy. Used to get into trouble a lot. Once served time in a Moroccan jail. Had his picture posted with the word "wanted" above it in several foreign countries.

"The old Ben never called home," Ben reminded his father.

"At least I knew he was out doing something exciting rather than fretting over my every move."

"I don't fret," Ben countered. "Besides, what could be more exciting than catching snippets of the erotic interlude of your liaison with a woman young enough to be your granddaughter?"

"Technically, my great-great-great-great-great-great-great-great-granddaughter, give or take a 'great,'" Paschal said, counting off the "greats" on his fingers.

"You're a strange old man."

Paschal snorted. "You don't live two hundred and

sixty years past your prime and not develop a few quirks. And unfortunately, our interlude was too brief to be considered anything more than an old man's error in judgment. Taught me a man needs to be at the top of his game to deal with Gemma. Bit of the old Ben wouldn't hurt, if you meet up with her. There's more to her than meets the eye."

"Shouldn't we be more worried about Farrow Pryce? He's the brains of the operation, isn't he?"

Paschal waved his hand weakly. "He's the money and the power, but brains, I'm not so sure. So long as he doesn't get his hands on the sword or realize we're onto his game, we'll stay one step ahead. Gemma's another story. There's something about her. . . . I can't say for sure, but I suspect that the blood running through her veins is more powerful than even she imagines. She's Rogan's direct descendant. That might explain . . ."

Paschal's voice drifted off while Ben tried to take his father's warning seriously, but it was hard to muster up fear of any so-called sorcerer who'd died centuries ago. It wasn't as if the K'vr, the cult dedicated to Rogan worship, had successfully taken over the world. Hell, Pryce hadn't even managed to take over the cult. Their run-in with the group nine months prior taught Ben and Paschal that factions remained within the organization and it had begun to crumble from within.

Which was why Pryce was so desperate to get his hands on the sword. With an object reported to possess Rogan's magic, he could become the definitive leader of an organization that was, according to the scant information he and Cat had been able to find, worth millions of dollars in devotions and tithes.

Ben understood that Rogan's magic had been formidable in its time. The proof—a man born in 1717— was lying on the bed across from him. But if Gemma Van Roan had even an ounce of her ancestor's power, why was she hanging out with a gangster like Pryce?

And why was her brother, also a blood descendant of the sorcerer, locked up in a Florida penitentiary awaiting trial for murder?

"I think we can handle Gemma Von Roan," Ben reassured him.

"Yes, but, why would we want to?"

Cat had slipped into the room, a steaming mug of strong-smelling tea cradled in her hands. "I met her. You didn't. And I think I'm still limping."

Paschal moved to sit up, slapping Ben away when he started to help.

"I'm not an invalid," Paschal barked.

"Funny how his energy came back the minute you came into the room," Ben muttered to Cat.

"I'm not deaf, either." Paschal leveled a murderous gaze on his son.

Cat grinned, and Ben couldn't help admiring the curve of her lips—and of her backside when she bent over to reward his father with the tea and a soft swipe of her hand across his forehead. "You are still clammy."

"You'd be clammy, too, if you were psychically jettisoned two hundred and sixty-one years into the past and then yanked back to the present to see your supposedly long-dead brother standing over the body of a naked woman."

"What are you talking about?" Ben asked.

Paschal sniffed the tea, clearly not happy with the strong herbal fragrance. He described his visions to them in surprising detail. At first he'd witnessed his brother's ride into Umgeben, the Gypsy village, during their fruitless search for their sister. He'd watched Aiden explore Rogan's armory, where'd he'd been sucked into a cursed sword. But then the scene had shifted, pulling Paschal into a vision he was sure took place in the here and now. The space was tight. The blond woman on the floor, nude. Wet. And Aiden was there, but not there—overcome by strife, even though Paschal could not see him.

Once the tale was told, Ben sneaked at glance at Cat, wondering if she'd seen any of these images when she'd shared the psychic experience with his father. Her expression remained stoic and blank.

"It was like I was tapping into him," Paschal said, his energy returning. "I've never experienced that before. I was concentrating only on the night our sister disappeared, but then this scene came through. I wasn't prepared; I'll admit it. His helpless rage was overwhelming."

"But was he free of the curse?" Ben asked.

Paschal frowned. "I could not tell."

Cat slid onto the bed and gestured for Paschal to take a sip. He did, bleching noisily once the brew touched his lips.

"One of your old family recipes?" he asked.

"Yes," she admitted.

"No wonder you're so thin," Paschal shot back.

Her mouth twisted into an expression halfway between a grimace and a grin. "It'll help restore psychic balance."

"I didn't know my psychic balance was off-kilter."

"Just depleted," she replied, kindly not pointing out that the rest of him wasn't doing so hot, either. "We may need you again. I'm afraid I wasn't very effective."

Ben's and Cat's eyes met, and the guilt on her face caught Paschal's attention.

Cat laid a calming hand on Paschal's wrist. "I piggybacked onto your psychic journey." She scooted nearer, her dark eyes wide and focused fully on his father. "It was amazing."

All sounds of reproach disappeared from Paschal's voice when he asked, "What did you see?"

"Snippets of what you saw," Cat replied. "You and

your brothers riding into the village. The emptiness. The sword."

"Did you see Aiden standing over the woman? Did you recognize her?"

Cat shook her head. "I'm sorry."

Ben turned away. Cat wasn't telling Paschal the whole story, but since she normally shot from the hip, she must have a damned good reason for playing coy.

Paschal pounded the bed, the tea splashing. "I've seen the woman before, but I can't seem to remember from where. But if we find her, we find Aiden. I'm sure of it."

In his exuberance, the rest of the foul-smelling tea sloshed over the side of the mug. Cat moved to mop it up, but knowing this action would only infuriate his father further, Ben grabbed her shoulder gently and drew her away. "What's one more woman to find? Right now you have to rest. Leave the detective work to us, okay?"

"I'm heartier than you think," Paschal said.

Ben rolled his eyes. "If I live to be two hundred and something, I hope I look half as good as you do. There. Satisfied?"

Cat added, "Why don't you let us handle the drudge work and you concentrate on regaining your strength. Once we find your brother, he might need our help to break the curse, like Damon did. You'll need to be stronger than you are now, and you know it."

Paschal pointed a gnarled finger accusingly at both of them. "I have your word that you won't leave me out because of some fool need to protect me?"

Cat glanced at Ben. The situation was shaving more and more time off his father's already extended life, but he knew he had no choice but to agree.

"You focus on recovering your strength," Ben said. "We'll focus on finding Gemma Von Roan."

Paschal smirked. "Concentrate on the other woman. Gemma will find me."

"And you know this how?" Cat asked.

Paschal tapped a finger to his temple, then closed his eyes, looking more peaceful than he had in weeks.

Ben followed Cat out of the room and onto the balcony overlooking the Atlantic Ocean. The suite atop the Crown Chandler property in St. Augustine kept them close to the source of Rogan's powerful magical haven, a castle he once owned, yet far enough away for them to retain their perspective. Rogan's castle had been moved over sixty years ago from the legendary Gypsy colony of Valoren to a supposedly haunted island off the coast of Florida. Now it was being renovated as a hotel—a high-priced resort no vacationer would set foot in until he and his uncle had mastered the Gypsy curse.

Now that Paschal had one brother back after six decades of trying to foil the dark magic, he had insisted on remaining close to the structure. He believed, perhaps naively, perhaps not, that all his brothers had been trapped by the same curse. He'd rededicated himself to finding and freeing them all, but so far, despite help from Ben and Cat, they'd made very little progress. Each time Paschal called upon his psychic skill to try to locate another brother, he grew weaker. Older. Ben couldn't help but wonder how much time his father had left before a family reunion was no longer possible.

"Heard from Alexa?" Ben asked after Cat leaned back against him, the exotic scent of her hair teasing his nostrils.

"A few hours ago," Cat replied. "She and Damon are being followed. Not sure yet by whom. They've stayed away from Valoren because they don't want to lead anyone back there. She's having a devil of a time keeping Damon in check, though. He's convinced the key to finding his brothers is back where it all began."

"Sounds reasonable. Maybe we should head there ourselves. Act as decoys."

Cat shook her head. "We're better off staying on the trail of the sword. We're so close."

Ben looked at her as if she'd lost her mind. "What are you talking about? We don't know where the sword is. We don't know where Farrow Pryce is. Or Gemma, for that matter. All we know is that Alexa and Damon met with an antiques dealer in Dresden who said he sold a sword matching the description of Rogan's to a rich American man and his beautiful wife over three years ago."

Cat arched a brow. "A beautiful *blond* wife. And I'll bet that same blonde is the woman from Paschal's vision. She has the sword. I saw it. It was lying on a table just a few feet away from her."

"Why didn't you tell Paschal you saw that part?"

Her frown answered his question. "He's in no shape to travel. Besides, this woman might be easy to find, but she's going to be hell to get close to."

She went into the suite and returned with a glossy magazine, one of those celebrity rags he saw tossed around the lobby of the hotel. On the cover was a statuesque blonde wearing a sparkly dress with some insipid headline about her apparently high-profile divorce.

"That's the woman he saw on the floor?" he asked.

"Yep. Lauren Cole," Cat replied. "She's one of Hollywood's hottest."

Ben smirked. "You told Paschal that you had seen only snippets of the experience."

Her lips quirked into an unrepentant smile. "I lied."

He had the overwhelming urge to tell Cat he loved her, but he squelched the instinct by dragging her into his arms and showing her instead with lips and tongue and hands.

All thoughts of swords and blondes and his father drifted out of his mind, replaced with the strong urge to divest Cat of her panties. Unfortunately she had a single-minded streak he'd rather not fight.

"Only problem is," she said, wiping her hand lovingly across her kiss-swollen mouth, "she was involved in some sort of accident today. Its all over the Internet. She's in the hospital in Los Angeles. We won't be able to get near her."

The mechanisms in Ben's brain clicked and whirled until he made a mind-blowing connection. "Do you think that's what he saw? Her accident? And Aiden was there? Didn't Alexa say that when she first released Damon she was knocked unconscious?"

Cat nodded. "Yes, but she came to rather quickly. Lauren Cole was much more severely injured. Some sort of electric shock. Either way, she's definitely released Aiden. At least partially. I felt a man standing over her, and he was very concerned. His soul felt very, very old."

"Could he have hurt her?"

When Damon had tapped into Rogan's magic, he'd become violent. Could Aiden suffer the same effect?

"I don't think so, but I don't know. We need to talk to Lauren Cole."

"Does Alexa know her?"

As the heiress to the Crown Chandler legacy, Alexa had more than just money and jets and hotel rooms at her disposal. She knew everyone worth knowing—including celebrities.

Cat smiled. "She booked us a suite at her Beverly Hills property. Lauren Cole uses their spa. The concierge is very well connected and should be able to wrangle us an introduction to her or, at the very least, someone in her entourage. Alexa wants to stay as far from this as possible. She doesn't want to tip off the people following her about what we're up to."

"What about Gemma Von Roan?"

Cat's grin turned into a hard frown. "That's the part you won't like."

"Why?"

"I called your friend Mariah."

Ben had trouble swallowing. The thought of his current lover talking to his former one did not make him happy.

"She's cool," Cat said.

Again he remained quiet. If cool equaled cold as ice, then Cat's assessment was on the money.

He took a chance. "And?"

Cat sidled away. "She used her aviation contacts and found out that Farrow Pryce's corporate jet has been used twice this week, both times heading to Los Angeles."

"He's closing in," Ben said. "He might already be close enough to beat us to the sword."

"Then we'd better hurry," Cat said, that sly look in her eye making his stomach do a little flip. "We leave in an hour."

13

The smell hit her first. Metallic and sterile, the odor lured Lauren from the darkness and into the pain. Images of white sleeves and pale hands faded, replaced by the fuzzy outlines of a man and a woman arguing at the foot of her bed. The woman she recognized immediately from the sheer venom in her voice—Helen. But she had to blink several times before she identified the soft-spoken man as her friend and director, Michael Sharpe.

"You can't let him in here," Helen insisted, slashing her hand inches from Michael's middle. Had her nails been sharpened, she might have disemboweled him.

"He's her husband."

"Her *ex*-husband. The divorce was final days ago."

Michael shoved his hands through his hair, bringing the white at his temples into sharp relief against his tan skin. "He's still the producer. He could shut down production, and then where would she be?"

"Don't be coy, Michael. It doesn't suit you," Helen spat. "The real question is, where would *you* be?"

Lauren moved her jaw, wondering if she had enough energy to open it and beg Helen to back off. Michael was a good guy, even if he was intimidated as hell by Ross. She couldn't blame him. Michael was a filmmaker, not a moneyman. Once known for costume dramas and quirky films that had earned him two Oscars and a Palme d'Or, he had signed on to direct the Athena films solely for the cash. Luckily for her his immense talent ensured that the four previous Athena films had been exciting, dramatic action thrillers rather than campy toga romps. Helen really shouldn't give him a hard time for kissing Ross's ass. Who in this town hadn't smooched that particular backside at least once?

"He just wants to check on her for himself," Michael explained to Helen. "He promised he won't stay long. If he pulls the plug—"

"I'd like to pull his plug," Helen snapped, and Lauren felt a chuckle burble inside her chest. "If he cancels this film he'll look like a vindictive, pussy-whipped asshole. He won't tarnish his prized reputation that way."

Michael frowned. "Depends on the spin."

Helen's grin sharpened with pure spite. "My point exactly. Ross Marchand is a powerful man, but what he knows about spin, I taught him. If he fucks with her, I'll give him so much spin he'll think he died and came back as a dreidel. I won't let him mess with her. Not today. Not when she almost—"

"Died?"

The word croaked from Lauren's parched lips.

"Lauren?"

Helen practically leaped into her arms, making Lauren feel a hell of a lot better about her long-term mortality. Clearly if she were moments from death, Helen would be treating her with kid gloves.

"You're alive. . . . I mean," she corrected, "awake."

"Apparently both," Lauren said, winded and achy. The roots of her hair hurt, as if someone were tugging on the strands and wasn't letting go. Every nerve ending in her body seemed to be set on hum, and the ringing in her ears gave a hollow quality to her voice when she spoke. She squirmed, hoping movement would alleviate the sensations, but the stiffness of the hospital bed beneath her only made it worse. "What happened?"

Helen's teeth caught on her berry-stained bottom lip. "We're not sure. Stan's looking into it."

And Stan was . . . who?

Her confusion must have shown.

"You remember Stan, don't you, sweetie? The set electrician? Whatever happened in your trailer cut the juice to half the soundstage. We nearly lost you."

Lauren shut her eyes tight and tried to remember. All she could see in her mind's eye was . . . Aiden. Warmth oozed over her body like heated massage oil, sensual and soothing. She could almost hear his voice whispering her name.

"Aiden," she murmured.

"No, honey. Stan. He's going to figure out what happened."

"We know what happened. Someone tried to kill you."

The voice boomed into the sterile hospital room and, if Lauren wasn't mistaken, shook the IV drip attached to her arm.

With each step Ross took into the room, Helen widened her stance until she looked like a linebacker about to block an oncoming tackle. "Leave her alone, Ross. She's been through hell."

Ross stared at Lauren, not sparing Helen a second glance. "She's been through worse before."

With any other man Helen might have unleashed her industry-famous temper, but with Ross she had to tread carefully. He was, after all, her boss on this film. And while Helen had clout to spare in her own right, she didn't need to be on the bad side of a mogul like Ross Marchand.

"It's okay," Lauren forced herself to say.

Helen spun on her, her eyes wide. "You sure?"

Lauren nodded. "Just don't go far."

Leaning in, Helen whispered, "If he so much as farts too loud, you call me."

Guessing that laughing would hurt like hell, Lauren kept her reaction to a reassuring smile. Before she left the room, Helen closed the curtain beside the empty bed near the window, then, after skewering Ross with a look of warning, exited the room. Michael, Lauren noticed, had already left.

"What do you want, Ross?"

She didn't want to look into his eyes, but something in his expression forced her attention there. Were they . . . glossy? Ross was a smooth operator, but he wasn't a very good actor. At least not with her. She looked away.

"You're really all right?" he asked.

She gave a light shrug. "I'm breathing."

"I called in a specialist. I'd have moved you to a better room, but the doctors wanted you—"

"I'm fine," she said, cutting him off. His obvious concern unnerved her almost as much as the tubes and monitors attached to her body. She couldn't help remembering a time, not so many years ago, when he'd come to her in a different hospital, shaking with the same anxiety and apprehension, sitting vigil at her bedside, professing a heart full of emotions while she drifted in and out of a drug-induced haze.

It had been the night she'd run away from him the first time. She'd just turned eighteen, and, after three years living with Ross and his wife, Donna, her whole world turned upside down. Ross announced that Donna had left him and then iced the shocking announcement by declaring his love for Lauren and asking her to marry him. Stunned and overwhelmed, she'd run away to West Hollywood, searching for her mother or her former friends, desperate to escape what even her very young mind knew was a bad idea.

Yeah, with Ross, she'd lived the high life in Malibu

and Beverly Hills, but running with the rich and famous came with a high price—her independence. Not to mention her self-respect.

Ross had been her teacher. A patient guide. Then, over time, he'd become more.

So cool. So manipulative. He'd convinced her that he could not only save her from the streets, but could also make her a star. He'd made good on his promises, too, arranging for her to appear in a few small independent films so she could learn the ropes without the whole industry watching. And since she hadn't embarrassed herself, she'd hung on Ross's every word after that—listened and learned and lived.

Her undeniable yearning for safety and security canceled out every bit of street smarts she'd ever learned. Years of depending on an undependable mother, squatting in abandoned buildings and foraging for food had broken her down to utter desperation. When his limo had popped a tire a few feet from where she was hanging on a street corner, she'd seen him as just another hotshot she could grift for lunch money.

But he'd found her act charming. Long after a second car had come to rescue him from the unwashed masses and return him to the golden vistas of the California coastline, he'd stayed with her, grunging his Armani slacks on the curb, asking her questions and listening to her bullshit answers.

And even after his wise-ass butler had coaxed him into leaving that day, he'd come back. Sometimes alone. Sometimes with Donna. His wife had blown Lauren away with her stylish smarts and fearless attitude. Lauren had never met a woman like her before. She wanted to be her. How could she not?

At the time, Lauren hadn't known what to make of these aliens from her own hometown. At first she'd figured they were just slumming, bringing her little gifts of gourmet cheese and imported crackers to appease their consciences for living such lives of excess. But after her mother lit out on some drug run to Tijuana, Lauren decided to screw her hand-to-mouth life and go with the Marchands back to the Hills. A couple of days turned into a week. Then a month. Then three years.

They taught her to dress properly and speak with correct pronunciation. They found her roles in the community theater they ran in West Hollywood, then had her audition for the parts in indie films. She earned her chops and, little by little, she transformed from a streetwise punk to a sleek, sophisticated actress who could believably spout lines from *Medea* as easily as the lyrics from the latest top-ten ballad.

But then Donna left, just days before Lauren turned eighteen. Ross's interest suddenly became personal—intimate. He had never, to her knowledge, looked at her that way, no matter how beautiful he'd told her she was or how handsome she'd found him.

How powerful.

How perfect.

Suddenly terrified by emotions and an attraction she'd never expected, Lauren had run back to the streets. She'd learned that her mother had OD'd, and the only friends she could remember had either gone to lockup or had moved on. She remembered meeting a guy—a runaway like her—and buying him dinner with the twenty dollars Ross had given her earlier in the day to tip her masseuse. Later that night she'd been jumped by five gang girls trolling for drug money. With each punch, kick and cut, she learned how much she no longer belonged in the hood. If not for the runaway who'd called the cops, she would have died in a stinking alleyway.

The kid had waited with her until the ambulance arrived, and then had abandoned her when she'd needed him most.

"Lauren, are you okay? Do you need more pain meds? I can get the doctor," Ross offered now.

Her own eyes filled with moisture. She took a

chance at raising her arm, which still felt as if she were being pricked by a thousand pins and needles, and swiped the tears away. The desperation of that moment all those years ago came flooding back. If only the kid had dragged her away instead of calling for help. If only he'd helped her escape, rather than leave her to fall once again under Ross's spell.

"What do you want, Ross? You can see I'm fine. The film will go on. I haven't talked to any doctors yet, but I'm sure the movie won't be delayed for more than a few days. The insurance—"

He cut her off with a hand over hers. She wanted to recoil, but didn't have the strength.

"I'm not worried about the movie."

No matter the pain, this time she couldn't prevent the laughter.

His grin was small and disarming, reminding her of how she'd once fallen so hard for him.

"Okay," he admitted. "I'm worried about the movie. But I'm more worried about you. First you break into my house and take something that isn't yours—"

It took all of her feeble strength, but she managed to yank her hand away. Beside her, one of the monitors beeped more quickly. It must be gauging her heart rate.

"Is that why you're here? Because of the sword? It's mine, Ross. You know it is. Your lawyer will tell you, or hasn't he already?"

"You can't prove it was a gift."

Any sentimental thoughts lingering in her brain burst into nothingness.

"Can't I?" she countered, trying to stretch so she at least looked as if she were sitting up taller in the damned bed. "Want me to produce the guy who owns the antiques shop? He's still there. He remembers us. He remembers the sword. Want to know how I know that?"

His spray-tan face paled. "The guy was a hundred years old," he claimed, but his voice quavered—just the tiniest bit, but enough to know she'd won this battle. At least for today.

She relaxed, closed her eyes for a moment and thought about Aiden. God, where was he? Where was the sword? If what Helen said was true, her trailer was probably swarming with people by now. Guys from the set. From the studio. From the insurance company. Anyone who took one look at the brilliant artistry of the sword wouldn't hesitate to steal it.

Maybe even Ross himself.

But he didn't have the weapon back yet or he wouldn't have come here to harass her. Nevertheless, for all she knew, Aiden Forsyth and the sword she'd coveted could be gone.

"I'm tired," she said. Her entire body ached, though she guessed that the liquid dripping into her arm was numbing the true brunt of her pain. She needed sleep. She needed to heal. She needed Ross to get the hell out. Even if she did have the sword, there was no way she was going to give it back.

He patted her hand, then let his palm sit atop her hand for a few minutes. A subtle shake vibrated from his fingers to hers . . . or was that just the aftereffect of her own injury? She opened her eyes and noticed, in this unguarded moment, that Ross's irises had a dark curtain drawn across them—a look she'd seen too often during their life together for her not to know that something was seriously wrong.

"Okay," she said with a sigh. "I'll bite. What's wrong?"

"I did this," he said.

She tensed, but did not move. "You tried to kill me?"

He blinked rapidly, as if he'd just realized what he'd said. "No, of course not. Damn it, Lauren. I'm pissed off at you for taking the sword, but I would never . . . You know I'd—"

"Then what are you talking about?"

He pressed his lips together, and the eyes she'd once gazed into with such admiration and trust blinked with uncertainty. "You need to watch yourself. You need a bodyguard. What was the name of that guy you used two years ago when you started getting those creepy letters?"

"The letters weren't creepy," Lauren said, her last words punctuated by an uncontrollable yawn. "And I don't need a bodyguard. This was an accident."

"You don't know that," he countered.

"And you don't know that it wasn't."

Ross moved away from the side of the bed, and Lauren was too tired to follow him, even with her eyes. She allowed her lids to drift closed and concentrated only on the sound of his shoes. Step. Step. Step. Step. Pacing. He always paced when he had a problem to work out. Step. Step.

Shuffle?

She forced her eyes open, blinking. Ross stood, eyes wide, frozen in place.

"Ross?"

He jumped. "What was that?"

Terror flashed in his eyes, but Lauren was too close to unconsciousness to care.

14

"Leave."

Aiden whispered the command into Ross's ear at such close range, the man's arms flailed through him in surprise. Aiden felt nothing. He wasn't exactly in one place, was he? He was . . . everywhere. He'd suspected that he could concentrate his spirit into a semblance of a translucent body if he so desired, but for now he existed everywhere and nowhere all at once, contained only by the walls of the sterile room.

The sword called to him. Helen had tucked the bag containing the weapon beneath the spare bed, and while he was grateful to be near the woman who'd awoken his soul, he wanted nothing more than to be separated from the forged metal, imbued as it was with Rogan's vile magic. While Ross was in the room he resisted the pull. Ross, who had kept Lauren from freeing Aiden for years. Ross, who had belittled her to his friends when she was not within earshot and had placated her with words of love he did not mean. Ross, who had had a most amazing woman as his wife, and yet had squandered her affections.

And now he sought to torment her when she should be recovering?

Not bloody likely.

The man had no honor. Had he still been in his own century, Aiden would have called him out. Instead he concentrated, drawing all the power and strength he possessed in this transitional state against Ross. The man jumped again when Aiden's invisible flesh pressed nearer.

"What the . . . ?"

Aiden focused on his fist, drawing all of his energy into the place where his hand and fingers and knuckles curled into one ball of pressure. But before he could betray his upbringing by striking a man without warning, a woman dressed completely in blue shot into the room.

She bypassed Ross and immediately attended to Lauren, who had fallen asleep again. After ensuring that her charge was unharmed, she tossed a suspicious glare at Ross, tempered only by her soft voice.

"Sir, are you all right?"

Aiden stood down. He supposed the man did look rather ridiculous, scrunched up against the presence of someone he could not see.

"Did you hear that?" Ross asked.

Aiden floated nearer to Lauren, who was now sleeping peacefully in the bed. Though she was still connected by various tubes and wires to machines, Aiden had learned that the soft, consistent beeps meant she was on the mend.

"Hear what?" the nurse asked, eyeing Ross suspiciously. "Ms. Cole is just fine. The doctor will be in—"

Aiden couldn't resist. He returned to Ross and used the energy he'd built around his hand to give the man a violent shove. Ross screamed like a lunatic, but when the nurse rushed to him, he shot out the door and disappeared. The nurse followed, shouting for him to stop, and then the door swung closed and the noise from outside faded away, leaving only Aiden's chuckle to compete with the sounds of the medical apparatus buzzing and beeping throughout the otherwise quiet room.

Soon after, the nurse returned, accompanied by a

doctor who had treated Lauren earlier. Fit and tall
and dressed in a crisp white coat, the man engendered
in Aiden confidence in the doctor's healing abilities.
He'd taken good care of Lauren so far. From what
he'd overheard, she'd come close to death and had
escaped that fate only because of something called
"CPR."

"Who was that you were chasing?" the doctor asked.

The nurse's brow furrowed even as she hovered
over Lauren, efficiently tending to her in ways that
did not wake her. "The husband."

Former husband, Aiden thought.

The doctor picked up a chart dangling from the end
of the bed and perused the information, then examined Lauren himself. She stirred this time, and Aiden
started at the jolt of pleasure he received when she
opened her eyes again.

"You're going to be fine, Ms. Cole."

The doctor explained the various procedures that
had been performed on her as a result of her injury.
He outlined the treatment, which, at this point, consisted mainly of rest.

"When can I leave?" she asked.

"Not for a few days, I'm afraid."

"I have a movie to shoot," she argued.

The doctor smirked. "You are the star, aren't you?
And you were injured on the set. I'm thinking no one
is going to complain if you take a few days to recover."

She opened her mouth as if she wished to comment
or ask more questions, but the doctor assured her he'd
return later, so she closed her eyes and drifted back to
sleep. Aiden felt his hold on his consciousness slipping.
Lauren lived. She would recover from the strange accident. He could no longer fight the pull of the sword.

Luckily, hours later, when the darkness descended on
the room like a veil, power drew back into Aiden's
soul and spread like lifeblood through his body. A not

wholly unpleasant tingle spread into his fingers and toes, and a thrumming in his ears pumped in time with his heart. In the same rush of life, magic burbled from the center of his chest and rushed into his veins, hot and thick and scented with metal, like polished steel.

Cold. Hard. Deadly.

The magic no longer belonged to Rogan, but the shadows of his influence remained. At the dawn of his reawakening, Aiden had sensed the crazed sorcerer's presence. Rogan had yoked him to a weapon he'd imbued with evil, and the vile blackness seemed wrought into his soul like the gold in the handle of the sword.

Shadows pulsed within him. He could feel them, just as he could feel the powerful weapon tucked into a bag beneath him.

From the other side of a curtain he heard a feminine mewl. Aiden swung off the spare bed, tore the fabric aside and then instantly stilled.

A white-coated man leaned over Lauren's bed. Instinctively Aiden stepped back, not wanting to reveal his presence to the doctor. But after a second he realized the lights in the room remained dim—too dim for a physician to examine a patient. Lauren made another noise, but this time, the sound was strangled. Through clenched teeth, the doctor hissed directly into Lauren's face, "Where is the sword?"

He was clutching her shoulder with one hand while a knife glinted in the other.

Aiden gave her no time to reply. He grabbed the man's wrist and twisted the joint until the slim knife flew from his grip, clattering to the floor.

The man wailed in pain and spun, his face hidden behind a mask, though his dark eyes flashed with rage.

"What the—"

Aiden heaved the man away from Lauren. The intruder sailed over a wheeled tray and tumbled to the ground with a metallic crash.

"Who are you?" Aiden demanded, positioning himself between Lauren and her attacker. He glanced over his shoulder. Her eyes were open, but unfocused. One hand grasped at her throat, but she did not speak.

The assailant scuttled toward the door.

In a flash Aiden blocked his path.

"Holy shit! How did you—"

Aiden snatched the man by the collar and lifted him to his feet, then higher, his shoes dangling and his clothing tightening around his neck.

"Tell me who you are before I tear your head from your shoulders with my bare hands."

Nothing but choking noises gurgled from the man's gasping mouth.

"Don't," Lauren croaked, her voice a forced whisper. "Don't kill him. I called . . . the nurse."

With a growl, Aiden flung him hard against the nearest wall.

"What is your purpose here?" he demanded, but the door behind him slammed open, and a nurse burst into the room. Aiden called on the magic to fade into the shadows, but the man on the ground continued to struggle with his now invisible assailant. The nurse screamed at the stranger on the floor, which brought a burly orderly into the room.

"Tried . . . to . . . kill . . ." Lauren forced the words out, and each syllable drained the color from the nurse's face.

"Get him! Hold him!" she commanded.

The orderly had him in a headlock so quickly, the attacker had neither time nor opportunity to say more.

In a rush of activity a uniformed officer appeared. The nurse positioned herself beside Lauren, her arms outstretched protectively as the attacker rambled and raged about a disappearing man.

"He attacked me! Nearly broke my neck! Then, 'poof,' he's gone. She saw him! Ask her!"

The nurse turned to Lauren.

"He's crazy," Lauren replied. "I woke up with him on top of me. He had a scalpel or something. He nearly killed me."

The guard was dragging the man out of the room when someone else forced his way inside—someone in a dark suit, with a clipboard and a pinched face—demanding to know who was causing the ruckus in his hospital. In the confusion, the attacker threw his head back hard, knocking the guard off of him, and bolted out the door. Aiden nearly sprang forward to pursue, but caught himself.

He could not go far. The sword saw to that. The orderly, the guard and the man in the suit gave chase. The nurse remained at her post, speaking in soothing tones, reassuring Lauren, whose blue eyes were wide with terror.

"You're all right. Please, Ms. Cole. You need to calm down."

"But security—"

"They'll catch him, I swear," the nurse said, but the quaver in her voice was not reassuring. "You need to lie back. Your heart might not be able to take another shock. Please, Ms. Cole, you need to lie back."

Lauren struggled against the nurse's hands, but she'd been weakened by the drugs. Aiden, still invisible by choice, leaned close to Lauren and whispered, "I'm here, my lady. Do not fight."

The nurse jumped back and spun around. "Who was that?"

She turned on the lights, then scrambled around the room, searching every possible hiding place for another intruder.

"Tell her to leave," Aiden suggested, this time pressing close to Lauren and speaking directly into her ear.

Lauren, who'd relaxed into the pillows with the curve of a smile on her lips, waved her hand at the frantic nurse.

"You're making me dizzy."

The nurse stopped. "I heard someone."

"Why don't you go see if they caught that man?"

"But I shouldn't leave you—"

The guard slipped back inside, panting. "Ms. Cole, are you—"

"Did you catch him?" she asked.

The guard glanced sheepishly at the ground. "Not yet. The hospital is in lockdown. We'll find him. But the chief wants me to stay with you until we're all clear."

Lauren shook her head. "I'm sure he meant for you to wait outside."

The guard shifted uneasily, but Lauren gave the nurse a quelling look, so she shooed the man out. "You can stay right outside by the door. I'll wait with—"

"No," Lauren interrupted. "I'll be fine. The other patients must need you. I just want to go back to sleep."

Reluctantly the nurse complied. Though alarms sounded and frantic voices from the other side of the door testified that the entire floor was in a panic, Lauren looked utterly bucolic the moment the nurse shut off the light and, with a promise to return when the attacker was caught, left the room.

Aiden made himself visible just as a twinkle of a smile danced across Lauren's face.

"You saved my life," she said. "Thank you."

He gestured at his now-solid body. "You did the same for me, my lady. I wonder, however, why your life is in such constant jeopardy."

"Never was before yesterday," she muttered. "He said he wanted the sword."

Aiden frowned. "So did your former husband. Perhaps he—"

"—hired someone to rough me up?" Lauren asked. "Doesn't seem like his style."

Aiden's chest filled with a rage that might have exploded had Ross Marchand been in the room. His veins sizzled with a bloodlust he hadn't experienced since the battlefields of Scotland, and which he had hoped he'd never feel again. "Perhaps his style has changed."

15

The moment the goon he'd sent into Lauren Cole's room slid, breathless and sweating, into the limousine parked a block away from the hospital, Farrow knew the idiot had failed.

"What happened?"

The man clutched at his chest, trying to pull enough oxygen into his lungs to speak. Farrow grabbed the collar of the man's stolen white coat and tugged him forward. Though he'd come with a reputation for being ruthless and wiry, the man's intense shaking made Farrow wonder if he'd been misled. Seriously misled.

"Breathe later," Farrow said evenly. "Talk now."

"Attacked. Appeared. Out of nowhere."

Farrow released the man and sat back into the plush leather seat and considered this odd turn of events. Could this be possible? Had Ross Marchand told him the truth when he claimed to have been accosted by an unseen force when in his ex-wife's hospital room?

Farrow had assumed the film producer had simply spent too much time sniffing coke with his A-list stars, or that he was concocting a wild tale to buy his ex-wife more time with the sword. Now Farrow had what appeared to be unbiased corroboration of a magical force at play.

"You didn't see the sword?"

The man shook his head furiously. "Looked everywhere. Nothing there. No one there. Then—"

Farrow held up his hand, instructed the driver to proceed, and then poured the man a finger of scotch, which he offered with a calm smile. The man was not a follower, so Farrow had no sway over him except that he'd promised him a generous payment for an hour's work. The K'vr had few contacts in Los Angeles, and with Lauren Cole being such a high-profile patient, he hadn't wanted any of his own men to risk breaking into a hospital they hadn't been able to reconnoiter. This man, at the very least, claimed to know the lay of the land.

"It was fucking messed up," he went on. "I've dealt with dudes who were fast, but this guy . . . he was a goddamned ghost. I checked the room before I grabbed her, man. Every inch. She was alone. But the minute I touched her he was there. Strong as a fucking bear. Could have thrown me through a wall. Would have snapped my neck, but she stopped him."

Farrow forced his expression to remain cool. "Tell me what you saw. Precisely."

For a man of less than average intelligence, he recounted the story with adequate detail. A forged security badge had given him access to Lauren's floor, and he'd quickly found her room. Luckily the security guard had been more interested in flirting with chatty nurses than standing vigil. When Farrow's man had finally slipped inside, Lauren Cole had been unconscious and drugged.

"I looked all over, but I couldn't find no sword. Decided I had no choice. Had to wake the bitch up. She was just coming to when this son of a bitch attacked. Came out of nowhere."

"When you say, 'out of nowhere,' do you mean—"

"I mean he fucking appeared where no one was before, got it? She started talking. Distracted him. I was almost out the door; then he just . . . appeared right in front of me. Black hair. Fucked-up gray eyes. Like ice, man. Like ice."

Farrow could feel his own eyes widening to saucers. All these years, all these generations, he'd heard tales of magic, but had never seen any evidence to make him a true believer. Former leaders of the K'vr, like Gemma's father, had often exhibited psychic talent that could not be explained—but he'd always considered the tricks mental sleight of hand.

Not that he didn't believe in the source of Rogan's magic—it was, after all, what had driven him to the leadership in the first place. History was littered with tales of talismans and charms that had increased the power and wealth of men cunning enough to exploit their magical properties. But he'd never imagined any magic that could allow a man to appear and disappear at will.

The possibilities made him dizzy.

"You've done very well," Farrow said with a grin. "Pull over behind that warehouse," he instructed his driver. Then he addressed the man again. "We'll let you off here."

He waited until the car was hidden on all sides before he nodded to his driver to let the man out. His useful envoy was now a loose end. But the problem was easily solved with a pistol and a silencer and one bullet.

Farrow instructed the driver to depart immediately as he mulled over the possibilities.

Magic.

Real magic.

Rogan's magic.

He slipped his cell phone out of his pocket and pressed a speed dial number.

"We need to get close to Lauren Cole," he said into the mouthpiece. "And when I say close, I mean *intimately* close."

*　　*　　*

" 'Tis not my sword," Aiden countered, incensed. He wanted nothing more to do with the weapon, and had so far enjoyed the fact that it had been hidden from sight. "The blade was forged by Gypsies and cursed by evil."

Lauren rubbed at her neck. "He couldn't have taken it, right? Because you're still here. But that's what he wanted. He wanted your sword."

Aiden swallowed a second denial of ownership and decided to allow the matter to rest. While she was under the influence of pain numbing drugs, sleep deprived and frightened, she was also in no state to be literal or rational. In the aftermath of the assault on her person, the guard around her would undoubtedly be doubled. And until sunrise, at least, Aiden would not leave her side.

For now, she was safe.

And so was the sword.

He retrieved the sword from beneath the bed. "Helen brought the sword from your trailer."

Lauren looked at him quizzically. "Why?"

"She struck me from the start as a very intelligent woman, but now I see her as crafty as a queen."

"She is that," Lauren agreed, though her voice drifted distractedly, her gaze snared by the dark canvas bag. "May I?"

After locking the door with a silent flick of his fingers, Aiden took the sword out of the bag and placed it gingerly in Lauren's hands. Even in the sparse light streaming in from beneath the door, the blade glowed cool and blue. The tiny rubies on the handle, however, sparkled with red flames.

"It's so beautiful," she said with a sigh.

Aiden scowled. " 'Tis evil."

She looked up, her expression confused. "But you aren't."

Even in the strange light, he could tell she had not yet regained her color. Her eyelids were heavy on her face, accentuated by dark circles around her sapphire irises and a thin white line around her lips.

And yet she was beautiful. Her tiny smile alleviated the sting of knowing how tightly bound he was to Rogan's magic—and to her.

"Thank you for coming back," she said.

"I never left," he replied.

"I know, but thanks for not disappearing entirely on me."

He nearly said, "I had no choice," but he kept the honest admission to himself. In another time, another place, another circumstance, Aiden would have pursued Lauren relentlessly. She was beautiful, smart and strong. But he'd learned his first night with her that seducing a woman of this century went beyond achieving sexual surrender. She'd made love with him, but had given up nothing.

The hours he'd spent invisible and ineffective as the world raged on around him convinced him more than ever that he needed to be free. *Completely* free. Free to pursue her as the man he once was. At least, the man he was before war shredded his soul.

With a soft grunt, Lauren pulled herself into a sitting position, the sword nestled beside her. "What's wrong?"

Aiden, with more effort this time, pushed unbidden, bloody images out of his mind.

"Besides the fact that you nearly died, twice, in my presence?"

" 'Nearly' being the operative word," she replied, running her hands down a thin wire and then pressing the mechanism at the end, which caused the back of the bed to rise perpendicular to the base.

As the bed moved, he swallowed a gasp of amazement. He had already seen more amazing wonders during his brief stay in this modern hospital than he had in a lifetime with the Gypsies of Valoren. Their magic, their healing skills, bore no equal to what he'd seen today. How many of his regiment might not have died on the bloody battlefield if doctors had had such magic at their disposal?

"How do you feel?" Aiden asked, focusing his entire attention on her.

"Like I was hit by a Mack truck," Lauren replied. She noticed his perplexed look and added, "It's a horseless carriage about the size of a small house."

"Horseless?"

After adjusting the pillows behind her, she relaxed against the starkly white sheets and closed her eyes until she stopped panting from the exertion.

"I have a lot to catch you up on," she said with a sigh.

Unable to resist, he eased as much of his body as he could beside hers on her bed, the sword nestled between them. Sometime before the attack, the nurses had removed her tubes and wires. IVs, they called them. And monitors. Except for a single transparent tube that pumped oxygen into her nostrils, she was free of the doctor's healing instruments, and while he wished to do nothing that would compromise her recovery, he could not fight the need to lie beside her, to feel her warmth. To have her feel his.

"You may fill me in on the details of modern life at another time," he told her, focusing on the exotic scent lingering in her hair, such a contrast to the alcohol essence so pungent around them. "The nurse insists you need rest."

Lauren turned so that her nose brushed against his. "Suddenly, rest is the last thing on my mind."

Though the light was deceiving, he imagined a flush of red in her cheeks. His sex stiffened at the deep, innuendo-laced huskiness in her voice, but while Aiden was a man of strong appetites, he'd also learned long ago how to control his desires.

"You need to sleep," he told her.

She opened her mouth to argue, but a yawn commandeered her face, and she shook her head, momentarily defeated. "Will you stay?"

He slid off the mattress, retrieved the sword and placed it into the crisscross metal frame beneath her bed. He then rejoined her in the crisp, stiff sheets and laid his hand possessively across her middle. "Of course."

After a moment of settling closer to each other, she asked, "You can't leave me, can you?"

"No," he answered honestly.

"Good," she said, then closed her eyes and fell almost instantly asleep.

After watching her for nearly an hour, Aiden wandered to the window and glanced out at the eerie, odd lights of the city. He'd never seen anything so confounding and strange. Red and white lights streaked by at alarming speeds. Lights of blue, gold and green sparked at him from signs that hawked services he did not understand. Tall, thin trees with tufts of spiked leaves stood sentinel beside lamps that threw a pinkish glow over roads that appeared smooth and slick in the night.

A crowd gathered below had burgeoned since the accident this afternoon. He'd heard Helen warn the hospital staff that her friend's celebrity was cause for concern. Though he could not see the faces of the people milling just beyond the building, he sensed their eyes, all trained on this window.

They wanted Lauren. They craved her. They needed her to fill some empty space in their souls they did not understand.

He knew the feeling.

16

"No, Cinda. They haven't found him yet, but the studio sent in an army of security specialists and they've been camped out by her room since the attack. No one will get anywhere near her again. Besides, the doctors are releasing her in a day, or two at the most," Helen said, standing by the emergency room entrance eyeing the paparazzi still staking out the front of the hospital, just behind the lights and cameras of the so-called "legitimate" media. Since the incident in Lauren's hospital room, which had been attributed to a crazed fan, the news trucks and cameras had multiplied sevenfold. Helen imagined the stench of morbid curiosity settling in around her, and she couldn't help but crinkle her nose in disgust. "Don't even try to come down here. The vultures are everywhere."

Lauren's assistant argued and cried on the other end of the phone, but Helen didn't budge. She'd checked on Lauren an hour ago and got the distinct impression that the star wanted to be alone, with no more hovering than absolutely necessary from either hospital staff or her friends.

"Just take care of the dog. Beast like that will tear the place apart if he's alone too long, and the helicopters hovering over her house must be driving him crazy. I'll call you tomorrow once I know what the doctor's orders are. And don't forget that confidentiality agreement you signed, either, got me?"

Through her sniffles, Lauren's assistant withered under Helen's threat and disconnected the call. It was cold and heartless to warn her, since the girl obviously worshiped the ground Lauren walked on, but trustworthiness was about as prevalent in this town as visible varicose veins.

In this business practically since birth, Helen had learned to insulate herself against feeling anything deep or real or warm for the people she worked with. Loyalties changed too easily and too often—if they existed at all. But she'd let her guard down with Lauren. She knew her secrets. Lauren wouldn't turn on her. If she did, Lauren would risk everything she'd accomplished in this dog-eat-dog industry that made people like Michael Vick look like Saint Francis of Assisi.

Helen spun back into the hospital, plowing into a hunk in scrubs. Even though she nearly landed on her ass, her insides gave a little quiver as his hand wrapped around her arm and kept her from falling.

Dr. Hard Body had a very nice grip.

"So sorry," the deliciously deep voice said. "I really should look where I'm going."

"Yes, you—" she snapped, but cut her tirade short when her gaze sliced into his.

Doctor, my ass.

"What are you, moonlighting on *Grey's*?"

David Drake's grin was just shy of illegal as he pulled off a pair of glasses and did the best Clark Kent–to–Superman imitation she'd seen in a long time. A sensual squeeze inside her panties drove the power of this guy's magnetism home.

"I was only one audition away from playing Dr. McSteamy myself, you know," he taunted.

If he weren't so clearly teasing, she might have written him off for making such an outrageous claim.

When it came to her job, Helen didn't screw around. No one got onto one of her sets without impeccable credentials. David Drake, while relatively new to the acting biz in L.A., had already scored several minor roles in New York, and Helen had worked with his agent before. He might not be McSteamy yet, but he had potential.

Definite potential.

"If you're so sought after," she asked, "what the hell are you doing sneaking around the hospital like a paparazzo?"

He rolled his eyes. "Do you see a camera?"

"Cameras can be very small these days," she replied.

He spread his arms out wide. "You can frisk me."

"You should be so lucky."

He snorted. "I was just trying to check on you. You were freaking out in my car after Lauren's accident."

"I don't freak out," she insisted.

"Not like other women do, I'll give you that. You've got a real good ice queen act going on. You pull it off very well."

"Word to the wise, hotshot," Helen assured him, "it's not an act."

He stepped closer and pressed his chest against hers. His impressive hardness extended from chest to thighs, including the best parts dead center.

"You? Icy? I don't think so."

His voice was liquid lava, hot and dangerous. She shouldn't. Really. She should go up and check on Lauren one more time, even though watching her sleep was getting old. After the attack, the doctors had upped Lauren's meds to ensure a restful night. Security had been tripled. No one would be bothering Lauren tonight. Helen knew she really should go home. Check e-mail. Take a bath. Grab a bite.

Or two.

She spied the hard sinews of David's neck and

shoulders and ran her tongue across the edge of her teeth.

His piercing gaze dropped down, skimming over the swell of her breasts, his thoughts clearly as lascivious as hers. "Too bad the audition was canceled."

She pulled reluctantly out of his grasp. "Crying shame."

Judging by the arrogant curve of his grin, he hadn't missed the breathless need lilting her voice. Damn, it had been a long, sucky couple of days. And David had suddenly given her a very naughty idea of how she could relieve her stress.

"So why are you dressed like a doctor?" she asked. "You're not stalking my star, are you?"

"Right. That's the best way to get a job. Stalk the star when she's lying vulnerable in a hospital room. Anyway, you told me someone else already got the gig."

She gave a nod, but said nothing more. She doubted an actor would risk his career just to pump her for information, but you never knew. News on Lauren's prognosis from a "source close to the star" could fetch a pretty chunk of change.

Still, he seemed sincere. And technically, his quick and levelheaded action had saved Lauren's life. As far as she knew he hadn't sold his story yet to the rags, and probably wouldn't if he wanted to work in Hollywood as anything other than a busboy.

"So, how is she?" he asked.

"She's recovering. Doctors say she just needs rest."

"Is that the truth or the official line?"

"Both. She just needs sleep and some TLC. She'll be back to herself in a few days."

"No short-term memory loss?"

"Are you really a doctor or do you just play one on TV?" Helen quipped.

"Just play one on TV," he admitted.

"Too soon to tell," she answered, "but I talked to her and she seemed okay."

"Then why are you heading back upstairs?"

"I don't want to leave her alone."

"Your office said you haven't left the hospital since her accident."

She cocked a brow, questioning his inside information.

"My agent called your office for me. I told you: I was concerned."

"Well, Lauren doesn't have any family, and she's not one of those stars who surrounds herself with admirers."

"So you've appointed yourself the royal guard? What more can you do? Since the attack, the hospital staff is already tripping all over themselves to make sure she has her privacy."

A shiver shot up Helen's spine.

"How do you know what they're doing inside her hospital room??"

He smiled sheepishly. "One of the plastic surgeons on call here was in my acting workshop last year."

Helen frowned, but her instincts told her to believe him. While he might be willing to go to extreme lengths to secure a part in the final Athena film by saving Lauren's life, she doubted he was a crazed fan.

Helen pocketed her cell phone and started toward the door. "This town is all about contacts."

"Exactly. So why don't you let me take you home?"

Helen eyed him pointedly. "My home or yours?"

He stepped onto the industrial rug in front of the door and, as the glass slid open, gestured gallantly inside. They'd have to cross through the ER to the parking garage on the other side of the campus. "Your choice."

A cool air-conditioned breeze hit them as they passed through the sliding glass doors. Helen watched

David out of the corner of her eye, and she had to admit that he looked utterly delicious in blue scrubs. But then, what man didn't? Since Patrick Dempsey and Goran Visnjic donned stethoscopes, scrubs had become the new tuxedo.

"I can call for a studio car," she said as they passed through the hallway that led to the parking garage.

"You can," he agreed, "but then I wouldn't be able to ply you with my charm and convince you to replace your new leading man with me."

She arched a brow. "Not trying to be sly about it?"

"You're too smart for that."

"Ah, flattery."

"Getting me anywhere?"

"Too soon to tell," she answered.

His car was nice. Clean, at least, if a bit nondescript. Older model. Chrysler. Ford. American-whatever, but kept in excellent condition. And large. Spacious, even. Her mind flickered with backseat fantasies, and she imagined she'd simply gone way too long between lovers again. Helen wasn't exactly promiscuous or insatiable, but she had a healthy sexual appetite like any other red-blooded woman. And she could certainly see the advantages of a binge with this hottie in the very near future.

He unlocked the car and, with a flourish that teetered on being hokey but didn't quite tumble over, opened the car door and handed her inside. She promised herself that if he reached across to buckle her seat belt, she'd bolt.

He didn't.

Damn it.

David Drake was turning out to be incredibly intriguing. Temptation like this was better than the pomegranate-chocolate-chip ice cream she'd stored in her fridge to satiate certain hungers that had nothing to do with sex.

Oh, who was she kidding? Everything in her per-

sonal life boiled down to sex. Getting it. Not getting
it. Wanting it. Even her professional life hinged on
lust. In Hollywood, "sex sells" wasn't a cute sound
bite, but a religious mantra. And she'd been practicing
that chant for a really long time.

David slid into the driver's seat and revved up the
engine.

"The part you wanted has been taken by a man
Lauren hand selected," she said. "And I'm not sure I
can find any other roles in this particular film that
would showcase your talent."

"A disappointing turn of events."

"Just so we're clear."

"Crystal," he said, his turquoise eyes twinkling.
"But you wouldn't make an actor sleep with you in
order to win a part anyway, right?"

"Make?" she asked, aghast. "Make? Do I look like
a woman who needs to *make* a man sleep with her
under any circumstances?"

"No, but the possibility could be pretty hot," he
replied. "Tough gal like you bossing around a tough
guy like me."

He eased out of the parking lot and paid the female
attendant with cash and a charming wink, as if he
suggested domination play to women he barely knew
on a regular basis.

"You into that sort of thing?" Helen asked skeptically. She'd met quite a few guys who were into kinky
shit, but this one gave off a vibe that said he liked his
loving hot and slow and intense—with no need for
accoutrements.

"Actually, I've never tried it," he admitted.

"But you want to?"

"Will I get a part in the movie if I do?"

She laughed. "No guarantees."

"Boy, your casting couch sucks," he quipped.

"Take it or leave it."

The silence was filled with regular traffic sounds.

Loud engines. Overzealous bass vibrations. Car horns. Tires on pavement. David trained his eyes on the road until they reached a stoplight. He threw the car into park, reached across and slid one hand behind her neck and the other up her skirt. In seconds, his lips were on hers and the world turned upside down.

Her nerve endings exploded from his quick and skilled assault. She couldn't stop herself from shifting in her seat so that his fingers pressed against her panties. Intent on exploring just as brazenly, she grabbed his crotch. He was rock hard—probably had been for quite some time. The minute his size registered in her brain, her body liquefied.

"Pull over," she told him.

"Right here?"

She squeezed his dick a little harder. "I don't care."

He tried to hide a grin as he looked around for a secluded spot, but she knew from the pulse in his cock that she'd made him an offer he wouldn't refuse. He accelerated the car with a lurch, then pulled into the parking lot of a grocery store.

She glanced around at the glaring lights streaming into the car.

"Not shy, are you?" she asked, rubbing him until his breath caught.

He peeled out and drove fast until they darted down a side street. The residential area wasn't exactly perfect for an automotive interlude, but the hotter and harder he got beneath her touch, the more impatient Helen became. She'd give him the damned job—any damned job—if he'd just find a place to stop the car.

"Perfect," he said finally, maneuvering the car into the driveway of a dark house with a FOR SALE sign prominent on the lawn and a computerized lockbox hanging off the front door.

She eyed the surroundings and figured this was good enough. If anyone was home, well, David would have to scoot them out of here in a hurry. But then, she wasn't planning on taking all night.

One after the other, they dove into the backseat. He barely had the drawstring scrub pants loosened when she tossed aside her thong and climbed atop him. He was inside her in one swift stroke.

"No . . . condom?" he asked, shifting in a delicious rhythm that nearly struck her blind.

Oh, yeah. That.

"You clean?" she asked, balancing on her knees so that when he moved, the tip of his head curved against her G-spot.

"Tested . . . last . . . year," he answered. He tore her blouse, grabbed at the bra until the lace cups yielded and then plunged his face between her breasts, inhaling her hot skin before he surrounded her right nipple with his mouth.

She smiled and increased the tempo, loving the feel of his hardness inside her and adoring the little swirly thing he was doing with his tongue.

"Me . . . too," she replied.

And that from that point on, all bets were off. Clothes disappeared. The windows fogged. After his first orgasm and her second, they toyed with the idea of getting dressed and leaving before anyone caught them, but when David pulled out a pack of cigarettes, they cracked the back window and lit up. Lounging against the backseat, David drew lazy circles around her areola as she lay against him, his soft but impressive cock nestled in the small of her back. She took a hard drag from the cigarette and enjoyed the buzz.

"So," he said, tweaking her nipple and then soothing the shot of pain with the pads of his fingers. "What part are you going to create for me?"

She laughed, then, tossing her hair with clichéd flair, leaned to the side and held the cigarette to his lips. "What part do you want?"

"Don't care," he answered. "I'd prefer a line or two, but I'm not particular."

He twisted to exhale out the window, and she noticed that the man had amazing lips. Not plush or plumped, but thin and straight. A man's mouth. Nice jaw, too. In fact, just about all of him was perfect, so she couldn't help but wonder why he was working so hard for a part that didn't exist.

"Why do you want on this film so badly?"

He plucked the cigarette out of her hand and tossed it outside. "Why did you want me so badly you'd do it in the backseat of my car? Doesn't feel like your typical venue. You seem more like the scented-oil-on-silk-sheets type to me."

"I'm impulsive and you're hot," she answered simply.

"So's Lauren Cole," he replied.

Helen inhaled quickly, but then covered her shock. Because, really, *was* she surprised? "I don't happen to swing that way, but I suppose you want to do her next?"

He shrugged. "I want to be in one of her films," he admitted.

"Because you're hot for her?"

"I was," he said, "until about twenty minutes ago."

A jolt of pride arched through her. So she wasn't his first choice. Did it matter?

"I can't compare to her," Helen said.

"Then don't," he replied, locking his fingers under her chin and forcing her to look into his dreamy, Pacific blue eyes. "You were straight up with me; now I'm being straight up with you. I pursued this role because of Lauren Cole. That hasn't changed just because you took about ten minutes to rock my world."

"I rocked your world?" She couldn't help it. The guy not only knew how to fuck, he knew how to talk to a woman afterward, even when he was confessing that he was attracted to her best friend.

"Couldn't you tell?" he asked.

"You're an actor."

"I don't do porn flicks," he countered.

"You should," she answered, but she was kidding. He flipped her around, and she could tell by his quirk of a smile that he got the joke. His dick was hard, but she wasn't in any hurry to do him again. The night was young, and so was he.

And so what if he was hot for Lauren? What man wasn't? But she certainly wasn't going to give in again so easily if he pined for someone else. Helen wasn't a prude, but she had her pride.

"So what about Lauren Cole makes you want a part in her film, beyond the obvious?"

Suddenly his eyes turned very hard and had their bodies not been squashed together, Helen might have backed away. "She owes me."

Swallowing deeply, Helen chased away a chill suddenly spreading across her skin.

"Everybody in this town owes somebody something," she assessed. "Why are you any different?"

"Well, let's just say that without me, Lauren Cole would not exist."

17

"Ms. Cole, I hear you're going home in the morning," the nurse said brightly, fluffing the newly changed pillow.

"That's the plan," Lauren replied, not breaking her gaze away from the shades of gray playing on the tinted glass of the window beside her bed. Three days cooped up in the hospital had been more than enough. She still had bouts of dizziness and her muscles felt like jelly, but she was counting the hours until the doctors signed her release and the studio arranged her escape. In anticipation, she'd insisted the nurse transfer her to the bed by the window, just so she could watch as the day faded into night—when Aiden would return.

After taking the quickest bath in the history of handheld hospital showerheads, she'd bundled in the robe Helen had brought her from home and waited for the sunset. She'd slept almost continuously since the attack, waking in short intervals during the night to either see Aiden standing over her bed or curled up beside her, or in the daylight, to feel his presence so near she could touch him wherever she placed her hands.

During an earlier visit, Helen had been frantic when she'd found the sword missing from the bag where she'd hidden it. Luckily Lauren had been lucid enough to assure her friend that the weapon was safe. Helen had offered to move it to Lauren's house, but of course, she'd refused.

She wanted Aiden close.

Hell, she just wanted Aiden.

Starting this afternoon she'd refused any more pain-killers. She wanted to remain alert. For days she'd dreamed about nothing but Aiden. Seeing him. Feeling him. Making love to him. But with a constant stream of doctors, nurses, studio executives, police and friends parading through her hospital room as if it were her suite during a press junket, she'd hardly had a chance to talk to him in the daytime, and the drugs had held her captive and quiet once night had fallen. She knew he was there, though. But for how long? What were the rules of this curse of his? What would happen if she didn't find a way to free him soon?

The nurse finished fussing, said something about hoping Lauren had enjoyed her stay at their hospital, as if it were some five-star resort, then headed toward the door.

"Can you keep out any visitors tonight?" Lauren asked. "Even staff? I'm disconnected from all the moni-tors, and if I need anything I can give you a buzz." She lifted the call button device and gave it a jaunty twirl.

The nurse stopped and turned, her eyebrows hitched up into her curly bangs. "Even that man?"

Lauren frowned. "What man? The one who at-tacked me?"

The police had made no progress in finding out who had sneaked into her room, and Lauren hadn't told anyone that he'd wanted the sword. Afraid the police would confiscate the weapon as evidence—or, worse, return it to Ross—she'd allowed everyone to subscribe to the crazed-fan theory. Once she was strong and recovered, she'd delve deeper into who knew about Aiden's sword, and who wanted it badly enough to attack a high-profile celebrity in a relatively public place, but in the meantime she just wanted one lucid night with Aiden.

"Oh, no," the nurse reassured her. "The man I keep hearing you talk to at night."

Lauren blushed. Exactly what had she been saying in her drug-induced sleep?

"I'm just running lines," she lied.

The woman beamed. "Then that's one movie I definitely want to see. From what I've heard you mumble, it's going to be hot."

Lauren rewarded the woman with her best red-carpet smile. "You have no idea."

The woman left with a spring in her step, and Lauren turned back to the window. The sky had definitely darkened. A full and sensuous quiet descended on the room, broken only by the hum of recycled air pushing through the vents and the muffled chatter from the hallway outside. Lauren ran her hand through her damp hair, and then, after taking a deep breath, whispered Aiden's name.

He did not reply or materialize.

How dark did it have to be before the sword released him?

Lauren settled into the mattress and closed her eyes. She was still tired, but, nestled in the brushed cotton of the robe, scrubbed clean and damp from her bath, she let her awareness of her body push to the forefront of her mind. No longer trapped in her dreams, memories of Aiden touching her in the shower just before the accident slipped into her consciousness. At the thought of his invisible tongue flicking inside her sex, a surge of desire swelled within her. She needed him to touch her, to make love to her, to fill her with the raw passion they'd exchanged just days ago—to remind her again that she was, indeed, alive.

"Aiden?" she whispered.

"You need not call me twice, my lady," he said.

Her eyelids fluttered. Aiden emerged from behind the curtain that separated her from the now empty bed near the door, where the sword remained stored.

Her mouth watered. She tried to remember the last time that merely setting her eyes on a man had caused such a flutter in her chest. And lower. Yes, she was achy. Her muscles were unsteady and her joints protested against most movement, but she still couldn't resist leaning toward him as he walked nearer.

Reaching out to him, she inhaled sharply when he took her hand in his and kissed her knuckles. The current that shot through her nerve endings had nothing to do with electricity, but with desire. His eyes, such a penetrating liquid silver, flashed at her from under thick, dark lashes.

"What have you been doing all this time? Just watching me sleep?" she asked.

She patted the bed, inhaling his rich, musky scent as he sat beside her. The essence of his maleness took her mind instantly off her pain. She couldn't help but lean a bit closer. God, he was like living, breathing Percocet.

"I've been listening," he replied. "Learning. This place offers much more information than the mantel in your husband's study."

"Ex."

"Pardon me?"

"Ex-husband. We're divorced, remember?"

"I do not forget, my lady. But I fear he has. His visits have been brief, but frequent."

Lauren shook her head, wholly unconcerned by the frequency of Ross's appearance at her bedside. "I'm just an investment to him now. He doesn't care about me."

"So your friend Helen says every time he appears," Aiden informed her. "She is one formidable woman."

Lauren smiled. Ross was probably kicking himself

now for hiring Helen all those years ago. She'd proved so damned good at her job, he'd had little choice but to keep her around. "It's part of her charm."

"You are also a formidable woman," he claimed. "From what the doctors and nurses have said, the"—he struggled for the word—"voltage you received could have killed someone of lesser physical strength."

She pulled her robe closer. She didn't want to think about how close she'd come to dying. Again. She'd been down this road before. Near-death experiences led to all sorts of inconvenient thoughts about mortality and unfulfilled goals and regrets, which had, in the past, spurred her to make less than wise decisions. For now, she wanted to focus only on Aiden. On his mysterious appearance in her life. On his increasingly sensual presence, and how one glance from those silver eyes of his set her heart racing.

"What else did you learn?" she said, hoping to change the subject.

"I learned that electricity, while useful," he said wryly, "is an extremely harmful substance."

He ran his hand up the length of her leg, brushing over the thick terry cloth of the robe and skirting just inches from the opening that would reveal her naked flesh. The sensation stole the moisture from her mouth, and she had to wet her lips before she could find the means to speak.

"When it's used incorrectly, yes," she said, marveling at the tiny sparks shooting through her nerve endings at his simple, lazy touch. Boldly, she scooted back the hem of her robe, exposing her bare leg. "But if you know how to use it right, electricity can be incredibly . . . hot."

His eyes met hers. His pupils dilated, and he licked his lips. She supposed sexual innuendo wasn't bound by time or space.

"You need your rest," he insisted.

The deep sensuality in his voice made her squirm.

"I've done nothing but rest for days."

"The doctor says you should not exert yourself."

"The doctor doesn't have the world's sexiest phantom haunting him."

His chuckle spawned a trail of gooseflesh across her skin. The sensations running down the opening of her robe, past the sensitized dip between her breasts, captured her attention. When his fingers lingered just above her navel, the pounding between her thighs flared.

"I may be the world's only phantom."

She grabbed his hand and forced it lower, inches from where her flesh throbbed for his touch.

"Lucky me," she replied.

He covered her mound with his palm, allowing his thumb to stray between the sensitive lips of flesh. She hissed as the sensations surged, then nearly buckled when he found her clit.

"If you cannot remain entirely still," he warned, "I will have to stop."

"No," she said, willing her body to remain as stationary as possible. "Please don't stop."

He grazed a succession of dull-edged fingernails over her sensitive nub, then pulled his hand away. "I cannot be responsible for waylaying your healing."

He was teasing her. The lilting edge in his voice told her he wanted her to beg. She was more than willing—and this surprised her most of all.

"You won't," she assured him. "I've spent two days dreaming about what you did to me in the shower, what you did to me on the mats."

"Ah, yes," he agreed, his hand smoothing over her inner thigh, up and down, up and down, with painful slowness, always stopping just half an inch short of where she wanted his touch the most. "I've been preoccupied with the same memories, though I have been entirely conscious, watching you sleep, knowing I could allow myself only the delight of brushing the hair away from your face, or perhaps, touching your cheek. I have ached for you, my lady, in ways you could not possibly know."

But when his finger finally dipped into her, she understood. Immediately her body wept from the excruciating wonder of his touch, from the jolts of pure delight streaking through her. One finger was followed by a second. Then a third. When he curled his hand so he could flick his thumb against her clit, she nearly leaped out of her skin.

"Shh," he whispered, his breath hot against her ear. "Remember, my lady: You must remain still."

But even as he chastised her, he coaxed her further into madness. Her body tightened around him. Orgasm was just a few excruciating, delicious moments away.

Her eyes locked with his. She focused not on the brilliant silver rim of his irises or the wide, unfathomable circles of his pupils, but beyond. She saw his jaw clench when she gasped, when the tiny moans of pleasure gathering from deep within her escaped unbidden and unrestrained. In his eyes she witnessed how her pleasure satisfied him to the deepest reaches of his soul.

His rhythm quickened, the pressure intensified and in seconds she exploded. When her cry grew too loud, he kissed her, luring her over the crest and into satiated bliss.

In the end he pressed his forehead against hers, and she realized he was panting nearly as strongly as she.

As her mind cleared, she wondered what to say, what to think. Ross had wanted her, groomed her into the perfect woman, gifted her with the life she'd always dreamed of, then thrown it all away. His lovemaking, while frequent and inventive over the course of their marriage, had been meant more to teach her how to please him rather than the other way around. Had she realized that before now?

Aiden, on the other hand, gave without taking. Only that wasn't entirely true. From her pleasure, he seemed to extract something deeply personal. Something he cherished. She could see it in his eyes.

Suddenly her own eyes burned. She blinked, but couldn't find the moisture to alleviate the sting. When she turned her head, Aiden took the cue and withdrew.

"You bring out the most wicked in me," he said, his lips curved in a smile even though his eyes remained intense and serious.

"Right back at you," she quipped, closing her robe. "If you scoot over a little closer, I'll return the favor."

But instead of moving closer, Aiden rolled off the bed entirely. "Is that how your new century deals with sexual matters? In barter and trade?"

She supposed he was trying to sound offended, but his chuckle betrayed him instantly. "Isn't that how it's always been? From the beginning of time, I mean? My generation certainly didn't invent sexual politics."

He crossed his arms, highlighting the powerful build of his chest and making her sigh in sated appreciation. "Nor did mine."

"But you play the game very well, 'cause right about now I'd do anything you wanted me to."

He arched a dark brow. "Anything?"

"Name it," she challenged.

His deep, measured laughter slipped right between her legs and aroused her with just as much skill as his deft and delicious fingers. "I intend to, when you are stronger."

She scooted closer to him. "I heal more quickly when I'm distracted. You know, when my mind is otherwise engaged."

He slipped his hand between the folds of her robe again and unabashedly tweaked her sensitized nipple. "Like this?"

"It's a start," she said with a sigh. "A very delicious start."

18

"Leave the towels by the door, will you?"

Paschal listened with half an ear while the maid shuffled across the plush carpet of the Crown Chandler penthouse suite, where Ben and Cat had left him to recover. Ignoring the luxury of having someone around to pick up after him, he typed another name into the search engine on his laptop computer and wondered why he'd waited so long to learn about the Internet. The information flowing through this remarkable wireless connection had been invaluable, even though Farrow Pryce had succeeded in keeping most of his activities on the q.t. Pryce had a certain amount of clout in the financial world, and his activities with the K'vr had, to the best of Paschal's knowledge, remained carefully hidden. Paschal had always known the man's name, always associated him with the K'vr—a group of Rogan worshipers who'd been nothing less than a pain in his patoot for over half a century—but he'd never known exactly how rich the man was. Now he could only wonder precisely how the K'vr had contributed to this fortune.

Pryce's extensive portfolio wasn't good news. Money equaled power, and apparently Pryce had plenty of both. Paschal now considered himself very fortunate to have escaped Pryce once, and though he doubted the man had any reason to pursue him again, he certainly had both means and motive to thwart Paschal in his quest to find Aiden—the brother he was now certain, thanks to his vision, was alive, though likely still trapped in his phantom state.

Paschal scanned a notation about Pryce in a stock trading magazine. Wasn't much here. Just a vague reference about his net worth.

Suddenly he became aware of someone standing directly behind him, reading over his shoulder.

"That's old news," a sultry voice informed him. "Pryce is worth twice that by now."

Paschal shifted his attention from the screen, but remained facing forward. The husky voice, the exotic perfume, the bold confidence told him that Gemma Von Roan had come for him, just as he'd suspected she would.

"So he finally kicked you out, and you've been reduced to cleaning hotel rooms for a living?"

She snorted. "That's a nice little fantasy you've got going on. Farrow did not kick me out. Yet. And until he does, I enjoy using his hard-earned cash to bribe my way into your hotel room."

"If Pryce is so wealthy," he asked coolly, "why does he need an old sword of comparatively low financial value?"

Gemma grabbed the back of his chair and swiveled him around. She was just as striking as ever, slim and sleek, from her short, cropped hair to her stiletto-heeled boots. Her icy blue eyes sparkled from beneath lashes heavily lined in black. "Because the sword holds a piece of my ancestor's magic. He knows you want it, and he's going to get it first. He's too close already. You need to act quickly unless you want to lose your advantage."

"And what advantage is that?"

"Me."

Paschal hardly had time to react when she moved to straddle him, but he managed a quick scoot backward and held up his hand.

"I'm not as young as I used to be," he admitted, torn between desiring to have her mount him and knowing the physical contact with her at this precise moment was not a good idea. He had been feeling his age lately, and though Gemma had fueled quite a few potent fantasies, he had to be realistic. Besides, he had suspicions about her latent abilities—magical talent he wasn't even sure she realized she had.

She frowned prettily. "It's only been nine months since I saw you last. Lost your taste for me already?"

"They say the taste buds are the first thing to go."

He braced his hands on the armrests of the swivel chair and wondered if he should risk standing and revealing the full breadth of his current weakness. He didn't have to decide when she laughed, ran her hands through her cropped black-and-blond hair and backed away.

"Nice suite," she commented, looking around.

He shrugged. "It's a room with a roof."

"A room with a roof conveniently owned by Alexa Chandler. Where is the heiress? I've always wanted to meet her."

"Don't you know? Farrow's having her followed."

Her pout lasted all of a split second, but Paschal noticed it all the same.

"He's left you out of the loop, hasn't he?"

"Let's just say that the unwavering trust we had before you came into our lives has . . . wavered. He's found it impossible to believe that a man over ninety could overpower a guard, take his gun, shoot his security guard and force me to drive him off the property."

Well, her story certainly had been inventive. "So why are you still with him?"

"He needs me. I'm a direct descendant of Rogan's

brother, Lukyan. Blood means a lot to the fellowship of the K'vr."

"But not as much as gender."

"It's an old organization, mostly underground, but the wealth the followers have amassed over the years is substantial. They're set in their ways. They've never had to consider a woman for leadership before."

"You sound as if you think you might change their minds."

"You never know until you try," she replied.

"And since Farrow's no longer keeping you under his wing, you're going to betray him and take the leadership for yourself?"

"That's always been my plan. And I suspect Farrow knows it. That's why he's in Los Angeles right now, negotiating with the last known owner of the sword. A man named Ross Marchand."

Paschal shook his head. The name did not sound familiar. "Our information tells us that the last buyer of the sword was a South American weapons collector involved in the drug trade. Alexa and Damon were headed that way as soon as—"

"Tell them not to waste their time," she interrupted. "You were led to believe that by a shady German antiques dealer whom Farrow paid a hefty price to throw any other collectors off the trail."

Paschal considered her expression and her words. He'd worked with enough less than reputable antiques dealers in his lifetime to find her story entirely believable.

"Why are you telling me this?"

"Isn't it obvious?" she asked, her eyes flashing. "I'm attracted to you."

"Try again."

She smiled slyly. "I'm trying to gain your trust. Apparently I'm not very good at it. Let me try again."

From inside a slim leather bag she'd slung over her

shoulder, she took out a series of photographs. Taking
her time and making sure she slid as close to him as
possible, she laid out each picture on the desk behind
him.

Paschal was almost afraid to look.

Almost.

There were ten pictures in all, each a high-quality
image of an item, one as old as the next. Most meant
absolutely nothing to him except that they appeared
Gypsy-made. The seventh picture, however, grabbed
his attention. It was a chalice—an adorned cup. He
fought the instinct to immediately pick it up when his
brain registered the symbol carved into the fine,
wrought silver of a hawk holding a fiery red opal in
its talons. He perused all the photographs a second
time, forcing his expression to remain impassive, before he met her eyes.

"Are you opening an auction house?"

She cursed. "There's no time to play games, old
man. I know you're looking for items associated with
Valoren. Each one of these items was handcrafted
by Gypsies in the early to mid-eighteenth century.
Most were found in and around the region of Germany where Valoren reportedly existed. This one"—
she slammed her red-tipped fingernail into the center
of the chalice—"bears the symbol of Rogan himself."

She turned and, in a move that nearly caused Paschal to rocket his chair across the room, tugged down
her slim slacks. On the area just above her smooth
pelvic bone was a tattoo—the hawk with the opal
clutched tight in its claws.

"Don't tell me you haven't seen this symbol before," she insisted.

He arched a brow. "Not presented like that, I
haven't. That secret passage where we were trapped
all those months ago was quite dark."

A red flush crept from her chin to her cheeks, surprising him. With a violent tug she pulled up her pants. "Tell me you're not interested."

"In which? You or the chalice?"

She smiled. "Either. Both. But I'm willing to show you more than photographs if you come with me. I have those items in a secure location. But you have to come now. Not later. Not tomorrow. Now. This is a take-it-or-leave-it offer."

"Why the rush?"

"I can't beat Farrow to the sword," she explained. "That battle is lost. But these items are mine. Or, at least, they will be. If you show me how to unlock their secrets, we'll both get what we want."

"How do you know I can unlock anything?"

She frowned deeply, as if he'd just insulted her intelligence. "Because you have before. You found a way into the castle where we could not. You unlocked that secret pretty handily. And you traced the sword before we did. Farrow only beat you to it because he paid that antiques dealer in Dresden an obscene amount of money to reveal who the buyer was and to throw whoever you've got sniffing after it off the scent."

Paschal arched a brow. He'd always suspected Gemma Von Roan possessed more than average intelligence. Now he was sure.

"What do I get in return for assisting you?"

"Name your price," she countered cockily, as if nothing were beyond her grasp.

"I so prefer showing to telling."

She grabbed his hand. "Let's go, then."

"I'll have to call my son."

"No way," she insisted. "That girlfriend of his has a bitch of a roundhouse kick. I'd rather this just be you and me."

"They'll come looking for me. And they'll find me. You know they will."

"You can leave a note."

Paschal shook his head. "Neither my son nor Catalina Reyes is a fool. They'll never believe I ran off with you willingly and only left a note."

The act of considering his demand seemed painful. She wasn't accustomed to compromise. Well, she'd learn.

"Fine. One phone call when we get there. But if you tell him what I have, the deal is off."

Paschal retrieved the cell phone Ben had left him, but eyed Gemma suspiciously. "How do I know you're not still loyal to Farrow?"

"I've never been loyal to Farrow." She touched his shoulder. In that instant Paschal felt a tingle of something electric, something so familiar he winced in response. The reaction broke their tentative contact, but her eyes narrowed. She'd felt it, too. "And you know it. Don't you?"

Her eyes widened. She took a step back.

"What was that?"

"Don't be afraid," he said.

She shoved her chin out defiantly. "I'm not afraid of you."

"You should be, my dear. You should be."

19

"I am your slave."

Lauren coughed, though it was more like a splutter than an innocent clearing of the throat. "Say again?"

Aiden glanced down at the parchment—er—paper, that Lauren had given him and rechecked the words he'd been instructed to recite. It was bad enough that the stage direction forced him to his knees in front of her. Then he had to declare his thrall as well?

He took a deep breath before speaking. "I am your slave," he repeated. This time each word was clipped and curt. He was quickly losing his patience with this folly, no matter what incentives she'd laid out for him.

She pressed her lips tightly together, suppressing, he suspected, the impulse to laugh. *Damnable woman.*

With a frustrated growl he threw the script to the floor. "I did warn you, my lady. I pride myself on honesty and forthright speech, not pathetic drivel. You ask me to pretend I am someone I am not and deliver declarations that are anathema to me, yet you chortle at my expense?"

"You're not trying," she insisted.

He cursed. "Lord, you are delusional. The fact that I am allowing such tripe to pass my lips denotes the greatest effort on my part."

She slapped a hand over her mouth, failing to cover her laughter. He had the sudden urge to break something. An actor! Ludicrous! The entire premise of her film lacked credulity. A warrior on par with the likes of Achilles and Agamemnon driven by sexual need to subjugate himself to a woman?

"This man is a toy. No real soldier would make such a declaration."

She quelled her laughter. "He's not real. He's a figment of the writer's imagination, and I'm betting this scene was written by a woman who understands women's fantasies."

Pouting must have been invented for lips like hers, but he would not be swayed. At least, not yet. He required more convincing than she had yet offered, though her enticements so far had been incredibly persuasive.

"The only woman whose fantasies I wish to fulfill is you," he declared. "I suspect you need to find another fool to promenade like a lovesick peacock for all the world to see."

She dropped to her knees and placed a soft kiss on the tip of his chin, then one on each corner of his mouth. He held tight to his resolve and remained stoically disinterested. Unless she touched his cock. The damned body part would give him away. Otherwise he'd discovered that he could be a tolerable actor when given the right incentive.

"You only have four words to master tonight," she coaxed. "Then you'll have the rest of the night to help my body clock adjust to the night shift. It wasn't easy for me to convince Michael to shoot your scenes at night. He only gave in because he's still freaked out over my accident."

"Four inane words," he griped.

"You're just not in the right frame of mind, but if you let me"—she pressed close to him so that her nipples grazed his chest through her insubstantial attire—"I can help."

She snaked her hands around his neck, bracing her

thumbs just behind his ears and pulling his face so that his lips had no other option but to crash against hers. Instantly she parted her lips and thrust her tongue inside his mouth, with no other goal than to arouse him completely. And as with every other time she'd attempted such a diversion with Aiden, she was wholly successful.

Boldly she pressed her pelvis against his, undulating so that the friction caused an immediate rise in both his body temperature and his lower regions. With her curvaceous flesh draped in little but a swath of silk secured with a golden cord, her pale curves made his mouth water and his muscles tighten. A rush of hot blood through his veins topped off a lust-induced delirium he could barely resist. Now, this was insanity he could appreciate.

On the one hand, he was quite regretful that he had refused to don the costume she'd procured. With nothing more binding him than a few straps of leather and a swatch of fabric, he could be inside her right now, feeling her hot flesh encasing his, rather than fighting over meaningless words spoken by people who did not exist.

Then the vibration of her laughter against his mouth alerted him to the instantaneous change in his attire . . . followed by a cool breeze around his arse and her hand wrapped tight around his sex.

"See?" she teased. "I told you I could make you love your costume."

His brain battled between the pleasure shooting through his body as she stroked and the fact that he'd just changed into the costume with a single errant thought. Though he'd used Rogan's magic freely on the night Lauren had freed him, he'd been reluctant to invoke the power since. Rogan's sorcery was not to be trifled with. Like waves from a raging ocean, the sensations of the ebbing and flowing magic chilled him to the bone.

Luckily, Lauren seemed intent on stoking a fire that could melt steel.

"You're wicked," he teased her, turning his thoughts away from their dark direction.

She smiled. "You're only now noticing?"

Mercifully, she'd released his manhood and had turned her attentions to his bared backside. "What else can you do with the magic?"

"I do not want to know."

She pulled back, surprised. "Why not?"

Aiden considered her question and decided to answer honestly. "The magic stirs something within me that reminds me of war."

Her bottom lip dropped slightly. "I can't imagine."

"No, my lady," he said, an unfortunate snap in his voice. "You cannot. Men under my command died at my feet, their bowels torn open by the slash of a traitor's sword. Infantrymen I'd broken bread with but the night before spent the morning slaughtering the children of our enemy. Unlike your films and Rogan's magic, what I saw at Culloden, what I lived, was very real."

Silence reigned while she processed what he couldn't believe he'd said aloud. He'd never shared with anyone a single detail regarding the great battle at Culloden. Had time and distance given him the freedom to finally speak about what weighed so heavily on his heart?

Her hand shook as she slid her palm over his cheek. "Rogan's magic is real, Aiden. It's what brought you to me."

"It's evil."

"Only in the wrong hands. You've possessed the magic for days now, and you haven't turned into Rogan. He can't change who you are."

"You don't know that," he insisted. "With each day that passes, I feel a burning fire building within me.

A rage and resentment that, if unleashed, could harm you."

"But you haven't harmed me," she argued.

"Because when you touch me . . ." The hunger in his voice completed his thought. When she touched him, the memories faded and the burgeoning anger receded to a simmer he could control. But for how long?

She smiled sensually and slid her fingers into his hair. "Then I'll have to touch you more often, won't I?"

But a squeal from a box near the door waylaid her from fulfilling her delicious promise.

"Hold that thought," she instructed, crossing the room quickly and pressing a button on the base of the device. "Yes, Gino? Let them through."

Aiden closed his eyes and despite his increased ire, concentrated on restoring his waistcoat, breeches and shirt.

"And how am I supposed to explain eighteenth century clothing?" she asked, stalking across the room and scooping up one of the many fashion magazines she kept on her coffee table and shoving one into his hands. He thumbed through, found a look that wasn't entirely foreign—slim slacks and a shirt that buttoned down the front—and invoked the magic so that he wore exactly the same combination. A bubble of tar-like darkness stirred in his belly, but she kissed him long and hard until the sensation subsided.

With a twinkle in her eye, she broke away. "I think I'm going to like keeping the magic in line."

She turned toward the entryway, but as he had no idea who was coming up to the house in the dead of night, he changed her clothing as well.

She glanced down at the sufficiently modest frock and skewered him with a deadly look.

"You want a kiss for this? Not exactly Roberto Cavalli, are you?"

"Who?"

"My favorite . . . never mind. Look, why don't you stick to soldiering and allow me to choose my own wardrobe?"

She flipped through the magazine, pointed at a snug jacket worn over equally revealing pants and tapped her finger impatiently.

"Who calls on you at this late hour?" he demanded, crossing his arms and ignoring her request.

"Helen," she replied curtly.

He supposed he need not cover her completely for another woman. Unimpressed by her choice, he grabbed her hand, yanked her to him and kissed her soundly while he conjured the sleepwear she'd worn after her shower—loose-fitting drawstring pants and a cropped T-shirt. He'd found the combination casual, but sensual in a way that could, in his opinion, withstand public consumption.

She smacked her lips and spun around. "Once I get you trained, you're going to save me a bundle in haute couture."

Her laughter followed her into the hallway, but Aiden remained behind. His mood had instantly turned sour, and not because of the magic. If Helen, who'd planted the idea of Aiden's becoming an actor into Lauren's mind, could tend to her business without his involvement, his night would not be a total loss.

He glanced at the clock on the mantel and realized he had just shy of five hours of solid form left. He certainly did not want to waste such precious moments exchanging small talk with a woman who had absolutely no idea who he really was. She'd assumed—and Lauren had not corrected her—that he was simply some attractive lover Lauren had taken into her bed. Aiden saw no reason to challenge her asssumption, particularly since she wasn't entirely mistaken, though the breadth of his true identity, he guessed, she'd never truly believe.

Lauren's recovery had progressed nicely. Three days at the hospital followed by four in relative seclusion at home had restored her to her former strength and vigor, as well as given Aiden time to adjust to this new century. She'd told him what she could about technological advances, from air-conditioning to computers, and had, the night before, taken him on a drive through Los Angeles, a city that fed on the night just as he did. He had not yet processed all he'd seen and experienced, but the more he learned, the closer he came to determining his next move.

Though he tried to deny the truth, he had begun to realize how the curse yoked him tighter with each dawn. In the daylight he returned to his prison within the sword, and each sunset it was harder to throw off the resilient ugliness that seeped into his soul. To Lauren he must appear entirely insatiable, with the sexual appetite of a starving man, but in reality he was simply attempting to hold on to what was left of his humanity.

In the shadow hours, he wondered if any of his brothers had suffered this same fate. He tortured himself with the possibility that Rogan himself had beaten death and still existed in this world. And if that were the case, Aiden had no choice but to find him and destroy him. The years had not lessened his rage— they'd fed it to all-consuming proportions.

But to achieve his revenge, Lauren had to free him entirely, and while her mind was preoccupied with her recovery and with her film, she was not motivated to do more than enjoy his company when darkness fell. If he took this role in her film, he'd be one step closer to freedom from the sword. Yet the longer he toyed with Rogan's magic, the more lost to the darkness he feared he'd become.

With no other choices, he'd decided to do as she asked. However, giving in easily to her request would not elicit the unequivocal gratitude he might require from her. He'd never known a woman who needed him less. He had to balance the scales. He had no idea what sacrifices she'd have to endure to gain his release from the sword and the curse.

"Well, looks like you're off the hook," Lauren announced, strolling into the room with Helen on her arm, and behind them the man who'd pressed his lips against Lauren's when she had been knocked unconscious by the electric shock. From what Aiden had heard from the hospital staff, the man had saved Lauren by breathing into her lungs when she could not, but Aiden could not forget how he'd touched his mouth to hers with a passion that defied simple lifesaving techniques.

When they reached the center of the room, Lauren waved her hand lazily at the man.

"Helen apparently has found a replacement for you," Lauren announced

The man smirked.

Aiden crossed the room in measured strides.

"An impossible feat," he said, assessing the man boldly.

Helen slid in front of Lauren and slapped Aiden twice on the chest—the first time to garner his attention; the second with a whistle of appreciation.

"Yes, well," she said, unhanding him after catching his disapproving eye. "We heard you weren't exactly anxious to take to the screen, big guy, so I found someone who can't wait to be with Lauren. On the screen."

Aiden saw the challenge in Helen's gaze and decided not to rise to her bait.

"You could have hired this man from the start," Aiden assessed, folding his arms across his chest.

Helen arched a brow. "I needed convincing that he was the right man for the role. And trust me," she said, conspiratorially quiet, "he'll do the job just right. You, on the other hand," she said loudly, her voice switching from secretive to sugary, "seem much better suited to looking after Lauren in a more private capacity."

The way she could warp a few simple words into a sensual suggestion unnerved him. In his century, this Helen woman would have been either a courtesan or the mother of queens. Manipulation and cleverness brightened her eyes like jewels, though Lauren seemed so used to her friend's maneuvering, she yawned.

"So you wish me to relinquish my role as Lauren's on-screen lover, when my employment was initially your idea?" he asked.

She shrugged lazily. "It's a woman's prerogative to change her mind—or haven't you heard?"

Aiden's frown deepened when he noticed that the man who'd accompanied Helen into the house stood transfixed, unable to rip his gaze away from Lauren. His eyes gleamed with the kind of hunger that Aiden knew all too well. He arrested the man's attention with a pointed question.

"Who are you?" he demanded.

"This is—" Lauren started, but Aiden cut her off with a potent glare.

The man jumped as if startled, then tore his stare from Lauren and held out his hand. "David Drake."

Their greeting was a crash and pump of male assessment. While the man had features that would have looked stunning on a woman, David Drake also possessed a decent, steady grip.

"Lauren's new lover," Helen announced. "Or Athena's, at any rate."

Lauren's eyes flashed as she looked David over from head to toe in a manner completely unbefitting a woman.

"Then let's do it. Got the camera?"

Helen produced a small electronic device, which she aimed at Lauren and David before Aiden could open his mouth to protest. Helen pushed Aiden out of the way, and Lauren launched herself into David's arms. After a split second of surprise, the man relaxed and he melted into Lauren as if their bodies had been meant to meld together.

Then the bastard dropped to his knees, wrapped his arms around her legs and pressed his cheek to her thigh. "I am your slave."

Aiden's hand instantly shot to his waist, but he was without scabbard—without sword.

Lauren's hand snaked down, fingering through Drake's hair and around his jaw until she grasped his chin tightly and tugged him upward. He took his time rising, making love to every inch of her body with his eyes, lingering at her breasts, then staring into her sapphire blue irises with a mixture of devotion and power. Aiden fumed, suddenly feeling as if he had stumbled into a private rendezvous between lovers. He took a step forward, but Helen, who'd sidled up beside him, grabbed him by the elbow and held him in place.

"You had your chance, hotshot. I think they're fabulous together, don't you?"

Watching their kiss pushed Aiden beyond control. Before any of them could act, Aiden broke them apart and sliced the conjured sword perilously close to the usurper's traitorous neck.

"Aiden, no!" Lauren screamed.

"Where did that come from?" Helen asked.

Aiden did not reply.

"Take it easy, there, fella," David pleaded, his voice tremulous. "We're just acting."

"You will not touch her. Ever. Again," Aiden insisted, his teeth so tight his jaw ached.

"Aiden, let him go this instant or I'll . . ."

Without moving an inch except to turn his head and lock gazes with Lauren, Aiden spoke. "You'll *what*, my lady?"

Her mouth gaped, but no words emerged. With a

stare meant to convey the full depth of his displeasure, he focused on her until she closed her mouth. During their exchange David Drake, who clearly was not a fool, had backed away.

From behind him he heard applause. He turned to find Helen slapping her hands together and grinning from ear to ear.

"Now, that's machismo," she assessed. "And quick reflexes. I didn't even see the sword when we came in."

"That's . . . what?" Aiden lowered the weapon, perplexed. He glanced back at Lauren and caught her sniggering behind her hand.

Drake stood with his arms crossed cockily over his chest. "*Machismo*. Don't tell me you've never heard of it. You practically ooze with it."

Lauren's hand on his arm dispelled his increasing ire. Aiden Forsyth liked a good laugh as well as any man, but he certainly did not appreciate being the butt of the joke. "This was—"

Helen clapped him on the shoulder. "Acting. When I called earlier, Lauren told me you were having a bit of trouble drawing on the right emotions. So we set up this little scenario. Of course, I didn't expect you to nearly slice David in half."

Aiden frowned, unable to remember fetching the sword. It was as if his anger had summoned the weapon to him—and the rage had nearly caused him to draw innocent blood.

"I would not have harmed him," he said.

David's eyes widened. "I'd sure as hell like to believe that, man, but I'd feel a hell of a lot safer if you put that baby down."

Aiden complied and the moment he released the handle his fury drained. He eyed David warily, then glanced at Lauren, whose eyes, locked on the actor, had narrowed with what looked suspiciously like . . . suspicion.

"What is it?" Aiden asked her.

She nearly jumped out of her skin. "What?"

Aiden moved closer to her, speaking directly into her ear. "Did he harm you?"

"What? No," she insisted, laughing off his concern. "No, he just . . ." She faced David directly again. "You look really familiar."

David slipped his hands into his pockets and rocked on his feet in a move Aiden suspected was supposed to show careless confidence. "Well, I'm not a superstar like you are, but I have—"

"No," Lauren interrupted. "I don't mean from your work. I mean . . . Ross," she whispered. Shock turned her normally forthright voice into a quaver of uncertainty. "That night. Oh, God. Ross." She stepped around Aiden and pointed an accusing finger at David. "You were there."

David shook his head. "I don't know what you're talking about."

Lauren might have launched herself on him if not for Aiden grabbing her by the arms. He had no idea what had upset her so, but she'd gone from relaxed and casual to nearly hysterical in a heartbeat.

"You liar!" she screamed, as near to crazed as Aiden had ever heard her. "You were there . . . you were there the night I died!"

20

Lauren could hardly breathe. For the first time since she'd come home from the hospital, the room around her started to spin. If not for Aiden's viselike grip around her arms, she might have crumbled.

Helen waved David back, her eyes wide and frightened in a way that Lauren had never seen before. Good. She needed to be afraid. She'd brought this lying snake into her home. Into her life. David Drake, or whatever he called himself these days, had clearly tricked one of the savviest women in Hollywood. But why?

"Honey, yes," Helen said. "David saved you after your electrocution. He gave you CPR before the paramedics arrived. I told you about him in the hospital."

Lauren shook her head as a fuzzy recollection of Helen chattering by her bedside at the hospital skittered across her brain. "No," she insisted. "Not then. Before. A long time before!"

She stopped fighting Aiden, who pulled her back and pressed her to his chest. With one arm protectively across her, he held her steady as he spoke in an even tone. "I think you should both leave."

Helen's eyes flashed with anger. "Who the hell do you think you are? You don't own her."

"I do not claim to own her, but I have sworn to protect her," Aiden declared.

The heat emanating from his body wrapped Lauren in a cocoon so soothing, she couldn't resist folding herself into it and wishing for the rest of the world to go away. She'd tried so hard to forget that night—the night that had changed her life so dramatically. On the edge between life and death, she'd turned over her heart and soul and trust to Ross. She'd given up her sad and tragic childhood, changed her name and succumbed to Ross Marchand's overpowering need to possess her, body and soul.

All because the boy who saved her refused to spirit her away.

God, how she'd begged him. Through eyes swollen to slits and lips puffed up beyond recognition, she'd pleaded with the young man who'd come to her aid to take her away, drag her if he had to, anywhere she could either die or heal on her own. She didn't want the police called. They'd take her to the hospital and contact Ross. She didn't have the strength to fight him or his promises of fame and riches and love.

If only she could escape. Start over somewhere else.

But the boy who'd scared away her attackers had refused her one request. She'd hated him for years, even after she'd fallen in love with Ross. Even after her husband had made good on every single promise he'd made her, turning the onetime street rat into an international star. And yet, somewhere in the back of her mind, she'd always wondered what might have happened if that teenage runaway with courage enough to run off the gang who'd jumped her had listened to her pleading and helped her escape. Might she have achieved her success on her own?

Never in a million years would she have expected for him to sneak into her life this way. Her savior, her betrayer, holding her? Kissing her? Craving stardom at her side in the series of films that had bound her to Ross?

"I can't deal with this right now," Lauren decided.

"Get him out of my house. Get him out before I throw him out!"

David's face betrayed nothing, stoic as stone. Only his eyes hinted at some emotion he wisely suppressed. Before Lauren could form the sharp words she'd longed to unleash on him, he left.

Helen took a shaky step backward. "I don't understand. Do you know him? Honey, what did he . . . ?"

Lauren flinched when Helen's hand reached out to her.

Aiden tightened his embrace. "Perhaps you should go as well."

Helen's eyes narrowed to slits. "Back off, big boy. We've been friends longer than you've been around. You don't speak for her!"

Lauren shook her head. No, he didn't speak for her, even though he was saying exactly what she felt. "Helen, Aiden's right. I don't want to talk about this tonight. I didn't expect to ever see him again, and certainly not in my house, touching me. . . . Please."

She turned within Aiden's arms and pressed her face against his chest. She contained a sob, realizing she could deal with an electric shock better than she could an emotional one.

"But David saved your life," Helen reasoned. "He knew what to do when I was freaking out. I don't know who you think he is, but . . ."

Mustering all the strength she could, Lauren broke free of Aiden, even though he did keep one hand on her shoulder. She reached out, wanting to take Helen's hand, but the conflux of emotions crested and she pulled back. "Find out what he wants," she said. "Find out why he used you to get to me."

Helen's eyes glazed. "Used? *Me?*"

Lauren knew Helen would find this concept inconceivable. Helen had grown up in Hollywood, and as a result had a laundry list of trust-related tragedies in her past. Enough to keep her wary and careful and cool. But somehow David Drake had broken past her barriers in record time, and the fallout wasn't going to be pretty.

"Yes, you," Lauren insisted. "I can't believe you brought him here. I—"

Helen, her eyes glossy, left without another word.

Only after the door had clicked shut did Lauren rally her strength. She charged to the intercom, punched the button that buzzed the guardhouse and instructed her security staff to let no one else into the house until she said otherwise. No exceptions. After delivering the code word that assured her guards that she had given this order of her own accord, she flipped off the communication device, spun and flattened herself against the cold wall, then dropped inch by inch to the floor.

Aiden stared at her, his broad arms at his sides, his fists clenched. Ready for battle. Ready to protect her. Ready to take the pain shooting through her and grind it into nothing through sheer force of will.

She forced a smile. "I'm okay."

He tilted his head, his eyes such a piercing silver, he might as well have sliced straight through to her heart. "You may be an accomplished actress, but your claim rings false to me, my lady. Who was that man?"

She squeezed her eyes shut. God, she didn't want to remember. But what choice did she have? The memories were flooding her, threatening to drown her, jeopardizing the strength and independence she'd worked so hard to rebuild.

"A blast from the past," she answered.

"I do not understand," he replied. "Did he hurt you?"

Forced to consider all the circumstances in a few brief moments, she sighed before answering, "No. Helen was right. He did save my life. Twice, now."

"Then why did you react so cruelly?"

She shook her head, overwhelmed and confused,

though she'd always been one to surrender to her emotions before thinking a situation all the way through. When she'd finally seen the boy he'd once been in David's deceptively contact-colored eyes, she'd reacted from her gut—striking out from a mixture of shock, resentment and humiliation. She hadn't even known his name then. She'd never seen him before that night or, as far as she knew, afterward. Not until he'd marched into her home on Helen's recommendation, given a pass into her sanctuary on her best friend's word.

"He came under false pretenses," she explained. "I shouldn't have been so emotional, but I guess I . . ."

Aiden fell to his knees in front of her and smoothed his hand over her cheek. "You reacted on instinct. You have nothing to be ashamed of."

His gentle touch and tender tone reminded her of the boy who'd saved her, the man she'd just thrown out of her house. How could she have treated him like that? Okay, so he'd lied and misled people in order to get close to her—she supposed if he'd tried to contact her through normal channels, he might have revealed her sordid past to the press. She could only imagine how much cold, hard cash he could have gotten from the tabloids for the story. And yet he'd chosen instead to work his way into Helen's good graces and approach Lauren in private.

And he'd actually been a pretty damned good actor.

Guilt made her stomach hurt even worse.

"You don't know enough about me to understand," she said.

Aiden curled a lock of her hair behind her ear. "I know only what you have told me. If there is more to tell, then please, I am willing to listen."

The last couple of days were a blur, but she was pretty sure their pillow talk hadn't included anything significant about her shady past.

"I used to live on the street."

His eyebrows scrunched together as he mulled over her meaning. What must he think, this eighteenth-century son of a nobleman? In his century she probably would never have even exchanged a civil word with him, except, perhaps, for words of gratitude as payment for services rendered.

He slipped his hands into her hair, cradling her temples, pressing her head to his shoulder. His warmth surrounded her, but did not penetrate the images flitting through her mind. For a second, impressions of her in a dirt-encrusted dress with the décolletage yanked down and her skirts hiked up while Aiden pounded into her from behind became even clearer. More vivid. As if it were becoming real . . .

Then he yanked his hand away.

She met his eyes, which were wide with surprise.

"You are above such depravity," he snapped.

"What did you see?" she asked. "What just almost happened?"

Aiden pressed his palms to her cheeks and stared potently into her eyes. "I would never treat you as such," he replied. "I would never subject you to such—"

His words cut off as his gaze flashed toward the sword. The bright light in the room normally muted the shimmering blue glow of the blade, nestled among the cushions on the couch. But at this moment the steel had turned nearly cobalt, as if aflame, and the handle glowed a fiery red.

"What's happening?" she asked, breathless.

Aiden glanced at the sword, then stood, alarm darting across his face.

"I know not," he replied. "But I believe it is time we found out the true nature of Rogan's magic."

"But you said it was evil," she warned, her muscles bunched as Aiden stalked to the weapon.

He grabbed the hilt and held the sword aloft. "It is, but I believe the time has come to vanquish this evil once and for all."

21

The moment Lauren's door closed behind her, Helen nearly doubled over with an ache that was half anger, half humiliation. What had just happened?

Helen had never seen her friend so out of control. Not when she'd caught Ross with another woman. Not when she'd come to terms with the clause in her contract that required her to finish the last Athena film. Not when she'd confessed to Helen soon afterward how much of her life had been a total and complete lie. Enraged by the gash in her friendship with Lauren, Helen launched herself at David, who stood, stunned to silence, just feet from Helen's car.

"What did you do to her?"

David twisted her into a hold that pinned her arms to her body, but still left him one hand free to press over her mouth. Terrified by his constraint, she kicked harder and struggled until she propelled them backward against the car. He lost his footing on the gravel drive and they fell in a tangled heap.

"Calm down," he ordered.

She twisted and squirmed, but he was too strong for her. Forcing her mind clear of rage, she achieved a temporary calm—enough to assess her situation. He'd shifted her against him, but to the side, so that her butting back with her head would not gain her freedom. She tried going slack, but he countered her easily, tugging her hard underneath her rib cage.

"I'm not going to hurt you," he insisted. "And I wouldn't hurt her. Ever. If you'll just calm down, I'll explain. I swear."

She hadn't known David long, but she'd already decided that his acting skills were above par. How did she know that the sincerity in his voice now wasn't just another act? Well, she'd done her share of stage and film work between the ages of five and nineteen. She had the freaking Emmy to prove it. Mustering all her rage into a tiny, potent stone she could hold tightly in her hand, she allowed her body to relax to the point where he'd let her go.

And when he did, it took all her self-control not to either pummel him with her fists or run like hell, screaming for the security guards she knew were just fifty yards down the winding driveway. Instead she stood, dusted the gravel off her clothes and forced a single word through her clenched teeth.

"Explain."

He combed his hands through his thick hair. "I'm not here to hurt her. Or you."

Helen did not react, biting into her bottom lip from the inside to keep herself from interrupting.

"I knew Lauren years ago," he went on. "Well, 'knew' isn't accurate. I met her." He shook his head frantically, as if he had his own store of rage he was fighting to keep under control. "She wasn't even Lauren then, and I wasn't David Drake. We were both runaways. My first night on the damned strip, scared to frickin' death, spent my last dollar the day before. She showed up out of nowhere in expensive clothes. Bought me dinner—burgers, fries, the works. Hardly spoke the whole time, but there was something in her eyes—something special. Then she just left. An hour later I saw her getting the shit kicked out of her. I didn't know what to do. I made a racket, scared the punks away. Then I called the police and waited with her until they came; I talked to her, went with her to the hospital."

Helen listened, half disbelieving. She knew all about the night in question, but while Lauren had told her the story, she'd never mentioned any runaway savior.

"And for that she hates your guts?"

He shoved his hands into his pockets and stared at the ground as if he hoped it would open and swallow him. "I didn't expect her to recognize me. I've changed. A lot. On purpose. But I didn't think she'd be so angry just because I . . ."

"Just because you what?" This time he didn't fight her off when she grabbed his shirt and twisted the soft fabric around her fist. "What did you do to her?"

"I didn't help her run away. She begged me not to make her go back to Ross. Not to let the hospital call him. I didn't know what she was talking about. I thought she was delirious. Now I know she was afraid of him."

Helen shook her head. "Lauren's the bravest woman I know. She wasn't afraid of Ross. She was afraid of who she'd become if she stayed with him. God!" she exclaimed, spinning in frustration. "Why am I still talking to you? You're lying! Lauren told me everything about that night, and she never mentioned any runaway helping her or refusing to help her. What game are you playing?"

And yet Lauren had clearly recognized the man, and she couldn't imagine that he'd made up such an elaborate story on the spot. Only three people in the world could connect the attack on the Hollywood street kid who'd wandered back into her old haunts, only to be nearly killed, to the actress who now called herself Lauren Cole—Lauren, Ross and Helen. The doctors and nurses who had treated her that night knew her under her old name. Her real name. Even Helen didn't know what that real name was.

Lauren Cole had been Ross's creation, a name he'd helped her choose shortly after she'd been released to his care. Now that Helen thought about it, Ross's first wife must have known about the situation, too, but in all this time she'd never said a word to the press. She was, according to all accounts, living the high life as the wife of a New York politician, producing theater and winning Tony Awards. She'd divorced herself not only from Ross, but from any connection to Hollywood.

"Who sent you here?" she asked.

"No one," he said. "I came on my own."

"You used to be an actor in New York, where Ross's ex-wife produces plays. Maybe she's been waiting to exact revenge on Lauren for stealing her husband?"

"Stealing him?" David asked, incensed. "She was trying like hell to get away from that monster."

Helen nearly lost her footing. "How do you know that?" Recovering herself, she tightened her grip on his shirt and asked again.

"Lauren told him when he arrived at the hospital. His address had been on her driver's license, so the nurse called him. I grabbed scrubs and blended in so I could wait around. I heard her confess why she'd left him."

"You are some sort of crazy stalker."

"No," he answered. "No. I was just there. It was . . . just . . . how things happened."

The anger Helen had been holding inside shot spikes through her body. She released him and stepped back, afraid of the emotions roiling inside her. She'd never fought with Lauren. Never exchanged a cross word except in jest. They'd become friends in a way that Helen valued deeply. Now she'd been tossed out of Lauren's house, marked as a betrayer, because she'd foolishly brought a stranger with a hidden agenda into her friend's guarded life.

"Why are you here?"

"I just wanted a part in her movie."

"I don't believe you. You wanted to be near her. You told me so after you'd fucked my brains out, remember? You have some freakish fixation on her, don't you? Because you saved her once and . . . I don't know . . . maybe because the press has been making such a big fucking deal out of her divorce that you thought you'd save her again? That she'd fall in love with you? Maybe take you to bed and pay you back for helping her all those years ago?"

He didn't answer, and the silence sliced into Helen's lungs and wouldn't allow her to draw breath. Mustering all her pride, she dug into her pocket, extracted her keys and got into her car.

He jumped out of the way, which was a damned good thing, because she might have run him down if he'd given her the chance. At the end of the drive she slid to a halt long enough to alert the guards about David's presence and insist they run him off immediately. Then she left.

She didn't know where she was going. She didn't know what she was thinking. She just knew she had to get as far away from Lauren and David as possible, as fast as possible, or she might do something really stupid.

Like cry.

David pushed his hand through the tear in his shirt, then shot a dirty look at the security guards who'd just shoved him off Lauren's property and were now securing the gate.

Could this have gone any worse?

"Come anywhere near Ms. Cole again and you'll be serving time for stalking, got it?" the guard shouted from behind the bars.

He supposed he should be happy he hadn't been arrested. Now he was just stranded. Not that it mattered. He'd certainly been stranded in worse parts of Los Angeles than Beverly Hills. And for what he'd paid for his shoes, they could withstand a little wear and tear. He checked his pockets, but his cell phone was gone. Probably crunched under Helen's retreating tires. Looking up to get his bearings, he headed south.

He hadn't been lying when he told Helen that he hadn't expected Lauren to recognize him, but then he realized that the flaw in his plan started right there. He'd recognized her, hadn't he? The first time he'd sneaked into that movie theater, two years after bumming a cross-country ride from Los Angeles to New York, and caught sight of the blond babe playing Athena on the silver screen?

He'd known instantly it was her. The girl he'd met in Hollywood. The girl who'd shown him kindness in the face of utter fear. The girl whose life he'd saved, only for her to be shuttled off to some private facility by her rich sugar daddy. The girl who'd unwittingly kick-started his career.

His footsteps echoed on the sidewalk. From just over the side of the tall, manicured hedges and rustling palm trees of tony Beverly Hills, the colors and sounds of wild, unchained Los Angeles beckoned. The sensations of being terrified, hungry, desperate and alone flooded back over him. Leaving his mother's house with nothing but a dozen fading bruises and his dreams of acting seemed like a lifetime ago. His fantasy had been instantly cut short by the realization that he was only one of a thousand throwaway kids who'd been tricked into trading one tragic life for another, thanks to movie-manufactured delusions and illusions.

Only, David had made it. Lauren might not have had a chance to thank him for his help that night, but her benefactor had paid him pretty nicely, both for his good deed and for his silence. Ross Marchand had paid him several thousand dollars and given him a business card for a modeling agent who owed him.

Through pure grit and will, David had parlayed his reward into an Actors' Equity card and a letter of acceptance from the Screen Actors' Guild.

He'd promised Marchand that he'd never come back to Hollywood, and technically the boy who'd taken the money had not returned. Now he was someone else. Someone new. Someone worthy of Lauren's attention and gratitude and affection—someone whose past had just smacked him down yet again.

His mind lost in his humble beginnings, David was unaware of the car trailing slowly behind him until it revved forward and the passenger side window slid down.

"Get in," the driver said.

David didn't stop walking. "This is Beverly Hills, buddy, not the Spotlight. Pick up your boy toy somewhere else."

The car screeched to a stop and one tire ran up on the curb. Instinctively David jumped away, then froze, stunned when the driver leaned across the seat, opened the passenger-side door and looked up into the light from the street lamp.

Ross Marchand.

"I said, get in," he repeated.

David held his ground. "Why?"

"You want to work in this town or not?"

Though delivered with an amused tone, the hard truth in Ross's threat hit him like a fist to the gut. With a shrug, he did as the producer asked, sliding onto the leather seat of the Jag and slamming the door.

"So you've taken to staking out your ex-wife's house now?"

Ross gave him a smug glance, then turned his eyes back to the road and jumped the curb until they were gliding farther and farther away from Lauren. "Did you get what you came for? Or did you crash and burn, like I predicted?"

"I was walking home. What do you think?"

"I warned you that coming back here was not a good idea."

"Yes, you did."

"This town isn't so big. Everyone knows everyone, and secrets aren't worth squat."

"I can see that now." David forced the words out. He didn't want to talk to Ross Marchand, but what choice did he have? The moment his head shot and résumé had been short-listed for the part of Lauren's love interest, he'd been on the producer's radar. Like an idiot, he'd thought he could bypass the producer, get to Lauren on his own.

How wrong he'd been.

"So I suppose you're willing to play this my way now?" Ross said confidently.

David resisted the urge to pound his head on the dashboard. "Do I have a choice?"

"None at all, kid. None at all."

22

The sensation was akin to liquid metal dripping down Aiden's arm. The sword glowed with power Aiden knew he had to master, no matter the cost. He tensed against the pain. A strangled yelp behind him nearly made him falter, but he stayed his hand.

"Do not be afraid," he said, his stare captured by the colors gleaming off the sword. The magical blue from the blade and an intensified red from the inset stones in the handle merged into a powerful violet. The effect was at once fascinating and terrifying.

"Aiden, please . . . put it down," Lauren begged.

He pressed his lips tightly together. As she'd confessed her past, the magic had revealed a new secret to him—a new power. He'd seen her thoughts and had nearly brought them into being. What else could the sword do if only he took the time to give it a command?

He closed his eyes and concentrated, picturing himself walking in the daylight with Lauren at his side. Suddenly a natural heat warmed his face. He inhaled, and the scent of perfumed air teased his nostrils.

"Aiden!"

His arms vibrated from holding the sword aloft. A current of power set his nerve endings afire. He turned to her, but his fist remained tight around the hilt of the sword. What other secrets did the weapon possess?

In all the time since he'd emerged from the sword, he'd concentrated entirely on Lauren, first on her recovery, and then on filling his empty soul with her, making love to the woman he'd fantasized about for what seemed like the whole of his life. But in his attempt to indulge his private needs, had he missed a chance to secure his freedom?

Why had he hesitated?

The answer was obvious: Once he was free, he might never see her again. His life would be in another country, rebuilding the life he'd lost to Rogan's curse. She was just as determined to hold on to her independence, to focus on her career. She would not leave all she'd built to follow him to England. And how much loss could one man bear?

"The magic must be explored," he insisted, though picturing his freedom seemed to do nothing but rip at his soul.

In a wild grab, she curled her arms around him and held on tight. She was afraid. He could feel her shaking, but she remained where she was, attempting to help him despite her fear.

"What do I do?" she asked.

"Imagine us out in the daylight. Picture us walking in your garden with the sun shining in our faces. Accept the fact that I am free to walk this earth as a man."

She must have done as he asked, because a moment later, after a dizzying sensation, they were standing in the lush garden behind her house, beside the Grecian-themed fountain sparkling in the moonlight.

Not sunlight.

Moonlight.

He dropped the sword. It landed in the soft grass with a thud, and the gleam faded until the blade and handle were yet again only silver and gold.

Aiden pulled Lauren around to his chest and, after

tapping the sword with his foot, transported them back to her living room.

"Whoa," she said, tugging away uneasily.

"I apologize," he said automatically, his voice wooden with disappointment. "I only wanted to see if you could wish me free of this curse."

"No," she said. "I want to help you, Aiden. I really do. I don't know how I freed you from the sword. I only touched it."

He picked it up from the floor and held the blade toward her. She'd tried once before to manipulate the sword's magic, but that had been during the daytime. Perhaps now, in the night, when he was strongest . . . ?

She closed her eyes, her face taut with concentration, and placed her hand on the blade.

Nothing happened.

He dropped the weapon again and couldn't resist giving it a little kick. Dissatisfied, he kicked harder. The blade slammed across the room, and again Lauren yelped. He turned to find her staring at him with a hodgepodge of emotions playing across her face, the most obvious ones shock and disbelief.

"I'm—"

"Don't apologize again. I can feel your frustration. You want to be free. I want you to be free. It's just . . ." She looked around the room as if searching, her hands outstretched. After a moment with nothing to grab onto, she jabbed her fingers into her hair and laughed, then dropped onto the sofa and buried her head in her hands. "This is so weird. This is beyond weird. This is Ed Wood, Tim Burton, Quentin Tarantino all rolled into one big weird."

He had no idea about whom she was talking, but glancing alternately between the sword and Lauren, he retrieved the weapon and dragged it begrudgingly to where she sat on the floor. He squatted beside her, toying with the golden handle, until she peeked up at him from beneath her folded arms. "What just happened?"

"We failed to free me."

She shook her head. "Maybe I wasn't trying."

"Maybe I wasn't, either."

She nibbled on the tips of her fingernails for a second, then forced her hands to her sides. "Where will you go once you're free?"

The sadness in her eyes revealed her inner turmoil. Lifting his hand softly, he toyed with the hair draping across her cheek, then smoothed the errant lock behind her ear. The instant his fingertip touched her temple, the blade of the sword burned a purplish blue, and the flash of an image entered his brain. Lauren. Alone.

"You do not want to be alone," he said.

She chuckled mirthlessly and gave a nonchalant shrug. "Who does?"

He brushed his hand deeper into her hair. The contact was intimate, but not more so than the second impression he received from her private thoughts: She was standing on the doorstep of her home, and Aiden was walking away without turning back.

"You fear the aftermath of my desertion. Yes, Lauren, when I am free, I will leave to seek out what might be left of my family. I could lie to you and assure you that I will stay with you forever, but I venture you've had enough men lie to you over the years. I can only be truthful and say that once I am free, I have no idea what my future holds. I will admit that I hope that it will somehow include you."

Lauren listened intently; then her blue eyes widened in surprise. "Did you just see what I was thinking?"

"Yes," he replied.

She scooted away from him, breaking the contact of his fingers against her scalp. Her luscious mouth sucked in gasps of air, but her lungs did not seem to accept the breaths.

"Lauren, you must breathe."

She closed her mouth and inhaled deeply through her nose, her eyes closed. She repeated the action until the muscles along her neck and shoulders visibly relaxed.

Aiden tossed the sword aside, but the clank of metal against the floor did not interrupt her breathing. He'd expected that the sword, magicked by Rogan, would possess other mysterious properties he might not ever fully discover, but even he had not expected to possess the ability to glimpse into Lauren's mind.

Perhaps this had been the means by which the clever wizard had infiltrated Sarina's heart centuries ago. His sister had always been a dreamer, a child of whim and fancy who believed in magic because she experienced it daily with the Gypsies of Valoren. If Rogan had found the means to penetrate the young girl's innocent fantasies, he would have discovered a powerful key to seducing her away from her family.

"I would think," he said after clearing his throat, "that after I emerged from a magical sword—a phantom relegated to corporeal form only in the darkest hours of the day—that this new revelation of my ability to read your mind would be inconsequential."

She looked up in time to smirk at his grin.

"Can you read my mind right this minute?"

Turning her face, she watched him as if the smallest tic in his facial muscles would reveal the answer. He had not expected to slip into the images of her mind. The act, at first, had been unconscious. Natural. He'd only been listening to her, touching her, wanting to ease the regretful sound of her voice.

He wasn't sure he wanted to know what she was thinking right now, not when a frown was curving her lips so unpleasantly.

Still, he squinted and tried to forge a connection. "Are you intentionally blocking me?"

"I don't think so."

"Then no, I cannot read your mind."

"But you did," she said. "You saw what I saw. Before, when I was thinking about you and me and if I'd lived in your time . . ."

He nodded. "I saw who you *thought* you might have been in my time, my lady, but I beg to differ. A woman of your beauty and intelligence would never have fallen into such disrepute, no matter your parentage. You are a clever woman, Lauren Cole. You would have found other means."

"My name isn't even Lauren Cole."

The lost look in her eyes caught him unaware. How could a woman who wielded a sword with such skill and had nearly bested him in hand-to-hand combat only days before suddenly think herself of such little worth? Was the woman he'd met the night he emerged from the sword—the woman who'd made love with him with such abandon—but a mask for the real woman within?

The vulnerable woman?

The damaged one?

"Lauren Cole is a name Ross and I made up."

"What was your name before?"

Her mouth quirked involuntarily into a grin, which she immediately quashed. She shook her head.

He tipped a finger beneath her chin. "Tell me."

"Doesn't matter. She doesn't exist anymore. Hell, she didn't exist back then. She was a nobody. A mistake. Lauren Cole isn't just a persona that Ross invented for me anymore. It's who I want to be. It's who I've dreamed of being my entire life. Wealthy, powerful, sexy. Talented."

"Then you have achieved your greatest ambition." He moved to stroke her hair away from her face, but she started, as if afraid his touch would cause another connection into her mind. "Why, then, do you still fear the past?"

"For the same reason you still wish to avenge yours.

The past doesn't go away just because we've moved beyond it."

Aiden nodded, surprised that she understood both herself and him so thoroughly. Up until now, he had not cared about her past. He'd been entirely compelled by his own.

His quest for freedom stemmed from his centuries-old need to avenge the curse and the destruction of his family. Once he'd achieved that, he would search for whatever remnants of the Forsyth line still existed. But what if no one had survived? Of his brothers, only Rafe had had a child. But with his Gypsy lineage, he would not have been entitled to the earldom. And for all he knew, even that innocent babe had been slaughtered by the mercenary army the morning after Aiden's entrapment.

His mouth filled with the bitter taste of rage. "Tell me about your family," he requested, hoping to offset his anger.

She scoffed. "I'm like you, buddy. I don't have family."

"I still exist," he insisted. "Albeit in an insubstantial form. But my brothers were with me that day in the village. Perhaps they, too, fell victim to Rogan's curse. I could yet find them, once I am free of my bond to the sword."

Her smile was bittersweet. "Then you have something to look forward to that I don't. I never knew my father. Never even knew his name. Don't think my mother knew it, either. And I don't have any siblings. And my mother's dead." She made the admissions so matter-of-factly, he silently mourned for her emptiness. "She was a drug addict."

As she explained, he nodded, but remained quiet. Though he had not heard of the particular pharmaceutical abuses she spoke of, he'd seen soldiers misuse Dover's powder after injuries sustained on the battlefield. The aftermath had been ugly. Soldiers who'd succumbed never truly recovered, and their families suffered for it.

"She'd tried to clean herself up after I was born, or so she told me. Got a job. A place to stay. But once I was old enough to fend for myself, she dropped back into her old life. Just before my eleventh birthday we were living out of our car. By the time I was thirteen we didn't have even that. I was on my own while she turned tricks for drugs. I don't know much about the time you lived, but I'm pretty sure that the child of a two-bit whore would have become a two-bit whore herself."

Aiden inhaled deeply, his mood darkening as he imagined the dark turn Lauren's life could have taken. "Look around you. You would not have—"

"I couldn't have had any of this if not for Ross."

"And this disturbs you?"

She laughed, but the sound lacked humor. "Women today try not to marry solely for financial security," she explained. "They still do it—don't get me wrong—but I never wanted that life. I wanted to make my own way in the world. That's all I've ever wanted."

Aiden shifted on the couch, noting how she'd pulled her knees to her chest and wrapped her arms around her shins. Crouching in this tiny corner of her lavish home seemed to provide her with a sense of security. He toyed with her fingers gently, inviting her to take his hand. She did. He slid her closer to him, and for a long few minutes they sat in silence, curled together, expensive furniture and knickknacks all around them, though he knew the trappings of wealth meant both nothing and everything to Lauren all at the same time.

Since her release from the hospital, they'd been free to talk during the day and make love for most of the night. She'd told him and shown him everything she could about the current events, history and technology that made her world so incredibly foreign. But they'd also, he realized, avoided any topics that might reveal too much about themselves. He'd told her about the curse and his family and his career as a soldier, but he'd revealed nothing about his early days as a dueling rogue, or the horrors he'd witnessed at Culloden. Those events had shaped who he might have become, had he escaped from Valoren to live and die in his own century.

Fortunately, it didn't take much time for him to realize that in Lauren he'd found a woman who was more reluctant to talk about her past than he was. Yes, he knew about her career as an actress and her role of Athena and the importance of her completing this film so she could move on without any obligation to Ross, but beyond that they'd been mysteries to each other.

Until tonight.

"I'm not proud of marrying him," she said.

"A woman marrying above her station to improve her lot is not a new invention, my lady. You said as much yourself."

She grinned, but the dullness in her usually bright eyes hadn't diminished. "I've never thought of myself as an old-fashioned girl before."

"Perspective is difficult to hold on to when emotions are involved."

"Maybe that's why I reacted so badly tonight to David."

Quiet echoed in the room until she took a deep breath, then described to Aiden how she and David had been strangers, kids, both of them, on the night their paths had first crossed. She'd been barely eighteen, running away from Ross's unexpected marriage proposal, and David might have been sixteen. Skinny. Dirty. Hungry. She'd bought him dinner with the last twenty in her wallet, wanting to purge herself of everything Ross had given her. Everything Ross had wanted her to become.

"An hour later, this gang jumped me. They weren't happy that I was broke," she explained.

"I gather this attack is why you learned to fight," he guessed.

She snorted. "Getting your ass kicked is strong motivation to learn martial arts, yes. I wasn't bad in a fight before, but five to one wasn't exactly even odds. I was down. They were kicking me in the stomach, in the head, and then they were gone and David was there holding my hand, telling me to hang on, that I'd be okay. He must have scared them away. I don't know. I can't remember much, but I know he called the cops. All I could think about was wanting to get away. I wanted him to drag me out of sight so I could just die or live, I didn't care. I just didn't want Ross to find me. I remember thinking, 'How can I become anything now that I'm a lump of raw meat?' "

Aiden slipped his arm tighter around her shoulders. Images started to swirl in his head, but he knew better than to intrude unbidden.

"May I?"

She blinked, but no tears flowed. Their eyes met, and after a moment, she understood his request to enter her mind. She gave a little nod. He slid his hand into her hair, and after a split second of resistance, she relaxed and allowed the memories to flow. Impressions of the pain and the therapy and the scars flooded into his mind, along with mirror images that belied her present beauty. He fought not to yank his hand away in shock at her injuries.

"The hospital found Ross through the address on my driver's license," she went on. "He came right away. David disappeared. Ross paid for my surgeries, therapy and meds. When I'd started to recover, Ross promised to make the whole incident go away. And he did. He made up a new life for me. Everything before just disappeared. He erased my ugly past and created a new backstory that we sold to the press. He helped me forget. And I let him, but I might not have had to if David had only helped me escape. I realize now he was just a scared kid himself, but why is he back? And pretending to be an actor? I don't get what he wants from me."

"Perhaps he just wanted to know that you have recovered."

"He can read the trades and the gossip rags like everyone else."

"Maybe he wanted the truth."

That quieted her. Aiden had not been a part of her world for long, but her accident in the trailer had taught him how the people around Lauren would lie, manipulate and bully whomever necessary to protect her image and her privacy.

He, however, wanted the truth.

"Tell me about Ross," he coaxed. "About your marriage to him."

"You were there," she said.

"I was hanging on a wall in his study, only vaguely aware of what went on around me. I was not privy to your most private moments. I was not there when he wooed you to his bed."

On the edges of his mind, pictures started to form. Lauren, young and naked, staring at herself in a mirror, exploring her body with tentative hands. Ross, standing behind her, speaking words of encouragement even as his own nude body reacted to her discoveries.

Aiden released her.

"Could you see that?" she asked.

He shook his head. "Not by choice."

"No," she said, grabbing his hands tightly. "I want you to understand."

23

Her voice was flat with determination. Aiden closed his eyes, and the images rushed at him fast. Ross standing behind her. Directing her. Telling her where to touch herself. Cupping his hand around hers and sliding her fingers between her legs. Aiden could hear his deep voice, instructing her to part her feminine lips and find the tiny nub inside, to manipulate it with her fingers until she gasped in pleasure. He led her other hand to her mouth, had her suck her fingers wet, then grasp her young nipples until they were taut. He could hear him telling her to explain in excruciating detail the sensations running through her. Then he grabbed his own penis and stroked himself hard and long.

Aiden broke away. "No more!"

"Don't you see—"

"I don't want to witness that man touching you or pleasing himself at your expense. You were barely a woman. Did you not torture me enough tonight, forcing me to watch that David Drake paw his hands all over you, running his mouth up your body—"

She launched herself on him, connecting her mouth with his in a way that washed all thoughts of any other man out of both her brain and his. Desire overrode all other considerations until they were nearly undressed—not by magical means, but by the tugging and rending of clothes.

"I was his puppet, damn it," she said, her eyes glassy and her breathing ragged. "Everything I know came from him. Everything I am. Do you have any idea how hard that is to live with?"

Her hands clutched at him with a desperation that bespoke more than lust. Lauren wanted Aiden from deep in her soul. Because she desired him, not because she needed him. Not because he was directing her. Their mating came from a desire that was wholly and entirely hers, and Aiden would deny her nothing.

"Then live with it no more."

He scooped her up into his arms and carried her through the glass doors that led to a glistening pool of blue water behind her home. Surrounded by lush greenery and bright pink and red flowers of varieties he'd never seen, the patio provided a private oasis not unlike a dream. He set her down on her feet near the edge of the water, his tongue still dueling with hers, his hands filling themselves with the fullness of her buttocks and breasts.

Suddenly she pushed him away. Her laughter accompanied his backward fall, and he had only a split second to prepare himself for the splash. But though the water slapped hard on his back, the liquid was welcoming. His lungs tightened, but he remained beneath the surface, enjoying the clear, wet weightlessness.

Seconds later he heard another splash. He turned in time to see Lauren's body slice into the water like a knife into butter. She swam with confident athleticism, and her beauty exceeded his imagination. Lights implanted in the walls of the pool illuminated her in shades of blue and green. He might have thought her a mermaid or sea siren had he not known she was real. And for tonight she was his.

When she reached him underneath the water, she slid her hands up his chest, and together they broke the surface, gasped for as much air as their lungs could handle, then crashed in a kiss that drew them back into the depths of the pool. Aiden had never experienced such delicious sensations against his flesh—her hot skin, the cool water, the fluid motions stirring the pool into a tempest of wild fulfillment. She crested the water again, and, grabbing her around the waist, he lifted her high. She arched her back, and he suckled the water sluicing across her nipples until she cried out in pleasured release.

He was hard. Rock hard. He wanted inside her, but the minx broke free of him, swam to the opposite end of the pool and slithered up the stairs. He dove forward, grabbed her by the ankle and waylaid her escape. With a roll he had her atop him, his backside on the steps.

She straddled him. The water around them made her body resist until his touch spawned moisture from deep inside her that smoothed his path to ecstasy. Sheathed within her, he knew a bliss that was more than magic.

Her breasts glistened and his eyes feasted for a moment before his mouth took over the banquet of sensations. Her areola, so dark and round and centered with nipples that responded to his tongue and teeth, tempted him to madness. With one hand on the bar that led out of the pool and the other braced on his shoulder, she increased the tempo of their lovemaking until he could resist no more. He spilled into her hot and hard. When he was spent, he knew she had not crested.

A disappointed frown curved her luscious lips. He slid his hands into her hair at her temples and concentrated on glimpsing the images in her mind. He saw jets of water swirling in steam and foam.

Grinning, he lifted her, kissed her and swam them to the opposite side of the pool. The overflow from the artificial hot spring tucked into the corner spilled into the cool water. Her eyes widened expectantly.

"I could become accustomed to living with such delights," he said, climbing onto the edge and then extending his hand to her.

She accepted, and in one yank they were stepping into the sultry waves of the spring.

"I've hardly used this since I moved in," she said.

He stepped into the water and handed her down. "Then use it now, my lady."

He'd never dreamed of such decadence before, but the window into her mind had implanted a fantasy in him that he could not deny. He slid her in front of him and positioned her across from the hot, hard jets of water. He took hold of her breasts, placing lavish, hungry kisses along her neck while the water coaxed her to orgasm.

"Aiden," she whispered. "Oh, God."

She tried to move away, but he held her steady. "This is your fantasy, Lauren. Do not deny yourself this small pleasure."

She panted and cooed. With his body fully pressed against hers, he saw the actions she wanted from him only split seconds before he could comply. He tweaked her nipples tightly and held on until her body vibrated from deep within her and she shouted his name on a wave of utter ecstasy.

When she slumped against him, he twirled her around and settled them on the ledge, the hot, bubbling water bathing them from the neck down. When her breathing steadied, he realized he was hard again. She snuggled her buttocks against his cock.

"It's not fair," she said.

He breathed in the heady scent of her hair and skin, the fragrance heightened by the steam. "How so?"

"You know what I want," she whispered. "But what do you want?"

" 'Tis no mystery."

She turned and climbed onto his lap so that his sex nestled against hers. "Beyond the sex. I've told you things and shown you things I have never shared with another human being. What can I give you in return?"

"Only my freedom from the curse."

Her eyes darkened with disappointment, but only for an instant. She stood abruptly, splashed beneath the water, then popped up and found her footing. He moved to snag her back to him, but she slapped his hand away.

"No," she said decisively. "It's time to get down to business."

24

They had come to a crossroads. Up until now Aiden, despite the solid form he took in the night, had truly existed only in Lauren's fantasies. Yes, he was real . . . but only in the darkness and usually only in her bed. But after he'd seen the truth about her past and still cared about her, she knew she had to act.

Her contribution in freeing him from the sword only so he could live in the aftermath of the curse, fully aware of and tormented by its cruel limitations, was nothing to brag about. He could not move of his free will. He could not pursue his family or find retribution against the sorcerer who'd trapped his soul. He was her prisoner now—and as someone who craved freedom more than anything else, she could not stand by as his jailer for much longer.

She had to find a way to break the curse entirely. He'd helped her live again—love again. Now it was her turn to pony up. Her injury had pushed primary shooting on the film back, though she was scheduled to return to the set in the morning for rehearsals and meetings. If she were going to act, she had to do it now.

She swam to the edge of the pool and climbed up the stairs to the cabana, where she took out a terry-cloth robe for her and a large bath towel for him.

When she turned to hand it to him, she realized he had not followed.

"Aren't you coming?" she asked.

With a grunt, he got out of the Jacuzzi. "Apparently, not again. At least not tonight."

She laughed, and the muscles between her thighs gave an involuntary squeeze. "I'm not ruling out anything, but it's time we tackled this curse problem of yours with real determination."

With a reluctant nod, he pushed out of the water and stalked down the steps toward her, naked and glistening with steam from the spa. Her breath caught, and her nipples, chafing beneath her robe, constricted needfully. From his penetrating silver stare to his broad, perfect chest, thick-muscled legs and impressive package, the man was stunning. Involuntarily she licked her lips and fought the instinct to drop to her knees right here and suck him dry. She didn't know what was fueling that magic of his, but damn, she was having a hard time resisting.

Once they were dressed, she went inside the house and retrieved the sword. She heard Aiden's breath catch as she lifted the handle and pressed the blade flush against her leg, the sharp edge centimeters away from slicing her skin. For the third time she closed her eyes and concentrated, truly and honestly wishing for Aiden's freedom. She imagined them lounging by the pool in the daylight, sipping cool drinks and laughing over some silly article about her in the trades or running lines for the next day's shoot. She conjured the feel of his hand in hers as they zipped around Los Angeles with the top down, heading toward lunch at her favorite Italian trattoria, sipping wine at a sidewalk table, talking in whispers about what they would do next to find his family.

The atmosphere around her shifted. The air, cool and crisp moments before, warmed with the scent of musk and man. She spun around, fully expecting

Aiden to somehow look or feel different, but his quirk of a grin didn't reach his eyes.

"Nothing?" she asked.

He shook his head.

"Well," she said determinedly, "we're down, but we're not out. Time to stop trying to futz with this old-fashioned magic. I think we'll be better served by using the modern kind."

Lauren led Aiden into her home office and turned on the computer. She also activated her speakerphone and dialed her assistant, Cinda. She knew it was after midnight, but her assistant was paid big bucks to be available twenty-four/seven. And when Cinda answered with a jaunty "Hello!" she didn't even sound sleepy.

"How's my puppy?" Lauren asked. She'd missed her dog for days, but wasn't entirely sure how her massive rottweiler would react to Aiden's sudden appearances and disappearances. She didn't want to give either Aiden or the dog a heart attack, so had opted to leave him with Cinda for one more night.

"Missing you," Cinda replied. "He was fine for the first few days, but he's starting to pine."

Lauren glanced over at Aiden, who was watching the screen of her computer light up. "I'm feeling much better now. Why don't you bring him home first thing in the morning?"

"Is that why you called?" Cinda asked.

Lauren slid into her leather chair. "Actually, no. I'm wondering, if I want to research a family from the seventeen hundreds in England, how would I do it?"

"Research for a new part?" Cinda asked.

Lauren didn't bother to lie. Cinda read just about every script that crossed Lauren's desk. It was part of her job to weed out any film opportunity where Lauren's role would be nothing more than a cheap imitation of Athena, or that contained gratuitous sex, or where her character would be nothing more than arm candy to some superalpha male. Lauren had amassed a tidy sum playing Athena, and now that she was nearly free of Ross, she could afford to be choosy.

"No, this is personal. I wondered if there was any way to track down the descendants of a British nobleman."

"Is this about that sword?"

Lauren sat forward. She hadn't told Cinda anything about the sword. At least, not recently. She supposed she might have mentioned the weapon back when Ross still held it over her head, literally and figuratively, but she'd remained mum since she'd first decided to steal it.

"How do you know about the sword?"

"Ross."

"He called you?"

Her assistant snorted. "Right after the accident on the set. By the way, did you know the set electrician ruled it an accident? Said something about a loose wire making contact with the shower door?"

"Yeah, I did," Lauren replied, though after the attack in the hospital, she wasn't entirely sure she believed the studio's determination. "Tell me what Ross said about the sword."

"He wanted me to keep an eye out, let him know if you had it. I guess it's gone missing from his house or something."

"What did you tell him?"

"Well," Cinda said guiltily, "I told him I would, but that's just because I don't want him ruining my reputation or making it so I can't get a job someday down the road, you know? I wouldn't betray you, Lauren. You know that."

In the background, Lauren heard the tap-tapping of Cinda's fingers on her keyboard. A few seconds later Lauren's screen popped to a search engine. As she'd done in the past, Cinda had used the network connection between her computer and Lauren's to control what happened on both machines. Lauren motioned for Aiden to pull up a chair and prepared to tell Cinda what little she knew about the man she'd been sleeping with since he'd first materialized out of a strangely glowing sword.

"The name is Forsyth," Lauren announced, "from a place called Valoren."

Even as Cinda typed the name into a search engine, Aiden's frown deepened into a scowl.

"There's nothing," Cinda said.

"Nothing about Forsyth or nothing about Valoren?"

"Valoren is coming up empty. Is that in England?"

Aiden shook his head.

"No, skip Valoren," she said, remembering that Aiden told her it was the name of a Gypsy colony somewhere outside the country where he'd been born.

"There's a gazillion Forsyth hits," Cinda said. "Tell me more."

Aiden pressed his hand over the place on the phone where Cinda's voice echoed, but Lauren pressed the mute button instead.

"Can you trust her?"

Lauren took a deep breath. "She's been with me a long time. She's paid very well to be discreet, and she's never been anything but."

Aiden's expression told her he didn't share her optimism, but they really had no choice. Lauren was only barely computer literate. She had never had the time nor the reason to explore the information superhighway, but her assistant was a pro. If they needed information—and they needed it quickly—she had to go to Cinda.

"Sorry," she said, releasing the mute button. "I have someone with me. His name is Aiden Forsyth. He's doing research into his family tree."

"Isn't that the guy who's going to play—"

"Yes," Lauren interrupted. "We were running lines

and started talking about our family histories, and he told me he always wanted to know what happened to this British duke—"

"Earl," he corrected.

"Right, earl, whom he's distantly related to. Think you can help him?"

Cinda didn't miss a beat. "Sure! I love this stuff. Aiden, tell me what you know."

Aiden scooted his seat closer to the phone and proceeded to give Cinda the dates and names and locations that were his history. His family. His lineage. His legacy. Lauren listened intently, amazed at the fact that he knew so much about his history in comparison to the scant information she had about her own family. But her envy was short-lived. He might have blue blood and pedigrees, but in the big picture he was just as alone as she was.

Lauren left them to their exploration, went into the kitchen and prepared a plate with fruit and cheese and crackers, suddenly overwhelmed by her isolation. So she'd help Aiden find out what happened to his family, maybe even discover he had a great-great-great-grandson or something. Maybe she'd figure out how to free him from the curse. Then what?

He'd leave.

Of course he would.

And she couldn't go with him.

Not that I'd want to.

Right?

Lauren dug into her wine cooler, searching for a vintage Aiden might enjoy, then stopped. Was she doing it again? Letting a man rule her choices and preferences, even when he hadn't made one demand of her she hadn't wanted to comply with? Or was she using her past to keep her heart from connecting with Aiden's in such a way that his inevitable departure would be too hard to bear?

She didn't know. She wasn't sure she wanted to know.

After selecting a favorite Tuscan Sangiovese and downing a glassful herself before pouring a second for Aiden, she strolled back into the office in time to hear Cinda say, "Now, this is interesting."

A simple Web site filled the screen. It was nothing more than a listing of names and an e-mail link.

"This is my family," Aiden said, his voice hushed with awed surprise.

Lauren slid the wineglass in front of him and read the names on the screen aloud. " 'Damon, Aiden, Colin, Paxton, Logan, Rafe and Sarina.' Sarina!"

The sister who'd started this mess. Lauren frowned, but then realized that without this young girl's fickle flight of fancy, she would never have met this incredible, honorable, selfless man. She supposed this was what everyone meant when they talked about destiny. She'd always heard that things happened for a reason, but she'd never accepted such inevitability as a part of her life. She'd split her experiences into good luck and bad luck. How would she classify Aiden? She supposed she wouldn't know until after he'd left.

"Whose site is this?" Lauren asked, shrugging away the sudden uncomfortable clench in her stomach.

Another window popped up in the corner. Lauren watched Cinda execute a remote "Whois" search. "The Web site is owned by a Gypsy Enterprises, LLC."

She and Aiden exchanged surprised looks. "Gypsy?"

Then the screens started popping up faster and faster while Cinda worked her technical magic. The parade of shapes and colors stopped at a PDF file in a public records database that connected Gypsy Enterprises with the Chandler group.

"Gypsy looks like a small subsidiary of the con-

glomerate that owns the Crown Chandler hotels,"
Cinda explained. "Just formed a few months ago. No
officers listed. Wait. Here's one. Catalina Reyes. I'll
google her in a minute. But this Web site is so odd.
Just a listing of names. No links, except for the e-mail.
Aiden, do you know the Chandlers or this Reyes
person?"

Aiden shook his head, so Lauren provided the audible, "No, he doesn't."

"Well, that's just weird. Do you want me to
e-mail them?"

Perplexed, Aiden did not respond.

"That's okay," Lauren provided. "We'll take it from
here. Thanks, Cinda. I didn't mean to keep you up so
late. You're getting a bonus after all this crap you've
been through lately on my behalf."

"I wasn't the one who was nearly killed," Cinda
responded, a shiver in her voice. "I'm glad you're feeling better."

Lauren ran her hand across Aiden's arm. He was
still staring at the screen, a stern look mixed with surprise frozen on his face. "I'm feeling wonderful. I'll
see you in the morning."

She disconnected the call. The computer screen remained static.

"What do you think this means?" she asked.

That he had some kind of connection to the present? That he'd soon be leaving her to explore his
roots?

"While you were in the kitchen, Cinda showed me
how to do this."

Tentatively, he wrapped his hand around the mouse,
pointed the arrow on the screen toward a box on the
bottom of the window and clicked. Another screen
popped up. "She found this listing first."

Lauren read quickly. On the Web site devoted to
the history of the British House of Lords, they found
the archival evidence of Aiden's existence, a family

tree of the last Earl of Hereford. "Your father . . . your mother?" she asked, tracing her hands over the slim line that connected the names.

Aiden nodded.

"Then Damon and you . . ." she stopped reading out loud when she realized that each brother's name was followed by the date of his birth . . . and the date of his death. Aiden had been born on March the twenty-fifth. An Aries. Not exactly the perfect match for her classic Taurus tendencies.

"It says here that you all died in 1747. On the same day?"

"The day of the attack at Valoren."

"But your father lived thirty years longer."

Again, nothing but a nod.

Oh, God.

"Do you think . . ." She swallowed the dread lumped in her throat. "Do you think you're dead?"

She could not believe it. Now that she'd become accustomed to the magic that allowed Aiden to pop into her life with the sunset, she had a hard time thinking of him as a ghost. She didn't know much about spirits trapped on earth, but she'd certainly never heard even the vaguest claims that ghosts could attain corporeal form.

Except in the movies.

But that wasn't real.

"I still do not believe that I am dead," he said finally, slipping his fingers around the stem of the wineglass she'd brought and sliding it nearer, though he did not drink. "History, however, claims otherwise."

"Well, they had to write something," she said. "They couldn't very well just say you up and disappeared one night while messing with a magical sword. You should trace your father's line in another source. See if he had any more children, or if your brothers left any sons."

"Cinda already did so. She could not find anything.

The earldom died with my father, and the monarchy reclaimed his lands."

Lauren pressed her hand to her chest, trying to quell the sudden ache there on Aiden's behalf. "There's nothing left?"

"One estate is now a museum, but otherwise, no."

Lauren dropped into a chair and cursed under her breath. She'd acted without thinking in calling Cinda, dragging Aiden into exploring his past without first knowing what they'd find. To her, the deaths and loss of his lands happened hundreds of years ago, in a culture she didn't understand. But she wasn't so self-centered that she couldn't read the fresh pain in his eyes.

"I'm so sorry," she said. "I shouldn't have suggested we research your family until you were free of the curse and could check things out for yourself. We should concentrate on that. I'll bet Helen knows someone—a psychic or something. They're a dime a dozen in Hollywood, though I don't know how good any of them are. Maybe she can make some discreet inquiries. . . ."

Her enthusiasm did nothing to smooth out the lines of disappointment etched into his face. In fact, he'd hardly seemed to hear her at all.

He clicked back to the other Web page, the one that listed all of his family's names. "This one is different."

Lauren read through the names on the rudimentary Web site, then reached across to the mouse and clicked back to the official family tree. "Wait a minute. The family tree doesn't mention Rafe or Sarina. This one does."

Aiden's mouth tightened. "Yes, I noticed this as well. Rafe and Sarina were born of my father's second wife. His secret wife. Alyse was Romani—one of the banished. Such a union between her and my father would have been unacceptable at court, and the scandal would have been quite ugly. I always thought that was why he never considered leaving his governorship, not even after the king recalled his garrison of soldiers or after Rogan moved in and took over the Gypsies' enterprises. I'm quite certain that my father never told anyone in England about his marriage to Alyse or about the children he had with her. So why are their names here?"

"Someone knows about them," she replied. "Someone survived the attack that supposedly killed you, and told someone about your Gypsy brother and sister. And another someone connected to Chandler Enterprises—this Catalina Reyes, perhaps—put this information up on the Web, though I can't imagine why."

"To find us."

Standing, he clasped his hands behind his back and stalked away from the computer. After he'd paced the room a half dozen times without speaking, Lauren snagged his hand and pulled him back.

"Who would even know to look for you?"

His eyes turned such a stormy gray, she gasped as if the air had just been sucked from the room. "My brothers."

Lauren's head swam. "Do you really think someone in your family is alive?"

"I am here, am I not? Could it not be possible then that one of my siblings suffered the same fate as I while in the village, but is now free and searching for the rest of us using this technology your world so relies upon?"

"I suppose. . . ."

He jabbed his finger at the monitor. "No one associated with my father would have known about Rafe and Sarina except for family. Even if some of the Gypsies survived, they would not have returned to England, and they certainly would not have reported on the earl's family to anyone of consequence. Servants would have been well paid to keep the secret, and even if they told, who would have cared enough to record Rafe's and Sarina's names? My father was disgraced. The king sent mercenaries to reclaim his lands, but the mission went awry. The Gypsies had mysteriously disappeared. This could explain why there is no record of Valoren or the experiment to colonize the Gypsies outside of England. Only kings have the power to change history. And to erase it."

"What about his wife?" she asked. "She would have kept records of her children's birth."

He rubbed his chin, thinking hard. "Alyse was a pragmatic woman, but illiterate. And Gypsies, for the most part, did not keep written records. If Alyse lived beyond that night and returned with my father to England, she would have insisted she take a place in my father's household to keep their marriage a secret. He loved her. He would not have abandoned her. But this information shows that he never again served in the House of Lords once he returned from out of the country. The museum site says he lived a quiet, secluded life until the end of his days, meaning he shut himself away with his secret wife, mourning the loss of his children. Never knowing about the curse. Never knowing we lived, although, with us in a state so crude and cruel, knowing might have been more punishment than believing we were dead."

He looked up, and his eyes gleamed silver with both determination and regret. Lauren's heart ached, thinking about how the earl had grieved for seven children— his entire legacy—without knowing that they'd never truly died.

His voice snapped her back to the present.

"I have to go to London," he said decisively. "The answers must be there."

Lauren's stomach dropped. "Yes, but you can't. I mean, I can't. And you can't go without me."

He scowled, his hands balled into tight fists. "You

told me about your modern means of travel. We could be there by tomorrow."

She covered her mouth, certain her sudden queasiness came from the fact that she could not give him what he so desperately wanted. "I can't go now. Rehearsals start tomorrow. We shoot the first scenes in a few days. I can't just pick up and leave right before we start the movie. Making the arrangements to film your scenes only at night has already pushed my limits."

"Then call back that David Drake. Have him take the part. Send the sword with your assistant. You claim you trust her. Tell her my secret. Order her to help me find my family."

Lauren's eyes widened. The thought of telling Cinda about Aiden tore at her insides like swallowed glass. It was one thing to believe in magic herself, because she'd seen it with her own eyes, but it was something else to share this insane tale with a girl who'd pinned her Hollywood ambitions on the stability of Lauren's career. She'd asked Cinda to do so much already— wasn't this above and beyond?

Or was she just making an excuse?

Was jealousy, perhaps, keeping her from acting as Aiden asked?

She wanted to help him. *She* wanted to be there for him when he found the freedom he so desperately needed.

For once, she wanted to be the one to help someone else, rather than the other way around. Wasn't that what her karma required to undo the years of taking while she'd lived with Ross?

"I can't drag Cinda into this," she decided. "It's too much to ask of her. Someone has already attacked me trying to get your sword. I can't put her in danger."

He continued to pace as she spoke, his hands clasped behind his back.

"Is that truly your reasoning, or do you simply not wish to help me? Perhaps I am just a means to an end for you. A reason not to confront David Drake or your past?"

A lick of fury fired her belly. "This has nothing to do with David."

"Then call him," Aiden insisted, pointing at the phone. "Tell him he can play your lover in your insignificant film. Or can you not, because he knows your secret? That you were once a child of the streets who lifted herself to greatness through the calculated lust of a man who never loved you, but wanted only to possess you? Does your greatness now embody that same cold selfishness?"

Lauren's eyes burned, and in her chest a sensation much like a crack bled icy resentment around her heart. He was right. She was being selfish. Selfishness had gotten her this far, hadn't it? If she hadn't been selfish, she would have ended up just like her mother—dead on a dirty L.A. street corner. Unwanted. Unloved.

Better to have a fake name than a name no one would ever know, right?

"Fine," she answered coolly. "I'll make sure David is hired for the part, but I still can't take you to England or put anyone else at risk. I have obligations of fulfill. People are counting on me. I have a contract."

"Break it."

"I can't." Her pride couldn't withstand the heartbreak in his eyes, and her voice cracked. "Why can't you understand? My whole career was built by Ross. Planned, manufactured, executed. This is the first film I've made without him pulling my every string. If I'm unreliable and cost the studio millions, I'll never work in this town again. What am I going to do then with my life?"

He shot across the room and grabbed her by the

arms. His gaze captured hers with such ferocity, her heart slammed hard against her chest.

"Be with me."

She couldn't stop the tears. They dripped down her cheeks like plump raindrops, splashing off the tip of her chin. How could he understand? They were from two different worlds. Two different centuries. Any delusions she might have had, unspoken and unnamed, about a future with Aiden were ripped from her by his easy, insistent reply.

She swallowed her disappointment and forced out three simple words of her own: "That's not enough."

His scowl broke her heart, but the way he dropped his hands from her and gave her a curt bow cut even deeper.

She blinked. He was gone. She gasped and fought for breath, even as she dashed into the living room and found the sword. Dropping to her knees beside the couch, she fought the instinct to grab the handle or touch the blade.

He did not want to be with her anymore. She would not give him what he wanted, even though she wished with all her soul that she could. He deserved freedom, but damn it, so did she. Clearly the fact that she wanted to help him, that she cared about him more than she could say, wasn't enough. He wanted more than just her love. He wanted her to give up everything she'd worked for—which was more than she had the capacity to give.

25

Cat recognized Helen Talbot immediately, not from her days as a child star—the woman barely resembled the fresh-faced, blond-haired, blue-eyed teen queen she'd once played on television—but from the cunning and suspicious look on her face as she entered the hotel bar. Their brief conversation on the phone, facilitated by Amber Rose, the most connected concierge Cat had ever met, had nearly ended ten words after "Hello." Mentioning the name Aiden Forsyth had convinced the woman to meet with her. And Ben, of course. Clearly, the casting agent and reported close friend of Lauren Cole was a natural-born skeptic with no time for bullshit. And what she and Ben had come to tell her wouldn't exactly be easy to swallow.

"I think you should do the talking," Cat said out of the corner of her mouth while Ms. Talbot chatted with the pretty blond concierge as she pointed in their direction.

Ben's eyebrows shot up. "I thought you were the silver tongue and I was the brass knuckles."

She stifled a laugh. To the rest of the world Ben looked more like Indiana Jones about to lecture to his lovelorn students rather than a man who could jump chasms and work magic with a whip, but Cat knew differently. From the widening of her big blue eyes as she approached, Helen Talbot noticed the delicious maleness of Cat's lover as well. The woman raked Ben with a blatantly appreciative stare. Appreciative, but still wary.

Ben stood.

The concierge made the introductions. "Dr. Ben Rousseau, this is Ms. Talbot. And this is . . ."

Cat extended her hand. "Catalina Reyes. It's a pleasure to meet you."

Helen's hand was in and out of hers so quickly, Cat didn't have a chance to register a single emotion other than impatience. But the woman did give Ben more than ten seconds worth of attention before sitting down.

Amber excused herself. The hotel bar, with its rich paneling and warm candlelight, possessed a seductive atmosphere even in the middle of the day. Cat suddenly felt a bit like a third wheel, which prompted her to speak.

"Thank you so much for agreeing—" she began.

The casting director quickly interrupted. "You wanted to meet with me regarding Aiden Forsyth?"

"We're looking for him," Cat replied.

Helen glanced at Ben. "Why is that?"

"He's my uncle."

Helen snorted, accepting what looked like a pomegranate martini that a waiter delivered before anyone had even ordered. Clearly, the woman was a regular.

"He's younger than you are," Helen said.

A muscle in Ben's jaw ticked, but his smile was smooth as glass. "My father—his much older brother, had me very late in life."

Her eyes remained narrow and assessing. "You don't have the same last name."

Ben leaned forward. Cat could only imagine what Ben's potent sandalwood cologne was doing to Helen's senses.

"Not a very trusting person, are you?" Ben challenged.

"This is Hollywood," she answered simply. "What was it Jay Leno said? If God doesn't do something about Hollywood, he owes Sodom and Gomorrah an apology."

Ben chuckled. "Then you'll understand when I tell you that my father had some questionable dealings in his past that forced him to change his name. But Aiden is still his brother. Clearly, you know him . . ."

She waved her hand as if she would not verify this fact one way or another.

". . . or you know how we can contact him," Ben continued. "If you can arrange a meeting as soon as possible, he'll verify that we're family. Trust me."

Helen took a smooth sip of her drink and laughed. "Well, at least I've verified that you are indeed new to this town. Only an out-of-towner would ask me to do that."

With a snap, she instructed the waiter to bring over drinks for Ben and Cat. She filled the silence between ordering and delivery with innocuous questions about their stay in Los Angeles, turning the topic back to Aiden only after all three of them had vodka-pom concoctions sitting in front of them. "So, your uncle . . . or whatever. Is he in trouble of some sort?"

Ben eyed her quizzically. "Why would you ask that?"

"Just wondering why you had to go through a stranger in order to make contact with a relative. Couldn't you call his cell phone?"

Ben smiled again. "Pretty sure he doesn't have one. He's an old-fashioned guy."

Helen's eyebrows lifted, as if Ben's words had just verified that he did indeed know the man he claimed was his uncle.

"And you have no other way to reach him?"

After a sip of the tart martini, Ben shook his head with just the right touch of vulnerable charm. Cat had to squelch the instinct to reach over and pat his hand. Man, he was good.

"I'm afraid he hasn't been in touch with his family for what seems like centuries."

He kept his eyes trained on Helen.

"Family squabble?" she asked.

"Something like that. He and my father haven't spoken for a very long time. And, to be honest, my father isn't doing well, health-wise, so I took a chance in coming out here and seeing if I could work out some sort of reunion."

Cat lifted the martini glass to her lips to hide her grin. Damn, but Ben really was brilliant. And handsome. And sexy. After a mouthful of flavored vodka passed over her lips, she gave herself a little shake and concentrated again on how smart he was. Keeping to the truth would bypass the highly tuned bullshit detector Helen Talbot seemed to have plugged in to her sharp blue eyes.

"We heard that he came out here to see Lauren Cole," Ben continued. "But she's not exactly in the white pages. Cat is practically family with Alexa Chandler, who, of course, owns this hotel, so we came out and had the concierge help us track you down in hopes of making contact with Ms. Cole and, subsequently, my uncle."

Helen rubbed a fingertip along the edge of her glass. "I don't know. Ms. Cole is very busy."

Cat decided to turn up the heat. "We're not asking for a private audience. We just need to get a message through to Aiden. *Uncle* Aiden."

Helen turned to Cat, folding her arms in the process. "How do I know you're not from the tabloids, trying to get an inside source to verify some torrid affair?"

"Anyone on the hotel staff, all the way up to the manager, will verify that we're personal friends of Alexa Chandler," Cat explained. "She's out of the country, but she's reachable by phone if you wish to speak with her directly."

Helen finished the rest of her drink, then stood.

Ben did the same. "Ms. Talbot, we realize that you have to be very careful about facilitating contacts between strangers and someone as famous as Lauren Cole, but we really don't need to speak to her so much as we need to speak to my uncle. Maybe if you give him this, he'll know that I am who I say I am."

Ben pulled a gold button out of his pocket and pressed it into Helen's hand.

"What is this?" she asked.

"A family heirloom," Ben replied. "It's become something of a lucky charm for my father, though it once belonged to Aiden. Please give him this and explain to him that we need to see him. That we can help him win the freedom he's looking for."

With an expression that hovered somewhere between a skeptical smile and an out-and-out smirk, Helen slid the button into the pocket of her slacks, gave them both a curt nod, then turned to leave. About five steps out, she spun back. "I can reach you here?"

Ben flashed a golden-boy grin. "Absolutely."

"Wait for my call, then," she announced. "I'll see what I can do."

Once Helen Talbot had disappeared out of the bar, Cat relaxed into her seat. She expected Ben to follow suit, but instead he remained standing, staring after Helen Talbot as if he could will her to act on their behalf.

"Ben?"

"She's seen him."

Cat gave a little tug until Ben sat down again. "Well, it looks that way, but she didn't really say for sure. She was pretty sly about it, actually."

Ben downed the last of his drink, then signaled the waiter for another. "If she's seen him, you know what that means?"

"That other people may have seen him as well."

"If he's already in the phantom state, we don't have much time to find him. He doesn't have the protection of the castle to keep him from being stolen by the K'vr."

"But he has the magic," Cat reassured him.

"And if it's still as corruptible as what Damon had to fight against . . ."

His voice drifted away. He was thinking. Formulating. Planning. Meshing together all the information they had and trying to work out a plan. Unfortunately, Cat knew there was nothing they could do unless Helen Talbot came through. Aiden simply had to fight the infectious nature of the magic on his own.

26

"Lauren? What are your thoughts?"

Lauren snapped to attention, mortified. Michael Sharpe, her director, as well as the writers, the production assistants and the principal cast, were gathered in a conference room adjacent to the soundstage, waiting for her input on . . . what? She had no idea. She'd managed to keep her head in the game long enough to complete two read-throughs of the new scene Michael had just added to the screenplay, but somewhere amid an argument over stage directions, she'd lost her train of thought. She'd struggled to keep on track since leaving this morning without so much as a whispered word from Aiden. Now anticipation and doubt hung thick in the air as everyone waited for her to speak.

"I'm sorry, Michael. I'm still a little fuzzy. What was it you asked?"

She hated blaming her recent injury for her inability to concentrate, but Michael smiled, and the rest of the crowd chimed in with understanding words and claims that she'd come back to work too soon. She needed to focus. To earn the respect and consideration everyone seemed so willing to blindly give. Hadn't she learned that merging her personal and professional lives was not a good idea? She had to carry this film. They all depended on her to make this film a success, especially now that Ross wasn't choreographing her every move.

But instead of giving Lauren a chance to redeem herself, Michael called for a break. They had been working for three hours straight. She supposed she could use a moment alone.

Really alone. She'd left the house this morning without Aiden's sword, opting to lock the silent weapon in her bedroom safe. Since then, no matter how many people were chattering to her or around her, a cold silence hung heavy in the air—an emptiness that made her stomach ache. She had to learn to fill that stillness with her character of Athena and no one else or she was going to flop.

She'd barely risen from the table when Cinda appeared at her side. "Can I get you anything?"

Lauren forced a smile. "No, I just need a few minutes."

Cinda hung back while Lauren worked her way through the people milling around the room or heading toward craft services for a snack. She spied her trailer from across the soundstage and lowered her head, hoping to get there without anyone waylaying her. She had her hand on the doorknob when someone grabbed her by the arm.

"I'm sorry, I—"

She cut off her polite brushoff when she registered who had his hand on her.

"Let go of me," she spat.

Ross released her. "No need to be testy, sweetheart. You're the high queen of this little court now, aren't you? You don't have any reason to hate me anymore."

She opened her mouth to list all the reasons she still had to despise him, but thought better of it. Not because he was her producer, but because she didn't have the energy to care.

"What do you want, Ross?"

"My sword."

For a split second she considered handing over the damned thing and being done with it. No more phantom to force her with his keen gray stare to look at her life. No more lover to complicate her ambitions or step in the way of her path to her future. No more man to try to tell her what she could do or what she should do or when.

But the confused and selfish moment passed quickly. She wouldn't turn Aiden over to Ross for all the freedom the world had to give.

"What else can I help you with?" she asked.

"You're turning out to be rather clever, you know, showing the video of you using the sword to Michael and the art director. I thought both of them were going to jack off right in front of me, though honestly I couldn't tell if it was you or the sword that was turning them on."

"Probably both," she snapped, though holding tight to her overconfident attitude wasn't easy when she knew *she* hadn't shown that video to anyone. The last time she'd had it in her possession had been shortly before her accident in the shower. She'd locked it up after watching it, hadn't she? Who had found it? Helen had the combination, but she'd never show something so personal to Michael and the art director. Or would she?

"Yes, well, that brings up my other reason for being here," Ross said. "I'd like to meet the man who shared that little bit of theatrics with you."

Judging by the continued cool confidence in Ross's tone, he hadn't seen the whole tape. Still, Lauren's lungs were constricted to the point where even a sigh of relief would hurt like hell.

"He's not here."

"Yes, I gathered as much, since the sun is shining. You know, Lauren, I've heard of actors making outrageous demands before, but do you have any idea how much it will cost me to pay the union to run production all night long?"

"He's not in every scene. Besides, you can afford it," she said.

Ross's focused gaze faltered for a split second, instantly alerting her. She'd been with Ross too long not to know when something was wrong.

"You *can* afford it, can't you?"

His grin was classic Ross—overconfident and condescending. "What if I couldn't?"

Lauren took an instinctive step forward and met Ross's gaze dead-on. He glanced aside, and she cursed.

"Ross, what did you do?"

"I don't know what you're talking about."

Lauren grabbed his shirt with one hand and opened her trailer door with the other, shuttling them both inside and then locking any prying ears out of their private conversation. She released him the moment she knew they were alone. "You never joke about money."

"Who was joking?"

" 'What if I couldn't?' you said. As in, maybe your financing isn't as strong as what you reported to the studio?"

"The financing on this film is fine. I'd never put the Athena franchise in jeopardy."

"No, but unlike me, you've invested in more than just this franchise. My whole future is riding on Athena. You have your hand in dozens of other pies. If you're in trouble, Ross, tell me now."

"Why? So you can help? Turn the tables on me and make me beholden to you after all the years that I taught you, supported you, made you a star?"

Lauren inhaled deeply. She hadn't wanted this showdown. Hadn't asked for it. Wasn't even prepared for it. But now that it was here, she was surprised to find she was up to the task.

"I repaid you for your help and then some, and you know it. You've made enough money on my last four films to finance a war, so don't come crying to me if you have to spend a little more this time around to make me happy. You want me to admit that you made me what I am? Fine. I'll admit it. You made me. The good and the bad. Because of you, I can't trust a single man who comes into my life, not even if he's honorable and funny and sexy and would lay down his life for me if he could."

Her voice caught, but before Ross could call her on the unbidden show of emotion, she grabbed a bottled water from her fridge, twisted off the top with a yank and chugged. He was speechless, so she decided to finish her tirade and unburden her soul.

"Because of you, all of Hollywood is circling me like vultures, waiting for me to screw up so that they can say I was never for real, never talented—that I was just a product designed and marketed by you to sell to the world. Because of you, I'm willing to betray my own personal happiness just so that I don't fall on my face in this last Athena movie. I left you. I divorced you. And yet I'm still tied to you with iron bands that . . ."

She faltered. The parallels between her inextricable bond to Ross and Aiden's cursed connection to the sword hit her hard. She didn't only have to free him. She had to free herself. She withdrew a second bottled water from the refrigerator and held the cold plastic to her increasingly hot face. "Do you have any idea how that feels?"

Ross slumped onto the couch behind him and took a long minute to answer, staring at his hands while she panted with released rage.

"Yes, I know how that feels."

His voice quavered. She half expected that when he looked up at her, he'd have tears in his eyes.

But when his hazel met her blue, his face was bone dry and his mouth was a slash of resentment and cruelty. "Welcome to my world."

"Fuck you."

"I did. And you enjoyed it."

"I didn't know any better," she shot back.

"Now you do?"

Images flashed in her mind. She and Aiden in the workout room. In the shower. In the hospital. In the pool. In her bed. Sensations spawned a spark of need within her that she'd fought all night long, knowing Aiden was near, but that he no longer wished to make love with her. She would change that, damn it. She'd find a way to make him understand or else free him, so he could find a woman who could be the lover he needed, even if she couldn't. He deserved that much.

Maybe more.

She sighed heavily, finished with Ross in so many ways, she couldn't begin to count.

"What do you want from me, Ross?"

"I want to meet your new lover."

"You mean my costar?"

"Isn't he one and the same?"

She narrowed her eyes and was thankful she'd left the sword at home. She couldn't imagine that Aiden would not have found a way to interrupt this conversation at some point, and she, for one, was glad she'd spoken her piece, even if Ross was still acting like a self-serving idiot.

"I told you, he's not available."

Ross stood. "When will he be available?"

She leveled her gaze directly into his. "His first scene isn't scheduled until tomorrow night. I guess you'll meet him then."

Though she gestured toward the door, Ross made no move to leave. "I've done background checks and

as far as I can tell, the man doesn't even exist. He's
not even SAG."

"Trust me, he exists," she answered haughtily, even
though, truth be told, she had no idea whether Aiden
was going to appear in the film at all.

For all she knew, she'd never see him again.

As for the little details of Aiden having no identity
in the modern world, she'd find a way to solve that
problem as well. *If* he let her.

"He'd better check out," Ross said, pointing a finger accusingly at her.

She smiled prettily. "Bite me."

"I have," he snapped back. "The putrid taste still
lingers on the palate."

Enraged, Lauren lobbed her water bottle, hitting
the door just as he left, rattling the walls so that a few
photographs dropped off the wall. When her throat
hurt from containing a scream of frustration, she
opened her mouth, prepared to let loose, when the
door opened again.

"What?"

"Sorry!" Cinda said apologetically.

"No," Lauren said, trying to steady her breathing
with deep lungfuls of air. "I'm sorry. I thought you
were Ross again."

"Is everything all right?"

"Is anything ever all right when that man is around?"

Cinda didn't reply, which was just as well.

"Does Michael want me back?"

"What? Oh, no. Not yet. But Helen called."

Lauren nearly doubled over from another emotional
blow to the gut. Helen. She'd been meaning to reach
out to her all day, but had secretly hoped that her
friend would simply show up on set and act as if nothing nasty had transpired between them the night before. No such luck, she supposed. She really needed
to check her horoscope, because so far this day had
truly sucked.

"Is she on her way?"

"To your place, yes," Cinda replied.

"My place? Why?"

"Oh! The security company called. Someone broke in."

27

Aiden sensed the presence almost instantly, alerted by a strident beep. He knew the sound. Lauren had shown him how the device that monitored the security of her house worked. The noise meant, under the current circumstances, that someone who had no business inside Lauren's house had entered.

She'd left only a short while ago. An hour. Perhaps two? It was hard for him to measure time while in this insubstantial state, particularly without Lauren there to mark the progression. This was the first situation since she'd touched the blade that he'd been without her during the daylight hours. The isolation unnerved him—rattled him to the core.

But though he had not spoken to her directly since their disagreement last night, he knew from her conversation this morning with Cinda that neither she nor her assistant was expected back until late in the evening. And yet someone was here.

Previously she'd told him that while she employed two guards to watch her property and occasionally make rounds to ensure that the house was secure, they never came inside unless called. And if they did enter the house, they did not know the code to disengage the alarm, ensuring that the local police would be alerted to any and all unauthorized intruders.

Five successive beeps rocked the silence, followed by a long whistle.

Her security device had been deactivated.

This was not good.

Angry at Lauren's inability to fully appreciate the severity of his situation, Aiden had acted uncharacteristically last night when he'd abandoned Lauren in her study and retreated to the garden for the duration of the darkness. Instead of spending the remainder of the night making love to the beautiful, deceptively fragile woman who'd devoted the better part of her evening researching the fate of his family, he'd thrown himself into seclusion, listening to the trickle and splash of the fountain and recounting memories of people and situations he'd spent centuries forgetting.

Only when daylight had been moments from dawning did he realize how he'd brooded more like his brothers Damon and Rafe might have. The eldest and the youngest Forsyth sons had earned reputations for dwelling on injustice beyond a reasonable period. Aiden, on the other hand, had been as likely as Logan or Paxton to drown his troubles with a pint of ale and perhaps the company of a lovely lady. Yet by the time Aiden had recognized his boorish behavior, the sun had risen and he'd retreated, unwillingly, into nothingness.

And yet, as the sunlight had streaked through her windows, he'd hovered above her bed, watching her fitful sleep, cursing himself for acting so much like her former husband that he was forced to wonder why she didn't ship the sword off to some unknown land and banish him from her life forever. Her refusal to leave her home and ambitions behind to take him on a fool's journey to England—where he might not find any more information about his family than he had on the Internet—had stung. Even after two centuries, he was not yet used to a woman denying his every whim and desire. In that regard he did not much like this new millennium.

Or perhaps he simply had to realize that some women deserved to honor their own heart's desire over that of a lover. Lauren's ability to focus on her own needs in sexual situations had excited him, but now, when his agenda contradicted hers, he questioned her choices and her loyalty.

He was no better than Rogan.

Except that he truly cared for Lauren in ways he had not experienced with any other woman. He might even love her, if he had any real notion of what that might mean.

But now he could prove his devotion by protecting her—or, at the very least, guarding her possessions. Though he suspected only one possession would be at risk.

The squeak of shoes announced the thief's path across the marble floor in her foyer. The steps were tentative. Uncertain. Someone with permission to be inside would not walk with such a hesitant stride. And yet whoever had breached her security did so with knowledge and forethought. They had clearly entered the correct security code—and they knew she wasn't at home.

With the risen sun blinding him anytime he ventured too close to the windows, he employed Rogan's magic to search the house, sensing the interloper in the living room. Aiden manifested, invisible, just behind the couch. The man had masked his face in thick black wool. His eyes were unrecognizable slits.

The intruder bypassed several items Aiden had learned cost Lauren a considerable amount of gold—a television, several collectible art pieces small enough for a thief to pocket, and a diamond bracelet Lauren had been wearing last night, but had removed and left on the coffee table when it had twice snagged her costume. Clearly the burglar was not here for ordinary treasure.

The thief turned toward the staircase. Though Aiden wasn't exactly sure where Lauren had stashed the sword, he'd felt a tug during the night that made him believe she'd taken it upstairs. With a thought, he positioned himself on the middle step. When the thief approached, Aiden focused all his power into his midsection, so that after the intruder bumped into him, he lost his footing and skittered down several steps before catching himself on the banister.

"What the f—"

Aiden *tsk*ed. "Such language," he chastised.

The man dropped on his arse down two more stairs.

"Who's there?"

"Leave," Aiden ordered. "Now."

The message seemed simple enough, but the thief merely screamed in a tone not unlike a woman's. Only when the interloper yanked off his mask to see more clearly was Aiden sure that his initial guess as to the gender of the intruder was correct.

A man. But not just any man.

Aiden's smile seemed to fill his insubstantial body with needs he'd squelched for over two centuries. Like the need for revenge and retribution and justice.

"Nigel."

Ross Marchand's nasty butler nearly leaped out of his skin. He skidded the rest of the way down the stairs and landed in a heap on the marble floor.

"Who's there?" he asked again, his voice cracking with fear.

Aiden chuckled. "Your conscience, Nigel. You've been a very naughty boy, haven't you? Treating Ms. Cole with such rude disdain."

"She's an upstart! With no class and no . . ."

The butler stopped when he realized, judging by the look on his face, that he was talking to nothing but air. Muttering about medication, he made a mad dash up the stairs, passing through Aiden on his way, loudly questioning his sanity with every step. He stopped at

the top, swung around and, with both hands braced
on either side of the banister, waited.

"Come out, if you're there!" he ordered.

Aiden remained utterly silent, the only noise a light
scratching at the patio door two rooms away.

Aiden theorized that Lauren might have once
owned this home with Ross. That would explain why
Nigel knew the security codes and his way around.
Aiden wondered about the guards, but as they were
stationed on the far perimeter of the house, he could
do nothing to alert them.

No, best to take care of this situation on his own.

Well, maybe not entirely alone.

The scratching intensified, followed by a hungry
whine.

In his mind, Aiden pictured the glass door to the
patio. With a mental twist and a push, the portal
swung open. He heard the telling beep, followed by
the scruffle and click of four thick paws on the floor.
He'd always been impressed by his lover's choice of
canine companions—especially when he recalled the
enmity between the dog and the butler when they resided at the house overlooking the ocean. Aiden could
only hope that absence hadn't made the heart grow
fonder.

Aiden whistled softly.

The dog stalked into the foyer, then turned his massive black and brown head quizzically toward the staircase, sniffed, then growled—a sound that was both
low and menacing.

Aiden moved to the top of the stairs and whistled
again.

The dog inched forward, then stopped dead and
growled more loudly.

"Come now, Apollo. There's a tasty morsel up here
for you."

The dog bent backward, his square jaw nearly
touching the ground even as his hindquarters were

raised high, the dog struggling between the instinct to protect and attack, and the fact that he could not see the man who had called him.

"Have it your way. I'll bring your breakfast to you, then." Aiden thought a moment before moving into the bedroom, where he found Nigel rifling beneath Lauren's bed.

The man truly had no shame.

"Where is it?" he asked aloud. "Look at me, acting like a common thief. And . . ."

Nigel stopped his rant when he retrieved a long, flat box from underneath Lauren's bed and whooped triumphantly. He pried off the top, threw aside a layer of thin tissue paper, then gasped, pulling out what looked like a man's private parts, cast in a rather authentic substitute for real skin.

"How disgusting!"

Aiden kicked out. The box skittered back under the bed and Nigel yelped in surprise. The cock and balls flew into the air. Aiden had no idea why Lauren owned such an authentic representation of a man's family jewels, but he sniggered all the same.

He hovered so close to Nigel, he could smell kippers on his breath.

"Boo," he whispered.

Nigel slammed backward, knocking the lamp off Lauren's bedside table. He screamed, then scrambled out of the room and bolted down the stairs. Aiden did not need to watch what happened next. He heard the barks, the growls, the screams and the rending of clothes. With a yawn born of the time of day, Aiden settled into the nothingness and, satisfied, drifted into a deep and dreamless sleep.

Helen cursed. The last vehicles she wanted to see parked outside Lauren's house were two police cars and an ambulance. From behind the wheel of her Jeep Cherokee she scanned the street, looking for the paparazzi, but beyond two women with fluffy dogs and a guy chatting on his cell phone, none of the ravenous photogs had descended on the scene just yet. But they had police scanners, the vultures. They'd hear Lauren's address and be here any minute. Helen could only hope that Lauren was still at the studio.

She parked on the curb and dashed by a uniformed officer to one of Lauren's security guards, Gino, who was sitting on a stool beside his guard stand with a paramedic hovering over him and an ice pack pressed to the base of his skull.

"What happened?"

"Damned fool knocked me out."

"What damned fool?"

Another set of paramedics was rolling a gurney toward them, and Helen's heart jammed into the back of her throat. Only when she saw that an older man was lying prone and bloody on it did she regain her ability to breathe.

He looked vaguely familiar.

"Who was that?"

"Nigel," Gino replied.

"Ross's butler?"

Gino nodded, but the action made him wince. "Idiot drove up an hour ago. Used an old code to open the gate, then nearly ran me down when I blocked the driveway. Said Mr. Marchand had left something in the house that he needed or some shit, but I knew Ms. Cole didn't want her ex or any of his employees anywhere near the place, so I told him to move along. He got out of the car. Must have had a tire iron hidden behind his back. He clocked me. Knocked me out cold."

The paramedic pushed Helen aside and rechecked Gino's pupils, declared him to be suffering from a slight concussion and insisted he get into the ambulance.

"I'll be fine," he claimed, but Helen could tell he was just being typically male.

"Go with the ambulance. I'll call the studio and have them send over a detail to watch the house until you're back."

Unsteadily, Gino stood. Helen was watching him go toward the ambulance when she spied Nigel again.

"Wait! Gino, how'd he get so beat up if you didn't—?"

"Apollo," he replied. "Good thing Cinda brought him home this morning."

Helen's knees weakened. Police were traipsing up and down Lauren's driveway. Another squad car had just pulled up. She could only imagine what they'd done to Lauren's dog if he'd threatened the boys in blue when they first arrived. She started running up the driveway, hampered by her three-inch heels, only to find Gino's counterpart, Billy or Bruiser or someone or other, holding the dog by the collar on the front porch while petting him soothingly.

Relief gave way to anger.

"Okay," Helen said to the second guard, "your partner got clocked and the butler broke in. Looks like Apollo stopped him from taking anything, but where the hell were you?"

"Taking a leak," the man shot back. "Bad timing, I guess."

"Looks like."

Helen bent down and gave Apollo's ears a scratch. "You're an ugly, scary beast, but that's why Lauren loves you, isn't it?"

The dog sighed, dropped to four paws with his head in the security guard's lap and watched with keen eyes and a still tail as the strangers roamed his domain. Thank God he was well trained. Relieved that she didn't have to break the news to Lauren that the police had shot her dog, Helen made her way into the house.

"No press," a uniformed officer said.

Helen smirked. "Do I look like press?"

"Anchorwoman, sure," the cop said, flirting.

She rolled her eyes. She was so through with men. "I'm the owner's best friend. Was anything taken?"

"Doesn't look like it, but you might want to give your friend a call so we can be sure."

Helen pulled out her cell phone and reached Cinda on Lauren's phone. After instructing the assistant to get Lauren home as quickly and quietly as possible, she disconnected the call and took a look around. Over the next twenty minutes the cops filed outside one at a time, speculating about whether the man who'd bypassed the security system was a crazed fan, or wondering who else had spied the dildo lying on Lauren's bed.

Great. Just fucking great. Helen made a quick call to Lauren's publicist, and they hammered out a game plan for how to handle that little bit of choice news once it was leaked to the press, which would be in less than an hour, by normal Hollywood standards. Some cop would think it was funny to list that item in the police report and the rest would be history.

Helen decided to march up the stairs and make sure none of L.A.'s finest decided it would be a fun idea to take the sex toy into evidence or to sell it on eBay. Once in the bedroom, she spotted it immediately, peeking out from between some pillows.

She leaned forward to get a closer look.

"I think I bought that for her," she said.

"Why on earth would you do that?"

Helen jumped and spun, expecting to see Aiden behind her. But he wasn't there. No one was. But she'd clearly heard his voice.

"Aiden?"

She leaned into the hallway. It was deserted. She explored the nearby rooms and found them all unoccupied. Had she imagined his voice?

It was possible, she supposed. She reached into her

pocket and retrieved the tarnished gold button Ben Rousseau had given her just a few hours before. Okay, so she'd had two pomegranate martinis. She certainly wasn't drunk. After her meeting she'd stopped into the hotel spa for a quick manicure and pedicure, allowing herself plenty of time to sober up before she got into the car. Unsure when Lauren was expected on the set and unable to reach her on the cell, she'd swung by the house on her way to the studio, hoping to smooth any residual hard feelings from the night before and to talk to her about Aiden's long-lost nephew and his request for contact. She'd stumbled onto the break-in purely by accident.

She heard movement downstairs. Just in case some nosy photographer had sneaked past the cops, she picked up a pillow and tossed it over the vibrator.

A voice echoed up the stairs. "Helen?"

"Lauren?"

She moved toward the door and suddenly was over-come by the scent, smell and feel of a man. She stopped dead, then spun around, expecting once again to see Aiden somewhere nearby, but the place was empty. First she'd heard his voice and now she'd recognized his scent?

She clutched the button tighter in the palm of her hand.

"Helen?"

"I'm up here!" she called.

Lauren met her halfway up the stairs.

"What happened? The police said Nigel broke into my house."

"Good thing Cinda brought back your watchdog. He took a nice hunk out of Nigel's snooty hide."

Lauren pressed her lips together, trying not to laugh. "Did Nigel get—"

"The sword? I don't think so. The police didn't find anything out of place except your . . . well, your . . ."

Why she was suddenly shy, Helen had no idea, but

she grabbed Lauren's arm and marched her up the stairs into the bedroom, where she uncovered the sex toy with a certain flourish.

Lauren cursed, then laughed. "Oh, dear God. Who saw that?"

"All the police who traipsed through this room, I'm assuming. But what I want to know is why you need that anymore when you have the real deal in the form of Aiden Forsyth."

A rumbling male voice caused an explosion of gooseflesh on Helen's skin: "I was wondering precisely the same thing."

28

Helen stumbled backward and fell onto the bed. Lauren, on the other hand, slammed her fists onto her hips and stared into the not-so-empty air. She knew he was probably still ticked off about last night, but that didn't give him an excuse to give her best friend a heart attack.

"What the fuck was that?" Helen shouted, her voice high-pitched with terror. "That's the second time I've heard Aiden's voice when he's not here. Lauren, what the hell is going on?"

Lauren waited to see if Aiden was going to answer again, because if he opened his big mouth one more time she might never forgive him. She dropped her arms lazily to her side and tried to look casual.

Luckily for her, he remained silent.

"What do you mean?" Lauren asked innocently.

Helen's eyes narrowed. "Don't pull that shit with me, Lauren Cole. You heard him. You had to hear him, unless you've suddenly gone deaf."

Lauren slid onto the bed beside Helen and pulled out her trump card. "Two-martini lunch again?"

With a sputter, Helen tried to stand. Lauren grabbed her by the blouse and, with a quick yank, sent her tumbling back onto the bed.

"You did that!"

"Did what?" Lauren lowered her chin and conjured

up her most reproachful expression. "Honey, you really shouldn't indulge so early in the day, especially with all the stress we've both been under. About last night, you know, with David. I was out of line. I'm really sorry."

"Don't try to distract me with apologies. Where is Aiden? Is he hiding in your closet?"

She leveraged herself off the bed and dashed toward the door to the walk-in, tearing it open and flipping on the light. The spacious room overflowed with clothes and shoes, which Helen tore into as if she were again missing the little Dolce & Gabbana skirt that Lauren often borrowed.

"Where is he?"

"I couldn't tell you," Lauren replied. "But no more vodka for you before happy hour. You're hearing things."

As she slammed the closet door shut, something slipped out of Helen's hand and clattered across Lauren's hard wood floor. It was small and gold. An earring?

"What was that?" Lauren said.

"What, now it's your turn?" Helen snapped, still shaking.

"You dropped something."

Helen pressed the heels of her hands against her temples. "Must have been my brain, because I've clearly lost my mind."

Lauren threw a reproachful look to nowhere in particular, not knowing exactly where Aiden was. She turned to Helen, who was doing her best to straighten her now rumpled clothes.

"Wait a minute," Helen said. "Where's the sword?"

"In my safe. I locked it up before I left. That's what Nigel was looking for."

"Too bad he was too late," Helen gloated. "I don't know if you heard, but I sold the idea of using the sword to the art director. He wants to see it in person first thing tomorrow so he can run some lighting tests. And he wants to get the prop guys started on making copies."

"So *you* showed them the video," Lauren said.

Helen grinned. "I edited out all the good parts."

"When did you have time to do all that?"

"While you were still recuperating in the hospital. I figured getting everyone excited about using the sword in the film would not only rub your possession in Ross's face, but it would keep him from trying to take it back."

Like her, Helen could be self-absorbed and single-minded when it came to her own success, but when it came to moving heaven and earth to be Lauren's friend, Helen was the bomb. Lauren's stomach lurched with guilt. "If you're trying to make me feel like a bitch for the way I reacted last night, you've succeeded."

"Good. You *were* a bitch," Helen verified. "But it's understandable. You were blindsided by David, and that was my fault. I should have checked more thoroughly into his background."

Lauren shook her head. "No, there's nothing you could have seen. Look, he's a good guy, deep down. He made some mistakes. Haven't we all? But he did save my life. Twice. I just wasn't prepared to see him. I reacted badly. I owe him a huge apology."

Helen didn't look convinced. "No, you don't. He could have come clean to both of us about who he really was and what he really wanted."

Her voice crackled with resentment, so Lauren decided to let the matter drop. More than likely she'd never see David Drake—or whatever his name used to be—ever again.

Helen returned to the bed, this time drawing her legs underneath her, as if she were afraid for her feet to dangle too close to the edge. She was creeped out. Lauren couldn't blame her. Disembodied voices tended to do that to people.

"You really didn't hear Aiden's voice?" Helen asked again.

Not wanting to lie outright, Lauren gave an innocent shrug.

"I'm losing my mind," she muttered.

"You're just drinking too early. Where'd you go?"

Helen took a moment to accept Lauren's explanation, lame as it was, then replied, "I had a meeting at the Crown Chandler with a friend of the owner."

"Alexa Chandler?"

Could this be a coincidence? Helen and Lauren both regularly frequented the posh hotel and its spa, but though Lauren had probably been introduced to the heiress Alexa Chandler at some party or premiere, they did not travel in the same circles, and Lauren couldn't remember anything about her. How convenient was it that Helen would take a meeting with someone associated with the company that owned the Web site listing Aiden's family tree?

"Yeah," Helen replied, still unnerved and glancing around the room suspiciously, as if she expected Aiden to jump out and scare them at any moment—which, Lauren supposed, he could. "I met this professor, Ben Rousseau. He claims to be Aiden's nephew."

"He knows about Aiden?"

"Why, is he a secret?"

Lauren forced a laugh. "I mean, he *knows* Aiden?"

A moment later Lauren felt an invisible hand slide over her shoulder. Her body responded instantly—every muscle warmed to a steady heat, her heartbeat accelerated and her chest constricted with a wash of emotions ranging from lust to regret to worry to love. Yes, love. Or at least a deep, intense caring that made her question everything about her life and ambitions. She hadn't realized until that moment how desperately she'd missed his touch—missed him. She leaned her cheek down toward her shoulder and inhaled deeply, invigorated by the subtle scent of him lingering in the air: musk and soap and leather and man.

Her man.

"Lauren?"

Aiden's insubstantial fingers wound into the hair along her nape. When a swish of lips brushed against the exposed flesh on her neck, her insides melted. How could she deny him anything? Ever?

"Lauren?"

She shook off the erotic sensations spiking through her body and cleared her throat.

"Are you all right?" Helen asked.

"Yes," she said, charging to the bathroom to splash water on her face. "Tell me more about this supposed nephew of Aiden's. I don't think he knows he has any family left."

After staring at her skeptically for a second, Helen proceeded to fill her in on her midday meeting with the college professor and expert in Gypsy lore, and his girlfriend, a paranormal researcher.

"Paranormal, huh?" Lauren asked.

That could not be a coincidence.

"Yeah," Helen said, though she seemed not to have paid much attention to the girlfriend. "So, the professor gives me this button, but . . ." She glanced down at her hands. "Oh, shit. Maybe that's what I dropped."

They were both on the floor searching when Helen's cell phone trilled, and she cursed.

"Who is it?"

Helen glanced at the caller ID. "The big, bad wolf."

"Ross?"

"Think he heard about Nigel?"

Lauren rolled her eyes and groaned. "Oh, yeah."

"Then why's he calling me?"

"No clue. Answer it outside, will you? I've had my fill of him today."

She waited until Helen had disappeared down the hall; then, from her place on the floor, she kicked the door closed. When the latch clicked, she called for Aiden in an urgent whisper.

"Answer me. I know you're here."

"Are we speaking to each other yet?"

Lauren sighed with relief. "Of course. Look, about last night—"

"Please, my lady, can we discuss our disagreement at a later time? I am more interested in hearing about my nephew."

"You think that's real?"

"I have no idea. Perhaps if I could see the button?"

Lauren dropped flat to the ground and looked under the bed, where she spied her private box open and disheveled. She dragged it out from her obviously inadequate hiding place.

"Did you do this?" she asked.

The pillow on the bed popped to the ground, revealing a thick purple plastic erection pointed out from between her pillow shams. "No more than I am responsible for this. I do not suppose you care to explain the modern usage of such a—"

"No," she snapped, yanking the battery-powered dildo off the bed and shoving it back in the box. "I suppose Nigel tried to ransack my room in search of the sword."

Aiden's chuckle seemed to vibrate straight into her skin.

"I attempted to distract him," he claimed.

"Yeah, well," she said, making a mental note to discuss dust bunnies with her housekeeper as she slapped powdery dirt off her hands. "I distinctly remember leaving Apollo out on the patio for the day."

"Clever dog, finding his way inside all on his own," Aiden claimed, his innocent tone exaggerated.

She laughed, relieved that her unwillingness to drop

her life to shuttle Aiden off to England hadn't resulted in a loss of his sense of humor. "It's not under here."

"Perhaps I can assist."

She waited, and as if a wave of heat had flashed through the room, she felt a sudden explosion of warmth, followed by the impression that Aiden had just touched her everywhere and nowhere all at the same moment. A tiny gold disk skittered out from behind her dresser. She lifted it into her palm, then held it out to the air.

"Well?"

He was silent for a long moment before he said, " 'Tis mine."

A chill spread through the room, rippling through her with the same force as the warmth had a moment before. "What does that mean?"

"I am not sure."

The door opened and Helen peeked her head in. "I thought I heard Aiden's voice again."

"I'm starting to think you've got a thing for him," Lauren replied.

"I'm starting to think there's something about this guy that you're not telling me."

"What did Ross have to say?"

"That you're needed on the set—with the sword."

"Now that his minion failed, I suppose he's going to try to get it back on his own."

"Ross was never one to get his hands dirty. He didn't even ask about Nigel. Maybe he doesn't know."

"Did you tell him?"

Helen frowned. "That's *so* not in my job description."

"So now I can tell him when we get back to the set?"

"Sounds like a plan."

Lauren felt a little push on the back of her shoulder, and her hand, still holding the button, jumped. "Oh, about Aiden's supposed nephew. Where is he?"

"Staying at the Crown Chandler, waiting for my call."

"Call him. And send a car. Have him and his girl-friend meet us on the set."

"But where is Aiden?"

When the urging sensations she'd felt a moment before shifted into intimate caresses, Lauren knew that no matter how they'd argued the night before, Aiden wasn't about to abandon her any more than she would abandon him.

"I have a feeling he'll meet us there."

29

Through the glass doors in the lobby, Cat watched Ben pace the length of the hotel's driveway, attempting again to reach his father. They'd called the hotel late last night, with no answer, but had figured Paschal had simply gone to bed. This morning Ben had started to worry. Now that they'd received a call from Helen Talbot, inviting them to the set of Lauren Cole's latest film with the promise of a chance to meet Aiden as soon as he arrived, they'd been desperate to reach Paschal and share the amazing news.

He'd returned no phone calls and no one had seen him in days. Every call from Paschal to Ben in Los Angeles had been from his cell.

Ben had left strict instructions for his father to stay put, but that might have been his first mistake. Paschal didn't like to be bossed around any more than his son did, which was the only reason Cat had been biting her tongue.

Not that she was any expert in interfamily relationships, but Ben's inability to treat his father as anything but a fragile old man had already taken a toll on the iffy trust the two shared. She didn't have to use her psychic powers to get the feeling that the more this quest played out, the more tentative the connection between father and son would become. Paschal didn't have a lot of time left, and she knew from her own experiences that Ben was going to kick himself for years if Paschal died while they were at odds, particularly over something insignificant.

"Ms. Reyes?"

Catalina turned. Amber Rose, the hotel's concierge, stepped up to her, bearing an overnight-mail envelope. Her curly blond hair was tamed in an upswept do that brought out the startling green of her eyes. It was no wonder the woman had a reputation for providing guests with anything they needed—Cat couldn't imagine anyone being able to tell the woman no.

"So, how's your stay so far?" the concierge asked.

"Very productive."

"Have you managed a trip to our spa yet? Ms. Chandler insisted I comp a full spa day for both you and Dr. Rousseau."

The idea of lounging in a mud bath or having a couples massage intrigued Cat, but so far they hadn't had the time. "Maybe tomorrow. We're keeping fairly busy."

"So your meeting with Ms. Talbot went well?"

Cat nodded. It had been the one bright spot of the entire morning. "She just called. She's sending over a studio limousine for us so we can meet with Lauren Cole."

"That's fabulous. She's really down-to-earth. You'll like her." As she spoke, she held out the overnight-delivery envelope. "This just came for you at the front desk. You seemed to be on your way out, and I suspected you might want it before you took off for the afternoon."

Cat thanked the concierge and made a mental note to tell Alexa that the woman deserved a raise. She'd been instrumental in arranging their upcoming meeting with Lauren Cole—a meeting that could change everything. Cat hurried across the lobby and sat, watching Ben out of the corner of her eye as she

ripped open the envelope and took out a collection of
crisp eight-by-ten glossies.

The moment she handled the photograph of an or-
nate pewter chalice, Cat knew where Paschal had
gone. She scooped up her purse and dashed outside
just in time to hear Ben say, "What do you mean, you
left with her? Have you lost your mind?"

Cat's stomach suddenly dropped to her knees. "Is
that your father?"

Ben spared her a quick glance, and the fear on his
face told her everything she needed to know.

The photograph of the chalice had last been handled by Paschal, and the psychic impressions she'd gotten had been immediate and powerful. He wanted that
chalice. He craved it with a hunger that meant only
one thing—he was willing to do anything to get it.
Anything.

Including make a deal with the devil.

"You can't trust her," Ben insisted. "You told me
so yourself."

Cat wished she could hear the other half of the
conversation, but she didn't really need to. She knew
what Paschal had done—run off with Gemma Von
Roan.

"I know that you're not a child, but you're not exactly a young man anymore, either. She could kill
you."

Whatever Paschal said in response turned Ben's naturally tanned skin a distinctive shade of green. "Don't
be crass. That's not what I meant, and you know it.
But now that you mention it . . ."

Cat winced. She grabbed Ben's arm. "Tell him
we're going to see Lauren Cole. Tell him we think
she has the sword and that Aiden has been released."

Ben did as she asked, and for a split second the
look on Ben's face reflected hope that they'd changed
Paschal's mind about staying with Gemma—because

that was just too dangerous. Cat was certain that the
woman had lured Ben's father with the photographs
he'd in turn sent to her—and Cat had no doubt that
the chalice in particular had been bait that Paschal
could not refuse. But now they were closer to the
sword—to Aiden—than they'd ever been before.
Surely knowing that they were less than an hour away
from potentially meeting his brother would change
his mind.

"Dad, please."

Ben dropped his hand, the phone hanging by a
few fingers.

Cat grabbed the device, but when she held it to her
ear and called Paschal's name, her worst fear came
to pass.

The line was dead. Paschal was gone.

"We have to find him," Ben said.

She shook her head. "It won't be so easy this time."

"Why not? You can connect with him psychically,
like you did before."

Cat hit the end button on the phone and handed it
back to Ben. "Last time he wanted to be found. He
doesn't this time, does he?"

Ben shoved the phone in his pocket. "Old fool. She
must be offering him something amazing to keep him
from joining us here to go after the sword."

Cat handed him the picture. "She's offering him
this."

"It's a cup."

"It's a chalice. And look at the etching on the side.
It's a hawk holding a gemstone."

"A fire opal?"

"This is Rogan's sign," Cat verified. "We've found
references and depictions all over the castle. Rogan
emblazoned his crest wherever he could. I've no doubt
this chalice, if authentic, belonged to him."

Ben cursed and stalked away, fighting the urge to
crumple the photograph and toss it in the trash. His

father was a damned old fool. Then again, what did that make him? Ben was savvy enough to know that this whole quest to reunite brothers cursed into obscure magical objects couldn't end happily. With the added dimension of the K'vr and Gemma Von Roan, someone was going to die—and the most likely candidate was his father.

Cat gave him some space, not moving from where he'd left her, even after a black stretch limousine pulled up the hotel's circular drive. They had no time to make a choice. They were too close to Aiden to turn back now, and if Paschal didn't want to be found, as Cat suggested, then returning to Florida now would be of no use.

When the driver stepped out of the car holding a sign that said, ROUSSEAU, Ben knew time had run out.

"Ben," Cat called. "Our ride is here."

He gave the car a cursory glance, then stomped back toward her.

"My father said that Farrow Pryce has the sword."

"Then why would Helen Talbot arrange this meeting?"

Ben scowled. "She knows we want Aiden, not the sword. Maybe the two aren't connected any longer."

"That doesn't make the sword any less powerful as a magical item. There's no telling what Pryce has planned once he has some of Lord Rogan's magic at his disposal. Either way, we have to stop him. We have to get the sword back."

Ben nodded, agreeing not out of altruism, but out of genuine dislike for this Lord Rogan and anyone associated with him. He'd been a hell of a lot of trouble to Ben's family for centuries.

Cat snuggled closer to him, and the warmth of her skin dispelled some of the cold hatred brewing inside him. "I still don't understand why your father would leave before he met his brother again."

The situation made no sense to him either, but he

never could comprehend the workings of his father's mind. "Gemma's convinced him that the sword is a lost cause and that she has the upper hand in finding something else associated with Valoren. Something Pryce doesn't know about. The items in the pictures, I suppose."

Cat fanned through them again. "I'm only feeling something off this photograph of the cup. Paschal isn't interested in the rest."

"I should have let you talk to him," Ben replied. "You would have been able to tell if he was speaking under duress."

Cat laid her hand on his arm, and her touch, while not unwelcome, injected him with a calmness he didn't want to feel at the moment. He fought the instinct to tug away. "He wants the chalice, Ben. He left a powerful imprint."

"Just because he wants it doesn't mean he went with her willingly."

"Did he use the code word?"

With a growl, Ben stalked a few feet away, spun on his heel, then returned. He and Paschal had fought her suggestion that they implement a code word before they parted to secretly alert the other if they were in trouble, but Cat had insisted. Ben couldn't fight a wave of disappointment when he realized his father had not signaled for help. Paschal had walked away willingly with a woman who was intimately involved with Pryce, who'd previously kidnapped and nearly killed him. Was his father so desperate that he'd make such a foolish mistake?

"No," he replied. "He didn't say it."

Cat laced her hand into his, urging him toward the studio car. "Then you just have to trust that he knows what he's doing."

"How am I supposed to do that?"

Cat kissed him on the cheek. Her simple and sweet response took the edge off the emotional maelstrom simmering beneath his skin. After a moment his breathing steadied and the red haze clouding his vision retreated. He'd never met anyone like her. She could be calm when necessary. Wise at the ideal moment. Sexy nearly all the time, and still reckless and exciting enough for him to never know what to expect. Why was he messing around searching for old Gypsy relics and long-lost cursed brothers when he could be starting some semblance of a life with the woman of his dreams?

"Paschal has already survived about two hundred years beyond a normal life expectancy," Cat said, her obsidian eyes sparkling. "Like you, your father has more than one trick up his sleeve. Maybe we should be more worried about that Von Roan woman."

"But she's dangerous," Ben reminded her.

"She's got a glass chin," Cat claimed with a mischievous grin. "He can probably take her."

"This isn't the time to joke," he replied, though the memory of Cat kicking the woman in the face after freeing his father last spring did lighten his mood.

"I don't know," she mused. "Seems to me that when a situation sucks, that's the best time to joke."

Though worried to his bones, Ben cupped Cat's elbow, leading her toward the limousine. The possibility of contacting his uncle was too real for him to back away now.

The driver came around and opened the passenger door. After gathering the pictures Paschal had sent and stuffing them into the cardboard envelope, Cat slid inside the limousine. Ben gave the dour-faced driver a nod, then climbed in after her.

Something about the driver's expression raised his hackles, but he was sure his father's decision to run off with Gemma was making him jumpy. "Let me see those pictures again," he said to Cat once the car pulled slowly away from the hotel.

He flipped through the dozen photographs, trying

to plug into the stores of knowledge he'd amassed while working first as an antiquities trader and then as his father's assistant. Of the twelve objects, eleven were undoubtedly Gypsy-made. He recognized the techniques, the lines and the mode of decoration as either from the mid–eighteenth century or, at the very least, based on it. He'd have to handle the objects in order to know which were authentic and which were reproductions.

"Recognize any of them?" Cat asked.

He chewed on his lower lip. "These are definitely from the right time period, and the style is clearly Gypsy, nearly identical to many of the artifacts my father collected. But I've never seen any of them before."

Cat frowned as she fished out the picture of the chalice again. "Only this one gives off your father's vibe. He was excited when he held it. I can't say he recognized it, but with Rogan's symbol on the cup, he clearly knew he'd found something significant. I don't understand, though. This chalice seems religious in nature, but the Gypsies follow their own faith, don't they?"

"Yes, but cups such as these could have been used merely for drinking. According to Damon, Rogan was ostentatious. I think I saw a very similar cup depicted in one of the mosaics back at the castle—you know, the ones Rogan designed to reflect the day-to-day life in the castle and village."

"You've got a fabulous memory," she complimented him.

"My brain is filled with useless knowledge."

"Not so useless right now," she reassured him. "Paschal wouldn't have taken off with Gemma if she didn't have this cup in her possession, don't you think?"

"She could be lying."

"I think he'd know," Cat said. "But just because

this cup belonged to Rogan doesn't mean that one of his brothers is trapped inside."

"I suppose we could say the same about the sword," he surmised.

Cat shoved the photographs into the envelope, then settled back as if prepared to enjoy the comfort of the limousine, which Ben had only just noticed had crisp leather seats, dark windows and a minibar area, though it hadn't been stocked with so much as an ice cube.

"No, Aiden's in that sword," Cat reassured him. "Or he was. Now we just have to hope he believes you when you tell him who you are."

Ben glanced out the window, which, though tinted, allowed him a fairly clear view of the outside. He wasn't a native of Los Angeles or even a frequent visitor, but he had taken the time to map the route to the movie studio earlier, out of curiosity about how long their trip would take. And from what he could tell, they were going in the wrong direction.

He pulled out his cell phone and tapped into the GPS system, confirming his suspicions. They were going the wrong way. After a quick glance toward the dividing glass, he showed the results to Cat.

"What's going on?" she asked, her voice hushed.

Ben shrugged, unwilling to act on his instincts just yet. He could think of no reason why Helen Talbot would send them on a wild-goose chase. Before he jumped to conclusions, he'd look for the logical explanation, no matter how the hairs on the back of his neck were standing on end.

He tapped on the window until the driver slid it a quarter of the way down.

"Excuse me, but I thought you were taking us to the studio where the Athena film is shooting."

The driver did not take his eyes off the road. "There's a location shoot this afternoon."

Cat grabbed his shoulder from behind and shook

her head. He had no idea whether she was relying on her psychic abilities or some piece of information she hadn't shared with him, but either way, his urge to bolt was too strong to ignore. The driver was lying.

"Okay, fine, then," Ben replied, his grin forced.

The driver replaced the partition.

"I have a bad feeling about this," Cat said quietly.

The car had just eased onto the freeway and was picking up speed.

"Looks like we've gotten ourselves into a bit of a pickle," Ben said, trying to keep his tone jaunty even while his heart was thudding against his chest. He didn't mind dangerous situations. He'd been in more than his share of scrapes in his lifetime. But he didn't like dragging Cat into the danger zone.

As if sensing his fear on her behalf, she curled her hand around his arm and beamed at him. The trust in her eyes steadied his heartbeat just enough for his brain to free up and work on a solution.

"And we'll just have to figure out a way to get ourselves out," he declared.

Suddenly the car swerved into the emergency lane and braked. Cat flew forward, tumbling, and Ben had just grabbed her hand and was pulling her toward the door when the handle popped out of his grip and a second man—not the driver—slid into the backseat, a 9mm handgun aimed at Cat's head.

"I say we all sit tight," the man said. "You want to arrive alive, don't you?"

"Arrive where?" Cat asked boldly.

But the man didn't answer, and, seriously, Ben wasn't sure he wanted to know.

30

"What do you mean, they weren't there?" Helen barked into her cell phone.

Lauren dropped the glass she'd been holding, but it stopped an inch short of the ground, then settled softly onto the carpeted floor, upright.

She whispered, "Thanks."

They had a good two hours until sundown, but Aiden had been patient, remaining quiet and still while the sword had been handled, photographed, measured, weighed and fawned over by several of the workmen and artisans associated with the film. The art director, as Helen had predicted, had nearly wet himself with glee over the beauty of the weapon, though as Lauren handled the sword for the awestruck stunt coordinator, she could sense that Aiden took no pride in the compliments. She supposed that to him the sword was nothing more than a prison.

"I am weary," Aiden murmured into her ear.

She understood. Remaining active while in this insubstantial state wiped Aiden out.

"Rest now," she encouraged him. "We've got everything under control. I'll see you soon."

And after the thrill of what felt like the soft pressing of lips against hers, Lauren sensed Aiden withdrawing, pulling completely into the sword until sunset.

After dumping into the sink the water she'd nearly

spilled, Lauren stared at Helen and hoped her plan to connect Aiden with his supposed nephew was still on track. She'd done everything in her power to clear everyone from the costumer to the hairstylists, assistant directors and screenwriters out of her trailer in anticipation of the meeting with Ben Rousseau.

On the ride from the house to the studio, Helen had filled her in entirely on what Ben had told her during the meeting at the Crown Chandler, though Lauren suspected Ben knew more than he'd revealed over martinis. Cinda had done her magic on the computer and learned that a Paschal Rousseau, Ben's father, was a professor of Romani studies at a university in Texas. They'd found no photograph of him, so it was impossible for Aiden to determine any family resemblance, but they guessed the Gypsy connection could not be a coincidence.

And after questioning, Helen volunteered Ben's girlfriend's name—Catalina Reyes. The same woman, Lauren guessed, as the one associated with the Crown Chandler subsidiary responsible for the Forsyth family tree Web site. Cinda's research also revealed that the Reyes woman was a respected paranormal researcher, with a lineage tied deep into the world of the unexplainable. Between Rousseau's knowledge of the Gypsies and Reyes's apparent expertise in the supernatural, they had to possess some clue about how to free Aiden once and for all.

But since neither Lauren nor Helen was big on trusting strangers, whoever they might be, they'd arranged to meet the pair in a fairly public place. Here on the soundstage, surrounded by cast and crew, they'd have a modicum of protection in case, like Nigel and whoever had attacked Lauren in the hospital, Rousseau and Reyes were simply trying to get their hands on a valuable and much-sought-after sword.

Helen had disconnected her call and was dialing again. In between buttons she informed Lauren that when the studio limo showed up to fetch their guests, they were not there.

"Why would they leave?"

Helen shrugged, then said, "Amber? Hi, this is Helen Talbot."

When this second call was over, Helen frowned deeply. "She says they left in another limousine about ten minutes before the studio car showed up."

"What? Why would they do that?"

Helen waved her hand, as if this odd turn of events meant nothing dire. Lauren had not told Helen the truth about Aiden, but her friend understood that the sword was a commodity that someone was pretty desperate to get their hands on.

"The concierge at the Crown Chandler gave me Rousseau's cell phone number," Helen explained. "I'll call him and find out what happened. It's probably just a misunderstanding."

But the call wasn't answered. Helen left a message, then jumped when someone knocked hard on the door but didn't wait for an answer before barging in to Lauren's trailer.

"What do you want?" Lauren asked before Ross had even shut the door behind him.

"I want to know what Nigel was looking for at your house."

Lauren laughed humorlessly. "He's your lapdog. Why did you send him to my house?"

"I didn't," Ross insisted, and from the anxious look on his face, she knew he wasn't lying.

Helen, however, seemed to miss the nuance of his expression. "Who are you trying to con, Marchand? You sent him to steal the sword. Just like that guy who attacked Lauren in the hospital."

Ross's mouth was a thin, unyielding line. Helen sidled up beside Lauren, which seemed to spark a fire in Ross's muddy hazel eyes. "I need to talk to my wife alone."

In unison, Lauren and Helen both said, "Ex."

Ross cursed. "Fine. Ex. Ex-wife. Satisfied? Clear out, Talbot. What I have to say is for her ears alone."

Helen narrowed her gaze, then glanced at Lauren, who gave her a confident nod.

"Don't worry. I can take care of myself."

Helen headed to the door. "I won't go far. I'm going to keep trying to get in touch with our friends. I'll let you know what happened as soon as I know."

Once they were alone, Ross jammed his hands into his hair and marched to the couch, where he sat beside the weapon. Just to be on the safe side, Lauren moved the sword to the bar area. She did not feel Aiden's presence, and in a small way she was thankful. After what had happened with Nigel this morning, she wanted to hear what Ross had to say. She didn't need Aiden running him off on her behalf.

Ross groaned. "I'm not here to steal that cursed hunk of steel."

"Cursed?"

Did he know something?

He sneered at the weapon. "More trouble than it's worth. I shouldn't have given in to you at that antiques store. Maybe if I hadn't, we wouldn't be in this mess."

"What mess?"

With a huff, he sank back into the cushions of the couch. "Nigel, for starters."

Not that she tried, but Lauren couldn't muster a shred of sympathy for Ross's butler. He'd treated her like something he'd accidentally smeared on the bottom of his shoe since the first minute she'd moved into the Marchand household. The fact that the dog she'd bought for protection had attacked him didn't make her feel guilty in the least.

"I assume he'll live, even without the part of his ass that Apollo had for breakfast?"

Ross grinned at her quip, despite the fact that he shouldn't. "Sit down, Lauren."

She crossed her arms over her chest and remained standing.

After a second he looked up. Again, she saw remorse in his eyes. And again, she couldn't ignore it.

"Please," he said more sincerely, "sit down."

With a frown, she realized she had nothing to lose by getting off her feet. She squeezed by him and sat on the opposite side of the couch.

He sat up straight, as if gearing himself up for a complicated explanation. "First, you have to know that I had nothing to do with Nigel breaking into your house this morning."

"Nigel doesn't do anything without your ordering him to."

"That used to be true," he muttered.

"It isn't anymore? Why?"

He bit his bottom lip before responding. "My circumstances have changed. I'm in trouble, Lauren. Financial trouble."

She scoffed. "I saw your financials during the divorce, Ross. You're doing fine."

"One doesn't usually admit to their accountant the kind of debts I'm talking about."

"What kind of debts?"

Lauren had known Ross to mix with business associates who could have stepped straight out of a Francis Ford Coppola flick, but he'd been fairly careful, separating his personal taste for rubbing shoulders with wise guys from his formidable status as a producer. Ross's reputation wouldn't inspire real respect if he laundered cash for criminals.

"You remember that series of movies I did in Mexico?"

"How can I forget? You were gone for nearly a year while I was shooting the second Athena movie."

"It was a risky enterprise," he said, repeating words she'd heard him say a hundred times back when they were practically newlyweds. "Shooting three movies concurrently in a rough part of a corrupt country. I had to pay some serious *dinero* to some big-time players to get those movies made without my actors being kidnapped or my sets torched. All of it had to be under the table, too. I thought with the star power I'd brought in, all three films would have been smash hits, but, well . . ."

His voice trailed away. Lauren didn't need to remind him that the first two movies in the series had been so critically panned and publicly ignored that the third one had gone direct to video. The idea behind the series had been sound, the script fascinating and the actors top-notch, but the director had lost his marbles in the editing, and the flops might have ruined Ross entirely if not for the soaring success of the Athena franchise. Lauren remembered watching, horrified, during the screenings, wondering how such a successful producer as her husband would put out not one dud, but three—with his name on them. Now she was starting to understand.

He didn't have a choice. The best he could do was make sure the director took all the blame for the horrendous failure of the series. As far as Lauren knew, the guy had never made another movie. Not in Hollywood, anyway.

It was Ross Marchand legend.

"Every producer loses money, Ross."

He took a deep breath, pushing it out as his fists clenched into tight white balls of flesh and bone that he pounded on his knees. "It was more than that. Look, Lauren, I don't want to tell you too much—not because I don't trust you or because I'm embarrassed, but because I don't want to drag you any deeper into my mess. And trust me, it's a big fucking mess. I still owe a lot of money to some very mean hombres, if you get my drift. The Mexicans wanted a cut of the series' gross, and they didn't care that the movies tanked. They left me alone for a long time, but I guess business isn't so good for them anymore, and they're looking to make me pay up. That's why I put so much pressure on you to make this last movie. I need my cut to pay off criminals I never should have gotten involved with."

Lauren's head was spinning. How could the man she'd always admired for being savvy in the business world have gotten himself into such deep shit?

"So you held the sword over my head to make sure I made the last film? Hate to break this news to you, Ross, but you've been holding that sword at arm's length from me since the moment I first saw it in that shop. In all the years I lived with you, in all the years we were married, I never asked you for anything that you gave me. Never. It was the one time I found something I really, truly wanted. I suppose I was stupid for wanting you to give it to me when I could have bought it for myself, but . . ."

Tentatively he reached over and placed his hand on hers, patting it twice before taking his touch away. "It was a test. I failed."

The gentle timbre of his voice told her he was sincere. They had a lot of baggage between them, but hashing out the past wasn't going to solve whatever crap he'd gotten himself into now. She'd opened her mouth to tell him to drop the whole subject, when he broke in with, "I knew our marriage was falling apart a long time before I slept with—"

"Don't say her name," Lauren begged. "I've moved beyond all that."

He didn't argue. "Our marriage was falling apart even before that sword. You'd been distancing yourself from me for a long time. I guess it was only natural. You didn't really need me anymore."

"I never should have needed you. I never should

have married you," Lauren said. "And you . . . you never should have asked."

She'd said the words to him before, but as she spoke them now, calmly and with the rancorous emotions between them having run their course during their divorce, Ross seemed to finally hear her.

"I can't change what was," he replied. "But you know I never wanted to hurt you. I never sent Nigel to your house, I swear, and I didn't have anything to do with that guy who broke into your hospital room. But I know who did."

Lauren's entire body tensed as she listened to Ross pour out his guts about his recent association with a man named Farrow Pryce. A secretive and well-connected businessman, Pryce had somehow found out about Ross's money troubles and had threatened to expose his deal with the Mexicans if Ross didn't cooperate in Pryce's quest for the sword.

"If you hadn't stolen the damned thing, I would have sold it to him and we wouldn't be in this mess."

"So now you're blaming me?"

She moved to stand, but he took her hands and, with surprising gentleness, tugged her back down. "No, that's not what I meant. I'm just trying to explain that I think Pryce sent that thug into your hospital room, and though he's not saying, I think he blackmailed Nigel into breaking into your house on my behalf. You know Nigel. He'd do anything for me."

"Including put my life in danger. He probably got a kick out of that. How did he bypass my security code, anyway?"

"You still using the numbers from your first paycheck as an actress as your code?"

She winced. Some habits died hard. "I suppose I should change that, huh?"

Ross nodded. "This Pryce guy is dangerous, maybe more dangerous than the guys I owe money to. Look, the prop guys photographed and measured that sword every which way from Sunday. They're going to come up with a copy in a few days that will be indistinguishable from the original. Just let me sell the sword to Pryce now, and after this movie premieres and I'm back in the black, I'll buy you twelve just like it. A whole collection."

"No," she said.

"Lauren, be reasonable."

"I don't have to be reasonable, Ross. The sword is mine. It's not yours to sell. Sell your damned house if you need to pay off someone, but I'm not parting with my . . ."

The lights flickered, then went black. Lauren waited for the emergency light above her door to turn on, but it did not.

"What the hell?" Ross said.

Using her hands to feel her way, she moved toward the bar and placed her palm on the handle of the sword. She heard Ross stumble to the door and wretch it open. It was just as black outside as it was within.

"Not again," Ross groaned. "Hey!"

Though it was black as night on the soundstage, it was certainly not as quiet. Shouts of frustration and fear from the sudden blackout drowned Ross's pleas for someone with a flashlight to come into the trailer. Then, with a grunt, she heard Ross leave, though she had a sinking suspicion that he hadn't done so by choice.

"Ross? Who's there?"

Lauren grabbed the sword. She held the blade parallel with her body, as eager to keep the weapon with her as she was to avoid accidentally running someone through in the dark.

No one answered. Even with the sounds from the melee outside, she thought she heard footsteps coming nearer. She feinted left, just in time to hear someone whisper, "I'm sorry," before something hard burst against her jaw and she fell to the ground.

31

"Not again," Lauren mumbled as awareness returned. She was on the floor, and her chin hurt like a mother. Someone had coldcocked her in the dark. For a pampered actress who played an action hero only on the silver screen, she was getting the shit kicked out of her a little too often.

She used the nearby bar stool to climb to her feet. The trailer, still dark, flashed with beams of light from the outside.

"Ms. Cole?"

She blinked, but saw who she thought was Marco blustering his way into the trailer. He shouted behind him for someone to help Mr. Marchand.

"What's wrong with Ross?" she asked, trying to stretch the pain out of her jaw.

Marco flashed the light directly in her face, wincing at what he saw. "Ice! I need ice!"

"Marco," Lauren said calmly. "What's wrong with Ross?"

"Knocked out cold. Looks like someone yanked him out of the trailer. Gash in his head. He's coming to, but we called the ambulance."

"Where are the lights?"

Another security guard handled Marco the ice tray from Lauren's freezer. He wrapped a handful of cubes in his handkerchief, gave it a few whacks on the bar to pulverize the ice, then pressed it to the swelling skin on her face. She recoiled from the cold, but then allowed the remedy to do its painful work.

"Someone cut the power to the soundstage. Place is a pitch-black madhouse. You're better off in here. What happened to you?"

"Someone hit me," she explained.

"Mr. Marchand?" Marco asked, shocked.

That would have been her first guess, too. Trouble was, she remembered that Ross had already been at the door when she'd heard someone else enter and say something to her before they'd knocked her out cold.

Something like . . . *I'm sorry.*

A voice in the dark. A voice that wasn't Aiden's. *Aiden!*

"Marco, let me have that light."

She took the handle from him and stood, focusing the beam on the top of the bar. As she feared, the sword was gone. She turned the light and searched as best she could, but she already knew what had happened. Someone had used the blackout in order to steal the sword—and that someone wasn't Ross. He was still lying on the floor, with several people attending to his injury. She could hear him cursing a blue streak.

"Marco, I need to find Helen Talbot," Lauren insisted.

"Can't find anyone until the emergency generators come on. Should be just a few more—"

As if on cue, the lights popped on. Blinded for a moment, Lauren shoved the flashlight back at Marco and looked around for her purse. *Damn.* She didn't even have her car. The studio had sent for her this morning, and Helen had driven her back after the break-in. When she heard Ross's voice rise to a booming crescendo, she made her decision.

The soundstage was in chaos. In the blackout several people had been hurt, equipment dropped and lighting destroyed. She bent down at the door to check on Ross, slipped her rusty but nimble thief's fingers into his pocket and extracted his keys.

"Where's Farrow Pryce, Ross?"

"Huh? What?"

Blood was trickling down from the gash above his eye, but she knew better than anyone that head wounds often looked worse than they actually were. "Tell me where to find this Pryce guy. The sword is missing, Ross, and I want it back."

His gaze met hers, and she was actually happy to see that his pupils were small and focused. "He moved in. Took over the place. I didn't have a choice."

She turned to Marco, who was staying close at her heels. Pressing her hand to his shoulder, she ordered, "Stay with Mr. Marchand. Make sure he gets to the hospital and receives the best care possible, got me?"

"But, Ms. Cole, if someone hit you, you need—"

"I need to know that Ross is going to be looked after, okay?"

But mostly she didn't need anyone else to slow her down.

With chaos reigning around her, she was able to slip out of the soundstage. She found Ross's car parked in his VIP spot and, with shaking hands, pushed the key into the ignition and revved the engine to life. When she flew backward out of the parking space, she heard a slam on the trunk. She spun around to see Helen holding up her hands.

Lauren pushed the gearshift into neutral. Helen ran around to the passenger side and jumped in. "Where do you think you're going?"

Shifting the car into drive before Helen had closed the door entirely, Lauren honked the horn at a group of people dashing across the narrow service road, then sped off toward the exit. "I'm going to get my sword back. Someone stole it."

She stopped at the security post and waited for the

gate to open. On a whim, she rolled down the window and beckoned the guard over, who smiled at her instantly in recognition.

"Can you tell me if a Farrow Pryce came into the studio this morning, headed for the Athena shoot?"

He checked his list. "No, ma'am. No Farrow Pryce."

"Did Mr. Marchand have any other guests he'd cleared for access?"

He rattled off a few names, all of which Lauren recognized as investors.

"What are you doing?" Helen asked.

She turned to her friend and said quietly, "Someone slugged me in the dark and stole the sword. I'm trying to figure out who it was. Whoever it was apologized to me before knocking me out cold."

"Apologized?" Helen glanced forward, squeezed her eyes shut, then leaned around Lauren to speak to the guard. "What about David Drake? Is he on the list?"

"You told me to take him off, Ms. Talbot," the guard said defensively. "He didn't come through while I've been here."

"Have you been here the whole time?" Lauren asked, knowing the guard took breaks.

"Well, no . . ."

"Can you check Mr. Marchand's list?" Helen continued.

He did so and verified that David had come to the studio two hours ago.

Lauren thanked the guard and tore off in the direction of the highway.

"Why would David be on the set?" Lauren asked. "Why would Ross have added him to the list?" she asked.

"Why does your ex-husband do anything?"

"To keep his ass alive and on top of the Hollywood food chain, that's why," she replied, then filled her friend in on what Ross had confessed about the Mexican movies, his overwhelming debt, Farrow Pryce and the man's outrageous bid for the sword.

"But Ross didn't steal the sword," Helen said. "He's still back there on the set. And you believe him when he says he didn't send Nigel to do his dirty work?"

"Yeah, I do. I think Farrow Pryce appealed to Nigel's sense of self-preservation and his desire to protect Ross at all costs and persuaded him to retrieve the sword himself. If he got caught, it would look reasonable, wouldn't it? The loyal butler retrieving a stolen item from the ex-wife who'd taken it?"

"But how is David tied in to all of this?"

Lauren used the pause at a red light to look around and ensure that she was headed in the right direction. "I have no idea, but if Farrow Pryce was using Ross's house as his drop-off point, we're about to find out."

Lauren hit the gas the second the light turned green. The car lurched forward, but a second shift had them riding smoothly onto the freeway. Traffic was piling up, but Lauren knew a shortcut to the house once they reached the right exit. With any luck, they'd arrive before David turned the sword over to Farrow Pryce.

"Damn it, Lauren, it's just a sword," Helen said, squeaking when Lauren swerved around a slow-moving truck. "Is it worth your life? Or, more important, is it worth mine?"

"It's not just a sword. My life . . . his life—they're tied together in a way I can't explain. I have to get him back."

"His? Him? Sweetie, what are you talking about?"

Lauren spared Helen a glance before darting into the emergency lane, advancing to the next gear and stomping her foot on the accelerator. "Put on your seat belt, Helen. I've got a story to tell you about my sword. One you aren't going to believe."

*   *   *

Farrow grinned, satisfied, as the pair who, up to an hour ago, had been his rivals in his quest for the Dresden sword were marched across the pool deck. The plan could have failed in so many ways, but for once it looked like he was finally going to get exactly what he wanted: not only the sword, but the knowledge of how to use it.

"Dr. Rousseau. Ms. Reyes. Please have a seat. The butler of this palatial home is no longer available to pour drinks, but feel free to help yourselves while we wait for the sword to arrive."

Farrow had placed K'vr followers at the Crown Chandler hotel, expecting someone associated with Alexa Chandler to come in search of the sword. After they'd flown in to extricate Paschal Rousseau from Farrow's compound last spring, he'd done his research. He now knew all about Ben Rousseau and Catalina Reyes. But now the time had come for formal introductions.

On his terms.

Close up, he realized that Ben Rousseau was much older than he'd assumed—probably close to forty— whereas Catalina Reyes stole his breath with her youthful obsidian eyes, straight black hair and lusciously curved figure. Stumbling onto Alexa Chandler's closest friend and the son of the man he'd kidnapped last spring had been a sign to Farrow that he was on the right track. Arranging the limousine to divert them here had been child's play.

"So," he said to Ben, though he had trouble tearing his eyes off his voluptuous companion. "I hear your father ran off with my former fiancée."

"I'd be reassessing my manhood if my fiancée chose to be with a guy old enough to be her grandfather over me," Ben shot back.

Farrow tapped down the slight rise in his temper by taking another sip of Marchand's delicious scotch. "Unlike you, reassessing my manhood under any circumstance would never occur to me, though I can see why you might be thinking in that direction, since you, a thief of some reputation in the archeological world, were unable to secure your freedom from my associates."

"That's not easy to do when your associates put a gun to my head," Cat pointed out. Her eyes burned with barely contained fury, sparking Farrow's interest even more.

He gestured to the seats across the table from him. "I'd hoped my driver wouldn't have to resort to violence, but it was either that or allow you and Mr. Rousseau to jump out of a moving car, or perhaps call the authorities. Either action would have delayed this very important meeting, which I've so looked forward to. We have but one more guest to arrive and then our afternoon will begin. And end."

His associates pushed Rousseau and Reyes into the seats, but neither captive partook of the scotch, which he considered their loss. Momentarily he wondered how Ross Marchand might react when he returned home to discover that Farrow had not only commandeered his home, but also his butler and his gofer. Ah, well. The man relied much too heavily on others. Too much delegation and not enough oversight. Farrow had learned his lesson with Gemma.

"So," Ben ventured, eyeing him with a confidence clearly born of his breeding rather than the current state of affairs, "why are we here?"

"I've come to understand that the two of you are quite versed in the history of Lord Rogan."

"You're bidding for the leadership of his cult," Catalina said, her words more like spitting than speaking. "Don't you know his history?"

"I know the legends as well as any other, but there's always more to learn," Farrow replied.

Though it was not a democratic organization, a council of elders had emerged over the decades within the K'vr. The twelve bestowed the title of Grand Apprentice to the person they deemed worthiest, nearly always a blood successor of Rogan, which Farrow was not. But with the death of Gemma's father and the incarceration of her brother, the mantle could fall only to Farrow. His father had served the last Grand Apprentice as his right hand. And Gemma, being a woman, had no right to lead, according to the Council.

If, however, Farrow found a relic he could tie directly to Lord Rogan—one that possessed undisputed magic powers—his path to the leadership would be clear. Then money, which he already had in abundance, would be inconsequential. He'd have power. Real, terrible power.

"In a decision I now understand was foolish, I relied too heavily on Gemma Von Roan to fill in the blanks of the legends and lore. She always took the historical context of her ancestor's life so seriously, why would I bother?"

Catalina and Ben exchanged looks. If he'd sounded bored with the minutiae of Rogan's life, it was because he was.

"You look surprised," he ventured.

Ben eyed him with a blend of skepticism and curiosity. "I'd think if your big goal in life is to inherit Lord Rogan's reputed magic, you'd learn whatever you could about the man and his powers."

"That's why you're here," Farrow said, taking another smooth, fiery sip of scotch. "And once I have the sword and know how to use it, I'll no longer need anyone."

"How do you know that?" Catalina challenged.

Farrow glanced up at the bright sun, which had lowered, but was still a good hour away from sunset. He'd hoped to have this entire matter wrapped up and be back on his plane by the time darkness fell. He wanted the leadership of the K'vr established by tomorrow. He'd waited long enough. And with the promised magic at his disposal, he planned to make his rise to power swift and decisive.

"I may not be versed in Lord Rogan's history, but I do know that in each generation, the leader of the K'vr, a man with Rogan's lineage, has possessed powers that could not be explained through traditional logic. Sometimes a psychic ability. Other times telekinesis or telepathy. Just enough of a magical connection to keep our followers believing. The K'vr has wisely remained small—exclusive even—exploiting the powers of the Grand Apprentice to our fullest financial potential or else"—he glanced at his guards—"offering physical strength in return for a comfortable living."

"That explains the lack of brains in your musclemen," Catalina cracked.

Farrow laughed. After years living with Gemma, he'd come to appreciate a woman with no sense of safe speech. Perhaps he could find some use for Catalina Reyes—after he had the sword.

Because in all honesty, Farrow was taking a great gamble in stealing the sword before he knew how to use it. He'd had no choice, however. Though Ross Marchand had been reluctant to give him any information Farrow could use against Lauren Cole to persuade her to part with the sword willingly, he had discovered how she'd manipulated the production team on her film so they would use the sword as a prop. Tying the weapon up in the multimillion-dollar production, where security would likely be intense once shooting began, had been a clever move. As it was, she kept the damned thing within ten feet of her at almost all times.

Marchand's butler had been easily convinced that his adored master would live a longer life if Nigel procured the sword on Farrow's behalf, but when he'd failed, Farrow had turned to Marchand's other lapdog, the actor, who'd been entirely more efficient.

Now, once this Drake fellow arrived, Farrow would

discover how to wrangle the magic that had made a man with reported superhuman strength appear out of nowhere.

"You shouldn't insult my associates, Ms. Reyes," Farrow warned. "They were responsible for bringing you here, just as they'll be responsible for taking you away. Your fate might lie entirely in their hands."

"You're running this show," Catalina contradicted. "Whatever happens to us will be on your head."

Farrow smiled, the thrill of power filling his veins so intensely, he couldn't imagine how magic would increase the sensation.

But it would. Yes, it would.

"All right, Ms. Reyes. So perhaps you should attempt to be just a bit nicer to me."

32

Lauren let loose a string of curses that had even Helen goggling with wide blue eyes.

"He beat us here," she said, gesturing toward the gate to Ross's house, where David Drake was chatting through his car window with the man at the entrance.

But Helen didn't respond. She hadn't said a word since Lauren had told her about Aiden and the sword. *Everything* about Aiden and the sword, including the part about him being a phantom cursed by a Gypsy and freed by her while in the workout room.

Helen shook her head, snapping out of her disbelieving reverie and adding a few choice words of her own. "I thought you knew a shortcut."

"L.A. traffic and shortcuts do not always mix," Lauren griped, sliding into a spot on a slanted curb across from her former home and throwing Ross's car into neutral.

As David eased his car beyond the gate, Lauren tried to figure out what to do. She'd never get past security. No amount of sweet talk or bribery could undo the fact that the last time she'd finagled her way inside, she'd stolen Ross's sword.

She unbuckled her seat belt. "Drive up to the gate."

"What?"

"Get in the driver's seat and drive up. If the guard won't let you in, make a big deal. Cause a stir."

"You mean a diversion."

Lauren smiled. "Yeah, that."

Helen stopped to think, then unbuttoned her blouse and gave a little shimmy. "How's this?"

"Irresistible."

Lauren and Helen got out of the car. Helen slid into the driver's seat and ducked Lauren down outside the passenger side of the car. Helen rolled down the window.

"What do I do if they let me in?"

"Use Ross's opener and drive into the garage. Tell them he asked you to deliver his car. Then lock the doors and use the OnStar to call the cops. Tell them you're inside Ross Marchand's Malibu mansion and there's been a break-in."

"Why don't we just call the cops now?"

"Um, hello? Not our house? The cops might consider it a crank. They know Ross has excellent security. And besides, I want to see what's going on. But once you're inside, use the phone in the garage. They'll have to come in and check things out. In the meantime, I'll try to get the sword back."

"What do I do if that guard still doesn't let me in?"

Lauren considered that possibility. The guard did not look like anyone who'd worked for Ross before. More than likely he was under the employ of Farrow Pryce.

"Give me five minutes tops and then drive away and call the cops from a safe distance. By then, I'll be inside. Tell them I'm in danger. Anything. Then find Ross. He's probably at the hospital, but he needs to know what is going on."

Helen pursed her lips. "Maybe he gave this guy permission to use his house."

Lauren shook her head. "He didn't. Trust your instincts. If you think the guard is going to hurt you, leave. I have to protect the sword for Aiden, at least until the sun goes down. After that, Aiden will be able to take care of himself."

Blowing out a pent-up breath, Helen shook her head despondently. "I can't believe I'm buying this story."

"You heard him," Lauren reminded her. "Twice."

"Three times, actually," Helen corrected.

At Lauren's disbelieving stare, her friend rolled her eyes. "On the day you were hurt in your trailer, I thought I heard a man scream. A straight-to-the-gut kind of scream. Coupled with the video where he appeared out of thin air, which I thought was a trick of bad lighting, and the fact that I know you've never once lied to me, what choice do I have but to believe you?"

Lauren reached into the car and patted Helen's hand. "Thanks. Now, go do your thing. I'll sneak in around the back and see if I cant put some of my Athena training to good use."

They wished each other good luck; then Lauren backed into a nearby oleander bush to remain out of sight while Helen pulled away. She'd considered waiting until night fell before attempting to retrieve the sword, but she had no idea how long this Farrow Pryce joker would stay at Ross's house once he had the weapon.

She simply had to act and try to buy enough time for Aiden to emerge. Once she had the sword, she didn't care if the police showed up and took it into evidence. At least Aiden would be safe from some cult-leader madman who might know more about the magic than anyone—including how to kill Aiden and steal the sword's magic for himself.

Not three minutes later Helen was out of Ross's car and throwing a world-class temper tantrum at the guard. Lauren used the diversion to sneak close to the gate, using the car as cover. The man keeping Helen from passing through was clutching something in his pocket. Lauren's heart skipped a beat, but she had to trust that Helen had the smarts to know when to walk away.

Lauren slipped on the gravel, but before the guard could turn, Helen leaned into the car and honked on the horn. "Ross! Ross Marchand! Call this Neanderthal guard of yours and tell him to let me in! You have no idea who I am, buddy, do you? You're going to be so fired once your boss finds out you wouldn't let me through. Ross! Ross!"

She continued honking, giving Lauren the sound cover she needed to dash behind the guard and disappear into the thick bushes that surrounded the estate. From there she could creep up to the house and then swing around the back, which was almost entirely windows. Then she would be able to figure out exactly what was going on.

Or at least she hoped she could. She had no other choice but to try.

Aiden became instantly aware of hands on the blade of the sword—hands that were not Lauren's. He expanded from the sword, both surprised and blinded by the vivid blue sky glistening above and around him. He was outside. But where?

Seeing in the light wasn't easy. Rogan's magic was more powerful in the dark. But he heard voices, though he recognized none.

The first voice oozed with an unctuous quality he found immediately distasteful. "You have succeeded where others failed. Congratulations."

"You'll leave Lauren alone now?"

That voice he placed. David Drake.

"I see no reason to bother Ms. Cole now that I have what I want," the oily voice responded.

"But, see, you've already bothered me by stealing my sword."

Aiden's entire being stiffened, if that was possible in this diaphanous state. Lauren, far away but drawing nearer, had added her presence to the mix. Unexpectedly, judging by David's curse. Where were they? Damn, but he could hardly see, though the sun was definitely moving downward toward the horizon. The blue of the sky was deepening, and streaks of red seemed to radiate from the sun. He could hear the familiar sound of waves crashing on rocks below them. He concentrated, pulling himself in from the wide-open space he seemed to inhabit now that he was awake and aware.

Chairs scraped as several people stood. Aiden felt the sword drop onto a hard surface. Outside, in the open, he had trouble drawing on the power of the sword. He needed walls. Boundaries.

"Ms. Cole," the voice said. "There was no need for you to involve yourself in this matter. Turn around now and leave. You won't be hurt."

She laughed lightly. Her voice dropped, and the cadence changed just enough for him to know that she was channeling her strength through the woman she played on film. Only this wasn't a movie or a play or a game. This was real. Danger swirled around Aiden like a fog: present, but too insubstantial to fight.

"I have no intention of leaving here without my sword, Mr. Pryce."

"Mr. Marchand told you about me, then."

"No, actually, Mr. Drake did."

A bluff? To what end?

Someone slid a hand over the blade, jolting Aiden with awareness. It wasn't Lauren. Nor was it this Pryce. The touch was decidedly female, and along with the tentative caress came an injection of understanding.

Farrow Pryce carried on the legacy of Lord Rogan. He sought the magic contained in the sword. Lauren and everyone around her was in danger, including

Drake. And the man beside him—the man who, at the woman's urging, touched the sword as well—came from the Forsyth line.

Aiden felt the connection almost instantaneously, then knew who the man must be—his so-called nephew, Ben, whom Helen had told Lauren about earlier. He had no idea how they could be related, but at this point, he did not care. The woman who'd transferred the information to him was clearly Catalina Reyes, the paranormal researcher. She possessed a magic he'd seen before only with the Gypsies—the gift of speaking with her mind. Aiden concentrated, traced a line up her arm, then across her shoulder to her neck.

"I am here," he whispered.

She started, and he could feel her flesh ripple beneath his touch. "He wants Rogan's magic," she whispered.

"He can have it," he replied.

"Not while you're still using it, he can't."

Shifting, Aiden experienced a thrill of fear. Someone had noticed she was talking.

"Don't speak," he said, his voice so soft it might have been the wind. "How do I free myself?"

You need to be solid, she replied in his mind. *Sunset is almost here.*

Aiden's strength surged. The moment he achieved corporeal form again, he was going to rip Farrow Pryce to shreds.

"Is that all?"

She has to love you. Her love will set you free.

Now, that, Aiden thought ruefully, *could be a problem.*

Lauren had never much cared about accolades or honors. She'd become an actress for the paycheck and the glamour, and because she sincerely loved transforming into someone else. But staring down two men with guns pointed at her, acting as if she weren't terrified, she deserved a damned Academy Award.

At the table just beyond the pool, and only a few yards from the drop-off that gave Ross one of the most stunning views of the Pacific in all of Malibu Beach, was a stunning Latina she assumed was Catalina Reyes and a man whose piercing eyes instantly reminded her of Aiden's. Ben Rousseau. Each of them had a hand on the sword, and they both looked as terrified for her as she felt. She doubted they were here of their own free will.

The only person who looked cooler than an Aspen ski slope was Farrow Pryce, who had seated himself again after warning her away. Everyone remained still except David, who charged toward her so that she broadened her stance and drew up her arms, prepared to fight.

"You have to leave," he said.

"I don't have to do anything, David, except maybe pay you back for this," she said, tilting her head so he could see the bruise she was certain now colored her jaw.

"I'm sorry. I didn't have a choice."

"That's what you said last time, wasn't it? No choice but to take Ross's money and leave me to marry a man twice my age?"

David took another step nearer, but stopped when she jerked her hands a little higher in response.

"How did you—"

"Helen told me," she replied.

"I was a kid then," he said dolefully.

"What's your excuse now?"

"He said he'd kill you," David whispered, nodding toward Pryce, who chuckled loudly.

"He's not lying, Ms. Cole. This young man acted entirely on behalf of your continued good health. I don't care about you or your former husband. I merely want the sword. I've been willing to pay you for it from the beginning. We've no need for violence."

"Too late for that, don't you think?" she challenged.

He ignored her, snapping his fingers. One of the men pointing a 9mm toward her holstered the gun and withdrew a checkbook.

This was her chance.

She glanced at David, who grew paler by the minute. Yes, she was angry with him. Furious, really. But fighting with him—and forgiving him—were best left for another day. She had to concentrate on Aiden. On the sword. On finding a way to outsmart this violent man who had no compunction about using people like Ross, David and Nigel to do his dirty work.

"I have money," Lauren replied, sliding around David, entirely aware that the second guy still had his gun gripped tight. He moved to ensure that his barrel remained trained on her. The first man dashed to Pryce's side and handed him the checkbook and a pen.

"There's always room in your bank account for more."

"Let David go," she said, hoping for one less distraction as well as one less person she did not trust.

"You're hardly in a position to make demands," Farrow pointed out, gesturing toward his armed guards.

"No, but you're in a position to show me a little goodwill. Murdering a major movie star is going to bring down some serious interest from the police, Mr. Pryce. Might seriously mess up whatever you have planned if you have to dodge cops. And the press. Ross isn't here, but he knows you are. If anything happens to me, you'll be the first person the cops will question."

A muscle in his jaw ticked below his thin line of a mouth, but after a few seconds he smiled. "Well played, Ms. Cole, well played. You may go, Mr. Drake. Your purpose has been fulfilled. Do remember to keep your mouth shut about our interaction. I wouldn't want to have to hunt you down once my transaction with Ms. Cole is complete."

The sneer in his voice told Lauren he intended to do just that. She wondered if David would make it as far as the gate. Yet if he stayed, she doubted he'd live long. Farrow Pryce didn't look like the type to leave loose ends.

David stepped forward and grabbed for Lauren's arm. "I'm not—"

Lauren spun out of his reach. "Don't be a fool. Get the hell out of here, or I swear to God, I'll make sure that the only acting job you get in the next ten years is in commercials for erectile dysfunction."

He hesitated, but she put every ounce of her determination into her eyes and stared him down, trying to broadcast her fears in her expression. His gaze flicked toward Pryce's men. After a curt nod, he walked away, his pace increasing as he turned the corner. There. He'd saved her life. She'd just saved his. Debt repaid.

Farrow Pryce made no move to hamper David's escape, so she turned her attention toward her original goal.

Lauren walked forward into the inner circle, beneath the wide awning that shaded the table where Farrow had laid the sword. She thought, for an instant, that she felt Aiden somewhere near, but since they'd never interacted during the daytime while outside, she wasn't entirely sure.

Sunset loomed. The sky was now more purple than blue. The lowest curve of the sun kissed the horizon. She had to keep Farrow talking for just a while longer.

Farrow grinned up at her. He'd already filled in her name and the date on the check, as well as signed his name. He had only to fill in the amount.

"And why would I take a check from you?" she

asked. "How do I know it won't just bounce, or that you won't stop payment?"

He twirled the pen around his long fingers. "Because then our transaction would not be legal. That could cause the very messy and annoying involvement of people like lawyers and bankers and, dare I say, law enforcement. No, no, Ms. Cole. I assure you my money is quite good."

She crossed her arms over her chest, careful to position them so that her breasts were nicely emphasized. "Then let's talk price."

Only a few streaks of blue lingered in the sky that was now a blazing, fiery red—not unlike the opal set in the handle of the sword. Lauren spared the weapon a glance and saw the gemstone sparkle.

Unfortunately, the blade itself had also started to glow.

Lauren twisted her body, leaning against the table with her hands behind her, shifting so that Farrow Pryce was eye level with her waist and his view of the sword was blocked.

"How much?" she asked.

"How much would you like?"

"How much did you offer Ross?"

When he repeated the price, she laughed. "You must really, really want this sword. You know, swords are considered a major phallic symbol. Think that has anything to do with . . . ?"

Farrow ignored her remark and started to fill in the amount. Lauren leaned closer and stayed his hand. "I want more than you offered Ross. If we're going to keep this whole matter hush-hush, I'm going to have to pay off those Mexicans for him."

"You're a generous woman," Farrow whispered. "How about if I tack on an extra million for your trouble? Will that satisfy you?"

She smiled seductively, inching just a bit closer, knowing that as the sky darkened around them, the sword's glow would become more dazzling and more impossible to ignore. "Takes a lot more than money to satisfy me. Make it two."

He inhaled deeply, then turned to write, but one of the guards must have noticed the sword, because he made a squeaking noise and nearly knocked over an urn positioned near the table when backing away. Farrow noticed, threw his pen aside and jumped to his feet, motioning wildly for everyone to move away, including Catalina, who seemed reluctant to release the blade.

"Don't touch it! Let go! What are you doing?"

Ben grabbed Catalina by the shoulders and pulled her hard against his chest.

The blue and red lights emanating from the sword intensified. Connected to darkness sensors, the lanterns strung on the pool deck bloomed to life. Suddenly Lauren could feel Aiden's presence strengthening. Unfortunately both of Farrow's guards had pulled their guns out again in an instinctive reaction to the unknown.

"What's happening?" Farrow asked, his eyes wide with such a mixture of wonder and pleasure, Lauren suspected he was going to orgasm right there.

The darker the sky became, the more pronounced the sapphire glow on the blade and the reddish glow from the handle. The effect was awe-inspiring and hypnotic, but Lauren tore her gaze away to make eye contact with Ben. He moved Catalina farther away from the table.

Lauren, however, took a step forward. When Aiden emerged to confront Pryce, she wanted a front-row seat.

33

Power surged through him like a deep inhalation of air. His form concentrated into a central point, growing stronger and more solid with each extinguished flame of the setting sun. Knowing he'd soon appear, Aiden focused on the space directly across the table from Farrow Pryce and manifested there. Instantly his hand was on the hilt of the sword, and before anyone could even gasp in surprise, he had the weapon in his hand, leveled at the heir to his centuries-old enemy.

Pryce reacted quickly, grabbing Lauren and pulling her in front of him like a shield, a small pistol suddenly in his hand where there was none before. The guards who'd transported Ben and the psychic to this place also had weapons, but as Ben and Catalina were prepared for what was about to happen, the couple took the advantage. Ben struck with his fists, knocking the first man in the face so hard his head snapped back and his gun went flying. Catalina relied on an elbow to the midsection of her assailant, paired with a backward head butt and a spinning kick to the groin.

She faltered, but retrieved the weapon nonetheless, as Ben had. Now three of them were armed against one enemy—Pryce.

"You are outgunned," Aiden warned.

Pryce held the gun to Lauren's temple, his hand

clutched around her upper arm so tightly she hissed
with pain.

"I don't care who you kill," Pryce taunted, sneering
at the men Ben and Catalina had ordered to the
ground. "But I daresay you'll care if I blow this woman's brains out. Who are you? What are you? Are
you Rogan?"

Aiden held the sword steady, even though he could
not strike at this distance. Yet he knew, as he'd not
known since the day he boarded a schooner bound
for England from the bloody battlefields of Scotland,
that he could kill a man without regret. Though
Lauren remained in the blackguard's grasp, he saw no
fear in her eyes. He saw only trust. And, dared he
believe, love?

"I am Aiden Forsyth, sir. Let her go."

Farrow laughed. "Not likely. What are you?"

"Your worst nightmare," Lauren said quietly.

Aiden grinned.

Farrow jammed the pistol's tip harder into her
temple.

"Tell me! Did he trap you in the sword? Are you
his minion, held by the magic to do his bidding?"

Farrow's gaze was wide and wild, but did not waver.
Aiden knew that when he acted, he'd have to be quick
or else Lauren could die.

"I am his heir," Farrow claimed haughtily. "You
will obey me."

Lauren exhaled audibly. "You, sir, have been watching too many movies."

Her brazen comment distracted Farrow for the split
second Aiden needed to act. He concentrated, and the
table between them shimmered and then disappeared.
He took a step nearer, but Farrow tightened his hold
on Lauren and jammed the gun barrel deep into her
flesh, making her yelp.

"Obey you?" Aiden sneered. "I was Rogan's greatest enemy, sir, and no man's slave."

Aiden held out his other hand, called to the gun with his mind, and seconds later it flew from Farrow's grip and landed in his. Lauren exploited Farrow's surprise, then mimicked Catalina's effective elbow and spinning kick, sending Farrow flying backward into the pool.

Lauren rushed toward Aiden, but he shunted her aside. Extending the sword over the glistening blue water, he called to the magic to seal the top of the water so that Farrow Pryce remained beneath the surface, which now glowed with an otherworldly luminescence.

"Don't do it," Ben warned.

Aiden spared him a glance. Ben's eyes blazed with warning.

"The police are coming," Catalina said. "Listen."

In the distance Aiden heard a persistent whine.

Below him, Farrow Pryce was pounding his hands against the invisible barrier that kept him beneath the water. The instinct to drown the man, to watch the life eke out of his body, appealed to Aiden in ways that surprised even him. He'd left Culloden convinced he was not cut out to be a killer. But now his actions and desires contradicted that belief.

Murder felt good.

Just.

Deserved.

Until Lauren ran her hand along the length of his arm.

"Don't," she said softly.

"He is Rogan's heir."

"No, he's not," Ben supplied. "He wants the organization dedicated to Rogan's corrupt magic, but he's not of his blood. Rogan's heir is named Gemma Von Roan, and as of this morning she kidnapped my father—your brother Paxton."

"Paxton?"

Aiden lowered the sword. The violet glow firing

across the pool burned out, and Farrow Pryce burst
to the surface, heaving in great gulps of air. But he
floundered, chopping at the water, too disoriented to
swim to the edge. Aiden turned, uncaring now
whether Pryce lived or died. He might not have Rogan's cursed blood running through his veins, but he
was associated with the sorcerer and had put Lauren
in grave danger. Aiden handed her the pistol he'd
magicked away from Pryce and charged toward Ben.

"Paxton is alive?"

The man Ben had been holding at bay moved to
run, spurred, no doubt, by the increasing volume of
the sirens now rending the air with their droning
squeal. With a thought, Aiden conjured ropes that
wound instantly around him and his compatriot until
they were trussed and squirming on the grassy lawn.

"That's cool," Ben said, impressed.

Aiden glanced at his hands. The power to manipulate Rogan's magic was convenient, but he paid a price
every time he called up the magic. Something chipped
at his soul. Something dark. Something evil.

"It is Rogan's magic," Aiden spat. "Not mine. Tell
me of my brother."

Lauren was coaxing Pryce to the edge of the pool,
holding the gun steady and promising all manner of
punishments and indignities once he was in the cus-
tody of the authorities. He had no doubt she could
handle that pitiful man while he learned whether what
he'd dreamed was true.

A brother? Alive?

"He's old," Ben answered.

"But very strong," Catalina assured him.

"Old?"

"He was freed from the curse over sixty years ago.
It's a long story. One he should tell you himself," Ben
finished regretfully.

"Where is he?"

The sirens stopped. Voices on the other side of the house echoed across the expanse of lawn.

"Aiden, put down the sword," Lauren warned.

"What?"

Lauren had yanked Farrow Pryce onto the white pool deck, but left him hacking on the ground as she joined Ben, Catalina and Aiden. "Put your guns down. Don't you guys watch action flicks? The cops are on their way, and anyone with a weapon isn't going to be treated like royalty."

She tossed her gun into the pool. Ben and Catalina did the same. Aiden, however, held tight to the sword. It was his lifeline and his prison.

Lauren grabbed his shirt just above his heart. "They'll take it as evidence," she said. "This whole mess started with the sword. If they take it, you'll go with them. We won't be able to explain why you're haunting the police station."

"Free him," Catalina said.

"What?" Lauren said.

Catalina grabbed Ben's arm possessively. "Free him from the sword. Completely. Make him human again. Just tell him you love him."

"That's all she must do?" Aiden asked.

But his heart ached nonetheless. Though he and Lauren had made love many times since she'd touched the blade and released him into a phantom state between life and loneliness, they'd never admitted that depth of emotion. He loved her. He knew he did. How could he not when she was everything a man could want, but could not possibly have? She, on the other hand, guarded her heart with swords deadlier and more razor-sharp then any he'd wielded in his lifetime.

"She just has to mean it," Ben confirmed.

Aiden's brain swarmed confusingly as Lauren tugged him closer and kissed him with such passion he dropped the sword to his side. Their tongues intertwined in a familiar dance of sensations that he could lose himself in forever. But just as he slid his hands along her waist and tugged her close, she broke away.

"I love you," she said. "I never thought I could ever love a man again, but you didn't give me any choice."

Their second kiss was a burst of awareness that shot through his veins like molten fire. In a flash of red light he lost his ability to stand, his ability to hold her, his ability to breathe. Distantly he heard his name screeched in terror, but he could not think, could not respond. Deep in his midsection he felt a rip not unlike the tearing of flesh, yanking his innards in a gush of blinding pain.

And then, again, the blackness.

"Aiden?" Lauren dropped to his side. He was white. Stark white. Clammy and cold. It was as if he'd never seen sunlight, never breathed air. Moisture drenched him, but when she touched her hand to his cheek, there was very little heat.

"What's happening?" she asked desperately.

Catalina dropped down beside her and placed her hand on his shoulder. "He'll be fine. Just give him a—"

It happened all at once. They were all so concentrated on Aiden that they did not hear the police come around the side of the house, or see Farrow Pryce crawling across the pool deck on his way toward the sword. By the time the cops yelled for everyone to remain still, he'd grabbed the sword and taken off toward the infinity edge of the pool.

He was going to . . .

Jump.

He was there.

And then he was gone.

Ben made a move toward the drop-off, but the police yelled for everyone to stay where they were.

Lauren didn't need to be told. She didn't care what happened to Pryce or the damned sword. She only wanted Aiden, alive, solid. Permanent.

She shifted so that his head was in her lap. It was so dark. The glow from the lanterns hardly gave her enough light to see anything, especially once she realized that her eyes were filled with tears. She swiped them away and patted Aiden's cheeks.

"Aiden, I know my admitting that I love you came as a huge shock, but you're giving me a complex here. I went to all the trouble of opening my heart; the least you can do is tell me you love me back."

His lips twitched, then, millimeter by millimeter, curved into a cocky smile. "You couldn't resist me."

She nearly shot back with some stupid, snarky remark, but instead she kissed him, both hands cupping his face, and her hair curtaining them from view.

In the background she heard Catalina sniffle, then Ben assuring the police that they were all fine and encouraging them to pursue Farrow Pryce. Someone shouted for spotlights. The scuffle of Farrow's thugs being dragged to their feet, protesting and shouting about crazy magic and invisible ropes and flying guns, was noise she barely registered as she concentrated on the feel of Aiden's mouth on hers. Slowly the coolness of his skin surrendered under an intense heat, and when she pressed her cheek against his chest and allowed her tears to flow freely, the heartbeat beneath her ear blocked out every other unimportant sound.

He wrapped his arms around her, and though she was holding him, Lauren had never felt so cradled, so protected in her entire life.

"Ma'am, is he all right? Do I need to call an ambulance?"

Lauren looked up. The policeman, dressed in black and helmeted, threw back his night-vision visor.

"He'll be fine."

Aiden groaned as he untwined from Lauren and

tried to get to his feet, but with a quick assist from
the cop he was standing, just as strong and proud as
he had when he'd first emerged from the sword.
"Thank you, sir," he said to the policeman. "I merely
took a bad fall."

"Not as bad as your friend," the cop replied, thumb-
ing toward the cliff. "No way he survived that drop.
We're going to need a statement, if you'll all take a
seat over there. Nice costume, by the way. Doing a
period piece next, Ms. Cole?"

"Something like that," she replied.

Aiden chose the chair at the head of the granite
table, where Farrow had held court, then tugged her
into his lap. He kissed her thoroughly, his hands intent
on touching every part of her, as if he were assuring
himself that she was real. That he was real. That they
were both alive and free of any curse, magical or
otherwise.

Lauren lost all track of time until someone cleared
his throat.

She blinked and focused on Ben, who was sitting
behind Catalina, his arms wrapped possessively around
her shoulders.

"Sorry to interrupt," Ben said sheepishly.

"No, he's not," Catalina amended. "The police are
busy searching for that maniac, but they'll be back
soon. You need a cover story."

Aiden looked perplexed.

"It's not every day the Malibu police meet a man
in eighteenth-century clothing who has no identifica-
tion, no job, no address," Lauren explained.

" 'Tis untrue! I shall soon have documents from the
Screen Actors Guild that will say precisely who I am.
I heard Helen tell you as much. So apparently in this
century I am an actor. And if I'm not mistaken, my
address is a rather tony home in an area you call
Beverly Hills."

Lauren's heart swelled. This couldn't be happening.

Aiden, no longer a phantom cursed and bound to the sword, had the whole world to explore, and yet he seemed to want to stay with her. Could this be possible?

"You're not mistaken," she managed to say, her voice squeaking only a little. "But what about finding your brother? Avenging Rogan's heirs for the curse they put on your family?"

His expression became serious. Turning to Ben, he asked, "Where is Paxton?"

Ben frowned. "Missing, but he went willingly with a woman named Gemma Von Roan to try to find other objects that could contain your other three brothers."

"You mean four," Aiden corrected.

"No, three," Catalina insisted. "Your brother Damon—he's already free."

Aiden's chest stiffened. Lauren curled her arms around his neck just a bit tighter, hoping to offset some of the shock.

"Where is he?"

"Europe, but he'll head back here as soon as he knows you're alive. He's been looking for you and your brothers as well. And for Rogan's heirs. Paxton—who now goes by the name Paschal Rousseau—is the only one he's found."

Quickly, and in hushed tones, Ben and Cat, as she told them she preferred to be called, filled them in on the wild tale of their journey thus far to reunite the cursed Forsyth clan. When they had finished answering as many questions as they could, the police came with the news that Farrow was nowhere to be seen, and though they'd initiated a search of the rocky beach below, they did not expect that he was alive.

Once the group was alone again, with instructions to stay put until the police took their official statement, Aiden and Ben exchanged a long stare that caused a chill to run up Lauren's spine.

"What?"

"Pryce was holding the sword when he jumped," Ben said.

"So? They're both gone. Good riddance," Lauren said, though she figured there was going to be some serious fallout on the set over the loss of the sword. Well, they had a gazillion pictures. They could make a replica, though she wasn't sure if she wanted to touch anything associated with the curse now that it was finally broken.

Aiden and Ben, however, did not seem relieved at the absence of Rogan's weapon. Cat winced, as if she'd finally figured out what concerned them, though Lauren had not caught on. "If someone doesn't—"

"The magic," Cat said. "The magic could have saved him."

Lauren could not breathe. "He's still alive? We have to tell the—"

But she cut herself off. They'd all be carted off to the psychiatric ward if they started telling tales about magic and sorcerers and curses. Farrow Pryce might have escaped, but he also might not have. That was a worry for another time and place.

After Ben and Cat went inside to talk to the cops about their kidnapping, Aiden and Lauren were left alone on the cool pool deck, the water still and the night blossoming with possibilities.

"There's so much," Aiden said simply.

She nodded, still curled in his lap, thinking there was nowhere in the world she'd rather be. "We'll sort it all out. We cheated death in a big way. I can't think of anything we can't weather from this point on."

"Even love?" he asked.

She stared into those silvery gray eyes of his and lost herself in the emotion so evident there. "Especially love. You know, I told you I loved you and look what happened. I broke a centuries-old curse. What do you think will happen when you tell me you love me?"

For a split second, though it felt like several long moments, Aiden did not speak. Then he slid his hand gingerly around her cheek, kissed the bruise with a soft brush of his lips, and whispered words she hadn't known she'd longed to hear until he spoke them.

"I do love you, Lauren Cole. And I believe—no, I *know*—that the entire world will be ours for the taking so long as we remain together."

"The whole world? That's pretty ambitious," she teased, kissing him along his jawline, across his forehead, on the tip of his nose.

"That's the least of what you deserve, my lady."

And when he wrapped his arms around her and kissed her as if the sun would never set again, she completely and thoroughly believed him.

Read on for a preview
of Julie Leto's next book,
coming soon from Signet Eclipse.

"Don't touch it, Mariah."

With dexterous skill bred of one too many close shaves with police all over the globe, Mariah Hunter pocketed the stone she'd spent the last half hour digging out of the craggy earth and traded it for the Walther P38 pistol she'd bought in a Berlin pawnshop. The warning had come from the last person she'd wanted to catch up to her. And considering the dangerous and desperate people who were currently on her trail, even in the middle of this godforsaken wasteland, that was saying a lot.

Bending her knee to cover the gaping hole, Mariah stood. With her boot directly over the spot where she'd found the stone, Ben Rousseau couldn't see that his warning had come too late. She hadn't had a chance to notice anything about the stone other than its glossy red surface and the odd markings carved along the edges, but the find was clearly valuable or Ben wouldn't have taken a chance with a confrontation.

He held his open palms at shoulder height. "I'm not armed."

"Then you're an idiot," Mariah replied, flipping off the Walther's safety. She spared a split-second glance at the thick copse of trees directly behind Ben; the massive sentinels of pines curved around the tight, oblong clearing. She saw no sign that Ben had brought backup, but she couldn't imagine that her former lover had come after Mariah without someone to watch his back. She'd bet money that Catalina Reyes, the paranormal researcher who'd been sharing Ben's bed for the last year, was out there somewhere, probably training her sights on Mariah while Ben attempted to sweet-talk her out of her hard-earned treasure. Mariah could only hope that Cat remembered how she'd helped her out a few months ago, providing key information about a big, bad guy threatening to outmaneuver Ben and Cat to some Gypsy artifact. She had no idea how that situation had been resolved; she knew only that the stone now nestled in her bomber jacket wasn't going anywhere without a fight.

Ben took a step forward, but she stopped him with a shot that missed his big toe by a quarter inch. He jumped back and cursed, but not before Mariah heard a soft squeak of surprise from the trees to her left.

Bingo.

"Hey! I said I was unarmed," Ben said, sidestepping. To the left. Protecting his lady love.

How sweet.

Blech.

"And I beat you to this dig, Rousseau. Finders keepers. Back off now while you still have all your body parts."

Ben's gaze dropped slyly to his crotch. Maybe he wasn't as stupid as he looked. He'd zeroed on where she might have shot him ten years ago, after their disastrous relationship and fiery breakup. Now she simply wanted to keep what was hers.

Though he didn't lower his hands, Ben's posture relaxed and his mouth curved into an infuriatingly lazy grin. "Threats? I'm just trying to keep you from falling into a quagmire of trouble you really don't want right now. From what I'm hearing, you have enough on your plate."

He wasn't talking out of his arse on that, was he? If not for her own thick *quagmire* of trouble, she wouldn't be in this godforsaken wasteland digging up rocks and threatening a former lover with a gun.

"Listen to the bloody professor," she said haughtily, stepping back and to the right, lining up her body to make the quickest escape. "You may have lost your nerve for the antiquities game, but I haven't. And whatever trouble I'm in, I'll get out without any help from you. I always have."

Ben's gaze, darkened only by a flash of regret, raked down her body. She shivered at the cold, calculated perusal. Unlike a decade ago, his intention wasn't the least bit sexual. He was looking for bulges that would give away the stone. The little bauble she'd unearthed must be more than a hunk of glass or else Ben wouldn't have crossed the Atlantic to try to beat her to it.

"Some artifacts are worth coming out of retirement for," he replied, with an annoying hint of cockiness that contradicted his current situation. The man never did know when an ounce of humility would do him good.

"But this place," he explained. "It's cursed, Mariah."

"So was that cave near the Oasis at Dakhla. That didn't stop either one of us from scooping up the statue of Sekhmet and selling it to the questionable collector in Yemen."

"This is different. Trust me—"

She snorted. "Trust *you*?"

"Anything taken from this area," he insisted, ignoring her justified doubts, "could contain very powerful black magic, and there are some really dangerous—"

Mariah could no longer contain her laughter. She couldn't imagine for one minute that Ben thought his warning would scare her off. Not after all they'd seen together. Not after all they'd survived.

"This isn't funny, Mariah."

She raised the gun to his chest. "Look, after what I've been through, I take my laughs where I can get them. Now pipe down. I thought I heard something."

Ben's darting eyes again revealed what she suspected was Cat's location, if indeed his cohort had joined him on this jaunt across the pond. Even if Ben did have his bedmate with him, she might not be a good shot. And though there was a fair amount of bad blood between her and her former partner and lover, he didn't want her dead or she'd be a corpse by now.

The wind, sharp with an icy nip, whistled through the pines. Tucked in a corner of Germany as yet undeveloped and wild, the area had been dubbed Valoren, which the locals told her translated loosely into, "land of the lost." Made perfect sense. From the sharp, jutting ridges of the mountains that surrounded them to the mossy soil beneath their feet, the area was a perfect place to hide treasures like the palm-size stone she now had in her pocket.

Under the circumstances, she didn't imagine that Ben would tell her why this stone—or whatever else she might have found here—was so sought-after. Even the people she'd met in the nearby village were perplexed by the recent interest in their poor and undeveloped corner of Germany. As a result, the locals had become suspicious and secretive. She'd considered it a major coup that she'd found a local artisan with Gypsy roots who'd given her a place to start in her quest for the stone.

"Look," Mariah said reasonably, "I've got my own troubles that have nothing to do with you. I highly suggest that once I pack up, you don't follow me."

"What makes you think I'm going to let you leave with what you found?"

"Who's going to stop me, you?"

Mariah fired the weapon again, missing Ben purposely and splintering the trunk of a nearby tree to his right.

Ben spun and started toward the trees on the left, giving Mariah the opening she needed.

She dove into the tangled forest. Behind her Ben shouted for her to stop. She didn't look back, but focused on leaping over rocks, ducking behind boulders and sliding over fallen tree trunks. Finally she spilled out onto the path where she'd stored her transportation—a dirt bike she'd bartered for in the village. It wasn't pretty and it was as loud as a cyclone, but it would get her out of here in a hurry.

She rode for nearly a quarter of a mile before she caught sight of her pursuers, roaring up behind her in an open-topped Jeep. She cursed, leaned forward, downshifted and swerved off-road, sending dirt and gravel flying. She wasn't expertly familiar with the terrain, and she certainly preferred to travel by air rather than ground, but she'd scoped out the area well enough to map out a few escape routes. Behind her, the Jeep's horn honked. Did they really expect her to stop?

She careened around an outcropping of boulders and under a canopy of trees that would lead to a river if she could avoid dropping over any of the cliffs that dotted this region. The overhang threw her into shadows. She could hear nothing but the roar of the bike's engine, the kick of the rocks beneath her wheels and the pump of her heartbeat in her ears.

As the path narrowed and she had to slow down or crash, she cursed. She'd come here on a lark. She'd grabbed a chance to beat Ben to a valuable piece of history and sell it to pay off the debt she'd acquired after liberating a certain stash of Mayan coins for a collector. She would have scored big on that operation, but she'd had to dump the package in the Chiapas jungle rather than risk arrest by the Mexican police. Trouble was, the tracking device she'd attached

to the coins in order to retrieve them later wasn't
working. Her collector wanted either the coins or the
cash he'd paid her up-front to facilitate her operation.

She had neither.

But now she had the stone. She could only hope
that Ben's persistence meant the ruddy thing was valuable enough to buy her out of this mess.

Distracted by her worries, she hit a root at top
speed and nearly flew over the handlebars. She corrected, scattering twigs, leaves and dirt behind her, but
avoided running into a tree and kept the bike upright.
The forest undergrowth was too thick for her to continue. She should have chosen another route. *Damn.*
She stopped, fighting to catch her breath as she pow-
ered down the engine and listened for her pursuers.

She didn't have to listen long. They were getting
closer.

She might have offered to sell the stone to Ben right
there, but she had no way of knowing a fair price until
she'd examined the find more closely. She patted her
jacket, surprised to find that the spot where she'd
stashed the rock seemed warm. Without time to wonder about the phenomenon, she hid the bike behind
a thick oak, grabbed her dilly bag and crashed deeper
into the brush on foot. She'd find a hidey-hole until
they gave up, then make her way back to the bike
and hightail it to the next village before trading up to
a car that would get her to the nearest airstrip. From
there she'd be free.

She tried to find a balance between speed and
stealth as she made her way deep into the cover. Her
heart racing more from exertion than fear, she focused
on her escape, ignoring the emotions that threatened
to distract her. She'd thought she'd moved above
wanting to one-up Ben, to show him who was the
more clever thief.

She was wrong.

Spying a narrow ledge she guessed might lead her

to a lookout, she moved carefully along the edge, digging her fingers into the mossy rocks as handholds. When the flat rock beneath her feet curved around an outcropping above a deep ravine, she nearly turned back. Her breath caught. Being a pilot she wasn't afraid of heights, but her talents did not extend to mountaineering.

She cursed. She'd have to go back down and find another route. But in her hurry to change directions, her ankle twisted and she lost her footing. When she tried to recover she found nothing beneath her. Nothing but air.

The *gadje* woman was going to get herself killed.

Infuriated, Rafe Forsyth tried to tune out the woman's emotions. For years he'd existed in peace. Centuries. His curse had not, until now, included experiencing the feelings of others, as he had so naturally in life. It had been his gift as much as his curse. But, unpracticed at bearing the onslaught of emotions, he could not tune her out. Despite his efforts to remain alone, he could not ignore the warmth of her flesh so near his, could not resist reacting when a jolt of fear shot into his soul like flaming glass.

Suddenly the ground beneath them disappeared. Her terror spiked, and the image of an impending plummet caused him to yell out the Romani word for "fly." A sensation of weightlessness suddenly surrounded him, surrounded her. Movement sleek and swift like a bird on a wing propelled them forward. Then her fear gave way to surprise and, a second after her feet gently touched the ground, relief.

He saw none of this, but he sensed it. Sensed it all.

"What the bloody hell?" she said, her voice muffled even as she dug into her pocket. He heard the rustle of fabric, and then a yank of limitless force grabbed at his middle and pulled. She'd wrapped her hand completely around the stone that contained him, and instantly he was injected with an essence of woman that stirred his blood. Spiked his awareness. Tempted him to sin.

Concentrating, he fought the wrench of the magic, the all-encompassing drag of the dark sorcery that had bound his soul to the stone for what he guessed had been hundreds of years. Rogan had not controlled him in life; or would he now, despite Rafe's entrapment by the curse.

How had this woman found him?

Why?

From the moment she'd brushed her fingers across the stone that had become his prison, he'd been awakened by a power he'd instantly recognized as the same dark magic that had entrapped him so many years ago. He'd used all his might to resist. The urge to materialize from his prison, to expand from the containment of the stone, pounded at him, but he would not succumb. The magic had tempted his sister, stolen his life and resulted in the murder of the only woman he'd ever loved.

And yet now, in the open, with sunlight dappling across hair the color of fine mahogany, he couldn't help inhaling, breathing in the essence of her. The woman named Mariah. He sensed no fragrances except her own natural musk, mixed with the rich scent of the earth and the sweet smell of torn leaves. For an instant, before he met her startled amber eyes and the pale arch of her cheek that bore none of the signs of his people, he wondered if she might be Romani, like himself.

She turned the stone that contained him over in her palms, fascinated by what he imagined was the same fiery glow that had drawn him to the marker so long ago. He pushed the memory aside and concentrated on the woman holding him, examining him, her entire being seized by a boundless curiosity unlike any he'd ever experienced.

What was this stone? Had it given her the ability to fly and saved her from certain death? Was it magic? Or was it truly cursed?

He had no answers. Only regrets.

At the sound of distant voices she released him. Sudden darkness engulfed him once more. An intense burst of energy told him she was again on the run.

This time she suppressed her fear with a thrill of adventure and a burst of confidence. The lure of her tugged at his core, but again he resisted.

He had no desire to leave his prison.

No desire for anything but quiet. Peace. Solitude. Forgetfulness.

Gifts he suspected he'd never experience as long as this woman possessed him.

Also Available

Phantom Pleasures

Julie Leto

Hotel developer Alexa Chandler wants to turn an abandoned island into an exclusive resort. Then she unwittingly unleashes a phantom cursed centuries ago—Damon Forsyth, a spectral man who turns her secret desires into reality...

"A sexy page-turner you won't want to miss!"
—*New York Times* bestselling author
Gena Showalter

Available wherever books are sold or at penguin.com